ALSO BY ERNEST HEMINGWAY

In Our Time
The Torrents of Spring
The Sun Also Rises
Men Without Women
A Farewell to Arms
Death in the Afternoon
Winner Take Nothing
To Have and Have Not
The Fifth Column and Four Stories of the Spanish Civil War
The Short Stories of Ernest Hemingway
For Whom the Bell Tolls
Across the River and Into the Trees
The Old Man and the Sea
The Snows of Kilimanjaro and Other Stories
A Moveable Feast
Islands in the Stream
The Nick Adams Stories
Selected Letters 1917–1961
On Writing
The Dangerous Summer
Dateline: Toronto
The Garden of Eden
The Complete Short Stories of Ernest Hemingway
By-Line: Ernest Hemingway
True at First Light
Hemingway on Fishing
Hemingway on Hunting
Hemingway on War
A Moveable Feast: The Restored Edition
A Farewell to Arms: The Hemingway Library Edition
The Sun Also Rises: The Hemingway Library Edition
Green Hills of Africa: The Hemingway Library Edition

Ernest Hemingway

◆

THE SHORT STORIES OF ERNEST HEMINGWAY

THE HEMINGWAY LIBRARY EDITION

Foreword by PATRICK HEMINGWAY

Edited with an introduction by SEÁN HEMINGWAY

SCRIBNER

New York   London   Toronto   Sydney   New Delhi

SCRIBNER
An Imprint of Simon & Schuster, Inc.
1230 Avenue of the Americas
New York, NY 10020

Foreword copyright © 2017 by Patrick Hemingway
Introduction copyright © 2017 by Seán Hemingway
Hemingway Library Edition copyright © 2017 by the Hemingway Copyright Owners

First Scribner trade paperback edition July 2018

SCRIBNER and design are registered trademarks of The Gale Group, Inc.,
used under license by Simon & Schuster, Inc., the publisher of this work.

For information about special discounts for bulk purchases,
please contact Simon & Schuster Special Sales at 1-866-506-1949
or business@simonandschuster.com.

The Simon & Schuster Speakers Bureau can bring authors to your live event.
For more information or to book an event contact the Simon & Schuster Speakers
Bureau at 1-866-248-3049 or visit our website at www.simonspeakers.com.

Interior design by Brooke Zimmer

Manufactured in the United States of America

7   9   10   8   6

ISBN 978-1-4767-8762-6
ISBN 978-1-4767-8767-1 (pbk)
ISBN 978-1-4767-8772-5 (ebook)

Interior photograph credits: p. 15: EH on the beach of a lake in Michigan, summer
1916, Ernest Hemingway Photo Collection, John F. Kennedy Presidential Library and
Museum; p. 23: EH in the courtyard of 113 rue Notre Dame des Champs, 1924, Ernest
Hemingway Photo Collection, John F. Kennedy Presidential Library and Museum; and
p. 179: EH at his typewriter in Key West, 1929, R. M. Munroe, Ernest Hemingway
Photo Collection, John F. Kennedy Presidential Library and Museum.

Contents

Foreword by Patrick Hemingway   vii

Introduction by Seán Hemingway   ix

"The Art of the Short Story" by Ernest Hemingway   1

I

1. Judgment of Manitou   17
2. Untitled Milan Story   19

II

3. Up in Michigan   25
4. A Very Short Story   49
5. Indian Camp   55
6. The Three-Day Blow   69
7. Soldier's Home   81
8. Big Two-Hearted River   97
9. The Killers   129
10. In Another Country   153
11. Hills Like White Elephants   165

III

12. The Sea Change   181
13. A Way You'll Never Be   193

14. A Clean, Well-Lighted Place   221
15. Fathers and Sons   231
16. The Short Happy Life of Francis Macomber   263
17. The Snows of Kilimanjaro   301
Acknowledgments   349
Notes   351

Foreword

My father, in his wonderful short stories, very much made use of his one and only well-examined life. Why Nick Adams? I don't know about Nick, but I am certain about Adams. He wished to echo another distinguished American's well-examined life from one generation before him.

When as a young person I had, through his generosity, the summer-vacation opportunity to visit France on my own, he gave me a copy of *Mont-Saint-Michel and Chartres* by Henry Adams and *A Little Tour in France* by Henry James. These set a high bar for what I should get out of my own little tour in France and opened my eyes to what Henry Adams meant to my father.

Here is an example of the four-corner billiards he could play, taken from the dust jacket of *My Life and Hard Times* by James Thurber (Harper, 1933):

> Ernest Hemingway says: "I find it far superior to the autobiography of Henry Adams. Even in the earliest days when Thurber was writing under the name of Alice B. Toklas we knew he had it in him if he could get it out."

As you read these stories, do take note of the four-corner billiards and the great little tour these stories provide of the hard-featured landscape of the twentieth century.

Patrick Hemingway
January 2017
Bozeman, Montana

Introduction

Ernest Hemingway is widely recognized as one of the greatest writers of the twentieth century. His writing, with its powerful, understated prose and economy of words, has influenced countless writers. More than any other writer of his time, Hemingway changed the course of literature and furthered the written expression of the human condition. His novels, such as *The Sun Also Rises*, *A Farewell to Arms*, and *For Whom the Bell Tolls*, have entered into the canon of world literature, but it is arguably his contributions to the art of the short story that are his greatest literary achievement. This volume features a selection of Ernest Hemingway's short stories from 1916 to 1936, during which time he mastered the short story form. The stories are accompanied by early drafts and notes, taken primarily from the archives of the Ernest Hemingway Collection at the John F. Kennedy Presidential Library and Museum in Boston, where approximately 90 percent of my grandfather's literary manuscripts are preserved. There were two guiding principles to the selection. First, the stories with the best manuscript material to illuminate Hemingway's writing methods are included. Second, the selection focuses squarely on his finished body of work so that the reader may see how a consummate short story writer honed his craft from first draft to final publication. In the following pages are many of Ernest Hemingway's finest short stories. His early drafts, notes, alternate titles, and false starts provide a unique window into the author's creative process.

I

The first section of this book presents two of Ernest Hemingway's earliest short stories, written when he was just sixteen and nineteen years old. The first story in this volume is Hemingway's first published story, "Judgment of Manitou." It appeared in the Oak Park High School literary magazine, *Tabula*, in the February issue of 1916, when he was in his junior year. It is a dark tale about two fur trappers in the wilderness who experience friendship, revenge, gruesome death, and poetic justice. The title, which refers to the great Native American spirit Manitou, sacred to the Ojibwe tribe of northern Michigan, where Hemingway spent his summers as a boy, adds an element of mysticism to the story.[1]

The second story, untitled and preserved in a single handwritten manuscript on American Red Cross Hospital stationery (fig. 1), was written sometime in the later part of 1918 while Hemingway was recuperating at the hospital in Milan (fig. 2) after the traumatic wound he received from a trench mortar shell at the front at Fossalta on July 8 of that year. The story draws heavily on Hemingway's own wartime experiences. It's set in a hospital in Italy on Armistice Day, November 11, 1918, when the Allies marked their victory over Germany and the end of World War I. The main character is a wounded soldier named Nick Grainger, who converses with a nurse about the celebrations that must be going on back home in the United States as they listen to the revels in the streets outside the hospital.[2] The bottle of bichloride of mercury—a medicine used to heal wounds but which is also a deadly poison—that Nick steals is a telling detail. The secreting of the poison and his somber final words after looking at his medals for valor on the battlefield that resulted in his left arm and both legs being badly wounded foreshadow his suicide.

Collectively, my grandfather's first stories reveal early literary influences such as O. Henry, Rudyard Kipling, Ring Lardner, and Jack London.[3] Hemingway published two more stories in the high school magazine *Tabula*, and there are some twelve additional stories preserved in manuscript form that he wrote between 1918 and 1921 before he set off to Paris with his wife, Hadley.

To my mind, the two stories included here are the best of the lot, and neither is a remarkable piece of writing. They effectively demonstrate how much Ernest Hemingway would develop his talent for writing and the short story genre.

Journalism was an important early influence on Hemingway's short story writing. This also began at Oak Park High School, where Hemingway was an editor for the school newspaper, the *Trapeze*, and contributed articles, sometimes using the byline Ring Lardner Jr. After graduation, he went to work as a cub reporter for the *Kansas City Star* for seven months before leaving in May 1918, at age eighteen, to join the war effort as an ambulance driver for the Red Cross in Italy. Hemingway later acknowledged the value of his training at the *Kansas City Star* and how he learned there to write simple, declarative sentences.[4] Its style guide (fig. 3) contained many useful dictums: use short sentences; use short first paragraphs; use vigorous English; be positive, not negative; be sparing of extravagant adjectives; avoid superfluous words.[5] Hemingway continued to write journalism in Paris as a foreign correspondent for the *Toronto Star* until 1924. He would cable his dispatches to the paper and had to pay for the cable by the word—another trade discipline that reinforced his belief that every word needed to count. His assignments in Turkey, Greece, Italy, France, and Spain provided invaluable source material for his stories.

II

Paris was my grandfather's true training ground, a place where he met and learned from so many luminaries, from Gertrude Stein and Ezra Pound to Ford Madox Ford and James Joyce. The second section of this volume presents short stories from Ernest Hemingway's Paris years, in many ways the most productive time of his short-story-writing career. The first story in this section, "Up in Michigan," was the leading work in his first collection, *Three Stories and Ten Poems*, published in Dijon by Robert McAlmon in August 1923. A preliminary mock-up of the cover by the author (fig. 4) is remarkably close to the final version and shows Hemingway's detailed involvement in every aspect of the publication. Authors rarely have controlling influence on a book cover's design. Hemingway would not have as much input into the covers of his books again, although he was never shy about voicing his opinions.

The manuscripts of Hemingway's short stories show that his typical writing process was to compose a first draft of a story by hand, often writing in pencil. He then normally had one or more typed drafts that he continued to edit, frequently by hand, sometimes with lengthy additions or alternate drafts of passages. Most often, he tended to cut during his revision process, and he would continue to revise in the proof stage as well, using every opportunity to make a story as good as it could be.[6] The manuscripts of "Up in Michigan" represent a special case and reflect the unusual literary history of this provocative early story.

The first preserved draft of "Up in Michigan" is a heavily edited typed draft (3a) that was likely written in Chicago in the early fall of 1921 or possibly soon after Hemingway arrived in Paris in December of that year, as he himself remembered years later. A poignant addendum to this manuscript are two alternate endings, one of which adds an anguished scene of the female protagonist the next morning worrying if she is now pregnant (3c, fig. 6). Although Hemingway ultimately cut this ending, it shows his sensitivity to the female character as he navigated the difficult terrain that he was trying to portray in the story.

In *A Moveable Feast*, Hemingway famously recalled showing the story in March 1922 to Gertrude Stein, who called it "inaccrochable."[7] It's an interesting term that literally means a painting that cannot be hung; it is unsuitable for public viewing. In their early conversations at her home at 27 rue de Fleurus, Stein was also educating Hemingway about painters and painting, and the phrase clearly resonated all the more with Hemingway as he sat in her salon surrounded by masterpieces of early modern painting from Cézanne to Picasso. Stein did not understand why Hemingway would write a story that would not be published. It seemed obviously unsuitable to her because of its subject of date rape. The second typed manuscript (3b), which bears the title written by hand (fig. 5), is most likely the one Hemingway shared with Gertrude Stein, and it has been plausibly argued that some of the edits, which appear on its pages in another person's hand, are by Gertrude Stein herself.[8]

Although only three hundred copies of *Three Stories and Ten Poems* were printed in 1923, "Up in Michigan" would not appear in print again because of its sensitive subject matter until Scribner's collected edition of Hemingway's short stories in 1938. Another manuscript (3d), hand-edited tear sheets of the story from *Three Stories and Ten Poems*, must date from after 1923— perhaps to 1926, when Hemingway considered revising "Up in Michigan" for inclusion in the short story collection *Men Without Women*. A quite clean handwritten manuscript (3e) probably dates to the summer of 1930, when Hemingway returned to the story to see if he could revise it to the satisfaction of his American publisher for inclusion in a new edition of *In Our Time*. In this late draft, he changes the names of the locale and the characters and also attempts to rework the final scene. Hemingway ultimately abandoned this repeated exercise in editing because he felt that to cut the material would ruin the story. When "Up in Michigan" finally reappeared in 1938, the text remained true to his first publication. The story still retains its edginess today, and the subject matter is as thought-provoking as when it was written.

Hemingway wrote to Sherwood Anderson that he and Gertrude Stein "were just like brothers," and there is no denying that she was an important early mentor.[9] Hemingway's first European literary publication in March 1923 was a glowing review in the Paris *Tribune* of Gertrude Stein's *Geography and Plays*.[10] She inscribed his reviewer's copy "To Hemingway, whom I like young and will like older, Always, Gertrude Stein," and he kept it his entire life. Stein's words were not prophetic—the two of them would have a falling-out after her publication of *The Autobiography of Alice B. Toklas*, with its overreaching claims of influencing Hemingway's work.

In those early Paris days, Hemingway was developing his talent rapidly. His next book was *in our time*, a collection of eighteen vignettes published as part of Ezra Pound's "Inquest into the state of contemporary English prose" in 1924 by Three Mountains Press in a limited edition of 170 copies. A truly bold, experimental work, *in our time* was a critical success. Edmund Wilson wrote that "in the dry compressed little vignettes of *in our time* [Hemingway] has almost invented a form of his own . . . and below its cool objective manner [it] really constitutes a harrowing record of barbarities: you have not only political executions, but criminal hangings, bullfights, assassinations by the police, and all the cruelties and enormities of the war. . . . He is showing you what life is, too proud an artist to simplify. And I am inclined to think that this little book has more artistic integrity than any other book that has been written by an American about the period of the war."[11] A good example of the manuscripts from this project is chapter 10 (here 4a–c), which Hemingway reworked slightly into "A Very Short Story" for an expanded version of the book. The new work, titled *In Our Time*, published in 1925 by Boni & Liveright, interspersed the vignettes with fifteen stories.[12] "A Very Short Story" is a highly personal account of a failed love affair between a soldier and a nurse in Milan during World War I. It is based largely on Hemingway's own first adult love affair with a nurse named Agnes von Kurowsky while he was convalescing at the American Red Cross hospital in Milan. The original title in a false start was "Personal," which became "Love" (4a, fig. 7) to fit in with a series of titles for the vignettes that he later abandoned (4c).[13]

"Indian Camp" is Ernest Hemingway's early masterpiece about the young Nick Adams, the youthful protagonist in many of Hemingway's Michigan stories. Nick accompanies his father to assist a Native American woman who is having great difficulty giving birth to her child. The manuscripts show how carefully Hemingway revised the story, wisely cutting a lengthy beginning conceived in the first handwritten draft (5a, fig. 8), which was published posthumously as a separate short story entitled "Three Shots."[14] Hemingway continued to refine the story in two further edited typescripts (5b, 5c). Robert Paul Lamb's recent thoughtful analysis explores the story in nearly exhaustive detail.[15] How to understand the suicide of the baby's father remains open to interpretation. Jeffrey Meyers's suggestion that his suicide may have been rooted in his own tribal beliefs is a compelling idea that merits further inquiry.[16] Perhaps the father's apparently selfish act of suicide was actually meant as a way to save the mother and child by taking his life in their place.

Hemingway vividly recalled writing "The Three-Day Blow" in a café on Place Saint-Michel in his memoir *A Moveable Feast*:

> It was a pleasant café, warm and clean and friendly, and I hung up my old waterproof on the coat rack to dry and put my worn and weathered felt hat on the rack above the bench and ordered a *café au lait*. The waiter brought it and I took out a notebook from the pocket of the coat and a pencil and started to write. I was writing about up in Michigan and since it was a wild, cold, blowing day it was that sort of day in the story. I had already seen the end of fall come through boyhood, youth and young manhood, and in one place you could write about it better than in another. That was called transplanting yourself, I thought, and it could be as necessary with people as with other sorts of growing things. But in the story the boys were drinking and this made me thirsty so I ordered a rum St. James. This tasted wonderful on the cold day and I kept on writing, feeling very well and feeling the good Martinique rum warm me all through my body and my spirit.[17]

A partial handwritten manuscript of the story (6a), likely the very draft Hemingway describes writing in the café on the Place Saint-Michel, is preserved, and it is powerful to see the actual pages of the story (fig. 9) that Hemingway describes writing so movingly. He mentions a notebook in his later recollection, and he often did write in notebooks, but these pages are individual sheets of paper bearing a Paris stationery watermark, and they are in ink rather than pencil.[18] "The Three-Day Blow" is a poignant portrayal of the simple pleasures of outdoor life among young friends growing up in northern Michigan in the early twentieth century.

The earliest manuscript of "Soldier's Home" (7a) is written in pencil on two sheets of telegram-form paper (fig. 10). One imagines the young Hemingway using whatever paper was at hand, perhaps when he was at the cable office sending a dispatch to the *Toronto Star*. On this paper he worked out his first thoughts about this indelible story of a World War I veteran returning home to the Midwest and having a hard time readjusting to civilian life. This tale of a young man deeply affected by post-traumatic stress disorder after serving his country remains harrowingly relevant, with the horrors of war ever present around the globe and American soldiers returning from combat in Afghanistan and the Middle East. In the first complete draft (7b) and two later manuscripts, the protagonist, Krebs, goes home to Kansas. In the second draft, Hemingway added the fact that Krebs went to a Methodist college in Kansas before he left for the war. In the final version, Hemingway changed Krebs's home state from Kansas to Oklahoma. These revisions add layers of complexity to the character: Krebs chose to leave home for a college in a neighboring state, and a religious school at that. The addition of such details shows how Hemingway thoughtfully reshaped and enriched his story to give it the greatest impact.

Hemingway eloquently describes in the essay that follows this introduction how "Big Two-Hearted River" is also a story about the war but with no mention of it. It is for him an example of his iceberg principle of writing:

> If a writer knows enough about what he is writing about he may omit things that he knows and the reader, if the writer is writing truly enough, will have a feeling of those things as strongly as though the writer had stated them. The dignity of an ice-berg is due to only one-eighth of it being above water.[19]

Hemingway's iceberg principle is especially relevant to short story writing, in which the author must keep the narrative short due to the limited amount of space dictated by the medium. The manuscripts of "Big Two-Hearted River" (fig. 11) show that Hemingway had started the story with Nick and two friends on a fishing trip (8a) but quickly gave up on it.[20] More significantly, Hemingway considered a very different ending that expounded on his philosophy of writing (8c) and that linked Nick Adams directly with Ernest Hemingway, through the writing of "My Old Man." In the end, Hemingway wisely cut this long passage and reworked the ending (8d), preferring to leave the focus on Nick's healing commune with nature and the splendid trout fishing.

In 1925, after *In Our Time* was published and Hemingway heard that his parents had returned the copies they had ordered, he wrote to his father, Clarence, from Paris to explain what he was trying to accomplish with his writing:

> You see I'm trying in all my stories to get the feeling of actual life across—not to just depict life—or criticize it—but to actually make it alive. So that when you have read something by me you actually experience the thing. You can't do this without putting in the bad and the ugly as well as what is beautiful. Because if it is all beautiful you can't believe in it. Things aren't that way. It is only by showing both sides—3 dimensions if possible 4 that you can write the way I want to.[21]

Short stories were the medium that Hemingway began with and favored early on in his career. The next month, Hemingway wrote to his future editor Maxwell Perkins:

> Somehow I don't care about writing a novel and I like to write short stories and I like to work at the bull fight book so I guess I'm a bad prospect for a publisher anyway. Somehow the novel seems to me to be an awfully artificial and worked out form but as some of the short stories are now stretching out to 8,000 and 10,000 words maybe I'll get there yet.[22]

Hemingway knew that, in the publishing world, commercial success lay in writing novels, and that he would need to publish a novel in order to make it as a writer—which he did with *The Sun Also Rises* in 1926.[23] Perkins suggested that Hemingway follow on the success of *The Sun Also Rises* with another book of short stories while he worked toward his next novel. It is no accident that this next project, *Men Without Women*, was largely formed while Hemingway was divorcing his first wife, Hadley, and at Hadley's request went through a voluntary exile from his future wife, Pauline Pfeiffer. Published in October 1927, *Men Without Women* included fourteen stories.[24]

One of Hemingway's early mentors was F. Scott Fitzgerald.

Fitzgerald was among the first to champion Hemingway's writing in America and was instrumental in connecting him with Scribner's, who would become his lifelong publisher. Fitzgerald offered sage advice on the editing of *The Sun Also Rises* that Hemingway heeded, and Hemingway often shared his early work with Fitzgerald. On Fitzgerald's advice, Hemingway cut the original beginning (fig. 12) of "Fifty Grand," but always regretted this decision, as he explains in the essay following this introduction.

Prominently featured in *Men Without Women*, "The Killers" is the first great American gangster story and perhaps the best example of how Hemingway uses dialogue to shape and move a tale, one of his enduring contributions to the art of short story writing.[25] The earliest preserved draft (9a) opens with a completely different setting, which Hemingway later rejected. He crafted the story during a marathon writing session in Madrid on May 16, 1926, as he noted on his second draft typescript, "written between 2:15 and 8 pm, Madrid—May 1926," which is included in this edition (9b). A third manuscript, an uncorrected carbon typescript, is preserved in the Houghton Library of Harvard University and is very close to the final published text, which appeared in *Scribner's Magazine* in the March issue of 1927.[26]

In my opinion, "In Another Country" has the best opening sentence of any war story ever written: "In the fall, the war was always there, but we did not go to it any more."[27] In simple, direct prose, Hemingway captures all of the complexity of the story that is to follow. The first sentence begins his second typewritten draft (included here as section 10a; see also fig. 13), just as it appears in the final version. The handwritten edits in this draft—for example, when Hemingway writes about the major and the loss of his wife—masterfully improved the text through subtle but important revisions. The story is among Hemingway's finest war stories. The tragic effect of war on the combatants was a subject Hemingway explored throughout much of his writing.[28]

More than for any other Hemingway short story, the manuscripts for "Hills Like White Elephants" illuminate the painterly quality of Hemingway's creative process. My grandfather liked to compare his writing to Cézanne's painting.[29] He said that he learned how to write landscapes from Cézanne (see 8c), whose work he saw in Paris as a young man. Hemingway's earliest manuscript for "Hills Like White Elephants" (11a) appears to be a straightforward nonfiction account of himself traveling with Hadley by train through Spain and stopping at a station where they see hills in the distance that look like white elephants, an analogy that Hemingway makes, but not in conversation. There is none of the tense dialogue between the two protagonists that appears in the finished short story (11b). Hemingway uses his own experience to provide a realistic background for the scene, recognizing it as a perfect setting for the story he would invent and weaving in the symbolic and ghostly metaphor of the hills. In Pieter Bruegel the Elder's masterpiece *Landscape with the Fall of Icarus* (ca. 1555), now in the collection of the Royal Museums of Fine Arts of Belgium in Brussels, the main scene is but a small feature of the canvas, which is dominated by a vast and amazingly detailed landscape. Hemingway's story is like Bruegel's painting in reverse. The dialogue between the two protagonists dominates the scene, which is set so carefully in its beautiful, impressionistic landscape.

III

In 1931, Ernest and Pauline Hemingway bought the residence at 907 Whitehead Street in Key West, Florida, and made it their primary home, the place where Patrick and my father, Gregory, grew up.[30] It was a good place to write, and Hemingway continued to alternate longer writing projects with collections of short stories. His next book would be *Death in the Afternoon*, published in 1932, followed by another book of short stories, *Winner Take Nothing*, which appeared in 1933. The 1930s were an exciting period in Hemingway's life. He commissioned the construction of his fishing boat, the *Pilar*, discovered Cuba, and explored the Gulf Stream; he continued to hunt and fish in the American West and went on his first big-game safari in East Africa; he returned to Spain to cover the Spanish Civil War; and by the end of the decade he had moved into his beloved home, the Finca Vigía, in the hills outside Havana with his future third wife, Martha Gellhorn. The final section of this book features short stories written by Ernest Hemingway during this period, which include some of his most famous works.

The epigraph for *Winner Take Nothing* reads: "Unlike all other forms of lutte or combat the conditions are that the winner shall take nothing; neither his ease, nor his pleasure, nor any notions of glory; nor, if he win far enough, shall there be any reward within himself." Hemingway invented this "neomedieval" quote and the title for his fourth, and perhaps least well-known, collection of short stories.[31] Yet the surprising and less-than-genteel subjects that he chose for the stories in this collection created new horizons for the American short story.

"The Sea Change" is a story about heterosexual, bisexual, and lesbian love. Two lovers, a man and a woman, talk in a bar about the woman's infidelity with another woman, which is not over. The manuscripts include a heavily revised first draft in pencil (12a), a second draft in ink, and three additional related fragments, one of which contains an alternate ending (12b). The title comes from Ariel's song to Ferdinand about his dead father in Shakespeare's *The Tempest*:

> *Full fathom five thy father lies,*
> *Of his bones are coral made,*
> *Those are pearls that were his eyes,*
> *Nothing of him that doth fade*
> *But doth suffer a sea-change*
> *Into something rich and strange.*[32]

What is so remarkable to me about the story, aside from its bold subject matter for literature in the 1930s, is that one thinks at the outset that it is the woman who has had a sea change, but by the end of the story it becomes clear that it is the man who has undergone a significant transformation.

"A Way You'll Never Be" is one of Hemingway's less heralded short stories but one well worth close reading. It is particularly interesting for this collection because its first draft (13a) differs significantly from the final version that was published in *Winner Take Nothing*. The story draws heavily on Hemingway's experiences in Italy during World War I. In the earliest preserved draft, published here in its entirety for the first time and probably written in the late 1920s, the focus is more on the troubled experiences of other soldiers badly affected by combat, just as Hemingway would have learned of them, since he was not a combatant.[33] In the final version, Nick Adams becomes more fully the focal character, one who is clearly damaged both physically and psychologically from his combat experiences. Hemingway explained that he intended the title to cheer up his friend Jane Mason, who was in the midst of a mental breakdown when he completed the story in 1932, since Nick Adams was much crazier than she would ever be.[34]

In its spare prose and emphasis on dialogue, "A Clean, Well-Lighted Place" offers a poignant vignette of life in the form of two waiters talking in a café about an elderly patron who has recently attempted suicide. Hemingway presents the essence of the story without a lot of detail and with such clarity that it has a universal quality to which many of us can relate. Yet Hemingway's distinctive practice of writing dialogue without identifying the speaker has led to a prolonged scholarly controversy over which waiter spoke the line "You said she cut him down" and whether it is the younger waiter who knows the details of the old man's suicide or the older waiter. When it was first published in *Scribner's Magazine*, the line was attributed to the older waiter. The present text, as changed in 1965 in response to scholarly criticism, attributes the line to the younger waiter. Scholars have looked to the original manuscripts for answers, but the first preserved handwritten draft (14a) adds this line in an edit whose precise placement is open to interpretation (fig. 14), and the typed manuscript that was presumably used for typesetting has the text as it was first published.[35] In 1956, Hemingway stated in response to the scholarly questioning of a copyediting error that he thought the story made perfect sense as it was first published.[36]

"Fathers and Sons" is another highly personal Nick Adams story that draws on Hemingway's own experiences with his father and with his oldest son, Jack. Originally entitled "The Tomb of My Grandfather" (15b) and first written in the first person, the preserved drafts contain extensive revisions that are characteristic of Hemingway's writing when he approaches a highly personal subject about which he still has mixed emotions.[37] The manuscripts (15a–e) show Hemingway's difficulty in establishing the emotional distance from his subject that a writer needs to write clearly, which Hemingway finally overcame through editing and rewriting.

When asked once what his best short story was, Hemingway responded that "The Short Happy Life of Francis Macomber" was as good as any, and it was among those that he liked best.[38] It is a masterpiece of short fiction, as perfect in every detail as Vermeer's *The Art of Painting* or Bruegel's *The Harvesters*. The manuscripts are incomplete, but what is preserved is most interesting. Two early false starts (16a–b) for the story show Hemingway working out the main characters and how to begin.[39] In the essay following this introduction, my grandfather explains how he wrote the story, inventing from what he knew, including his own experiences on safari in East Africa in 1933–34. In notes written on his second African safari of 1953–54, he stated that he had given the professional hunter the appearance of Philip Percival but the habits of Bror von Blixen-Finecke, two professional hunters whom he befriended while in Africa.[40] I believe my grandfather took the name of the central character from the first page of George Eastman's *Chronicles of an African Trip*, in which a certain Frank Macomber sees the Kodak film millionaire off to the train station in Rochester, New York, at the beginning of his African safari and then is not mentioned again.[41] The manuscripts also include a list of sixteen possible titles for the story (fig. 15, 16c), an exercise that Hemingway often did for his novels, typically after he had finished writing. Among them was one close to the final title, "The Short Life of Francis Macomber," and the more humorous "In Darkest Marriage," a play on the journalist explorer Henry M. Stanley's famous two-volume work *In Darkest Africa* (New York: Charles Scribner's Sons, 1890).

The last story included in this collection is "The Snows of Kilimanjaro," Hemingway's second African short story, and one of his most famous. As Hemingway recalls in the following essay, "The Snows of Kilimanjaro," with its flashback and dream sequences taking place while the protagonist lies dying in bed, draws on many significant episodes from Hemingway's life. The wait for the plane and the final dream sequence of the flight were inspired by Hemingway's bout with amoebic dysentery on safari and his rescue flight, which are chronicled in the journal that his wife, Pauline, kept on that safari, published in the Hemingway Library Edition of *Green Hills of Africa*.[42] Hemingway left this embarrassing but significant event out of his account in *Green Hills of Africa* but improved on it through invention to make it a central element in "The Snows of Kilimanjaro." The masterful story reflects on a writer, how he lived, and what he accomplished and failed to accomplish in a life cut short. The earliest preserved manuscript (17a) shows that Hemingway added the celebrated epigraph only after he wrote the story. In fact, he considered including two epigraphs (fig. 16, 17c) contrasting a man's challenge to attain the summit of Kilimanjaro with the leopard's mysterious quest.[43] The working title for the story was "The Happy Ending." Hemingway changed the title to "The Snows of Kilimanjaro" in the final draft, which is preserved in the Harry Ransom Center of the University of Texas at Austin.[44]

Ernest Hemingway's manuscripts tell us a great deal about his writing technique, especially how he worked to perfect the beginnings and endings of his stories and how he continued to refine them through multiple drafts. Of particular interest is the way Hemingway was able to draw from the well of his own experience to create powerful stories that were then perfected through his storytelling craft. The manuscripts reveal that Hemingway sometimes started stories in the first person but then invented a great deal to improve them and make them as good as they could be. Time and again, through careful editing, he purposefully cut a significant amount of material to make each story as tight and concise as possible. Even when Hemingway was working from a story that was told to him, the manuscripts elucidate how much he worked to revise the telling to make the stories works of art in their own right.

Luckily for us, Hemingway explains his technique in his essay "The Art of the Short Story." Written in 1959, the essay was originally intended as an introduction for students to his short stories, and it reads like an informal lecture from a master. Mary

Hemingway thought it was too condescending and smug, and perhaps too personal a presentation, like Lillian Ross's interview for the *New Yorker*, which caused a sensation when it came out in 1950.[45] She suggested major edits that Ernest rejected. The manuscript, which is preserved in three drafts with corrections, changes, and additions, shows that he was satisfied with it. He even sent it to Charles Scribner, although it was never published during my grandfather's lifetime. The essay is pure Hemingway. It contains a great deal of fascinating information about his thoughts on the short story genre, how to write a short story, and even personal anecdotes about many of the stories featured in this book.[46]

Seán Hemingway
January 2017
Maplewood, New Jersey

The Short Stories of Ernest Hemingway

The Art of the Short Story

Gertrude Stein who was sometimes very wise said to me on one of her wise days, "Remember, Hemingway, that remarks are not literature." The following remarks are not intended to be nor do they pretend to be literature. They are meant to be instructive, irritating and informative. No writer should be asked to write solemnly about what he has written. Truthfully, yes. Solemnly, no. Should we begin in the form of a lecture designed to counteract the many lectures you will have heard on the art of the short story?

Many people have a compulsion to write. There is no law against it and doing it makes them happy while they do it and presumably relieves them. Given editors who will remove the worst of their emissions, supply them with spelling and syntax and help them shape their thoughts and their beliefs, some compulsive writers attain a temporary fame. But when shit, or *merde*—a word which teacher will explain—is cut out of a book, the odor of it always remains perceptible to anyone with sufficient olfactory sensibility.

The compulsive writer would be advised not to attempt the short story. Should he make the attempt, he might well suffer the fate of the compulsive architect, which is as lonely an end as that of the compulsive bassoon player. Let us not waste our time considering the sad and lonely ends of these unfortunate creatures, gentlemen. Let us continue the exercise.

Are there any questions? Have you mastered the art of the short story? Have I been helpful? Or have I not made myself clear? I hope so.

Gentlemen, I will be frank with you. The masters of the short story come to no good end. You query this? You cite me Maugham? Longevity, gentlemen, is not an end. It is a prolongation. I cannot say fie upon it, since I have never fied on anything yet. Shuck it off, Jack. Don't fie on it.

Should we abandon rhetoric and realize at the same time that what is the most authentic hipster talk of today is the twenty-three skidoo of tomorrow? We should? What intelligent young people you are and what a privilege it is to be with you. Do I hear a request for authentic ballroom bananas? I do? Gentlemen, we have them for you in bunches.

Actually, as writers put it when they do not know how to begin a sentence, there is very little to say about writing short stories unless you are a professional explainer. If you can do it, you don't have to explain it. If you can not do it, no explanation will ever help.

A few things I have found to be true. If you leave out important things or events that you know about, the story is strengthened. If you leave or skip something because you do not know it, the story will be worthless. The test of any story is how very good the stuff is that you, not your editors, omit. A story in this book called "Big Two-Hearted River" is about a boy coming home beat to the wide from a war. Beat to the wide was an earlier and possibly more severe form of beat, since those who had it were unable to comment on this condition and could not suffer that it be mentioned in their presence. So the war, all mention of the war, anything about the war, is omitted. The river was the Fox River, by Seney, Michigan, not the Big Two-Hearted. The change of name was made purposely, not from ignorance nor carelessness but because Big Two-Hearted River is poetry, and because there were many Indians in the story, just as the war was in the story, and none of the Indians nor the war appeared. As you see, it is very simple and easy to explain.

In a story called "The Sea Change," everything is left out. I had seen the couple in the Bar Basque in St.-Jean-de-Luz and I knew the story too too well, which is the squared root of well, and use any well you like except mine. So I left the story out. But it is all there. It is not visible but it is there.

It is very hard to talk about your work since it implies arrogance or pride. I have tried to get rid of arrogance and replace it with humility and I do all right at that sometimes, but without pride I would not wish to continue to live nor to write and I publish nothing of which I am not proud. You can take that any way you like, Jack. I might not take it myself. But maybe we're built different.

Another story is "Fifty Grand." This story originally started like this:

"'How did you handle Benny so easy, Jack?' Soldier asked him.

"'Benny's an awful smart boxer,' Jack said. 'All the time he's in there, he's thinking. All the time he's thinking, I was hitting him.'"

I told this story to Scott Fitzgerald in Paris before I wrote "Fifty Grand" trying to explain to him how a truly great boxer like Jack Britton functioned. I wrote the story opening with that incident and when it was finished I was happy about it and showed it to Scott. He said he liked the story very much and spoke about it in so fulsome a manner that I was embarrassed. Then he said, "There is only one thing wrong with it, Ernest, and I tell you this as your friend. You have to cut out that old chestnut about Britton and Leonard."

At that time my humility was in such ascendance that I thought he must have heard the remark before or that Britton must have said it to someone else. It was not until I had published the story, from which I had removed that lovely revelation of the metaphysics of boxing that Fitzgerald in the way his mind was functioning that year so that he called an historic statement an "old chestnut" because he had heard it once and only once from a friend, that I realized how dangerous that attractive virtue, humility, can be. So do not be too humble, gentlemen. Be humble after but not during the action. They will all con you, gentlemen. But sometimes it is not intentional. Sometimes they simply do not know. This is the saddest state of writers and the one you will most frequently encounter. If there are no questions, let us press on.

My loyal and devoted friend Fitzgerald, who was truly more

interested in my own career at this point than in his own, sent me to *Scribner's* with the story. It had already been turned down by Ray Long of *Cosmopolitan Magazine* because it had no love interest. That was okay with me since I eliminated any love interest and there were, purposely, no women in it except for two broads. Enter two broads as in Shakespeare, and they go out of the story. This is unlike what you will hear from your instructors, that if a broad comes into a story in the first paragraph, she must reappear later to justify her original presence. This is untrue, gentlemen. You may dispense with her, just as in life. It is also untrue that if a gun hangs on the wall when you open up the story, it must be fired by page fourteen. The chances are, gentlemen, that if it hangs upon the wall, it will not even shoot. If there are no questions, shall we press on? Yes, the unfireable gun may be a symbol. That is true. But with a good enough writer, the chances are some jerk just hung it there to look at. Gentlemen, you can't be sure. Maybe he is queer for guns, or maybe an interior decorator put it there. Or both.

So with pressure by Max Perkins on the editor, *Scribner's Magazine* agreed to publish the story and pay me two hundred and fifty dollars, if I would cut it to a length where it would not have to be continued into the back of the book. They call magazines books. There is significance in this but we will not go into it. They are not books, even if they put them in stiff covers. You have to watch this, gentlemen. Anyway, I explained without heat or hope, seeing the built-in stupidity of the editor of the magazine and his intransigence, that I had already cut the story myself and that the only way it could be shortened by five hundred words and make sense was to amputate the first five hundred. I had often done that myself with stories and it improved them. It would not have improved this story but I thought that was their ass not mine. I would put it back together in a book. They read differently in a book anyway. You will learn about this.

No, gentlemen, they would not cut the first five hundred words. They gave it instead to a very intelligent young assistant editor who assured me he could cut it with no difficulty. That was just what he did on his first attempt, and any place he took words out, the story no longer made sense. It had been cut for keeps when I wrote it, and afterwards at Scott's request I'd even cut out the metaphysics which, ordinarily, I leave in. So they quit on it finally and eventually, I understand, Edward Weeks got Ellery Sedgwick to publish it in the *Atlantic Monthly*. Then everyone wanted me to write fight stories and I did not write any more fight stories because I tried to write only one story on anything, if I got what I was after, because Life is very short if you like it and I knew that even then. There are other things to write about and other people who write very good fight stories. I recommend to you "The Professional" by W. C. Heinz.

Yes, the confidently cutting young editor became a big man on *Reader's Digest*. Or didn't he? I'll have to check that. So you see, gentlemen, you never know and what you win in Boston you lose in Chicago. That's symbolism, gentlemen, and you can run a saliva test on it. That is how we now detect symbolism in our group and so far it gives fairly satisfactory results. Not complete, mind you. But we are getting in to see our way through. Incidentally, within a short time *Scribner's Magazine* was running a contest for long short stories that broke back into the back of the book, and paying many times two hundred and fifty dollars to the winners.

Now since I have answered your perceptive questions, let us take up another story.

This story is called "The Light of the World." I could have called it "Behold I Stand at the Door and Knock" or some other stained-glass window title, but I did not think of it and actually "The Light of the World" is better. It is about many things and you would be ill-advised to think it is a simple tale. It is really, no matter what you hear, a love letter to a whore named Alice who at the time of the story would have dressed out at around two hundred and ten pounds. Maybe more. And the point of it is that nobody, and that goes for you, Jack, knows how we were then from how we are now. This is worse on women than on us, until you look into the mirror yourself some day instead of looking at women all the time, and in writing the story I was trying to do something about it. But there are very few basic things you can do anything about. So I do what the French call *constater*. Look that up. That is what you have to learn to do, and you ought to learn French anyway if you are going to understand short stories, and there is nothing rougher than to do it all the way. It is hardest to do about women and you must not worry when they say there are no such women as those you wrote about. That only means your women aren't like their women. You ever see any of their women, Jack? I have a couple of times and you would be appalled and I know you don't appall easy.

What I learned constructive about women, not just ethics like never blame them if they pox you because somebody poxed them and lots of times they don't even know they have it—that's in the first reader for squares—is, no matter *how* they get, always think of them the way they were on the best day they ever had in their lives. That's about all you can do about it and that is what I was trying for in the story.

Now there is another story called "The Short Happy Life of Francis Macomber." Jack, I get a bang even yet from just writing the titles. That's why you write, no matter what they tell you. I'm glad to be with somebody I know now and those feecking students have gone. They haven't? Okay. Glad to have them with us. It is in you that our hope is. That's the stuff to feed the troops. Students, at ease.

This is a simple story in a way, because the woman, who I knew very well in real life but then invented out of, to make the woman for this story, is a bitch for the full course and doesn't change. You'll probably never meet the type because you haven't got the money. I haven't either but I get around. Now this woman doesn't change. She has been better, but she will never be any better anymore. I invented her complete with handles from the worst bitch I knew (then) and when I first knew her she'd been lovely. Not my dish, not my pigeon, not my cup of tea, but lovely for what she was and I was her all of the above which is whatever you make of it. This is as close as I can put it and keep it clean. This information is what you call the background of a story. You throw it all away and invent from what you know. I should have said that sooner. That's all there is to writing. That, a perfect ear—call it selective—absolute pitch, the devotion to your work and respect for it that a priest of God has for his, and then have the guts of a burglar, no conscience except to writing, and you're in, gentlemen. It's easy. Anybody can write if he is cut out for it and applies himself. Never give it a thought. Just have those few requisites. I mean the way you have to write now to handle the way now is now. There was a time when it was nicer, much nicer and all that has been well written by nicer people. They are all dead and so are their times, but they handled them very well. Those times are over and writing like that won't help you now.

But to return to this story. The woman called Margot Macomber is no good to anybody now except for trouble. You can bang her but that's about all. The man is a nice jerk. I knew him very well in real life, so invent him too from everything I know. So he is just how he really was, only he is invented. The White Hunter is my best friend and he does not care what I write as long as it is readable, so I don't invent him at all. I just disguise him for family and business reasons, and to keep him out of trouble with the Game Department. He is the furthest thing from a square since they invented the circle, so I just have to take care of him with an adequate disguise and he is as proud as though we both wrote it, which actually you always do in anything if you go back far enough. So it is a secret between us. That's all there is to that story except maybe the lion when he is hit and I am thinking inside of him really, not faked. I can think inside of a lion, really. It's hard to believe and it is perfectly okay with me if you don't believe it. Perfectly. Plenty of people have used it since, though, and one boy used it quite well, making only one mistake. Making any mistake kills you. This mistake killed him and quite soon everything he wrote was a mistake. You have to watch yourself, Jack, every minute, and the more talented you are the more you have to watch these mistakes because you will be in faster company. A writer who is not going all the way up can make all the mistakes he wants. None of it matters. He doesn't matter. The people who like him don't matter either. They could drop dead. It wouldn't make any difference. It's too bad. As soon as you read one page by anyone you can tell whether it matters or not. This is sad and you hate to do it. I don't want to be the one that tells them. So don't make any mistakes. You see how easy it is? Just go right in there and be a writer.

That about handles that story. Any questions? No, I don't know whether she shot him on purpose any more than you do. I could find out if I asked myself because I invented it and I could go right on inventing. But you have to know where to stop. That is what makes a short story. Makes it short at least. The only hint I could give you is that it is my belief that the incidence of husbands shot accidentally by wives who are bitches and really work at it is very low. Should we continue?

If you are interested in how you get the idea for a story, this is how it was with "The Snows of Kilimanjaro." They have you ticketed and always try to make it that you are someone who can only write about theirself. I am using in this lecture the spoken language, which varies. It is one of the ways to write, so you might as well follow it and maybe you will learn something. Anyone who can write can write spoken, pedantic, inexorably dull, or pure English prose, just as slot machines can be set for straight, percentage, give-away or stealing. No one who can write spoken ever starves except at the start. The others you can eat irregularly on. But any good writer can do them all. This is spoken, approved for over fourteen I hope. Thank you.

Anyway we came home from Africa, which is a place you stay until the money runs out or you get smacked, one year and at quarantine I said to the ship news reporters when somebody asked me what my projects were that I was going to work and when I had some more money go back to Africa. The different wars killed off that project and it took nineteen years to get back. Well it was in the papers and a really nice and really fine and really rich woman invited me to tea and we had a few drinks as well and she had read in the papers about this project, and why should I have to wait to go back for any lack of money? She and my wife and I could go to Africa any time and money was only something to be used intelligently for the best enjoyment of good people and so forth. It was a sincere and fine and good offer and I liked her very much and I turned down the offer.

So I get down to Key West and I start to think what would happen to a character like me whose defects I know, if I had accepted that offer. So I start to invent and I make myself a guy who would do what I invent. I know about the dying part because I had been through all that. Not just once. I got it early, in the middle and later. So I invent how someone I know who cannot sue me—that is me—would turn out, and put into one short story things you would use in, say, four novels if you were careful and not a spender. I throw everything I had been saving into the story and spend it all. I really throw it away, if you know what I mean. I am not gambling with it. Or maybe I am. Who knows? Real gamblers don't gamble. At least you think they don't gamble. They gamble, Jack, don't worry. So I make up the man and the woman as well as I can and I put all the true stuff in and with all the load, the most load any short story ever carried, it still takes off and it flies. This makes me very happy. So I thought that and the Macomber story are as good short stories as I can write for a while, so I lose interest and take up other forms of writing.

Any questions? The leopard? He is part of the metaphysics. I did not hire out to explain that nor a lot of other things. I know, but I am under no obligation to tell you. Put it down to *omertá*. Look that word up. I dislike explainers, apologists, stoolies, pimps. No writer should be any one of those for his own work. This is just a little background, Jack, that won't do either of us any harm. You see the point, don't you? If not it is too bad.

That doesn't mean you shouldn't explain for, apologize for or pimp or tout for some other writer. I have done it and the best luck I had was doing it for Faulkner. When they didn't know him in Europe, I told them all how he was the best we had and so forth and I over-humbled with him plenty and built him up about as high as he could go because he never had a break then and he was good then. So now whenever he has a few shots, he'll tell students what's wrong with me or tell the Japanese or anybody they send him to, to build up our local product. I get tired of this but I figure what the hell he's had a few shots and maybe he even believes it. So you asked me just now what I think about him, as everybody does and I always stall, so I say you know how good he is. Right. You ought to. What is wrong is he cons himself sometimes pretty bad. That may just be the sauce. But for quite a while when he hits the sauce toward the end of a book, it shows bad. He gets tired and he goes on and on, and that sauce writing is really hard on who has to read it. I mean if they care about writing. I thought maybe it would help if I read it using the sauce myself, but it wasn't any help. Maybe it would have helped if I was fourteen. But I was fourteen one year and then I would have been too busy. So that's what I think about Faulkner. You ask that I sum it up from the standpoint of a professional. Very good writer. Cons himself now. Too much sauce. But he wrote a really fine story called "The Bear" and I would be glad to put it in this book for your pleasure and delight, if I had written it. But you can't write them all, Jack.

It would be simpler and more fun to talk about other writers and what is good and what is wrong with them, as I saw when you asked me about Faulkner. He's easy to handle because he talks so much for a supposed silent man. Never talk, Jack, if you are a writer, unless you have the guy write it down and have you go over it. Otherwise, they get it wrong. That's what you think until they play a tape back at you. Then you know how silly it sounds. You're a writer aren't you? Okay, shut up and write. What was that question?

Did I really write three stories in one day in Madrid, the way it said in that interview in *The Paris Review* and *Horizon*? Yes sir. I was hotter than a—let's skip it, gentlemen. I was laden with uninhibited energy. Or should we say this energy was canalized into my work. Such states are compounded by the brisk air of the Guadarramas (Jack, was it cold) the highly seasoned bacalao vizcaíno (dried cod fish, Jack) a certain vague loneliness. (I was in love and the girl was in Bologna and I couldn't sleep anyway, so why not write.) So I wrote.

"The stories you mention I wrote in one day in Madrid on May 16 when it snowed out the San Isidro bullfights. First I wrote 'The Killers' which I'd tried to write before and failed. Then after lunch I got in bed to keep warm and wrote 'Today is Friday.' I had so much juice I thought maybe I was going crazy and I had about six other stories to write. So I got dressed and walked to Fornos, the old bull fighter's cafe, and drank coffee and then came back and wrote 'Ten Indians.' This made me very sad and I drank some brandy and went to sleep. I'd forgotten to eat and one of the waiters brought me up some bacalao and a small steak and fried potatoes and a bottle of Valdepeñas.

"The woman who ran the Pension was always worried that I did not eat enough and she had sent the waiter. I remember sitting up in bed and eating, and drink the Valdepeñas. The waiter said he would bring up another bottle. He said the Señora wanted to know if I was going to write all night. I said no, I thought I would lay off for a while. Why don't you try to write just one more, the waiter asked. I'm only supposed to write one, I said. Nonsense, he said. You could write six. I'll try tomorrow, I said. Try it tonight, he said. What do you think the old woman sent the food up for?

"I'm tired, I told him. Nonsense, he said (the word was not nonsense). You tired after three miserable little stories. Translate me one.

"Leave me alone, I said. How am I going to write it if you don't leave me alone. So I sat up in bed and drank the Valdepeñas and thought what a hell of a writer I was if the first story was as good as I'd hoped."

I have used the same words in answering that the excellent Plimpton elicited from me in order to avoid error or repetition. If there are no more questions, should we continue?

It is very bad for writers to be hit on the head too much. Sometimes you lose months when you should have and perhaps would have worked well but sometimes a long time after the memory of the sensory distortions of these woundings will produce a story which, while not justifying the temporary cerebral damage, will palliate it. "A Way You'll Never Be" was written at Key West, Florida, some fifteen years after the damage it depicts, both to a man, a village and a countryside, had occurred. No questions? I understand. I understand completely. However, do not be alarmed. We are not going to call for a moment of silence. Nor for the man in the white suit. Nor for the net. Now gentlemen, and I notice a sprinkling of ladies who have drifted in attracted I hope by the sprinkling of applause. Thank you. Just *what* stories do you yourselves care for? I must not impose on you exclusively those that find favor with their author. Do *you* too care for any of them?

You like "The Killers"? So good of you. And why? Because it had Burt Lancaster and Ava Gardner in it? Excellent. Now we are getting somewhere. It is always a pleasure to remember Miss Gardner as she was then. No, I never met Mr. Lancaster. I can't tell you what he is really like but everyone says he is terrific. The background of that story is that I had a lawyer who had cancer and he wanted cash rather than any long term stuff. You can see his point I hope. So when he was offered a share in the picture for me and less cash, he took the more cash. It turned out badly for us both. He died eventually and I retained only an academic interest in the picture. But the company lets me run it off free when I want to see Miss Gardner and hear the shooting. It is a good picture and the only good picture ever made of a story of mine. One of the reasons for that is that John Huston wrote the script. Yes I know him. Is everything true about him that they say? No. But the best things are. Isn't that interesting.

You mean background about the story not the picture? That's not very sporting, young lady. Didn't you see the class was enjoying itself finally? Besides it has a sordid background. I hesitate to bring it in, on account of there is no statute of limitations on what it deals with. Gene Tunney, who is a man of wide culture, once asked me, "Ernest, wasn't that Andre Anderson in 'The Killers'?" I told him it was and that the town was Summit, Illinois, not Summit, N.J. We left it at that. I thought about that story a long long time before I invented it, and I had to be as far away as Madrid before I invented it properly. That story probably had more left out of it than anything I ever wrote. More even than when I left the war out of "Big Two-Hearted River." I left out all Chicago, which is hard to do in 2951 words.

Another time I was leaving out good was in "A Clean Well-Lighted Place." There I really had luck. I left out everything. That is about as far as you can go, so I stood on that one and haven't drawn to that since.

I trust you follow me, gentlemen. As I said at the start, there is nothing to writing short stories once you get the knack of it.

A story I can beat, and I promise you I will, is "The Undefeated." But I leave it in to show you the difference between when you leave it all in and when you take it out. The stories where you leave it all in do not re-read like the ones where you leave it out. They understand easier, but when you have read them once or twice you can't re-read them. I could give you examples in everybody who writes, but writers have enough enemies without doing it to each other. All really good writers know exactly what is wrong in all other good writers. There are no perfect writers unless they write just a very little bit and then stand on it. But writers have no business fingering another writer to outsiders while he is alive. After a writer is dead and doesn't have to work any more, anything goes. A son of a bitch alive is a son of a bitch dead. I am not talking about rows between writers. They are okay and can be comic. If someone puts a thumb in your eye, you don't protest. You thumb him back. He fouls you, you foul him back. That teaches people to keep it clean. What I mean is, you shouldn't give it to another writer, I mean really give it to him. I know you shouldn't do it because I did it once to Sherwood Anderson. I did it because I was righteous, which is the worst thing you can be, and I thought he was going to pot the way he was writing and that I could kid him out of it by showing him how awful it was. So I wrote *The Torrents of Spring*. It was cruel to do, and it didn't do any good, and he just wrote worse and worse. What the hell business of mine was it if he wanted to write badly? None. But then I was righteous and more loyal to writing than to my friend. I would have shot anybody then, not kill them, just shoot them a little, if I thought it would straighten them up and make them write right. Now I know that there is nothing you can do about any writer ever. The seeds of their destruction are in them from the start, and the thing to do about writers is get along with them if you see them, and try not to see them. All except a very few, and all of them except a couple are dead. Like I said, once they're dead anything goes as long as it's true.

I'm sorry I threw at Anderson. It was cruel and I was a son of a bitch to do it. The only thing I can say is that I was as cruel to myself then. But that is no excuse. He was a friend of mine, but that was no excuse for doing it to him. Any questions? Ask me that some other time.

This brings us to another story, "My Old Man." The background of this was all the time we spent at the races at San Siro when I used to be in hospital in Milan in 1918, and the time put in at the tracks in Paris when we really worked at it. Handicapping I mean. Some people say that this story is derived from a story about harness racing by Sherwood Anderson called "I'm a

Fool." I do not believe this. My theory is that it is derived from a jockey I knew very well and a number of horses I knew, one of which I was in love with. I invented the boy in my story and I think the boy in Sherwood's story was himself. If you read both stories you can form your own opinion. Whatever it is, it is all right with me. The best things Sherwood wrote are in two books, *Winesburg, Ohio* and *The Triumph of the Egg*. You should read them both. Before you know too much about things, they are better. The best thing about Sherwood was he was the kind of guy at the start his name made you think of Sherwood Forest, while in Bob Sherwood the name only made you think of a playwright.

Any other stories you find in this book are in because I liked them. If you like them too I will be pleased. Thank you very much. It has been nice to be with you.

Ernest Hemingway
June 1959
La Consula
Churriana
Malaga, Spain

1.

Judgment of Manitou

1916

Dick Haywood buttoned the collar of his mackinaw up about his ears, took down his rifle from the deer horns above the fireplace of the cabin and pulled on his heavy fur mittens. "I'll go and run that line toward Loon River, Pierre," he said. "Holy quill pigs, but it's cold." He glanced at the thermometer. "Forty-two below!" "Well, so long, Pierre." Pierre merely grunted, as, twisting on his snow shoes, Dick started out over the crust with the swinging snowshoe stride of the traveler of the barren grounds.

In the doorway of the cabin Pierre stood looking after Dick as he swung along. He grinned evilly to himself, "De tief will tink it a blame sight cooler when he swingin' by one leg in the air like Wah-boy, the rabbit; he would steal my money, would he!" Pierre slammed the heavy door shut, threw some wood on the fire and crawled into his bunk.

As Dick Haywood strode along he talked to himself as to the traveler's of the "silent places." "Wonder why Pierre is so grouchy just because he lost that money? Bet he just misplaced it somewhere. All he does now is to grunt like a surly pig and every once in a while I catch him leering at me behind my back. If he thinks I stole his money why don't he say so and have it out with me! Why, he used to be so cheerful and jolly; when we agreed at Missainabal to be partners and trap up here in the Ungava district, I thought he'd be a jolly good companion, but now he hasn't spoken to me for the last week, except to grunt or swear in that Cree lingo."

It was a cold day, but it was the dry, invigorating cold of the northland and Dick enjoyed the crisp air. He was a good traveler on snowshoes and rapidly covered the first five miles of the trap line, but somehow he felt that something was following him and he glanced around several times only to be disappointed each time. "I guess it's only the Koutzie-ootzie," he muttered to him-self, for in the North whenever men do not understand a thing they blame it on the "little bad god of the Crees." Suddenly, as Dick entered a growth of spruce, he was jerked off his feet, high into the air. When his head had cleared from the bang it had received by striking the icy crust, he saw that he was suspended in the air by a rope that was attached to a spruce tree, which had been bent over to form the spring for a snare, such as is used to capture rabbits. His fingers barely touched the crust, and as he struggled and the cord grew tighter on his leg, he saw what he had sensed to be following him. Slowly out of the woods trotted a band of gaunt, white, hungry timber wolves, and squatted on their haunches in a circle round him.

Back in the cabin Pierre as he lay in his bunk was awakened by a gnawing sound overhead, and idly looking up at the rafter he saw a red squirrel busily gnawing away at the leather of his lost wallet. He thought of the trap he had set for Dick, and spring-ing from his bunk he seized his rifle, and coatless and gloveless ran madly out along the trail. After a gasping, breathless, choking run he came upon the spruce grove. Two ravens left off picking at the shapeless something that had once been Dick Haywood, and flapped lazily into a neighboring spruce. All over the bloody snow were the tracks of My-in-gau, the timber wolf.

As he took a step forward Pierre felt the clanking grip of the toothed bear trap, that Dick had come to tend, close on his feet. He fell forward, and as he lay on the snow he said, "it is the judg-ment of Manitou; I will save My-in-gau, the wolf, the trouble."

And he reached for the rifle.

2.

Untitled Milan Story

1918

Item 604, Ernest Hemingway Collection, John F. Kennedy Library and Museum, Boston. Untitled short story written in the fall of 1918. Autograph manuscript on stationery of the American Red Cross, Milan, Italy. Four pages of text written in pencil on both sides of two sheets of stationery.

[I]

Nick lay in bed in the hospital while from outside came the hysterical roar of the crowd milling through the streets. "Viva La Pace! Viva La Pace!," came the voice of the crowd through the closed glass doors, and as the mob waving flags, blowing horns, carrying torches made of twisted paper boiled into the street of the American hospital it cried "Viva America!" and then "Viva Wilson!"

"Gee," Nick grinned at the nurse. "Those horns sound like Halloween! Some time back in the States tonight, eh Sister?"

"Oh wouldn't it be wonderful on Broadway!," said the nurse ecstatically.

"I don't know about Broadway but I'll bet things are popping up in Petoskey Michigan where I'm from. I didn't know you were a New Yorker."

II

"Oh I'm not really. I'm from Fort Wayne Indiana. It's on the G.R. and I. and that runs to Petoskey. But you know how everyone talks about Broadway!"

"Sure I've used that stuff too. Well good night Sister. Fort Wayne will look pretty good in a couple of months eh?"

"Don't talk about Broadway to me!," the nurse smiled back over her shoulder as she closed the door.

Nick reached out a thin hand[,] grasped a bottle on the table by his bed and shoved it under the bed clothes.

In a moment the nurse reappeared.

"I wonder where that bottle of bichloride is. I was certain I left it here. Did Miss Becker take it Mr. Grainger?"

"She must have," said Nick.

On the little iron table by the bed were two oblong red Moroccan leather boxes.

III

Nick opened the first one and took out a round silver medal on a plain blue ribbon. The second box revealed a bronze cross. Nick studied the two medals turning them over and over with his right hand. Then he picked up a typewritten paper and read it to himself.

"Some flowery translation Giovane did on this. 'Although previously wounded in the left arm and not recommended for active duty, he volunteered for the offensive while his arm was not yet of a complete cure. Wounded twice by the machine guns of the enemy he continued to advance at the head of his platoon with the greatest coolness and valor until struck in the legs by the shell of a trench mortar. For his intrepid bravery and noble example the state has conferred the Medaglia D'Argento per Valore. The Croce al Merito Di Guerra has been previously been conferred.'"

IV

Nick folded the paper and smiled a crooked smile. "That counterfeit dollar represents my legs and that tin cross is my left arm. I had a rendezvous with Death—but Death broke the date and now it's all over. God double crossed me."

II

3.

Up in Michigan

1923

Jim Gilmore came to Hortons Bay from Canada. He bought the blacksmith shop from old man Horton. Jim was short and dark with big mustaches and big hands. He was a good horseshoer and did not look much like a blacksmith even with his leather apron on. He lived upstairs above the blacksmith shop and took his meals at D. J. Smith's.

Liz Coates worked for Smith's. Mrs. Smith, who was a very large clean woman, said Liz Coates was the neatest girl she'd ever seen. Liz had good legs and always wore clean gingham aprons and Jim noticed that her hair was always neat behind. He liked her face because it was so jolly but he never thought about her.

Liz liked Jim very much. She liked it the way he walked over from the shop and often went to the kitchen door to watch for him to start down the road. She liked it about his mustache. She liked it about how white his teeth were when he smiled. She liked it very much that he didn't look like a blacksmith. She liked it how much D. J. Smith and Mrs. Smith liked Jim. One day she found that she liked it the way the hair was black on his arms and how white they were above the tanned line when he washed up in the washbasin outside the house. Liking that made her feel funny.

Hortons Bay, the town, was only five houses on the main road between Boyne City and Charlevoix. There was the general store and post office with a high false front and maybe a wagon hitched out in front, Smith's house, Stroud's house, Dillworth's house, Horton's house and Van Hoosen's house. The houses were in a big grove of elm trees and the road was very sandy. There was farming country and timber each way up the road. Up the road a ways was the Methodist church and down the road the other direction was the township school. The blacksmith shop was painted red and faced the school.

A steep sandy road ran down the hill to the bay through the timber. From Smith's back door you could look out across the woods that ran down to the lake and across the bay. It was very beautiful in the spring and summer, the bay blue and bright and usually whitecaps on the lake out beyond the point from the breeze blowing from Charlevoix and Lake Michigan. From Smith's back door Liz could see ore barges way out in the lake going toward Boyne City. When she looked at them they didn't seem to be moving at all but if she went in and dried some more dishes and then came out again they would be out of sight beyond the point.

All the time now Liz was thinking about Jim Gilmore. He didn't seem to notice her much. He talked about the shop to D. J. Smith and about the Republican Party and about James G. Blaine. In the evenings he read *The Toledo Blade* and the Grand Rapids paper by the lamp in the front room or went out spearing fish in the bay with a jacklight with D. J. Smith. In the fall he and Smith and Charley Wyman took a wagon and tent, grub, axes, their rifles and two dogs and went on a trip to the pine plains beyond Vanderbilt deer hunting. Liz and Mrs. Smith were cooking for four days for them before they started. Liz wanted to make something special for Jim to take but she didn't finally because she was afraid to ask Mrs. Smith for the eggs and flour and afraid if she bought them Mrs. Smith would catch her cooking. It would have been all right with Mrs. Smith but Liz was afraid.

All the time Jim was gone on the deer hunting trip Liz thought about him. It was awful while he was gone. She couldn't sleep well from thinking about him but she discovered it was fun to think about him too. If she let herself go it was better. The night before they were to come back she didn't sleep at all, that is she didn't think she slept because it was all mixed up in a dream about not sleeping and really not sleeping. When she saw the wagon coming down the road she felt weak and sick sort of inside. She couldn't wait till she saw Jim and it seemed as though everything would be all right when he came. The wagon stopped outside under the big elm and Mrs. Smith and Liz went out. All the men had beards and there were three deer in the back of the wagon, their thin legs sticking stiff over the edge of the wagon box. Mrs. Smith kissed D. J. and he hugged her. Jim said "Hello, Liz," and grinned. Liz hadn't known just what would happen when Jim got back but she was sure it would be something. Nothing had happened. The men were just home, that was all. Jim pulled the burlap sacks off the deer and Liz looked at them. One was a big buck. It was stiff and hard to lift out of the wagon.

"Did you shoot it, Jim?" Liz asked.

"Yeah. Ain't it a beauty?" Jim got it onto his back to carry to the smokehouse.

That night Charley Wyman stayed to supper at Smith's. It was too late to get back to Charlevoix. The men washed up and waited in the front room for supper.

"Ain't there something left in that crock, Jimmy?" D. J. Smith asked, and Jim went out to the wagon in the barn and fetched in the jug of whiskey the men had taken hunting with them. It was a four-gallon jug and there was quite a little slopped back and forth in the bottom. Jim took a long pull on his way back to the house. It was hard to lift such a big jug up to drink out of it. Some of the whiskey ran down on his shirt front. The two men smiled when Jim came in with the jug. D. J. Smith sent for glasses and Liz brought them. D. J. poured out three big shots.

"Well, here's looking at you, D. J.," said Charley Wyman.

"That damn big buck, Jimmy," said D. J.

"Here's all the ones we missed, D. J.," said Jim, and downed his liquor.

"Tastes good to a man."

"Nothing like it this time of year for what ails you."

"How about another, boys?"

"Here's how, D. J."

"Down the creek, boys."

"Here's to next year."

Jim began to feel great. He loved the taste and the feel of whiskey. He was glad to be back to a comfortable bed and warm food and the shop. He had another drink. The men came in to supper feeling hilarious but acting very respectable. Liz sat at the table after she put on the food and ate with the family. It was a good dinner. The men ate seriously. After supper they went into the front room again and Liz cleaned off with Mrs. Smith. Then Mrs. Smith went upstairs and pretty soon Smith came out and went upstairs too. Jim and Charley were still in the front room. Liz was sitting in the kitchen next to the stove pretending to read a book and thinking about Jim. She didn't want to go to bed yet because she knew Jim would be coming out and she wanted to see him as he went out so she could take the way he looked up to bed with her.

She was thinking about him hard and then Jim came out. His eyes were shining and his hair was a little rumpled. Liz looked down at her book. Jim came over back of her chair and stood there and she could feel him breathing and then he put his arms around her. Her breasts felt plump and firm and the nipples were erect under his hands. Liz was terribly frightened, no one had ever touched her, but she thought, "He's come to me finally. He's really come."

She held herself stiff because she was so frightened and did not know anything else to do and then Jim held her tight against the chair and kissed her. It was such a sharp, aching, hurting feeling that she thought she couldn't stand it. She felt Jim right through the back of the chair and she couldn't stand it and then something clicked inside of her and the feeling was warmer and softer. Jim held her tight hard against the chair and she wanted it now and Jim whispered, "Come on for a walk."

Liz took her coat off the peg on the kitchen wall and they went out the door. Jim had his arm around her and every little way they stopped and pressed against each other and Jim kissed her. There was no moon and they walked ankle-deep in the sandy road through the trees down to the dock and the warehouse on the bay. The water was lapping in the piles and the point was dark across the bay. It was cold but Liz was hot all over from being with Jim. They sat down in the shelter of the warehouse and Jim pulled Liz close to him. She was frightened. One of Jim's hands went inside her dress and stroked over her breast and the other hand was in her lap. She was very frightened and didn't know how he was going to go about things but she snuggled close to him. Then the hand that felt so big in her lap went away and was on her leg and started to move up it.

"Don't, Jim," Liz said. Jim slid the hand further up.

"You mustn't, Jim. You mustn't." Neither Jim nor Jim's big hand paid any attention to her.

The boards were hard. Jim had her dress up and was trying to do something to her. She was frightened but she wanted it. She had to have it but it frightened her.

"You mustn't do it, Jim. You mustn't."

"I got to. I'm going to. You know we got to."

"No we haven't, Jim. We ain't got to. Oh, it isn't right. Oh, it's so big and it hurts so. You can't. Oh, Jim. Jim. Oh."

The hemlock planks of the dock were hard and splintery and cold and Jim was heavy on her and he had hurt her. Liz pushed him, she was so uncomfortable and cramped. Jim was asleep. He wouldn't move. She worked out from under him and sat up and straightened her skirt and coat and tried to do something with her hair. Jim was sleeping with his mouth a little open. Liz leaned over and kissed him on the cheek. He was still asleep. She lifted his head a little and shook it. He rolled his head over and swallowed. Liz started to cry. She walked over to the edge of the dock and looked down to the water. There was a mist coming up from the bay. She was cold and miserable and everything felt gone. She walked back to where Jim was lying and shook him once more to make sure. She was crying.

"Jim," she said, "Jim. Please, Jim."

Jim stirred and curled a little tighter. Liz took off her coat and leaned over and covered him with it. She tucked it around him neatly and carefully. Then she walked across the dock and up the steep sandy road to go to bed. A cold mist was coming up through the woods from the bay.

3a.

Item 800, Ernest Hemingway Collection, John F. Kennedy Library and Museum, Boston. Untitled typescript with pencil corrections. This is the earliest preserved manuscript of "Up in Michigan."

~~Jim [?] in his chin from his mother. Her name had been Liz Buell. Jim Dilworth married her when he came to Horton's Bay from Canada and bought the mill with A.J. Stroud.~~

Jim Dilworth came to Hortons Bay from Canada. He bought the blacksmith shop from old man Horton. Jim was short and dark with big mustaches and big hands. He was a good horseshoer and did not look much like a blacksmith even with his leather apron on. He lived upstairs above the blacksmith shop and took his meals at A.J. Strouds.

Liz Buell worked for Strouds. Mrs. Stroud who was a very big clean woman said Liz Buell was the neatest girl she'd ever seen. Liz had good legs and always wore clean gingham aprons and Jim noticed that her hair ~~never scraggled~~ was always neat behind. He liked her face because it was so jolly. Liz liked Jim very much. She liked it the way he walked over from the shop and often went to the kitchen door to watch for him to start down the road, she liked it about his mustache, she liked it about how white his teeth were when he smiled. She liked it very much that he didn't look like a blacksmith. She liked it how much A.J. Stroud and Mrs. A.J. Stroud liked Jim. One day she found that she liked it the way the hair was black on his arms and how white they were above the tanned line when he washed up in the wash basin outside the house. Liking that made her feel funny.

~~Liz and Jim were both bashful.~~ Hortons Bay the town was only four houses on the main road between Boyne City and Charlevoix. ~~There was~~ There was farming country and timber each way up the road. The general store and post office ~~with~~ had a high false front and ~~maybe~~ usually a ~~buggy~~ wagon hitched out in front. Stroud's house, Fox's house, Horton's house and Van Housan's house were all in a big grove of elm trees and the road was very sandy. Up the road a ways was the Methodist Church and down the road the other way was the township school. The blacksmith shop was painted red and faced the township school. A steep sandy road ran down the hill to the Bay through the timber. From Stroud's back door ~~you~~ Liz could look out across the timber that ran down to the bay and across the bay. It was very beautiful in the spring and summer, the bay blue and bright and usually white caps on the lake out beyond the point from the breeze blowing from Charlevoix and Lake Michigan. From Stroud's back ~~door~~ Liz could see ore barges way out in the lake going toward Boyne City. When she looked at them they didn't seem to be moving, but if she went in and dried some more dishes and then came out again they would be out of sight beyond the point.

All the time now Liz was thinking about Jim Dilworth. He didn't seem to notice her much. He talked about the shop to A.J Stroud and about the Republican party and about James G. Blaine. In the evenings he read the Toledo Blade and the Grand Rapids paper or went out spearing fish in the bay with a jacklight with A.J. Stroud. In the fall he and Stroud and Charley Weaver took a wagon and tent, grub, axes, their rifles and two dogs and went on a trip to the pine plains beyond Vanderbilt deer hunting. Liz and Mrs. Stroud were cooking for four days for them before they started. Liz wanted to make something special for Jim to take but she couldn't because she was afraid to ask Mrs. Stroud for the eggs and flour and afraid if she bought them Mrs. Stroud would catch her cooking them. It would have been allright with Mrs. Stroud but Liz was afraid.

All the time Jim was gone on the deer hunting trip Liz thought about him. It was awful while he was gone. She couldn't sleep well from thinking about him but she discovered it was fun to think about him too. If she let herself go it was better. The night before they were to come back she didn't sleep at all, that is she didn't think she slept because it was all mixed up in a dream about not sleeping and really not sleeping. When she saw the wagon coming down the road she felt weak and sick sort of inside. She couldn't wait till she saw Jim and it seemed as though everything would be all right when he came. The wagon stopped outside and Mrs. Stroud and Liz went out. All the men had beards and there were three deer in the back of the wagon with their thin legs sticking stiff over the edge of the wagon-box. Mrs. Stroud kissed Alonzo and he hugged her. Jim said, "Hello Liz!" and grinned. Liz hadn't known just what would happen when Jim got back but she was sure it would be something. Nothing had happened. They were just home that was all. Jim pulled the burlap sacks off ~~of~~ the deer and Liz looked at them. One was a big buck. It was stiff and hard to lift out of the wagon. "Did you shoot it Jim?" Liz asked.

"Yeah. Aint it a beauty?" Jim said and got it on his back to carry to the smokehouse.

That night Charley Weaver stayed to supper at Strouds because it was too late for him to go back to Charlevoix. The men washed up and waited for supper.

"Aint there something left in that crock Jimmy?" Stroud asked and Jim went out to the wagon and fetched in the jug of whiskey the men had taken hunting with them. It was a four gallon jug and there was quite a little left. Jim took a long pull on his way in. It was hard to lift such a big jug up to drink out of it. Some of the whiskey ran down on his shirt front. A.J. Stroud poured out three big shots in the front room.

"Here's how A.J." said Charley Weaver.

"~~The~~ That big buck Jim" said A.J.

"Looking at you A.J." said Jim and downed his liquor.

"Tastes good to a man."

"Nothing like it this time of year."

"How about another boys?"

"Next year A.J."

"Over the River boys."

"Here's to crime."

They had about three big drinks. Jim felt great. The men came in to supper from the front room feeling hilarious but acting very respectable. Liz ~~always~~ sat at the table after she put on the food and ate with the family. It was a good dinner. The men were jolly but nobody ever talked much at the table in Hortons Bay. After the meal they went into the front room again and Liz cleared off with Mrs. Stroud. Then Stroud and Mrs. Stroud went up stairs together and Jim and Charley stayed in the front room. Liz was sitting in the kitchen next to the stove reading a book by Mrs. Glaskell and thinking about Jim. She didn't want to go up to bed yet because she knew that Jim would be coming out and she wanted to see him as he went out so she could take the way he looked up to bed with her.

She was thinking about him hard and then Jim came out. His eyes were shining his hair was a little rumpled. She looked down at her book. Jim came over behind her chair and put his arms around her. Her breasts felt plump and firm and the nipples were erect under his hands. Liz was terribly frightened but she thought, "He's come to me finally. He's come to me."

She held herself stiff because she was so frightened and did not know anything else to do and then Jim kissed her. It was such a sharp wonderful ~~feeling~~ hurting feeling that she felt she couldn't ~~not bear~~ stand it and then something clicked inside of her and the feeling was warmer and softer. Jim held her tightly against the chair and whispered. "~~Do you want to~~ Come on for a walk?"

Liz took her coat off the peg on the kitchen wall and they went out the door. Jim had his arm around her and every little way they stopped and Jim kissed her. There was no moon and they walked ankle deep in the sandy road through the trees down to the dock and warehouse on the bay. The water was lapping in the piles and the point was dark out across the bay. It was cold but Liz was hot all over from being with Jim. They sat down in the shelter of the warehouse and Jim pulled Liz close to him. He stroked her breast with one hand and rested the other in her lap. She was very frightened but she snuggled close to him. Then he put a hand on her leg and moved it up.

"Don't Jim." Liz whispered. Jim slid the hand further up.

"You musn't Jim. You musn't." Liz said. Neither Jim nor Jim's big hand paid any attention to her. Jim had pulled her slip up all over her and was trying to do something to her. She wanted it and was afraid of it.

"You musn't do it Jim. You musn't."

"~~But~~ I love you Liz. ~~I've~~ I got to. You know I got to."

"I know Jim. I know. But it isn't right. And it's so big and it hurts so."

The hemlock planks of the dock were hard and splintery and cold and Jim was heavy and he had hurt her. Liz pushed him, she was so uncomfortable and cramped. Jim was asleep. She worked out from under him got to her feet straightened her skirt and coat and

~~arranged~~ tried to do something with her hair. Jim was sleeping heavily. She leaned over and kissed him. He kept on sleeping. She grabbed his coat and shook him. He ~~stirred and~~ rolled his head over. Liz started to cry. She walked over to the edge of the dock and looked into the water. She was cold and miserable and everything was gone. She walked back to where Jim was lying and shook him once more to make sure. "Jim." She said, "Jim. Please Jim." Jim curled a little tighter. Liz took off her coat and leaned over and covered him with it. She tucked it around him carefully. Then ~~shivering~~ she walked across the dock and up the steep sandy road to go to bed. It was cold and there was a mist coming up from the Bay.

3b.

Item 799, Ernest Hemingway Collection, John F. Kennedy Library and Museum, Boston. Titled typescript with corrections in pencil and ink. This is most likely the typescript that Hemingway shared with Gertrude Stein and some of the edits on it have been plausibly assigned to her. Hemingway's Paris address is typed at the top left of the first page.

Ernest M. Hemingway
74 Rue du Cardinal Lemoine
Paris.

Up In Michigan

Jim ~~Dilworth~~ Gilmore came to Hortons Bay from Canada. He bought the blacksmith shop from old Man Horton. Jim was short and dark with big mustaches and big hands. He was a good horse-shoer and did not look much like a blacksmith even with his leather apron on. He lived upstairs above the blacksmith shop and took his meals at A.J. ~~Strouds Moores Coates~~.

Liz ~~Buell~~ Coates worked for ~~Strouds Moores Coates~~. Mrs. ~~Stroud Moore Coates~~, who was a very big clean woman, said Liz Buell was the neatest girl she'd ever seen. Liz had good legs and always wore clean gingham aprons and Jim noticed that her hair was always neat behind. He liked her face because it was jolly but he never thought about her.

Liz liked Jim very much. She liked it the way he walked over from the shop and often went to the kitchen door to watch for him to start down the road. She liked it about his mustache. She liked it about how white his teeth were when he smiled. She liked it very much that he didn't look like a blacksmith. She liked it how much A.J. ~~Stroud~~ Moore and Mrs. ~~Stroud~~ Moore liked Jim. One day she found that she liked it the way the hair was black on his arms and how white they were above the tanned line when he washed up in the washbasin outside the house. Liking that made her feel funny.

Hortons Bay, the town, was only ~~four~~ five houses on the main road between Boyne City and Charlevoix. There was the general store and postoffice with a high false front and maybe a wagon hitched out in front, Moore's house, Stroud's house, Fox's house, Horton's house and Van Housan's house. The houses were in a big grove of elm trees and the road was very sandy. There was farming country and timber each way up the road. Up the road a ways was the Methodist church and down the road the other way was the township school. The blacksmith shop was painted red and faced the school.

A steep sandy road ran down the hill to the bay through the timber. From ~~Stroud's~~ Moore's back door you could look out across the woods that ran down to the lake and across the bay. It was very beautiful in the spring and summer, the bay blue and bright and usually white caps on the lake out beyond the point from the breeze blowing from Charlevoix and Lake Michigan. From ~~Stroud's~~ Moore's back door Liz could see ore barges way out in the lake going toward Boyne City. When she looked at them they didn't seem to be moving but if she went in and dried some more dishes and then came out again they would be out of sight beyond the point.

All the time now Liz was thinking about Jim ~~Dilworth~~ Gilmore. He didn't seem to notice her much. He talked about the shop to A.J. ~~Stroud~~ Moore and about the Republican party and about James G. Blaine. In the evenings he read the Toledo Blade and the Grand Rapids paper by the lamp in the front room or went out spearing fish in the bay with a jacklight with A.J. ~~Stroud~~ Moore. In the fall he and ~~Stroud~~ A.J. and Charley Weaver took a wagon and tent, grub, axes, their rifles and two dogs and went on a trip to the pine plains beyond Vanderbilt deer hunting. Liz and Mrs. ~~Stroud~~ Moore were cooking for four days for them before they started. Liz wanted to make something special for Jim to take but she couldn't because she was afraid to ask Mrs. ~~Stroud~~ Moore for the eggs and flour and afraid if she bought them Mrs. Stroud would catch her cooking them. It would have been all right with Mrs. ~~Stroud~~ Moore but Liz was afraid.

All the time Jim was gone on the deer hunting trip Liz thought about him. It was awful while he was gone. She couldn't sleep well from thinking about him but she discovered it was fun to think about him too. If she let herself go it was better. The night before they were to come back she didn't sleep at all, that is she didn't think she slept because it was all mixed up in a dream about not sleeping and really not sleeping. When she saw the wagon coming down the road she felt weak and sick sort of inside. She couldn't wait till she saw Jim and it seemed that everything would be allright when he came. The wagon stopped outside and Mrs. ~~Stroud~~ Moore and Liz went out. All the men had beards and there were three deer in the back of the wagon with their thin legs sticking stiff over the edge of the wagon box. Mrs. ~~Stroud~~ Moore kissed Alonzo and he hugged her. Jim said "Hello Liz" and grinned. Liz hadn't known just what would happen when Jim got back but she was sure it would be something. Nothing had happened. They were just home that was all. Jim pulled the burlap sacks off the deer and Liz looked at them. One was a big buck. It was stiff and hard to lift out of the wagon.

"Did you shoot it, Jim?" Liz asked.

"Yeah. Aint it a beauty?" Jim got it onto his back to carry to the smokehouse.

That night Charley Weaver stayed to supper at ~~Strouds~~ Moore's. It was too late for him to get back to Charlevoix. The men washed up and waited for supper.

"Aint there something left in that crock Jimmy?" A.J. ~~Stroud~~ Moore asked and Jim went out to the wagon and fetched in the jug of whiskey the men had taken hunting with them. It was a four gallon jug and there was quite a little left. Jim took a long pull on his way in. It was hard to lift such a big jug up to drink out of it. Some of the whiskey ran down on his shirt front. A.J. ~~Stroud~~ Moore poured out three big shots in the front room.

"Here's looking at you A.J." said Charley Weaver.

"That damn big buck Jimmy" said A.J.

"All the ones we missed A.J." said Jim and downed his liquor.

"Tastes good to a man."

"Nothing like it this time of the year for what ails you."

"How about another boys?"

"Here's how A.J."

"Over the river boys."

"Here's to crime."

They had three or four big drinks. Jim felt great. The men came in to supper from the front room feeling hilarious but acting very respectable. Liz sat at the table after she put on the food and ate with the family. It was a good dinner. The men were jolly but ate seriously. After the meal they went into the front room again and Liz cleared off with Mrs. ~~Stroud~~ Moore. Then ~~Stroud~~ Moore and Mrs. ~~Stroud~~ Moore went up stairs together and Jim and Charley stayed in the front room. Liz was sitting in the kitchen next to the stove pretending to read a book and thinking about Jim. She didn't want to go to bed yet because she knew Jim would be coming out and she wanted to see him as he went out so she could take the way he looked up to bed with her.

She was thinking about him hard and then Jim came out. His eyes were shining and his hair was a little rumpled. She looked down at her book. Jim came over back of her chair and stood there and she could feel him breathing and then he put his arms around her. Her breasts felt plump and firm and the nipples were erect under his hands. Liz was terribly frightened but she thought, "He's come to me finally. He's really come."

She held herself stiff because she was so frightened and did not know anything else to do and then Jim held her tight against the chair and kissed her. It was such a sharp, aching hurting feeling that she felt she couldn't stand it. She felt Jim right through the back of the chair and she couldn't stand it and then something clicked inside of her and the feeling was warmer and softer. Jim held her tight hard against the chair and whispered, "Come on for a walk."

Liz took her coat off the peg on the kitchen wall and they went out the door. Jim had his arm around her and every little way they stopped and pressed against each other and Jim kissed her. There was no moon and they walked ankle deep in the sandy road through the trees down to the dock and the warehouse on the bay. The water was lapping in the piles and the point was dark out across the bay. It was cold but Liz was hot all over from being with Jim. They sat down in the shelter of the warehouse and Jim pulled Liz close to him. She was frightened. He stroked her breast with one hand inside her dress and rested the other in her lap. She was very frightened but she snuggled close to him. Then he put a hand on her leg and moved it up.

"Don't Jim." Liz said. Jim slid the hand further up.

"You musn't Jim. You musn't." Neither Jim nor Jim's big hand paid any attention to her.

The boards were hard. ~~Jim had her dress up and was trying to do something to her. She was frightened but she wanted it.~~ She had to have it but it frightened her.

~~"You musn't do it Jim. You musn't."~~

~~"I got to do it. I'm going to. You know we got to."~~

~~"No we haven't Jim. We aint got to. Oh it isn't right. And it's so big and it hurts so. Oh Jim. Jim. Oh."~~

~~The hemlock planks of the dock were hard and splintery and cold and Jim was heavy and he had hurt her. Liz pushed him, she was so uncomfortable and cramped.~~ [Crossing out may have been done by Gertrude Stein. Hemingway wrote along the side of the crossed-out text, "Pay no attention to."] Jim was asleep. He wouldn't move. She worked out from under him and sat up and straightened her skirt and coat and tried to do something with her hair. Jim was sleeping with his mouth a little open. Liz leaned over and kissed him on the cheek. He kept on sleeping. She put her hands under his head and shook it. He rolled his head over and swallowed. Liz started to cry. She walked over to the edge of the dock and looked into the water. There was a mist coming up from the bay. She was cold and miserable and everything felt gone. She walked back to where Jim was lying and shook him once more to make sure.

"Jim" she said crying, "Jim. Please Jim."

Jim curled a little tighter. Liz took off her coat and leaned over and covered him with it. She tucked it around him neatly and carefully. Then she walked across the dock and up the steep sandy road to go to bed.

3c.

Item 801, Ernest Hemingway Collection, John F. Kennedy Library and Museum, Boston. Untitled typescript fragment with two texts continuing the story of "Up in Michigan."

In the morning Jim came over to breakfast. Liz kept from looking at him. Then she did and saw his eyes were red. He seemed ashamed and embarrassed. When Jim had gone off to the shop

Liz was frightened and sick when she got up to her room. She put on one of her unwell pads because she was afraid of blood getting on the sheets. She felt ashamed and sick and cried and prayed until she fell asleep. She woke up frightened and stiff and aching. It was still dark. "What if I have a baby?" She thought. It was the first time she had thought about it. It really was. She was so frightened the sweat ran down under her armpits. She was too frightened to cry. She thought about having a baby until it was morning.

3d.

Item 802, Ernest Hemingway Collection, John F. Kennedy Library and Museum, Boston. Four corrected pages taken from *Three Stories and Ten Poems* with pencil corrections and changes by Ernest Hemingway.

Jim Gilmore came to H̶Mortons Bay from Canada. He bought the blacksmith shop from old man H̶Morton. Jim was short and dark with big mustaches and big hands. He was a good horseshoer and did not look much like a blacksmith even with his leather apron on. He lived upstairs above the blacksmith shop and took his meals at A. J. Smith's.

Liz Coates worked for Smith's. Mrs. Smith, who was a very large clean woman, said Liz Coates was the neatest girl she'd ever seen. Liz had good legs and always wore clean gingham aprons and Jim noticed that her hair was always neat behind. He liked her face because it was so jolly but he never thought about her.

Liz liked Jim very much. She liked it the way he walked over from the shop and often went to the kitchen door to watch for him to start down the road. She liked it about his mustache. She liked it about how white his teeth were when he smiled. She liked it very much that he didn't look like a blacksmith. She liked it how much A. J. Smith and Mrs. Smith liked Jim. One day she found that she liked it the way the hair was black on his arms and how white they were above the tanned line when he washed up in the washbasin outside the house. Liking that made her feel funny.

HMortons Bay, the town, was only five houses on the main road between Boyne City and Charlevoix. There was the general store and postoffice with a high false front and maybe a wagon hitched out in front, Smith's house, Stroud's house, Fox's house, HMorton's house and Van Hoosen's house. The houses were in a big grove of elm trees and the road was very sandy. There was farming country and timber each way up the road. Up the road a ways was the Methodist church and down the road the other direction was the township school. The blacksmith shop was painted red and faced the school.

A steep sandy road ran down the hill to the bay through the timber. From Smith's back door you could look out across the woods that ran down to the lake and across the bay. It was very beautiful in the spring and summer, the bay blue and bright and usually white-caps on the lake out beyond the point from the breeze blowing from Charlevoix and Lake Michigan. From Smith's back door Liz could see ore barges way out in the lake going toward Boyne City. When she looked at them they didn't seem to be moving at all but if she went in and dried some more dishes and then came out again they would be out of sight beyond the point.

All the time now Liz was thinking about Jim Gilmore. He didn't seem to notice her much. He talked about the shop to A. J. Smith and about the Republican Party and about James G. Blaine. In the evenings he read the Toledo Blade and the Grand Rapids paper by the lamp in the front room or went out spearing fish in the bay with a jacklight with A. J. Smith. In the fall he and Smith and Charley Wyman took a wagon and tent, grub, axes, their rifles and two dogs and went on a trip to the pine plains beyond Vanderbilt deer hunting. Liz and

Mrs. Smith were cooking for four days for them before they started. Liz wanted to make something special for Jim to take but she didn't finally because she was afraid to ask Mrs. Smith for the eggs and flour and afraid if she bought them Mrs. Smith would catch her cooking. It would have been all right with Mrs. Smith but Liz was afraid.

All the time Jim was gone on the deer hunting trip Liz thought about him. It was awful while he was gone. She couldn't sleep well from thinking about him but she discovered it was fun to think about him too. If she let herself go it was better. The night before they were to come back she didn't sleep at all, that is she didn't think she slept because it was all mixed up in a dream about not sleeping and really not sleeping. When she saw the wagon coming down the road she felt weak and sick ~~sort of~~ inside. She couldn't wait till she saw Jim and it seemed as though everything would be all right when he came. The wagon stopped outside under the big elm and Mrs. Smith and Liz went out. All the men had beards and there were three deer in the back of the wagon, their thin legs sticking stiff over the edge of the wagon box. Mrs. Smith kissed Alonzo and he hugged her. Jim said "Hello Liz." and grinned. Liz hadn't known just what would happen when Jim got back but she was sure it would be something. Nothing had happened. The men were just home that was all. Jim pulled the burlap sacks off the deer and Liz looked at them. One was a big buck. It was stiff and hard to lift out of the wagon.

"Did you shoot it, Jim?" Liz asked.

"Yeah. Aint it a beauty?" Jim got it onto his back to carry to the smokehouse.

That night Charley Wyman stayed to supper at Smith's. It was too late to get back to Charlevoix. The men washed up and waited in the front room for supper.

"Aint there something left in that crock Jimmy?" A. J. Smith asked and Jim went out to the wagon in the barn and fetched in the jug of whiskey the men had taken hunting with them. It was a ~~four~~ two gallon jug and there was quite a little slopped back and forth in the bottom. Jim took a long pull on his way back to the house. It was hard to lift such a big jug up to drink out of it. Some of the whiskey ran down on his shirt front. The two men smiled when Jim came in with the jug. A. J. Smith sent for glasses and Liz brought them. A. J. poured out three big shots.

"Well here's looking at you A. J." said Charley Wyman.

"That damn big buck Jimmy." said A. J.

"Here's all the ones we missed A. J." said Jim and downed his liquor.

"That tastes good to a man."

"Nothing like it this time of year for what ails you."

"How about another boys?"

"Here's how A. J."

"Down the creek boys."

"Here's to next year."

Jim began to feel great. He loved the taste and the feel of whisky. He was glad to be back to a comfortable bed and warm food and the shop. He had another drink. The men came in to supper feeling hilarious but acting very respectable. Liz sat at the table after she put on the food and ate with the family. It was a good dinner. The men ate seriously. After supper they went into the front room again and Liz cleaned off with Mrs. Smith. Then Mrs. Smith went up stairs and pretty soon Smith came out and went up stairs too. Jim and Charley were still in the front room. Liz was sitting in the kitchen next to the stove pretending to read a book and thinking about Jim. She didn't want to go to bed yet because she knew Jim would be coming out and she wanted to see him as he went out so she could take the way he looked up to bed with her.

She was thinking about him hard and then Jim came out. His eyes were shining and his hair was a little rumpled. Liz looked down at her book. Jim came over back of her chair and stood there and she could feel him breathing and then he put his arms around her. Her breasts felt plump and firm and the nipples were erect under his hands. Liz was terribly frightened, no one had ever touched her, but she thought, "He's come to me finally. He's really come."

She held herself stiff because she was so frightened and did not know anything else to do and then Jim held her tight against the chair and kissed her. It was such a sharp, aching, hurting feeling that she thought she couldn't stand it. She felt Jim right through the back of the chair and she couldn't stand it and then something clicked went inside of her and the feeling was warmer and softer. Jim held her tight hard against the chair and she wanted it now and Jim whispered, "Come on for a walk."

Liz took her coat off the peg on the kitchen wall and they went out the door. Jim had his arm around her and every little way they stopped and pressed against each other and Jim kissed her. There was no moon and they walked ankle deep in the sandy road through the trees down to the dock and the warehouse on the bay. The water was lapping in the piles and the point was dark across the bay. It was cold but Liz was hot all over from being with Jim. They sat down in the shelter of the warehouse and Jim pulled Liz close to him. She was frightened. One of Jim's hands went inside her dress and stroked over her breast and the other hand was in her lap. She was very frightened and didn't know how he was going to go about things but snuggled close to him. Then the hand that felt so big in her lap went away and was on her leg and started to move up it.

"Don't Jim," Liz said. Jim slid the hand further up.

"You musn't Jim. You musn't." Neither Jim nor Jim's big hand paid any attention to her.

The boards were hard. Jim had her dress up and was trying to do something to her. She was frightened but she wanted it. She had to have it but it frightened her. [Hemingway wrote "stet" in the margin.]

"You musn't do it Jim. You musn't."

"I got to. I'm going to. You know we got to."

"No we haven't Jim. We aint got to. Oh it isn't right. Oh it's so big and it hurts so. You can't. Oh Jim. Jim. Oh."

The hemlock planks of the dock were hard and splintery and cold and Jim was heavy on her and he had hurt her. Liz pushed him, she was so uncomfortable and cramped. Jim was asleep. He wouldn't move. She worked out from under him and sat up and straightened her skirt and coat and tried to do something with her hair. Jim was sleeping with his mouth a little open. Liz leaned over and kissed him on the cheek. He was still asleep. She lifted his head a little and shook it. He rolled his head over and swallowed. Liz started to cry. She walked over to the edge of the dock and looked down to the water. There was a mist coming up from the bay. She was cold and miserable and everything felt gone. She walked back to where Jim was lying and shook him once more to make sure. She was crying.

"Jim" she said, "Jim. Please Jim."

Jim stirred and curled a little tighter. Liz took off her coat and leaned over and covered him with it. She tucked it around him neatly and carefully. Then she walked across the dock and up the steep sandy road to go to bed. A cold mist was coming up through the woods from the bay.

3e.

Item 798, Ernest Hemingway Collection, John F. Kennedy Library and Museum, Boston. Untitled handwritten manuscript in pencil beginning "A steep sandy road ran down the hill . . ." with some corrections and deletions. Hemingway probably wrote this in 1930 when he was considering revising "Up in Michigan" for inclusion in a new edition of *In Our Time*.

A steep sandy road ran down the hill to the bay through the timber. From ~~the~~ Smith's door she could look out across the woods that ran down to the lake and across the bay. It was very fine in the spring and summer, the bay blue and bright and usually whitecaps on the lake out beyond the point from the breeze blowing from Charlevoix and Lake Michigan. From the back door Mary could see ore barges out in the lake going toward Boyne City. When she looked at them they did not seem to be moving at all but if she went in and dried some more dishes and then came out again they would be out of sight beyond the point.

Mary Coates worked for the F.E. Smiths and ~~Jim~~ Fred Dutton took his meals there. Mrs. Smith who was a very large clean woman said Mary Coates was the neatest girl she'd ever seen. Mary Coates liked Fred Dutton very much. She liked ~~it~~ the way he walked over from the shop and often went to the kitchen door to watch for him to start down the road. She liked it ~~about how~~ that he was short and dark. She liked ~~it about~~ how white his teeth were when he smiled. She liked it about how much F.E. Smith and Mrs. Smith liked him. One day she found that she liked ~~it~~ the way the hair was black on his arms and how white they were above the tanned line when he washed up in the washbasin outside the kitchen. Liking that made her feel funny. All the time now she was thinking about Fred Dutton.

He did not seem to notice her much. He talked about how things went to F.E. Smith and about the Republican Party and about James G. Blaine. In the evenings he read the Toledo Blade and the Grand Rapids paper by the lamp in the front room or sometimes he went down to the bay to spear fish with a jacklight with F.E. Smith. Mary would wake in the night and hear them coming in. In the fall he and F.E. and Charley Wyman took a wagon and tent, grub, axes, their rifles and two dogs and went to the Pine plains beyond ~~the line of the Michigan Central~~ Vanderbilt deer hunting. Mary and Mrs. Smith were cooking up things for them for four days before they started.

All the time Fred was gone on the deer hunting trip Mary thought about him. It was awful while he was gone. She could not sleep well from thinking about him ~~but she discovered it was all right to think about him too. Anything she thought was better than not thinking at all.~~ The night before they were to come back she didn't sleep at all, that is she didn't think she slept. It was all mixed up in a dream about not sleeping and really not sleeping. When she saw the wagon coming down the road she felt weak and nearly sick ~~sort of~~ inside. She could not wait till she saw Jim and it seemed as though everything would be all right when he came.

The wagon stopped outside under the big elm and Mrs. Smith and Mary went out. The men all had beards and there were three deer in the back of the wagon, their thin legs sticking stiff over the edge of the wagon box. Mrs. Smith kissed F.E. and he hugged her. Fred said, "Hello Mary," and grinned. Mary had not known what would happen when Fred got back but she was sure it would be something. Nothing had happened. The men were just home; that was all. Fred pushed the burlap sacks off the deer and Mary looked at them. One was a big buck. It was stiff and hard to lift out of the wagon.

"Did you shoot it, Fred?" Mary asked.

"Sure," Jim said. "There. See the place?" Jim got it onto his back to carry to the smokehouse.

That night Charley Wyman stayed to supper at Smiths. It was too late to try to get back to Charlevoix. The men washed up and waited in the front room for supper to be ready.

"Is there anything left in that crock, Fred?" F.E. Smith asked and Fred went out to the barn and ~~fetched~~ brought in the jug of whiskey the men had taken hunting with them. It was a two gallon jug and there was still quite a little whiskey that slopped back and forth in the bottom. Fred took a long pull on his way back to the house. It was hard to lift such a big jug up to drink out of it and some of the whiskey ran down on his shirt front. The two men smiled when Fred came in with the jug. F.E. sent for glasses and Mary brought them and F.E. poured out three big drinks.

"Well here's looking at you, F.E.," said Charley Wyman.

"Here's to Freddy's big buck," F.E. said.

"Here's to next year," Fred said. They drank the three glasses.

"It's good all right."

"How about it?"

"You bet."

"Down the creek, boys," F.E. said.

"Here's to next year," said Fred.

Fred began to feel great. He loved the taste and feel of whiskey. He was glad to be back to a comfortable bed and warm food and his work. He had another drink and they all had one. The men came in to supper feeling hilarious but acting very respectable.

Mary sat at the table after she put on the food and ate with the family. It was a good dinner and the men ate seriously. After the meal they went into the front room and Mary cleared off with Mrs. Smith. Then Mrs. Smith went upstairs and pretty soon Smith came out and went upstairs too. Fred and Charley were still in the front room.

Mary was sitting in the kitchen by the stove pretending to read a book and thinking about Fred. She didn't want to go to bed yet because she knew Fred would be coming out and she wanted to see him as he went out so she could take the way he looked up to bed with her.

She was thinking about him hard and then Fred came out. His eyes were shining and his hair was a little rumpled. Mary looked down at her book. ~~but Fred had seen her look at him.~~ He came over in back of her chair and she could feel him ~~breathing~~ there although she did not look up and then he put his arms around her. Mary was terribly frightened. No one had ever touched her, but she thought, "He's come to me finally. He's really come."

She held herself stiff because she did not know anything else to do and then Fred pressed her tight against the chair and kissed her.

It was such a sharp, aching, hurting feeling that she thought she couldn't stand it. She couldn't stand it, she knew she couldn't stand it. But Fred held her tight hard against the chair and she could stand it now. She wanted him to hold her ~~tight~~ now and ~~Jim~~ Fred whispered, "Come on for a walk."

Mary took her coat off the peg on the kitchen wall and they went out the door. Fred had his arm around her and every little way they stopped and pressed against each other and Fred kissed her. There was no moon and they walked ankle deep in the sandy road through the trees down to the dock and the warehouse on the bay. The water was lapping in the piles and the point was dark across the bay. They sat down in the shelter of the warehouse and Fred pulled Mary close to him. She was frightened. One of Fred's hands went inside her dress and she felt it on her breast and the other hand was in her lap. She was very frightened and did not know how he was going to go about things but she snuggled close to him. Then the hand that felt so big in her lap went away and was on her leg and started to move up it.

"Don't Fred," Mary said.

"You musn't Fred. You musn't." Neither Fred nor Fred's big hand paid any attention to her.

The boards were hard. Fred had her dress up and was trying to do something to her. She was frightened but she wanted it. She had to have it but it frightened her.

"You musn't do it, Fred. You musn't."

"I got to. I'm going to. You know we got to."

"No we haven't, Fred. We aint got to. Oh it isn't right. We musn't. We musn't. ~~Oh it's so big and it hurts so.~~ You can't. Oh Fred. Fred. Oh."

The hemlock planks of the dock were hard and splintery and cold and Fred was heavy on her and he had hurt her. Mary pushed him, she was so uncomfortable and cramped. Fred was asleep. He wouldn't move. She worked out from under him and straightened her skirt and coat and tried to do something with her hair. Fred was sleeping with his mouth a little open. Mary leaned over and kissed him on the cheek. He was still asleep. She lifted his head a little and shook it. He rolled his head over and swallowed. Mary started to cry. She walked over to the edge of the dock and looked down to the water. There was a mist coming up from the bay. She was cold and miserable and everything felt gone. She walked back to where Fred was lying and shook him once more to make sure. She was crying.

"Fred," she said. "Fred. Please Fred."

Fred stirred and curled a little tighter. Mary took off her coat and leaned over and covered him with it. She tucked it around him neatly and carefully. Then she walked across the dock and up the steep sandy road to go to bed. A cold mist was coming up through the woods from the bay.

4.

A Very Short Story

1925

One hot evening in Padua they carried him up onto the roof and he could look out over the top of the town. There were chimney swifts in the sky. After a while it got dark and the searchlights came out. The others went down and took the bottles with them. He and Luz could hear them below on the balcony. Luz sat on the bed. She was cool and fresh in the hot night.

Luz stayed on night duty for three months. They were glad to let her. When they operated on him she prepared him for the operating table; and they had a joke about friend or enema. He went under the anæsthetic holding tight on to himself so he would not blab about anything during the silly, talky time. After he got on crutches he used to take the temperatures so Luz would not have to get up from the bed. There were only a few patients, and they all knew about it. They all liked Luz. As he walked back along the halls he thought of Luz in his bed.

Before he went back to the front they went into the Duomo and prayed. It was dim and quiet, and there were other people praying. They wanted to get married, but there was not enough time for the banns, and neither of them had birth certificates. They felt as though they were married, but they wanted every one to know about it, and to make it so they could not lose it.

Luz wrote him many letters that he never got until after the armistice. Fifteen came in a bunch to the front and he sorted them by the dates and read them all straight through. They were all about the hospital, and how much she loved him and how it was impossible to get along without him and how terrible it was missing him at night.

After the armistice they agreed he should go home to get a job so they might be married. Luz would not come home until he had a good job and could come to New York to meet her. It was understood he would not drink, and he did not want to see his friends or any one in the States. Only to get a job and be married. On the train from Padua to Milan they quarrelled about her not being willing to come home at once. When they had to say good-bye, in the station at Milan, they kissed good-bye, but were not finished with the quarrel. He felt sick about saying good-bye like that.

He went to America on a boat from Genoa. Luz went back to Pordenone to open a hospital. It was lonely and rainy there, and there was a battalion of *arditi* quartered in the town. Living in the muddy, rainy town in the winter, the major of the battalion made love to Luz, and she had never known Italians before, and finally wrote to the States that theirs had been only a boy and girl affair. She was sorry, and she knew he would probably not be able to understand, but might some day forgive her, and be grateful to her, and she expected, absolutely unexpectedly, to be married in the spring. She loved him as always, but she realized now it was only a boy and girl love. She hoped he would have a great career, and believed in him absolutely. She knew it was for the best.

The major did not marry her in the spring, or any other time. Luz never got an answer to the letter to Chicago about it. A short time after he contracted gonorrhea from a sales girl in a loop department store while riding in a taxicab through Lincoln Park.

4a.

Item 633, Ernest Hemingway Collection, John F. Kennedy Library and Museum, Boston. Earliest preserved draft of "A Very Short Story" when Hemingway was writing it as a vignette for inclusion in his second book, *in our time*, published in Paris in 1924. Three pages written by hand on both sides of two loose sheets from a notebook with numerous emendations and corrections.

Personal

~~One hot evening in Milan there were flocks of chimney swifts in the sky. The searchlights came out and they carried me out onto the roof.~~

Love

One hot evening in Milan they carried him up onto the roof and I could look out over ~~all the other roofs~~ the flat top of the town. There were chimney swifts in the sky. After a while it got dark and the searchlights came out. The others went down and took the bottles with them. We could hear them on the balcony. Ag sat on the bed. ~~I said, "I love you Ag," and pulled her against me. And she said, "I know it, Kid" and kissed me and got all the way up onto the bed. For thre[e]~~ She was cool and fresh in the hot night. She stayed on night duty for three months. They were glad to let her. When I had the big operation she ~~had to give me the enema~~ prepared me for the operating table and we had a joke about friend or enema. When I got crutches I used to take the temperatures so she ~~could sleep~~ wouldn't have to get up. Daytimes I slept and wrote letters for her to send downstairs when she got up from the bed. Before I went back to the front we went into the Duomo and prayed. It was dim and quiet. We wanted to get married but there ~~were too m~~ wasn't enough time ~~and we didn't~~ for publishing the banns and we didn't either have birth certificates. She used to send letters up to me by the charwoman. We loved each other very much. After the armistice I went home to get a job so we could get married and Ag went up to Torre di Mosta ~~to run a childrens~~ to run some sort of a show. It was lonely there and there was a battalion of Arditi quartered in the town. ~~She didn't marry the major as she wrote me she she after a while~~ When the letter came saying ours had been only a kid affair, I got awfully drunk. The major ~~didn't marry her after all~~ never married her ~~In the meantime I got the~~ and I got a dose of clap from a girl in Chicago riding in a yellow taxi.

4b.

Item 94a, Ernest Hemingway Collection, John F. Kennedy Library and Museum, Boston. Typescript of chapter 10, still titled "Love" for *in our time* (Paris: Three Mountains Press, 1924) with handwritten emendations.

Blank. Xx Sub-head -----Love.

One hot evening in Milan they carried him up onto the roof and he could look out over the top of the town. There were chimney swifts in the sky. After a while it got dark and the searchlights came out. The others went down and took the bottles with them. He and Ag could hear them below on the balcony. Ag sat on the bed. She was cool and fresh in the hot night.

Ag stayed on night duty for three months. They were glad to let her. When they operated on him she prepared him for the operation and they had a joke about friend or enema. He went under the anaesthetic holding tight on to himself so that he wouldn't blab about anything during the silly talky time. After he got on crutches he used to take the temperatures so she wouldn't have to get up from the bed. He thought of her in his bed as he walked back along the halls.

Before he went back to the front they went into the Duomo and prayed. It was dim and quiet and there were other people praying. They wanted to get married but there was not enough time for the banns and neither of them had birth certificates. They loved each other very much.

After the armistice he went home to get a job so they might be married. They quarrelled on the train from Padova to Milano and could not remember what it was about when they said goodbye in the station. Ag went back to Torre di Mosta to help open a hospital.

It was lonely and rainy there and there was a battalion of arditi quartered in the town. The major made love to her and she had never known Italians before and finally wrote to the States that theirs had been only a boy and girl affair. The major didn't marry Ag after all. She never got an answer to her second letter to Chicago saying it had all been a mistake about the major. ~~It was~~ quite a while after ~~that,~~ he ~~got a dose of clap~~ had gotten sick from a girl riding in a taxicab through Lincoln park.

4c.

The following is the first published version of "A Very Short Story," which appeared as chapter 10 of *in our time* (Paris: Three Mountains Press, 1924).

chapter 10

One hot evening in Milan they carried him up onto the roof and he could look out over the top of the town. There were chimney swifts in the sky. After a while it got dark and the searchlights came out. The others went down and took the bottles with them. He and Ag could hear them below on the balcony. Ag sat on the bed. She was cool and fresh in the hot night.

Ag stayed on night duty for three months. They were glad to let her. When they operated on him she prepared him for the operating table, and they had a joke about friend or enema. He went under the anæsthetic holding tight on to himself so that he would not blab about anything during the silly, talky time. After he got on crutches he used to take the temperature so Ag would not have to get up from the bed. There were only a few patients, and they all knew about it. They all liked Ag. As he walked back along the halls he thought of Ag in his bed.

Before he went back to the front they went into the Duomo and prayed. It was dim and quiet, and there were other people praying. They wanted to get married, but there was not enough time for the banns, and neither of them had birth certificates. They felt as though they were married, but they wanted everyone to know about it, and to make it so they could not lose it.

Ag wrote him many letters that he never got until after the armistice. Fifteen came in a bunch and he sorted them by the dates and read them all straight through. They were about the hospital, and how much she loved him and how it was impossible to get along without him and how terrible it was missing him at night.

After the armistice they agreed he should go home to get a job so they might be married. Ag would not come home until he had a good job and could come to New York to meet her. It was understood he would not drink, and he did not want to see his friends or anyone in the States. Only to get a job and be married. On the train from Padova to Milan they quarrelled about her not being willing to come home at once. When they had to say good-bye in the station at Padova they kissed good-bye, but were not finished with the quarrel. He felt sick about saying good-bye like that.

He went to America on a boat from Genoa. Ag went back to Torre di Mosta to open a hospital. It was lonely and rainy there, and there was a battalion of *arditi* quartered in the town. Living in the muddy, rainy town in the winter the major of the battalion made love to Ag, and she had never known Italians before, and finally wrote a letter to the States that theirs had been only a boy and girl affair. She was sorry, and she knew he would probably not be able to understand, but might some day forgive her, and be grateful to her, and she expected, absolutely unexpectedly, to be married in the spring. She loved him as always, but she realized now it was only a boy and girl love. She hoped he would have a great career, and believed in him absolutely. She knew it was for the best.

The Major did not marry her in the spring, or any other time. Ag never got an answer to her letter to Chicago about it. A short time after he contracted gonorrhea from a sales girl from The Fair riding in a taxicab through Lincoln Park.

5.

Indian Camp

1924

At the lake shore there was another rowboat drawn up. The two Indians stood waiting.

Nick and his father got in the stern of the boat and the Indians shoved it off and one of them got in to row. Uncle George sat in the stern of the camp rowboat. The young Indian shoved the camp boat off and got in to row Uncle George.

The two boats started off in the dark. Nick heard the oarlocks of the other boat quite a way ahead of them in the mist. The Indians rowed with quick choppy strokes. Nick lay back with his father's arm around him. It was cold on the water. The Indian who was rowing them was working very hard, but the other boat moved further ahead in the mist all the time.

"Where are we going, Dad?" Nick asked.

"Over to the Indian camp. There is an Indian lady very sick."

"Oh," said Nick.

Across the bay they found the other boat beached. Uncle George was smoking a cigar in the dark. The young Indian pulled the boat way up on the beach. Uncle George gave both the Indians cigars.

They walked up from the beach through a meadow that was soaking wet with dew, following the young Indian who carried a lantern. Then they went into the woods and followed a trail that led to the logging road that ran back into the hills. It was much lighter on the logging road as the timber was cut away on both sides. The young Indian stopped and blew out his lantern and they all walked on along the road.

They came around a bend and a dog came out barking. Ahead were the lights of the shanties where the Indian bark-peelers lived. More dogs rushed out at them. The two Indians sent them back to the shanties. In the shanty nearest the road there was a light in the window. An old woman stood in the doorway holding a lamp.

Inside on a wooden bunk lay a young Indian woman. She had been trying to have her baby for two days. All the old women in the camp had been helping her. The men had moved off up the road to sit in the dark and smoke out of range of the noise she made. She screamed just as Nick and the two Indians followed his father and Uncle George into the shanty. She lay in the lower bunk, very big under a quilt. Her head was turned to one side. In the upper bunk was her husband. He had cut his foot very badly with an ax three days before. He was smoking a pipe. The room smelled very bad.

Nick's father ordered some water to be put on the stove, and while it was heating he spoke to Nick.

"This lady is going to have a baby, Nick," he said.

"I know," said Nick.

"You don't know," said his father. "Listen to me. What she is going through is called being in labor. The baby wants to be born and she wants it to be born. All her muscles are trying to get the baby born. That is what is happening when she screams."

"I see," Nick said.

Just then the woman cried out.

"Oh, Daddy, can't you give her something to make her stop screaming?" asked Nick.

"No. I haven't any anæsthetic," his father said. "But her screams are not important. I don't hear them because they are not important."

The husband in the upper bunk rolled over against the wall.

The woman in the kitchen motioned to the doctor that the water was hot. Nick's father went into the kitchen and poured about half of the water out of the big kettle into a basin. Into the water left in the kettle he put several things he unwrapped from a handkerchief.

"Those must boil," he said, and began to scrub his hands in the basin of hot water with a cake of soap he had brought from the camp. Nick watched his father's hands scrubbing each other with the soap. While his father washed his hands very carefully and thoroughly, he talked.

"You see, Nick, babies are supposed to be born head first but sometimes they're not. When they're not they make a lot of trouble for everybody. Maybe I'll have to operate on this lady. We'll know in a little while."

When he was satisfied with his hands he went in and went to work.

"Pull back that quilt, will you, George?" he said. "I'd rather not touch it."

Later when he started to operate Uncle George and three Indian men held the woman still. She bit Uncle George on the arm and Uncle George said, "Damn squaw bitch!" and the young Indian who had rowed Uncle George over laughed at him. Nick held the basin for his father. It all took a long time. His father picked the baby up and slapped it to make it breathe and handed it to the old woman.

"See, it's a boy, Nick," he said. "How do you like being an interne?"

Nick said, "All right." He was looking away so as not to see what his father was doing.

"There. That gets it," said his father and put something into the basin.

Nick didn't look at it.

"Now," his father said, "there's some stitches to put in. You can watch this or not, Nick, just as you like. I'm going to sew up the incision I made."

Nick did not watch. His curiosity had been gone for a long time.

His father finished and stood up. Uncle George and the three Indian men stood up. Nick put the basin out in the kitchen.

Uncle George looked at his arm. The young Indian smiled reminiscently.

"I'll put some peroxide on that, George," the doctor said. He bent over the Indian woman. She was quiet now and her eyes were closed. She looked very pale. She did not know what had become of the baby or anything.

"I'll be back in the morning," the doctor said, standing up. "The nurse should be here from St. Ignace by noon and she'll bring everything we need."

He was feeling exalted and talkative as football players are in the dressing room after a game.

"That's one for the medical journal, George," he said. "Doing a Cæsarian with a jack-knife and sewing it up with nine-foot, tapered gut leaders."

Uncle George was standing against the wall, looking at his arm.

"Oh, you're a great man, all right," he said.

"Ought to have a look at the proud father. They're usually the worst sufferers in these little affairs," the doctor said. "I must say he took it all pretty quietly."

He pulled back the blanket from the Indian's head. His hand came away wet. He mounted on the edge of the lower bunk with the lamp in one hand and looked in. The Indian lay with his face toward the wall. His throat had been cut from ear to ear. The blood had flowed down into a pool where his body sagged the bunk. His head rested on his left arm. The open razor lay, edge up, in the blankets.

"Take Nick out of the shanty, George," the doctor said.

There was no need of that. Nick, standing in the door of the kitchen, had a good view of the upper bunk when his father, the lamp in one hand, tipped the Indian's head back.

It was just beginning to be daylight when they walked along the logging road back toward the lake.

"I'm terribly sorry I brought you along, Nickie," said his father, all his post-operative exhilaration gone. "It was an awful mess to put you through."

"Do ladies always have such a hard time having babies?" Nick asked.

"No, that was very, very exceptional."

"Why did he kill himself, Daddy?"

"I don't know, Nick. He couldn't stand things, I guess."

"Do many men kill themselves, Daddy?"

"Not very many, Nick."

"Do many women?"

"Hardly ever."

"Don't they ever?"

"Oh, yes. They do sometimes."

"Daddy?"

"Yes."

"Where did Uncle George go?"

"He'll turn up all right."

"Is dying hard, Daddy?"

"No, I think it's pretty easy, Nick. It all depends."

They were seated in the boat, Nick in the stern, his father rowing. The sun was coming up over the hills. A bass jumped, making a circle in the water. Nick trailed his hand in the water. It felt warm in the sharp chill of the morning.

In the early morning on the lake sitting in the stern of the boat with his father rowing, he felt quite sure that he would never die.

5a.

Item 493, Ernest Hemingway Collection, John F. Kennedy Library and Museum, Boston. Untitled handwritten ink manuscript with an eight-page start, which was deleted from the story. The beginning was published posthumously as "Three Shots" in *The Nick Adams Stories*.

~~It was a long time after supper. Nick had started to undress in the tent. He could see the shadows of his father and his uncle Joe on the wall of the tent. He did not feel very happy.~~

Nick ~~had started to undress~~ was undressing in the tent. He ~~could~~ saw the shadows of his father and uncle ~~Joe~~ George ~~on the wall of the tent cast by the fire~~ cast by the fire on the canvas wall. He felt very uncomfortable and ashamed and undressed as fast as he could, piling his clothes neatly. He was ~~undressing~~ ashamed because undressing reminded him of the night before. He had kept it out of his mind all day.

His father and uncle had gone off across the lake ~~in the canoe~~ after supper to fish with a jack light. Before they shoved the boat out his father told him that if any emergency came up while they were gone he was to fire three shots with the rifle and they would come right back. Nick went back from the edge of the lake through the woods to the camp. He could hear the oars of the boat in the dark. His father was rowing and his uncle was sitting in the stern trolling. He had taken his seat with his rod ready when ~~the boat~~ his father shoved the boat out. Nick listened to them on the lake ~~for a long time~~ until he could no longer hear the oars.

Walking back through the woods Nick began to be frightened. He was always a little frightened of the woods at night. He opened the flap of the tent and undressed and lay very quietly between the blankets in the dark. The fire was burned down to a bed of coals outside; Nick lay still and tried to go to sleep. There was no noise anywhere. Nick felt if he could only hear a fox bark or an owl or anything he would be all right. He was not afraid of anything definite as yet. But he was getting very ~~frightened~~ afraid. Then suddenly he was afraid of dying. Just a few weeks before at home in church they had sung a hymn ~~with~~ "Some day the silver chord will break." ~~This was the first time~~ While they were singing the hymn Nick had realized that someday he must die. It made him feel quite sick. It was the first time he had ever realized that he himself would have to die sometime.

That night he sat out in the hall under the night light trying to read Robinson Crusoe to keep his mind off the fact that someday the silver chord must break. The nurse found him there and threatened to tell his father on him if he did not go to bed. He went in to bed and as soon as the nurse was in her room came out again and read under the hall light until morning.

Last night in the tent ~~the same terrible fear had come over him~~ he had the same fear. He never had it except at night ~~except during the daytime~~. It was more a realization than a fear at first. But it was always on the edge of fear and became fear very quickly when it started. As soon as he began to be really frightened he took the rifle and ~~shot out three stepped to~~ poked the muzzle out the front of the tent and shot three times. The rifle kicked badly ~~but he knew how to hold it tight into his shoulder and~~. He heard the shots rip off through the trees. As soon as he had fired the shots it was all right.

He lay down to wait for his father's return and was asleep before his father and uncle had put out their jack light on the other side of the lake.

"Damn that kid," Uncle George said as they rowed back. "What did you tell him to call us in for? He's probably got the Heeby Jeebies about something."

Uncle George was an enthusiastic fisherman and his father's younger brother.

"Oh well. He's pretty small." His father said.

"That's no reason to bring him into the woods with us."

"I know he's an awful coward." His father said, "but ~~this is the~~ we're all yellow at that age."

"I can't stand him," George said, "He's such an awful liar."

"Oh well forget it. You'll get plenty of fishing anyway. ~~Besides jacklighting isn't much of a sport.~~"

~~"Anything that's worth doing is worth not being interrupted in."~~

"Forget it."

They came into the tent and Uncle George shone his flashlight into Nick's eyes.

"What was it Nickie?" Said his father. Nick sat up in bed.

"It sounded like a cross between a fox and a wolf and it was fooling around the tent." Nick said. "It was a little like a fox but more like a wolf." He had learned the phrase cross between that same day from his uncle.

"He probably heard a screech owl." Uncle George said.

In the morning his father found two big basswood trees that leaned across each other and made a squeaking sound when the wind blew them against each other so that they rubbed together in the wind.

"Do you think that was what made the noise it was Nick?" His father asked.

"Maybe." Nick said sheepishly. He didn't want to think about it.

"You don't want to ever be frightened in the woods Nick. There is nothing that can hurt you."

"Not even lightening?" Nick asked.

"No, not even lightening. If it lightenings there is a thunder storm get out into the open. Or get under a beech tree. They're never struck."

"Never?" Nick asked.

"I never heard of one." Said his father.

"Gee I'm glad to know that about beech trees." Nick said.

Now he was undressing again in the tent. He was conscious of the two shadows on the wall although he was not watching them. Then he heard a boat being pulled up on the beach and the two shadows were gone. He could heard his father talking with someone. Then his father shouted.

"Get your clothes on Nick."

He dressed as fast as he could. very excitedly His father came in and rummaged through the duffel bags.

"Put your coat on Nick." His father said absent mindedly.

At the lake shore there was another rowboat drawn up. Two Indians standing stood beside it.

Nick and his father got in the stern of the boat and the Indians shoved it off and one of them got in to row. Uncle George sat in the stern of the camp rowboat. The other Indian got in with him.

The two boats started off in the dark. Nick ~~could~~ heard the oar locks of the other boat quite a way ahead of them in the mist. The Indians rowed with quick choppy strokes.

Nick lay back with his father's arm around him. It was cold on the water. The Indian who was rowing them was working very hard but the other boat moved further ahead in the mist all the time.

"Where are we going Dad?" Nick asked.

"Over to the Indian Camp. There is an Indian lady very sick."

"Oh" said Nick.

Across the bay they found the other boat beached. Uncle George was smoking a cigar. He had given one to the young Indian who had cut it in half and ~~was chewing it~~ lit it as they came up. He pulled their boat way up the beach.

They walked up from the beach through a meadow that was soaking wet with dew following the young Indian who carried a lantern. Then they went into the woods and followed a trail that led to the logging road that ran back into the hills. It was much lighter on the logging road as the timber was cut away on both sides. The young Indian stopped and blew out his lantern and they all walked on ~~toward the camp where the Indian bark peelers lived.~~ along the road.

They came around a bend and a dog came out barking. Ahead were the lights of the shanties where the Indian bark peelers lived. More dogs rushed out at them but the two Indians sent them back to the shanties.

In the shanty nearest the road there was a light in the window and an old woman stood in the doorway holding a lamp. ~~One The young Indian went up to~~

~~From inside came a y~~

Inside on a ~~bed~~ wooden bunk lay a young Indian woman. She had been trying to have her baby for two days. All the old women in the camp had been helping her. The men had moved off up the road to sit in the dark and smoke out of range of ~~her screaming~~ the noise she made. She screamed just as Nick followed his father and his Uncle George into the ~~room~~ shanty. She lay in the lower bunk under a quilt. Her head was turned to one side. ~~She braced her feet against the wooden boards at one end of the bunk.~~ In the upper bunk was her husband. He had ~~nearly cut off his foot~~ cut his foot very badly with an ax three days before. He was smoking a pipe. The room smelled very bad.

Nick's father ordered some water to be put on the stove and while it was heating he spoke to Nick.

"This lady is going to have a baby Nick." He said.

"I know." Said Nick.

"You don't know." Said his father. "Listen to me. What she is going through is called being in labour. The baby wants to be born and she wants it to be born. All her muscles are trying to get the baby born. That is what is happening when she screams."

"I see," Nick said.

Just then the woman ~~moved under the quilt scream~~ cried out.

"Oh Daddy can't you give her something to make her stop screaming?" Asked Nick.

"No. I haven't any anaesthetic." his father said. "But her screams are not important. I don't hear them because they are not important."

The man in the upper bunk rolled over ~~and~~ against the wall.

The woman in the kitchen motioned to the Doctor that the water was hot. Nick's father went into the kitchen and poured about half of the water out of the big kettle into a basin ~~to wash~~. In what was left he put several things he ~~had took from his pocket~~ unwrapped from a handkerchief.

"Those must boil" he said and began to scrub his hands in the basin of hot water with a cake of soap he had brought from camp. Nick had never noticed his father's hands before. Now he watched them ~~under the kitchen lamps~~ scrubbing each other with the soap. While his father washed his hands he talked.

"You see Nick babies are supposed to be born head first but sometimes they're not. When they're not they make a lot of trouble for everybody. Maybe I'll have to operate on this lady. We'll know in a little while."

~~Then~~ When his hands were clean he went in and went to work.

"Pull back that quilt will you George?" he said, "I'd rather not touch it."

Later when he started to operate Uncle George and three Indian men held the woman down. She bit Uncle George on the arm and he said "Damn bitch of a squaw." And the young Indian who had rowed Uncle George over laughed at him. Nick held the basin for his father. It all took a long time.

His father picked the baby up and slapped it to make it breathe and handed it to the old woman.

"See it's a boy Nick." He said. "How do you like being an interne?"

Nick said "All right"

He was looking away so as not to see what his father was doing.

"There. That gets it" said his father and put something into the basin.

Nick didn't look at it.

"Now" his father said. "There's some stitches to put in. You can watch this or not Nick just as you like. I'm going to sew up the incision I made."

He finished and stood up. Uncle George and the three Indian men stood up. Nick put the basin out in the kitchen.

Uncle George looked at his arm. The young Indian smiled reminiscently.

"I'll put some peroxide on that George." Said the doctor.

He bent over the Indian woman. She was quiet now and her eyes were closed. She looked very pale. She did not know what had become of the baby or anything.

"I'll be back in the morning." He said. "The nurse should be here from St. Ignace by noon and she'll bring everything we need."

He was feeling ~~quite~~ jovial, like football players after a game.

"That's one for the book George." He said, "Doing a Caeserian with a jack-knife and sewing it up with nine foot, tapered gut leaders."

Uncle George was standing against the wall looking at his arm.

"Oh you're a great man all right." He said.

"Ought to have a look at the proud father." The Doctor said. "I must say he took it all pretty quietly. He's got an awful foot on him."

~~He stood on the edge of the lower bunk and~~

He pulled back the blanket from over the Indian's head. His hand came away wet. He mounted on the edge of the lower bunk with the lamp in one hand and looked in.

~~An open razor lay under the man's~~

The Indian lay with his face toward the wall. His throat had been cut from ear to ear. The blood had flowed down into a pool where his body sagged the bunk. His head rested on his left arm and the open razor lay just beyond this fingers.

"~~Get~~ Take Nick out of the shanty George." The Doctor said. ~~But it was too late.~~ There was no need of that. Nick standing in the door of the kitchen

~~had a good view of~~
~~was looking up at the~~

of the upper bunk when his father tipped the Indian's head back.

It was just breaking daylight when they walked along the logging road back toward the lake.

"I'm terribly sorry I brought you along Nickie." Said his father, all his post operation exhilaration gone.

"It was an awful mess to put you through."

"Do ladies always have such a hard time having babies?" Nick asked.

"No. That was very very exceptional."

"Why did he kill himself Daddy?"

"I don't know Nick. He couldn't stand things I guess."

"Do many men kill themselves Daddy?"

"Not very many Nick."

"Do many women?"

"Hardly ever." ~~Bitterly~~

"Don't they ever?"

"Oh yes. They do sometimes."

"Daddy?"

"Yes"

"Where did Uncle George go."

"~~He went~~ He'll turn up all right."

"Is dying hard Daddy?"

"No. I think it's pretty easy Nick."

They were seated in the boat. Nick in the stern his father rowing. The sun was coming up over the hills. A bass jumped making a circle in the water. Nick trailed his hand in the water. It felt warm in the sharp chill of the morning.

~~In the~~
~~Siting in the stern of the boat with~~

In the early morning on the lake sitting in the stern of the boat with his father rowing he felt quite sure he would never die.

5b.

Item 494, Ernest Hemingway Collection, John F. Kennedy Library and Museum, Boston. Carbon typescript with ink corrections, titled in ink: "One Night Last Summer." Penned in Hemingway's hand on page 1, published April 1924 in the *Transatlantic Review*, the first publication of "Indian Camp," where it was titled "Work in Progress." Page 1 of 7.

Ernest Hemingway
113 Rue Notre Dame de Champs
Paris VI
Puplished [*sic*] April 1924 in *Transatlantic Review*

(Title) One Night Last Summer.

At the lake shore there was another row boat drawn up. The two indians stood waiting.

Nick and his father got in the stern of the boat and the indians shoved off and one of them got in to row. Uncle George sat in the stern of the camp row boat. The young indian shoved the camp row boat off and got in to row Uncle George.

The two boats started off in the dark. Nick heard the oar locks of the other boat quite a way ahead of them in the mist. The indians rowed with quick choppy strokes. Nick lay back with his father's arm around him. It was cold on the water. The indian who was rowing them was working very hard but the other boat moved further ahead in the mist all the time.

"Where are we going Dad?" Nick asked.

"Over to the indian camp. There is an Indian lady very sick."

"Oh" said Nick.

5c.

Item 495, Ernest Hemingway Collection, John F. Kennedy Library and Museum, Boston. Typescript with ink corrections, titled: "Indian Story." Page numbered in ink. Page 1 of 7.

Ernest Hemingway
[1]

INDIAN ~~CAMP~~ STORY.

At the lake shore there was another rowboat drawn up. The two Indians stood waiting.

Nick and his father got in the stern of the boat and the Indians shoved it off and one of them got in to row. Uncle George sat in the stern of the camp rowboat. The young Indian shoved the camp boat off and got in to row Uncle George.

The two boats started off in the dark. Nick heard the oar locks of the other boat quite a way ahead of them in the mist. The Indians rowed with quick choppy strokes. Nick lay back with his father's arm around him. It was cold on the water. The Indian who was rowing them was working very hard but the other boat moved further ahead in the mist all the time.

"Where are we going Dad?" Nick asked.

"Over to the Indian camp. There is an Indian lady very sick."

"Oh," said Nick.

Across the bay they found the other boat beached. Uncle George was smoking a cigar in the dark. The young Indian pulled the boat way up the beach. Uncle George gave both the Indians cigars.

6.

The Three-Day Blow

1925

The rain stopped as Nick turned into the road that went up through the orchard. The fruit had been picked and the fall wind blew through the bare trees. Nick stopped and picked up a Wagner apple from beside the road, shiny in the brown grass from the rain. He put the apple in the pocket of his Mackinaw coat.

The road came out of the orchard on to the top of the hill. There was the cottage, the porch bare, smoke coming from the chimney. In back was the garage, the chicken coop and the second-growth timber like a hedge against the woods behind. The big trees swayed far over in the wind as he watched. It was the first of the autumn storms.

As Nick crossed the open field above the orchard the door of the cottage opened and Bill came out. He stood on the porch looking out.

"Well, Wemedge," he said.

"Hey, Bill," Nick said, coming up the steps.

They stood together, looking out across the country, down over the orchard, beyond the road, across the lower fields and the woods of the point to the lake. The wind was blowing straight down the lake. They could see the surf along Ten Mile point.

"She's blowing," Nick said.

"She'll blow like that for three days," Bill said.

"Is your dad in?" Nick said.

"No. He's out with the gun. Come on in."

Nick went inside the cottage. There was a big fire in the fireplace. The wind made it roar. Bill shut the door.

"Have a drink?" he said.

He went out to the kitchen and came back with two glasses and a pitcher of water. Nick reached the whisky bottle from the shelf above the fireplace.

"All right?" he said.

"Good," said Bill.

They sat in front of the fire and drank the Irish whisky and water.

"It's got a swell, smoky taste," Nick said, and looked at the fire through the glass.

"That's the peat," Bill said.

"You can't get peat into liquor," Nick said.

"That doesn't make any difference," Bill said.

"You ever seen any peat?" Nick asked.

"No," said Bill.

"Neither have I," Nick said.

His shoes, stretched out on the hearth, began to steam in front of the fire.

"Better take your shoes off," Bill said.

"I haven't got any socks on."

"Take them off and dry them and I'll get you some," Bill said. He went upstairs into the loft and Nick heard him walking about overhead. Upstairs was open under the roof and was where Bill and his father and he, Nick, sometimes slept. In back was a dressing room. They moved the cots back out of the rain and covered them with rubber blankets.

Bill came down with a pair of heavy wool socks.

"It's getting too late to go around without socks," he said.

"I hate to start them again," Nick said. He pulled the socks on and slumped back in the chair, putting his feet up on the screen in front of the fire.

"You'll dent in the screen," Bill said. Nick swung his feet over to the side of the fireplace.

"Got anything to read?" he asked.

"Only the paper."

"What did the Cards do?"

"Dropped a double header to the Giants."

"That ought to cinch it for them."

"It's a gift," Bill said. "As long as McGraw can buy every good ball player in the league there's nothing to it."

"He can't buy them all," Nick said.

"He buys all the ones he wants," Bill said. "Or he makes them discontented so they have to trade them to him."

"Like Heinie Zim," Nick agreed.

"That bonehead will do him a lot of good."

Bill stood up.

"He can hit," Nick offered. The heat from the fire was baking his legs.

"He's a sweet fielder, too," Bill said. "But he loses ball games."

"Maybe that's what McGraw wants him for," Nick suggested.

"Maybe," Bill agreed.

"There's always more to it than we know about," Nick said.

"Of course. But we've got pretty good dope for being so far away."

"Like how much better you can pick them if you don't see the horses."

"That's it."

Bill reached down the whisky bottle. His big hand went all the way around it. He poured the whisky into the glass Nick held out.

"How much water?"

"Just the same."

He sat down on the floor beside Nick's chair.

"It's good when the fall storms come, isn't it?" Nick said.

"It's swell."

"It's the best time of year," Nick said.

"Wouldn't it be hell to be in town?" Bill said.

"I'd like to see the World Series," Nick said.

"Well, they're always in New York or Philadelphia now," Bill said. "That doesn't do us any good."

"I wonder if the Cards will ever win a pennant?"

"Not in our lifetime," Bill said.

"Gee, they'd go crazy," Nick said.

"Do you remember when they got going that once before they had the train wreck?"

"Boy!" Nick said, remembering.

Bill reached over to the table under the window for the book that lay there, face down, where he had put it when he went to the door. He held his glass in one hand and the book in the other, leaning back against Nick's chair.

"What are you reading?"

"*Richard Feverel.*"

"I couldn't get into it."

"It's all right," Bill said. "It ain't a bad book, Wemedge."

"What else have you got I haven't read?" Nick asked.

"Did you read the *Forest Lovers?*"

"Yup. That's the one where they go to bed every night with the naked sword between them."

"That's a good book, Wemedge."

"It's a swell book. What I couldn't ever understand was what good the sword would do. It would have to stay edge up all the time because if it went over flat you could roll right over it and it wouldn't make any trouble."

"It's a symbol," Bill said.

"Sure," said Nick, "but it isn't practical."

"Did you ever read *Fortitude?*"

"It's fine," Nick said. "That's a real book. That's where his old man is after him all the time. Have you got any more by Walpole?"

"*The Dark Forest,*" Bill said. "It's about Russia."

"What does he know about Russia?" Nick asked.

"I don't know. You can't ever tell about those guys. Maybe he was there when he was a boy. He's got a lot of dope on it."

"I'd like to meet him," Nick said.

"I'd like to meet Chesterton," Bill said.

"I wish he was here now," Nick said. "We'd take him fishing to the 'Voix tomorrow."

"I wonder if he'd like to go fishing," Bill said.

"Sure," said Nick. "He must be about the best guy there is. Do you remember the *Flying Inn?*"

"'If an angel out of heaven
Gives you something else to drink,
Thank him for his kind intentions;
Go and pour them down the sink.'"

"That's right," said Nick. "I guess he's a better guy than Walpole."

"Oh, he's a better guy, all right," Bill said.

"But Walpole's a better writer."

"I don't know," Nick said. "Chesterton's a classic."

"Walpole's a classic, too," Bill insisted.

"I wish we had them both here," Nick said. "We'd take them both fishing to the 'Voix tomorrow."

"Let's get drunk," Bill said.

"All right," Nick agreed.

"My old man won't care," Bill said.

"Are you sure?" said Nick.

"I know it," Bill said.

"I'm a little drunk now," Nick said.

"You aren't drunk," Bill said.

He got up from the floor and reached for the whisky bottle. Nick held out his glass. His eyes fixed on it while Bill poured.

Bill poured the glass half full of whisky.

"Put in your own water," he said. "There's just one more shot."

"Got any more?" Nick asked.

"There's plenty more but dad only likes me to drink what's open."

"Sure," said Nick.

"He says opening bottles is what makes drunkards," Bill explained.

"That's right," said Nick. He was impressed. He had never thought of that before. He had always thought it was solitary drinking that made drunkards.

"How is your dad?" he asked respectfully.

"He's all right," Bill said. "He gets a little wild sometimes."

"He's a swell guy," Nick said. He poured water into his glass out of the pitcher. It mixed slowly with the whisky. There was more whisky than water.

"You bet your life he is," Bill said.

"My old man's all right," Nick said.

"You're damn right he is," said Bill.

"He claims he's never taken a drink in his life," Nick said, as though announcing a scientific fact.

"Well, he's a doctor. My old man's a painter. That's different."

"He's missed a lot," Nick said sadly.

"You can't tell," Bill said. "Everything's got its compensations."

"He says he's missed a lot himself," Nick confessed.

"Well, dad's had a tough time," Bill said.

"It all evens up," Nick said.

They sat looking into the fire and thinking of this profound truth.

"I'll get a chunk from the back porch," Nick said. He had noticed while looking into the fire that the fire was dying down. Also he wished to show he could hold his liquor and be practical. Even if his father had never touched a drop Bill was not going to get him drunk before he himself was drunk.

"Bring one of the big beech chunks," Bill said. He was also being consciously practical.

Nick came in with the log through the kitchen and in passing knocked a pan off the kitchen table. He laid the log down and picked up the pan. It had contained dried apricots, soaking in water. He carefully picked up all the apricots off the floor, some of them had gone under the stove, and put them back in the pan. He dipped some more water onto them from the pail by the table. He felt quite proud of himself. He had been thoroughly practical.

He came in carrying the log and Bill got up from the chair and helped him put it on the fire.

"That's a swell log," Nick said.

"I'd been saving it for the bad weather," Bill said. "A log like that will burn all night."

"There'll be coals left to start the fire in the morning," Nick said.

"That's right," Bill agreed. They were conducting the conversation on a high plane.

"Let's have another drink," Nick said.

"I think there's another bottle open in the locker," Bill said.

He kneeled down in the corner in front of the locker and brought out a square-faced bottle.

"It's Scotch," he said.

"I'll get some more water," Nick said. He went out into the kitchen again. He filled the pitcher with the dipper dipping cold spring water from the pail. On his way back to the living room he passed a mirror in the dining room and looked in it. His face looked strange. He smiled at the face in the mirror and it grinned back at him. He winked at it and went on. It was not his face but it didn't make any difference.

Bill had poured out the drinks.

"That's an awfully big shot," Nick said.

"Not for us, Wemedge," Bill said.

"What'll we drink to?" Nick asked, holding up the glass.

"Let's drink to fishing," Bill said.

"All right," Nick said. "Gentlemen, I give you fishing."

"All fishing," Bill said. "Everywhere."

"Fishing," Nick said. "That's what we drink to."

"It's better than baseball," Bill said.

"There isn't any comparison," said Nick. "How did we ever get talking about baseball?"

"It was a mistake," Bill said. "Baseball is a game for louts."

They drank all that was in their glasses.

"Now let's drink to Chesterton."

"And Walpole," Nick interposed.

Nick poured out the liquor. Bill poured in the water. They looked at each other. They felt very fine.

"Gentlemen," Bill said, "I give you Chesterton and Walpole."

"Exactly, gentlemen," Nick said.

They drank. Bill filled up the glasses. They sat down in the big chairs in front of the fire.

"You were very wise, Wemedge," Bill said.

"What do you mean?" asked Nick.

"To bust off that Marge business," Bill said.

"I guess so," said Nick.

"It was the only thing to do. If you hadn't, by now you'd be back home working trying to get enough money to get married."

Nick said nothing.

"Once a man's married he's absolutely bitched," Bill went on. "He hasn't got anything more. Nothing. Not a damn thing. He's done for. You've seen the guys that get married."

Nick said nothing.

"You can tell them," Bill said. "They get this sort of fat married look. They're done for."

"Sure," said Nick.

"It was probably bad busting it off," Bill said. "But you always fall for somebody else and then it's all right. Fall for them but don't let them ruin you."

"Yes," said Nick.

"If you'd have married her you would have had to marry the whole family. Remember her mother and that guy she married."

Nick nodded.

"Imagine having them around the house all the time and going to Sunday dinners at their house, and having them over to dinner and her telling Marge all the time what to do and how to act."

Nick sat quiet.

"You came out of it damned well," Bill said. "Now she can marry somebody of her own sort and settle down and be happy. You can't mix oil and water and you can't mix that sort of thing any more than if I'd marry Ida that works for Strattons. She'd probably like it, too."

Nick said nothing. The liquor had all died out of him and left him alone. Bill wasn't there. He wasn't sitting in front of the fire or going fishing tomorrow with Bill and his dad or anything. He wasn't drunk. It was all gone. All he knew was that he had once had Marjorie and that he had lost her. She was gone and he had sent her away. That was all that mattered. He might never see her again. Probably he never would. It was all gone, finished.

"Let's have another drink," Nick said.

Bill poured it out. Nick splashed in a little water.

"If you'd gone on that way we wouldn't be here now," Bill said.

That was true. His original plan had been to go down home and get a job. Then he had planned to stay in Charlevoix all winter so he could be near Marge. Now he did not know what he was going to do.

"Probably we wouldn't even be going fishing tomorrow," Bill said. "You had the right dope, all right."

"I couldn't help it," Nick said.

"I know. That's the way it works out," Bill said.

"All of a sudden everything was over," Nick said. "I don't know why it was. I couldn't help it. Just like when the three-day blows come now and rip all the leaves off the trees."

"Well, it's over. That's the point," Bill said.

"It was my fault," Nick said.

"It doesn't make any difference whose fault it was," Bill said.

"No, I suppose not," Nick said.

The big thing was that Marjorie was gone and that probably he would never see her again. He had talked to her about how they would go to Italy together and the fun they would have. Places they would be together. It was all gone now.

"So long as it's over that's all that matters," Bill said. "I tell you, Wemedge, I was worried while it was going on. You played it right. I understand her mother is sore as hell. She told a lot of people you were engaged."

"We weren't engaged," Nick said.

"It was all around that you were."

"I can't help it," Nick said. "We weren't."

"Weren't you going to get married?" Bill asked.

"Yes. But we weren't engaged," Nick said.

"What's the difference?" Bill asked judicially.

"I don't know. There's a difference."

"I don't see it," said Bill.

"All right," said Nick. "Let's get drunk."

"All right," Bill said. "Let's get really drunk."

"Let's get drunk and then go swimming," Nick said.

He drank off his glass.

"I'm sorry as hell about her but what could I do?" he said. "You know what her mother was like!"

"She was terrible," Bill said.

"All of a sudden it was over," Nick said. "I oughtn't to talk about it."

"You aren't," Bill said. "I talked about it and now I'm through. We won't ever speak about it again. You don't want to think about it. You might get back into it again."

Nick had not thought about that. It had seemed so absolute. That was a thought. That made him feel better.

"Sure," he said. "There's always that danger."

He felt happy now. There was not anything that was irrevocable. He might go into town Saturday night. Today was Thursday.

"There's always a chance," he said.

"You'll have to watch yourself," Bill said.

"I'll watch myself," he said.

He felt happy. Nothing was finished. Nothing was ever lost. He would go into town on Saturday. He felt lighter, as he had felt before Bill started to talk about it. There was always a way out.

"Let's take the guns and go down to the point and look for your dad," Nick said.

"All right."

Bill took down the two shotguns from the rack on the wall. He opened a box of shells. Nick put on his Mackinaw coat and his shoes. His shoes were stiff from the drying. He was still quite drunk but his head was clear.

"How do you feel?" Nick asked.

"Swell. I've just got a good edge on." Bill was buttoning up his sweater.

"There's no use getting drunk."

"No. We ought to get outdoors."

They stepped out the door. The wind was blowing a gale.

"The birds will lie right down in the grass with this," Nick said.

They struck down toward the orchard.

"I saw a woodcock this morning," Bill said.

"Maybe we'll jump him," Nick said.

"You can't shoot in this wind," Bill said.

Outside now the Marge business was no longer so tragic. It was not even very important. The wind blew everything like that away.

"It's coming right off the big lake," Nick said.

Against the wind they heard the thud of a shotgun.

"That's dad," Bill said. "He's down in the swamp."

"Let's cut down that way," Nick said.

"Let's cut across the lower meadow and see if we jump anything," Bill said.

"All right," Nick said.

None of it was important now. The wind blew it out of his head. Still he could always go into town Saturday night. It was a good thing to have in reserve.

6a.

Item 762, Ernest Hemingway Collection, John F. Kennedy Library and Museum, Boston. Untitled handwritten ink manuscript fragment from the beginning of "The Three-Day Blow." The text differs from the final version in several places.

[. . .] pocket of his Mackinaw coat.

The road came out of the orchard on to the top of the hill. There was the house, the porch bare, smoke coming from the chimney.

As Nick crossed the open field ~~on~~ above the orchard the door opened and Bill came out. He stood on the porch looking out.

"Well, Wemedge" he called.

"Hey, Bird" Nick said coming up the steps.

They stood together looking out across the country, down, over the orchard, beyond the road, across the fields and the woods of the point to the lake. The wind was blowing straight down the lake. It was the first of the big fall storms.

7.

Soldier's Home

1925

Krebs went to the war from a Methodist college in Kansas. There is a picture which shows him among his fraternity brothers, all of them wearing exactly the same height and style collar. He enlisted in the Marines in 1917 and did not return to the United States until the second division returned from the Rhine in the summer of 1919.

There is a picture which shows him on the Rhine with two German girls and another corporal. Krebs and the corporal look too big for their uniforms. The German girls are not beautiful. The Rhine does not show in the picture.

By the time Krebs returned to his home town in Oklahoma the greeting of heroes was over. He came back much too late. The men from the town who had been drafted had all been welcomed elaborately on their return. There had been a great deal of hysteria. Now the reaction had set in. People seemed to think it was rather ridiculous for Krebs to be getting back so late, years after the war was over.

At first Krebs, who had been at Belleau Wood, Soissons, the Champagne, St. Mihiel and in the Argonne did not want to talk about the war at all. Later he felt the need to talk but no one wanted to hear about it. His town had heard too many atrocity stories to be thrilled by actualities. Krebs found that to be listened to at all he had to lie, and after he had done this twice he, too, had a reaction against the war and against talking about it. A distaste for everything that had happened to him in the war set in because of the lies he had told. All of the times that had been able to make him feel cool and clear inside himself when he thought of them; the times so long back when he had done the one thing, the only thing for a man to do, easily and naturally, when he might have done something else, now lost their cool, valuable quality and then were lost themselves.

His lies were quite unimportant lies and consisted in attributing to himself things other men had seen, done or heard of, and stating as facts certain apocryphal incidents familiar to all soldiers. Even his lies were not sensational at the pool room. His acquaintances, who had heard detailed accounts of German women found chained to machine guns in the Argonne forest and who could not comprehend, or were barred by their patriotism from interest in, any German machine gunners who were not chained, were not thrilled by his stories.

Krebs acquired the nausea in regard to experience that is the result of untruth or exaggeration, and when he occasionally met another man who had really been a soldier and they talked a few minutes in the dressing room at a dance he fell into the easy pose of the old soldier among other soldiers: that he had been badly, sickeningly frightened all the time. In this way he lost everything.

During this time, it was late summer, he was sleeping late in bed, getting up to walk down town to the library to get a book, eating lunch at home, reading on the front porch until he became bored and then walking down through the town to spend the hottest hours of the day in the cool dark of the pool room. He loved to play pool.

In the evening he practised on his clarinet, strolled down town, read and went to bed. He was still a hero to his two young sisters. His mother would have given him breakfast in bed if he had wanted it. She often came in when he was in bed and asked him to tell her about the war, but her attention always wandered. His father was non-committal.

Before Krebs went away to the war he had never been allowed to drive the family motor car. His father was in the real estate business and always wanted the car to be at his command when he required it to take clients out into the country to show them a piece of farm property. The car always stood outside the First National Bank building where his father had an office on the second floor. Now, after the war, it was still the same car.

Nothing was changed in the town except that the young girls had grown up. But they lived in such a complicated world of already defined alliances and shifting feuds that Krebs did not feel the energy or the courage to break into it. He liked to look at them, though. There were so many good-looking young girls. Most of them had their hair cut short. When he went away only little girls wore their hair like that or girls that were fast. They all wore sweaters and shirt waists with round Dutch collars. It was a pattern. He liked to look at them from the front porch as they walked on the other side of the street. He liked to watch them walking under the shade of the trees. He liked the round Dutch collars above their sweaters. He liked their silk stockings and flat shoes. He liked their bobbed hair and the way they walked.

When he was in town their appeal to him was not very strong. He did not like them when he saw them in the Greek's ice cream parlor. He did not want them themselves really. They were too complicated. There was something else. Vaguely he wanted a girl but he did not want to have to work to get her. He would have liked to have a girl but he did not want to have to spend a long time getting her. He did not want to get into the intrigue and the politics. He did not want to have to do any courting. He did not want to tell any more lies. It wasn't worth it.

He did not want any consequences. He did not want any consequences ever again. He wanted to live along without consequences. Besides he did not really need a girl. The army had taught him that. It was all right to pose as though you had to have a girl. Nearly everybody did that. But it wasn't true. You did not need a girl. That was the funny thing. First a fellow boasted how girls mean nothing to him, that he never thought of them, that they could not touch him. Then a fellow boasted that he could not get along without girls, that he had to have them all the time, that he could not go to sleep without them.

That was all a lie. It was all a lie both ways. You did not need a girl unless you thought about them. He learned that in the army. Then sooner or later you always got one. When you were really ripe for a girl you always got one. You did not have to think about it. Sooner or later it would come. He had learned that in the army.

Now he would have liked a girl if she had come to him and not wanted to talk. But here at home it was all too complicated. He knew he could never get through it all again. It was not worth the trouble. That was the thing about French girls and German girls. There was not all this talking. You couldn't talk much and you did not need to talk. It was simple and you were friends. He thought about France and then he began to think about Germany. On the whole he had liked Germany better. He did not want to leave Germany. He did not want to come home. Still, he had come home. He sat on the front porch.

He liked the girls that were walking along the other side of the street. He liked the look of them much better than the French girls or the German girls. But the world they were in was not the world he was in. He would like to have one of them. But it was not worth it. They were such a nice pattern. He liked the pattern. It was exciting. But he would not go through all the talking. He did not want one badly enough. He liked to look at them all, though. It was not worth it. Not now when things were getting good again.

He sat there on the porch reading a book on the war. It was a history and he was reading about all the engagements he had been in. It was the most interesting reading he had ever done. He wished there were more maps. He looked forward with a good feeling to reading all the really good histories when they would come out with good detail maps. Now he was really learning about the war. He had been a good soldier. That made a difference.

One morning after he had been home about a month his mother came into his bedroom and sat on the bed. She smoothed her apron.

"I had a talk with your father last night, Harold," she said, "and he is willing for you to take the car out in the evenings."

"Yeah?" said Krebs, who was not fully awake. "Take the car out? Yeah?"

"Yes. Your father has felt for some time that you should be able to take the car out in the evenings whenever you wished but we only talked it over last night."

"I'll bet you made him," Krebs said.

"No. It was your father's suggestion that we talk the matter over."

"Yeah. I'll bet you made him," Krebs sat up in bed.

"Will you come down to breakfast, Harold?" his mother said.

"As soon as I get my clothes on," Krebs said.

His mother went out of the room and he could hear her frying something downstairs while he washed, shaved and dressed to go down into the dining-room for breakfast. While he was eating breakfast his sister brought in the mail.

"Well, Hare," she said. "You old sleepy-head. What do you ever get up for?"

Krebs looked at her. He liked her. She was his best sister.

"Have you got the paper?" he asked.

She handed him *The Kansas City Star* and he shucked off its brown wrapper and opened it to the sporting page. He folded *The Star* open and propped it against the water pitcher with his cereal dish to steady it, so he could read while he ate.

"Harold," his mother stood in the kitchen doorway, "Harold, please don't muss up the paper. Your father can't read his *Star* if it's been mussed."

"I won't muss it," Krebs said.

His sister sat down at the table and watched him while he read.

"We're playing indoor over at school this afternoon," she said. "I'm going to pitch."

"Good," said Krebs. "How's the old wing?"

"I can pitch better than lots of the boys. I tell them all you taught me. The other girls aren't much good."

"Yeah?" said Krebs.

"I tell them all you're my beau. Aren't you my beau, Hare?"

"You bet."

"Couldn't your brother really be your beau just because he's your brother?"

"I don't know."

"Sure you know. Couldn't you be my beau, Hare, if I was old enough and if you wanted to?"

"Sure. You're my girl now."

"Am I really your girl?"

"Sure."

"Do you love me?"

"Uh, huh."

"Will you love me always?"

"Sure."

"Will you come over and watch me play indoor?"

"Maybe."

"Aw, Hare, you don't love me. If you loved me, you'd want to come over and watch me play indoor."

Krebs's mother came into the dining-room from the kitchen. She carried a plate with two fried eggs and some crisp bacon on it and a plate of buckwheat cakes.

"You run along, Helen," she said. "I want to talk to Harold."

She put the eggs and bacon down in front of him and brought in a jug of maple syrup for the buckwheat cakes. Then she sat down across the table from Krebs.

"I wish you'd put down the paper a minute, Harold," she said.

Krebs took down the paper and folded it.

"Have you decided what you are going to do yet, Harold?" his mother said, taking off her glasses.

"No," said Krebs.

"Don't you think it's about time?" His mother did not say this in a mean way. She seemed worried.

"I hadn't thought about it," Krebs said.

"God has some work for every one to do," his mother said. "There can be no idle hands in His Kingdom."

"I'm not in His Kingdom," Krebs said.

"We are all of us in His Kingdom."

Krebs felt embarrassed and resentful as always.

"I've worried about you so much, Harold," his mother went on. "I know the temptations you must have been exposed to. I know how weak men are. I know what your own dear grandfather, my own father, told us about the Civil War and I have prayed for you. I pray for you all day long, Harold."

Krebs looked at the bacon fat hardening on his plate.

"Your father is worried, too," his mother went on. "He thinks you have lost your ambition, that you haven't got a definite aim in life. Charley Simmons, who is just your age, has a good job and is going to be married. The boys are all settling down; they're all determined to get somewhere; you can see that boys like Charley Simmons are on their way to being really a credit to the community."

Krebs said nothing.

"Don't look that way, Harold," his mother said. "You know we love you and I want to tell you for your own good how matters stand. Your father does not want to hamper your freedom. He thinks you should be allowed to drive the car. If you want to take some of the nice girls out riding with you, we are only too pleased. We want you to enjoy yourself. But you are going to have to settle down to work, Harold. Your father doesn't care what you start in at. All work is honorable as he says. But you've got to make a start at something. He asked me to speak to you this morning and then you can stop in and see him at his office."

"Is that all?" Krebs said.

"Yes. Don't you love your mother, dear boy?"

"No," Krebs said.

His mother looked at him across the table. Her eyes were shiny. She started crying.

"I don't love anybody," Krebs said.

It wasn't any good. He couldn't tell her, he couldn't make her see it. It was silly to have said it. He had only hurt her. He went over and took hold of her arm. She was crying with her head in her hands.

"I didn't mean it," he said. "I was just angry at something. I didn't mean I didn't love you."

His mother went on crying. Krebs put his arm on her shoulder.

"Can't you believe me, mother?"

His mother shook her head.

"Please, please, mother. Please believe me."

"All right," his mother said chokily. She looked up at him. "I believe you, Harold."

Krebs kissed her hair. She put her face up to him.

"I'm your mother," she said. "I held you next to my heart when you were a tiny baby."

Krebs felt sick and vaguely nauseated.

"I know, Mummy," he said. "I'll try and be a good boy for you."

"Would you kneel and pray with me, Harold?" his mother asked.

They knelt down beside the dining-room table and Krebs's mother prayed.

"Now, you pray, Harold," she said.

"I can't," Krebs said.

"Try, Harold."

"I can't."

"Do you want me to pray for you?"

"Yes."

So his mother prayed for him and then they stood up and Krebs kissed his mother and went out of the house. He had tried so to keep his life from being complicated. Still, none of it had touched him. He had felt sorry for his mother and she had made him lie. He would go to Kansas City and get a job and she would feel all right about it. There would be one more scene maybe before he got away. He would not go down to his father's office. He would miss that one. He wanted his life to go smoothly. It had just gotten going that way. Well, that was all over now, anyway. He would go over to the schoolyard and watch Helen play indoor baseball.

7a.

Item 708, Ernest Hemingway Collection, John F. Kennedy Library and Museum, Boston. Untitled pencil draft manuscript on postal telegraph paper with the earliest preserved draft opening to "Soldier's Home." Pages 1–2.

After he was discharged from the Marine Corps Krebs went home to Kansas. He got home too late. The ~~boys~~ young men from his town who had enlisted in the National Guard or been drafted had all come home months before. The war was well over. The reaction to the war time ~~hysteria~~ feelings had set in.

Krebs knew he was a hero. At least he had done for a long time what the other ~~men~~ soldiers from his town had done a little. He had been a good soldier in a good regiment in a division that had been ~~at the front long enough to~~ in all the big engagements. After the war he was on the Rhine.

7b.

Item 709, Ernest Hemingway Collection, John F. Kennedy Library and Museum, Boston. Titled ink and pencil, handwritten manuscript with corrections, earliest preserved complete draft of "Soldier's Home" with two false starts.

~~Krebs was born in a small town in Kansas. He had grown up~~
   ~~Krebs had gone through high school and three years of college in a Methodist college when the United States declared war in April 1917 and~~

Soldiers Home.

Krebs went to the war from a Methodist college in Kansas. There is a picture which shows him ~~in~~ among his fraternity brothers, all of them wearing exactly the same height and style collar. He enlisted in the Marines early in 1917 and did not return to the United States until the second division returned from the Rhine in the summer of 1919. There is a picture which shows him on the Rhine with another corporal and two German girls. ~~Both Krebs and the corporal are too big for their uniforms. The Rhine does not show in the picture.~~ Krebs and the corporal look too big for their uniforms. The German girls are not beautiful. The Rhine does not show in the picture.

By the time Krebs returned to his home town in Kansas the greeting of heroes was over. He returned much too late. The men from the town who had been drafted had all been welcomed elaborately on their return. There had been a great deal of hysteria. Now the reaction had set in. People seemed to think it was rather ridiculous for Krebs to be getting back so late, years after the war was over.

At first Krebs, who had been at Belleau Wood, ~~in~~ the Champagne, ~~at~~ Saissons, St. Michiel and in the Argonne ~~was q~~ did not want to talk about the war at all. Later he felt the need to talk but no one wanted to hear about it. His town had heard too many ~~atrocities~~ atrocity stories to be thrilled by actualities. Krebs found that to be listened to at all he had to lie and after he had done this twice he too had a reaction against the war and against talking about it. A distaste for everything that happened to him in the war set in because of the lies he had told. All of the ~~things~~ times that had been able to make him feel ~~fine and~~ cool and clear inside himself when he thought of them; ~~because of the fact that~~ the times so long back when he had done the one thing, the only thing for a man to do, easily and naturally when he might have done something else now lost their cool, valuable quality and then were lost themselves. ~~After h~~ His lies, ~~which~~ were quite unimportant lies and consisted in ~~assigning~~ attributing to himself things other men had seen, done, or heard of, and stating as facts certain apocryphal incidents. ~~even they fell rather flat in the~~ Even his lies were not sensational at the pool room. ~~[. . .] acquaintances who had heard~~ His detailed accounts of German women found chained to machine guns in the Argonne forest and who could not ~~picture~~ comprehend, or were barred by their patriotism from interest in, any German machine gunners who were not chained were not thrilled by his stories. Krebs acquired the nausea in regard to experience that is the result of untruth or exaggeration and when he occasionally met another man who had really been a soldier and they ~~exchanged a few~~ talked a few minutes in the dressing room at a dance he fell into ~~that~~ the easy pose of the old soldier among other soldiers; that had been badly, sickeningly, frightened all the time. In this way he lost everything.

During this time, it was late summer, he was sleeping late in bed, getting up to walk downtown to the library to get a book, ~~dropping in at the pool room~~ eating lunch at home, reading on the front porch until he became bored and then walking down through the ~~heat of the day~~ town to spend the hottest hours of the day in the cool, dark of the pool room. He loved to play pool.

In the evenings, he practiced on his clarinet, strolled downtown, read, and went to bed. He was still ~~very much~~ a hero to his two young sisters. His mother would have given him breakfast in bed if he wanted it. She often came in when he was in bed and asked him to tell her things about the war. But her attention always wandered. His father was noncommittal.

Before ~~he~~ Krebs went away to the war he had never been allowed to drive the family car. His father was in the real estate business and always wanted the car to be at his command when he ~~wanted~~ required it to take some one out into the country to show them a piece of farm property. The car always stood in the shade outside ~~his father's office on the second floor of the 1st National Bank building~~ the First National Bank building where his father had an office on the second floor. Now after the war it was still the same car ~~the Krebs family had owned before the war~~. Nothing was changed in the town except that the young girls had all grown up.

~~Insert~~

But they lived in such a complicated world of ~~special friendships~~ already defined alliances and shifting feuds that Krebs ~~felt barred by his lack of~~ did not feel the energy or the courage to break into it. He liked to look at them ~~however~~ though. There were so many good looking young girls. Most of them had their hair cut short. When he went away only little girls had their hair like that or gals that were fast. They all wore sweaters and skirt waists. It was a pattern. He liked to watch them ~~pass by along the walking under the shade of the trees~~ from the front porch as they walked on the other side of the street. He liked to watch them walking under the shade of the trees. ~~He liked less less seeing them in the Greeks ice cream parlor.~~ He liked the round dutch collars ~~of their~~

~~shirt waists~~ above their sweaters. He liked their silk stockings and flat shoes. He liked their bobbed hair. They were all a pattern. When he was in the town their appeal to him was not very strong. He did not like them when he saw them in the Greeks ice cream place. He did not want them themselves really. They were too complicated. There was something else. Vaguely he wanted a girl but he did not want to have to work ~~for her~~ to get her. He would have liked to have a girl but he did not want to have to spend a long time getting her. He did not want to get into the intrigue and the politics. He did not want to have to do any courting. He did not want to tell any more lies. It wasn't worth it. He did not want any consequences. He did not want any consequences ever again. He wanted to live ~~a lif~~ along without consequences. Besides he did not really need a girl. The army had taught him that. It was all right to pose as though you had to have a girl. Nearly everybody did that. ~~But~~ But it wasn't true. You did not need a girl. That was a funny thing. First a fellow boasted how girls meant nothing to him, that he never thought of them, that they ~~couldn't~~ not touch him. Then a fellow boasted that he ~~couldn't~~ not get along without girls, that he had to have them all the time, that he could not go to sleep without them.

That was all a lie. It was all a lie both ways. You did not need a girl unless you thought about them. He learned that in the army. Then sooner or later you always got one. ~~If~~ When you were really ripe for a girl you always got one. You ~~didn't~~ not have to think about it. Sooner or later ~~you~~ it would come ~~out all right~~. He had learned that in the army.

Now he would have liked a girl if she had come to him and not wanted to talk. But here at home it was all too complicated. He knew he could never ~~face~~ go through it all again. It was not worth the trouble. That was the thing about French girls and German girls. There was not all this talking. You couldn't talk much and you ~~didn't~~ not need to talk. It was simple and you were friends. He thought about France and then he began to think about Germany. On the whole he had liked Germany better. He did not want to leave Germany. He did not want to come home. Still he had come home. He sat on the front porch.

He liked the girls as they walked along on the other side of the street. He liked the look of them much better than French girls or German girls. But the world they ~~lived~~ were in was not the world he ~~lived~~ was in. He would like to have one of them. But it was not worth it. They were such a nice pattern. He liked the pattern. It was exciting. But he would not go through all the talking. He did not want one bad enough. He liked to look at them all. He liked the pattern. It was not worth it. Not now when things were getting good again. He sat there on the porch reading a book on the war. It was a history and he was reading about all the engagements he had been in. It was the most interesting reading he had ever done. He wished there were more maps. He looked forward with a good feeling to ~~the time when~~ reading all the really good histories, ~~would be out~~ with regimental papers and good maps. Now he was really learning about the war. He had been a good soldier. That made a difference.

After he had been home about two weeks his mother came into his bed room one morning and sat ~~down~~ on the bed. She smoothed her apron[.] "I had a talk with your father last night Harold." She said "and he is willing for you to take the car out in the evenings."

"Yeah?" said Krebs, who was not wholly awake, "take the car out? Yeah?"

"Yes. Your father has felt for some time that you should be able to take the car out in the evenings whenever you wished. But we only talked it over last night."

"I'll bet you made him[,]" Krebs said.

"No. It was your father's suggestion that we talk the matter over."

"Yeah. I'll bet you made him." Krebs sat up in bed.

"Will you come down to breakfast, Harold?" his mother said.

"As soon as I get my clothes on," Krebs said.

His mother went out of the room and he could hear her frying something downstairs while he washed, shaved and dressed to go down into the dining room for breakfast.

While he was eating breakfast his sister brought in the mail.

"Well Hare[,]" she said, "you old sleepy head. What do you get up at all for?"

Krebs looked at her. He liked her ~~very much~~. She was his best sister. "Have you got the paper?" he asked.

She handed him the Kansas City Star and he shucked off its brown wrapper and opened it to the sporting page. ~~He looked at it thoroughly and it seemed to satisfy him.~~ He folded it open and propped it against the water pitcher ~~behind his cereal~~ with his cereal dish to steady it so he could read while he ate.

"Harold," his mother stood in the kitchen doorway, "Harold please don't muss up the paper. Your father can't read his Star if it's been mussed."

"I won't muss it," Krebs ~~answered~~ said.

His sister sat down at the table and watched him while he read.

"We're playing indoor over at school this afternoon[,]" she said, "I'm going to pitch."

"Good[,]" said Krebs, "How's the old wing?"

"I can pitch better than lots of the boys. ~~I tell them all that you taught me.~~ I tell them all that you taught me. The other girls aren't much good."

"Yeah?" said Krebs.

"I tell them all you're my beau. Aren't you my beau Hare?"

"You bet."

"Couldn't ~~Really couldn't~~ your brother really be your beau just because he's your brother?"

"You better ask your mother[.]"

"I don't want to ask her. ~~You tell me Hare.~~ Couldn't you be my beau Hare if I was old enough and ~~we both~~ if you wanted to?"

"Sure. You're my girl now."

"Am I really your girl?"

"Sure. ~~Yes~~"

"Do you love me?"

"~~Yes~~ Uh huh[.]"

"Will you love me always?"

"~~Yes~~ Sure."

"Will you come over and watch me play indoor?"

"Maybe."

"You don't love me. If you loved me you'd want to come over and watch me play indoor."

Krebs' mother came into the dining room from the kitchen. She carried a plate ~~of~~ with two fried eggs ~~on it~~ and some slices of bacon on it and a plate of buckwheat cakes.

"You run along Helen[,]" she said. "I want to talk to Harold."

She put the eggs and bacon down in front of him and brought in a jug of maple syrup for the buckwheat cakes. Then she sat down across the table from Krebs.

"I wish you'd put down the paper a minute Harold," she said.

Krebs took down the paper and folded it.

"Have you decided what you are going to do yet Harold?" ~~She~~ His mother asked taking off her glasses.

"No[,]" said Krebs.

"Don't you think it's about time?" His mother did not say this in a mean way. She seemed worried.

"I hadn't thought about it[,]" Krebs said.

"God has some work for everyone to do[.]" His mother said. "There can be no idle hands in His ~~world~~ Kingdom."

"I'm not in his kingdom[,]" Krebs said.

"~~Oh~~ We are all of us in His kingdom."

Krebs felt embarrassed and resentful as always.

"I've worried about you so much Harold[,]" his mother went on. "I know the temptations you must have been exposed to, I know how weak men are, I know what your own dear grandfather, my own father, told us about the civil war and I have prayed for you. I pray for you all day long Harold."

Krebs looked at the bacon fat hardening on his plate.

"Your father is worried too." His mother went on. "He thinks you have lost your ambition, that you haven't got a definite aim in life. Charley Simmons ~~is in business~~ has a good job and is going to get married. The boys are all settling down, they're all determined to get somewhere, you can see that boys like Charley Simmons are going to be a real credit to the community."

Krebs said nothing.

"Don't look that way Harold[,]" his mother said. "You know we love you and I want to tell you for your own good how matters stand. Your father thinks you should be allowed to drive the car. If you want to take a nice girl out riding with you we are only too pleased. But you are going to have to settle down to work Harold. Your father doesn't care what you start in at. All work is honorable as he says. But you've got to make a start at something. He asked me to speak to you this morning and then you can stop in and see him at his office."

"Is that all?" Krebs said.

"Yes. Don't you love your mother dear boy?"

"No[,]" Krebs said[.]

His mother looked at him across the table. Her eyes were ~~bright~~

shiny, ~~then tears came out, then her eyes were red and she was crying~~ she started crying.

"I don't love anybody[,]" Krebs said. It wasn't any good. He couldn't tell her he couldn't make her see it. It was silly to have said it. He'd only hurt her. He went over and took hold of her arm. She was crying with her head in her hands.

"I didn't mean it[,]" he said. "I was just angry at something. I didn't mean I didn't love you."

His mother went on crying. Krebs put his arm on her shoulder.

"Can't you believe me mother?"

His mother shook her head.

"Please mother. Please, please believe me."

"All right[.]" His mother said cheerily. "I believe you Harold."

Krebs kissed her hair. She put her face up to him.

"I'm your mother[,]" she said. "I held you next to my heart when you were a tiny baby."

Krebs felt sick and almost nauseated.

"I know Mummie[,]" he said, "I'll try and be a good boy for you."

"Would you kneel and pray with me Harold?" His mother asked.

They ~~kneeled~~ knelt down beside the dining room table and Krebs' mother prayed.

"Now you pray Harold[,]" she said.

"I can't[,]" Krebs said.

"Try Harold[.]"

"I can't[.]"

"Do you want me to pray for you?"

"Yes."

So his mother prayed for him and then they stood up and Krebs kissed his mother and went out of the house. He had tried so to keep his life from being complicated. Still none of it had touched him. He had felt sorry for his mother and she had made him lie. He would go to Kansas City and get a job and she would feel all right about it. There would be one more scene maybe before he got away. He would not go down to his father's office. He'd miss that one. He would go ~~down~~ over to the school yard and watch Helen play indoor base ball. ~~Hd He'd He had wanted it to go smoothly. Well that was all over now anyway.~~

8.

Big Two-Hearted River

1925

PART I

The train went on up the track out of sight, around one of the hills of burnt timber. Nick sat down on the bundle of canvas and bedding the baggage man had pitched out of the door of the baggage car. There was no town, nothing but the rails and the burned-over country. The thirteen saloons that had lined the one street of Seney had not left a trace. The foundations of the Mansion House hotel stuck up above the ground. The stone was chipped and split by the fire. It was all that was left of the town of Seney. Even the surface had been burned off the ground.

Nick looked at the burned-over stretch of hillside, where he had expected to find the scattered houses of the town and then walked down the railroad track to the bridge over the river. The river was there. It swirled against the log spiles of the bridge. Nick looked down into the clear, brown water, colored from the pebbly bottom, and watched the trout keeping themselves steady in the current with wavering fins. As he watched them they changed their positions by quick angles, only to hold steady in the fast water again. Nick watched them a long time.

He watched them holding themselves with their noses into the current, many trout in deep, fast moving water, slightly distorted as he watched far down through the glassy convex surface of the pool, its surface pushing and swelling smooth against the resistance of the log-driven piles of the bridge. At the bottom of the pool were the big trout. Nick did not see them at first. Then he saw them at the bottom of the pool, big trout looking to hold themselves on the gravel bottom in a varying mist of gravel and sand, raised in spurts by the current.

Nick looked down into the pool from the bridge. It was a hot day. A kingfisher flew up the stream. It was a long time since Nick had looked into a stream and seen trout. They were very satisfactory. As the shadow of the kingfisher moved up the stream, a big trout shot upstream in a long angle, only his shadow marking the angle, then lost his shadow as he came through the surface of the water, caught the sun, and then, as he went back into the stream under the surface, his shadow seemed to float down the stream with the current, unresisting, to his post under the bridge where he tightened facing up into the current.

Nick's heart tightened as the trout moved. He felt all the old feeling.

He turned and looked down the stream. It stretched away, pebbly-bottomed with shallows and big boulders and a deep pool as it curved away around the foot of a bluff.

Nick walked back up the ties to where his pack lay in the cinders beside the railway track. He was happy. He adjusted the pack harness around the bundle, pulling straps tight, slung the pack on his back, got his arms through the shoulder straps and took some of the pull off his shoulders by leaning his forehead against the wide band of the tump-line. Still, it was too heavy. It was much too heavy. He had his leather rod-case in his hand and leaning forward to keep the weight of the pack high on his shoulders he walked along the road that paralleled the railway track, leaving the burned town behind in the heat, and then turned off around a hill with a high, fire-scarred hill on either side onto a road that went back into the country. He walked along the road feeling the ache from the pull of the heavy pack. The road climbed steadily. It was hard work walking up-hill. His muscles ached and the day was hot, but Nick felt happy. He felt he had left everything behind, the need for thinking, the need to write, other needs. It was all back of him.

From the time he had gotten down off the train and the baggage man had thrown his pack out of the open car door things had been different. Seney was burned, the country was burned over and changed, but it did not matter. It could not all be burned. He knew that. He hiked along the road, sweating in the sun, climbing to cross the range of hills that separated the railway from the pine plains.

The road ran on, dipping occasionally, but always climbing. Nick went on up. Finally the road after going parallel to the burnt hillside reached the top. Nick leaned back against a stump and slipped out of the pack harness. Ahead of him, as far as he could see, was the pine plain. The burned country stopped off at the left with the range of hills. On ahead islands of dark pine trees rose out of the plain. Far off to the left was the line of the river. Nick followed it with his eye and caught glints of the water in the sun.

There was nothing but the pine plain ahead of him, until the far blue hills that marked the Lake Superior height of land. He could hardly see them, faint and far away in the heat-light over the plain. If he looked too steadily they were gone. But if he only half-looked they were there, the far-off hills of the height of land.

Nick sat down against the charred stump and smoked a cigarette. His pack balanced on the top of the stump, harness holding ready, a hollow molded in it from his back. Nick sat smoking, looking out over the country. He did not need to get his map out. He knew where he was from the position of the river.

As he smoked, his legs stretched out in front of him, he noticed a grasshopper walk along the ground and up onto his woolen sock. The grasshopper was black. As he had walked along the road, climbing, he had started many grasshoppers from the dust. They were all black. They were not the big grasshoppers with yellow and black or red and black wings whirring out from their black wing sheathing as they fly up. These were just ordinary hoppers, but all a sooty black in color. Nick had wondered about them as he walked, without really thinking about them. Now, as he watched the black hopper that was nibbling at the wool of his sock with its fourway lip, he realized that they had all turned black from living in the burned-over land. He realized that the fire must have come the year before, but the grasshoppers were all black now. He wondered how long they would stay that way.

Carefully he reached his hand down and took hold of the hopper by the wings. He turned him up, all his legs walking in the air, and looked at his jointed belly. Yes, it was black too, iridescent where the back and head were dusty.

"Go on, hopper," Nick said, speaking out loud for the first time. "Fly away somewhere."

He tossed the grasshopper up into the air and watched him sail away to a charcoal stump across the road.

Nick stood up. He leaned his back against the weight of his pack where it rested upright on the stump and got his arms through the shoulder straps. He stood with the pack on his back on the brow of the hill looking out across the country toward the distant river and then struck down the hillside away from the road. Underfoot the ground was good walking. Two hundred yards down the hillside the fire line stopped. Then it was sweet fern, growing ankle high, to walk through, and clumps of jack pines; a long undulating country with frequent rises and descents, sandy underfoot and the country alive again.

Nick kept his direction by the sun. He knew where he wanted to strike the river and he kept on through the pine plain, mounting small rises to see other rises ahead of him and sometimes from the top of a rise a great solid island of pines off to his right or his left. He broke off some sprigs of the heathery sweet fern, and put them under his pack straps. The chafing crushed it and he smelled it as he walked.

He was tired and very hot, walking across the uneven, shadeless pine plain. At any time he knew he could strike the river by turning off to his left. It could not be more than a mile away. But he kept on toward the north to hit the river as far upstream as he could go in one day's walking.

For some time as he walked Nick had been in sight of one of the big islands of pine standing out above the rolling high ground he was crossing.

He dipped down and then as he came slowly up to the crest of the bridge he turned and made toward the pine trees.

There was no underbrush in the island of pine trees. The trunks of the trees went straight up or slanted toward each other. The trunks were straight and brown without branches. The branches were high above. Some interlocked to make a solid shadow on the brown forest floor. Around the grove of trees was a bare space. It was brown and soft underfoot as Nick walked on it. This was the over-lapping of the pine needle floor, extending out beyond the width of the high branches. The trees had grown tall and the branches moved high, leaving in the sun this bare space they had once covered with shadow. Sharp at the edge of this extension of the forest floor commenced the sweet fern.

Nick slipped off his pack and lay down in the shade. He lay on his back and looked up into the pine trees. His neck and back and the small of his back rested as he stretched. The earth felt good against his back. He looked up at the sky, through the branches, and then shut his eyes. He opened them and looked up again. There was a wind high up in the branches. He shut his eyes again and went to sleep.

Nick woke stiff and cramped. The sun was nearly down. His pack was heavy and the straps painful as he lifted it on. He leaned over with the pack on and picked up the leather rod-case and started out from the pine trees across the sweet fern swale, toward the river. He knew it could not be more than a mile.

He came down a hillside covered with stumps into a meadow. At the edge of the meadow flowed the river. Nick was glad to get to the river. He walked upstream through the meadow. His trousers were soaked with the dew as he walked. After the hot day, the dew had come quickly and heavily. The river made no sound. It was too fast and smooth. At the edge of the meadow, before he mounted to a piece of high ground to make camp, Nick looked down the river at the trout rising. They were rising to insects come from the swamp on the other side of the stream when the sun went down. The trout jumped out of water to take them. While Nick walked through the little stretch of meadow alongside the stream, trout had jumped high out of water. Now as he looked down the river, the insects must be settling on the surface, for the trout were feeding steadily all down the stream. As far down the long stretch as he could see, the trout were rising, making circles all down the surface of the water, as though it were starting to rain.

The ground rose, wooded and sandy, to overlook the meadow,

the stretch of river and the swamp. Nick dropped his pack and rod-case and looked for a level piece of ground. He was very hungry and he wanted to make his camp before he cooked. Between two jack pines, the ground was quite level. He took the ax out of the pack and chopped out two projecting roots. That leveled a piece of ground large enough to sleep on. He smoothed out the sandy soil with his hand and pulled all the sweet fern bushes by their roots. His hands smelled good from the sweet fern. He smoothed the uprooted earth. He did not want anything making lumps under the blankets. When he had the ground smooth, he spread his three blankets. One he folded double, next to the ground. The other two he spread on top.

With the ax he slit off a bright slab of pine from one of the stumps and split it into pegs for the tent. He wanted them long and solid to hold in the ground. With the tent unpacked and spread on the ground, the pack, leaning against a jackpine, looked much smaller. Nick tied the rope that served the tent for a ridgepole to the trunk of one of the pine trees and pulled the tent up off the ground with the other end of the rope and tied it to the other pine. The tent hung on the rope like a canvas blanket on a clothesline. Nick poked a pole he had cut up under the back peak of the canvas and then made it a tent by pegging out the sides. He pegged the sides out taut and drove the pegs deep, hitting them down into the ground with the flat of the ax until the rope loops were buried and the canvas was drum tight.

Across the open mouth of the tent Nick fixed cheesecloth to keep out mosquitoes. He crawled inside under the mosquito bar with various things from the pack to put at the head of the bed under the slant of the canvas. Inside the tent the light came through the brown canvas. It smelled pleasantly of canvas. Already there was something mysterious and homelike. Nick was happy as he crawled inside the tent. He had not been unhappy all day. This was different though. Now things were done. There had been this to do. Now it was done. It had been a hard trip. He was very tired. That was done. He had made his camp. He was settled. Nothing could touch him. It was a good place to camp. He was there, in the good place. He was in his home where he had made it. Now he was hungry.

He came out, crawling under the cheesecloth. It was quite dark outside. It was lighter in the tent.

Nick went over to the pack and found, with his fingers, a long nail in a paper sack of nails, in the bottom of the pack. He drove it into the pine tree, holding it close and hitting it gently with the flat of the ax. He hung the pack up on the nail. All his supplies were in the pack. They were off the ground and sheltered now.

Nick was hungry. He did not believe he had ever been hungrier. He opened and emptied a can of pork and beans and a can of spaghetti into the frying pan.

"I've got a right to eat this kind of stuff, if I'm willing to carry it," Nick said. His voice sounded strange in the darkening woods. He did not speak again.

He started a fire with some chunks of pine he got with the ax from a stump. Over the fire he stuck a wire grill, pushing the four legs down into the ground with his boot. Nick put the frying pan on the grill over the flames. He was hungrier. The beans and spaghetti warmed. Nick stirred them and mixed them together. They began to bubble, making little bubbles that rose with difficulty to the surface. There was a good smell. Nick got out a bottle of tomato catchup and cut four slices of bread. The little bubbles were coming faster now. Nick sat down beside the fire and lifted the frying pan off. He poured about half the contents out into the tin plate. It spread slowly on the plate. Nick knew it was too hot. He poured on some tomato catchup. He knew the beans and spaghetti were still too hot. He looked at the fire, then at the tent, he was not going to spoil it all by burning his tongue. For years he had never enjoyed fried bananas because he had never been able to wait for them to cool. His tongue was very sensitive. He was very hungry. Across the river in the swamp, in the almost dark, he saw a mist rising. He looked at the tent once more. All right. He took a full spoonful from the plate.

"Chrise," Nick said, "Geezus Chrise," he said happily.

He ate the whole plateful before he remembered the bread. Nick finished the second plateful with the bread, mopping the plate shiny. He had not eaten since a cup of coffee and a ham sandwich in the station restaurant at St. Ignace. It had been a very fine experience. He had been that hungry before, but had not been able to satisfy it. He could have made camp hours before if he had wanted to. There were plenty of good places to camp on the river. But this was good.

Nick tucked two big chips of pine under the grill. The fire flared up. He had forgotten to get water for the coffee. Out of the pack he got a folding canvas bucket and walked down the hill, across the edge of the meadow, to the stream. The other bank was in the white mist. The grass was wet and cold as he knelt on the bank and dipped the canvas bucket into the stream. It bellied and pulled hard in the current. The water was ice cold. Nick rinsed the bucket and carried it full up to the camp. Up away from the stream it was not so cold.

Nick drove another big nail and hung up the bucket full of water. He dipped the coffee pot half full, put some more chips under the grill onto the fire and put the pot on. He could not remember which way he made coffee. He could remember an argument about it with Hopkins, but not which side he had taken. He decided to bring it to a boil. He remembered now that was Hopkins's way. He had once argued about everything with Hopkins. While he waited for the coffee to boil, he opened a small can of apricots. He liked to open cans. He emptied the can of apricots out into a tin cup. While he watched the coffee on the fire, he drank the juice syrup of the apricots, carefully at first to keep from spilling, then meditatively, sucking the apricots down. They were better than fresh apricots.

The coffee boiled as he watched. The lid came up and coffee and grounds ran down the side of the pot. Nick took it off the grill. It was a triumph for Hopkins. He put sugar in the empty apricot cup and poured some of the coffee out to cool. It was too hot to pour and he used his hat to hold the handle of the coffee pot. He would not let it steep in the pot at all. Not the first cup. It should be straight Hopkins all the way. Hop deserved that. He was a very serious coffee drinker. He was the most serious man Nick had ever known. Not heavy, serious. That was a long time ago. Hopkins spoke without moving his lips. He had played polo. He made millions of dollars in Texas. He had borrowed carfare to go to Chicago, when the wire came that his first big well had come in. He could have wired for money. That would have been too slow. They called Hop's girl the Blonde Venus. Hop did not mind because she was not his real girl. Hopkins said very confidently that none of them would make fun of his real girl. He was right. Hopkins went away when the telegram came. That was on the Black River. It took eight days for the telegram to reach him. Hopkins gave away his .22 caliber Colt automatic pistol to Nick. He gave his camera to Bill. It was to remember him always by. They were all going fishing again next summer. The Hop Head was rich. He would get a yacht and they would all cruise along the north shore of Lake Superior. He was excited but serious. They said good-bye and all felt bad. It broke up the trip. They never saw Hopkins again. That was a long time ago on the Black River.

Nick drank the coffee, the coffee according to Hopkins. The coffee was bitter. Nick laughed. It made a good ending to the story. His mind was starting to work. He knew he could choke it because he was tired enough. He spilled the coffee out of the pot and shook the grounds loose into the fire. He lit a cigarette and went inside the tent. He took off his shoes and trousers, sitting on the blankets, rolled the shoes up inside the trousers for a pillow and got in between the blankets.

Out through the front of the tent he watched the glow of the fire, when the night wind blew on it. It was a quiet night. The swamp was perfectly quiet. Nick stretched under the blanket comfortably. A mosquito hummed close to his ear. Nick sat up and lit a match. The mosquito was on the canvas, over his head. Nick moved the match quickly up to it. The mosquito made a satisfactory hiss in the flame. The match went out. Nick lay down again under the blanket. He turned on his side and shut his eyes. He was sleepy. He felt sleep coming. He curled up under the blanket and went to sleep.

PART II

In the morning the sun was up and the tent was starting to get hot. Nick crawled out under the mosquito netting stretched across the mouth of the tent, to look at the morning. The grass was wet on his hands as he came out. He held his trousers and his shoes in his hands. The sun was just up over the hill. There was the meadow, the river and the swamp. There were birch trees in the green of the swamp on the other side of the river.

The river was clear and smoothly fast in the early morning. Down about two hundred yards were three logs all the way across the stream. They made the water smooth and deep above them. As Nick watched, a mink crossed the river on the logs and went into the swamp. Nick was excited. He was excited by the early morning and the river. He was really too hurried to eat breakfast, but he knew he must. He built a little fire and put on the coffee pot.

While the water was heating in the pot he took an empty bottle and went down over the edge of the high ground to the meadow. The meadow was wet with dew and Nick wanted to catch grasshoppers for bait before the sun dried the grass. He found plenty of good grasshoppers. They were at the base of the grass stems. Sometimes they clung to a grass stem. They were cold and wet with the dew, and could not jump until the sun warmed them. Nick picked them up, taking only the medium-sized brown ones, and put them into the bottle. He turned over a log and just under the shelter of the edge were several hundred hoppers. It was a grasshopper lodging house. Nick put about fifty of the medium browns into the bottle. While he was picking up the hoppers the others warmed in the sun and commenced to hop away. They flew when they hopped. At first they made one flight and stayed stiff when they landed, as though they were dead.

Nick knew that by the time he was through with breakfast they would be as lively as ever. Without dew in the grass it would take him all day to catch a bottle full of good grasshoppers and he would have to crush many of them, slamming at them with his hat. He washed his hands at the stream. He was excited to be near it. Then he walked up to the tent. The hoppers were already jumping stiffly in the grass. In the bottle, warmed by the sun, they were jumping in a mass. Nick put in a pine stick as a cork. It plugged the mouth of the bottle enough, so the hoppers could not get out and left plenty of air passage.

He had rolled the log back and knew he could get grasshoppers there every morning.

Nick laid the bottle full of jumping grasshoppers against a pine trunk. Rapidly he mixed some buckwheat flour with water and stirred it smooth, one cup of flour, one cup of water. He put a handful of coffee in the pot and dipped a lump of grease out of a can and slid it sputtering across the hot skillet. On the smoking skillet he poured smoothly the buckwheat batter. It spread like lava, the grease spitting sharply. Around the edges the buckwheat cake began to firm, then brown, then crisp. The surface was bubbling slowly to porousness. Nick pushed under the browned under surface with a fresh pine chip. He shook the skillet sideways and the cake was loose on the surface. I won't try and flop it, he thought. He slid the chip of clean wood all the way under the cake, and flopped it over onto its face. It sputtered in the pan.

When it was cooked Nick regreased the skillet. He used all the batter. It made another big flapjack and one smaller one.

Nick ate a big flapjack and a smaller one, covered with apple butter. He put apple butter on the third cake, folded it over twice, wrapped it in oiled paper and put it in his shirt pocket. He put the apple butter jar back in the pack and cut bread for two sandwiches.

In the pack he found a big onion. He sliced it in two and peeled the silky outer skin. Then he cut one half into slices and made onion sandwiches. He wrapped them in oiled paper and buttoned them in the other pocket of his khaki shirt. He turned the skillet upside down on the grill, drank the coffee, sweetened and yellow brown with the condensed milk in it, and tidied up the camp. It was a good camp.

Nick took his fly rod out of the leather rod-case, jointed it, and shoved the rod-case back into the tent. He put on the reel and threaded the line through the guides. He had to hold it from hand to hand, as he threaded it, or it would slip back through its own weight. It was a heavy, double tapered fly line. Nick had paid eight dollars for it a long time ago. It was made heavy to lift back in the air and come forward flat and heavy and straight to make it possible to cast a fly which has no weight. Nick opened the aluminum leader box. The leaders were coiled between the damp flannel pads. Nick had wet the pads at the water cooler on the train up to St. Ignace. In the damp pads the gut leaders had softened and Nick unrolled one and tied it by a loop at the end to the heavy fly line. He fastened a hook on the end of the leader. It was a small hook; very thin and springy.

Nick took it from his hook book, sitting with the rod across his lap. He tested the knot and the spring of the rod by pulling the line taut. It was a good feeling. He was careful not to let the hook bite into his finger.

He started down to the stream, holding his rod, the bottle of grasshoppers hung from his neck by a thong tied in half hitches around the neck of the bottle. His landing net hung by a hook from his belt. Over his shoulder was a long flour sack tied at each corner into an ear. The cord went over his shoulder. The sack flapped against his legs.

Nick felt awkward and professionally happy with all his equipment hanging from him. The grasshopper bottle swung against his chest. In his shirt the breast pockets bulged against him with the lunch and his fly book.

He stepped into the stream. It was a shock. His trousers clung tight to his legs. His shoes felt the gravel. The water was a rising cold shock.

Rushing, the current sucked against his legs. Where he stepped in, the water was over his knees. He waded with the current. The gravel slid under his shoes. He looked down at the swirl of water below each leg and tipped up the bottle to get a grasshopper.

The first grasshopper gave a jump in the neck of the bottle and went out into the water. He was sucked under in the whirl by Nick's right leg and came to the surface a little way down stream. He floated rapidly, kicking. In a quick circle, breaking the smooth surface of the water, he disappeared. A trout had taken him.

Another hopper poked his face out of the bottle. His antennæ wavered. He was getting his front legs out of the bottle to jump. Nick took him by the head and held him while he threaded the slim hook under his chin, down through his thorax and into the last segments of his abdomen. The grasshopper took hold of the hook with his front feet, spitting tobacco juice on it. Nick dropped him into the water.

Holding the rod in his right hand he let out line against the pull of the grasshopper in the current. He stripped off line from the reel with his left hand and let it run free. He could see the hopper in the little waves of the current. It went out of sight.

There was a tug on the line. Nick pulled against the taut line. It was his first strike. Holding the now living rod across the current, he brought in the line with his left hand. The rod bent in jerks, the trout pumping against the current. Nick knew it was a small one. He lifted the rod straight up in the air. It bowed with the pull.

He saw the trout in the water jerking with his head and body against the shifting tangent of the line in the stream.

Nick took the line in his left hand and pulled the trout, thumping tiredly against the current, to the surface. His back was mottled the clear, water-over-gravel color, his side flashing in the sun. The rod under his right arm, Nick stooped, dipping his right hand into the current. He held the trout, never still, with his moist right hand, while he unhooked the barb from his mouth, then dropped him back into the stream.

He hung unsteadily in the current, then settled to the bottom beside a stone. Nick reached down his hand to touch him, his arm to the elbow under water. The trout was steady in the moving stream, resting on the gravel, beside a stone. As Nick's fingers touched him, touched his smooth, cool, underwater feeling he was gone, gone in a shadow across the bottom of the stream.

He's all right, Nick thought. He was only tired.

He had wet his hand before he touched the trout, so he would not disturb the delicate mucus that covered him. If a trout was touched with a dry hand, a white fungus attacked the unprotected spot. Years before when he had fished crowded streams, with fly fishermen ahead of him and behind him, Nick had again and again come on dead trout, furry with white fungus, drifted against a rock, or floating belly up in some pool. Nick did not like to fish with other men on the river. Unless they were of your party, they spoiled it.

He wallowed down the stream, above his knees in the current, through the fifty yards of shallow water above the pile of logs that crossed the stream. He did not rebait his hook and held it in his hand as he waded. He was certain he could catch small trout in the shallows, but he did not want them. There would be no big trout in the shallows this time of day.

Now the water deepened up his thighs sharply and coldly. Ahead was the smooth dammed-back flood of water above the logs. The water was smooth and dark; on the left, the lower edge of the meadow; on the right the swamp.

Nick leaned back against the current and took a hopper from the bottle. He threaded the hopper on the hook and spat on him for good luck. Then he pulled several yards of line from the reel and tossed the hopper out ahead onto the fast, dark water. It floated down towards the logs, then the weight of the line pulled the bait under the surface. Nick held the rod in his right hand, letting the line run out through his fingers.

There was a long tug. Nick struck and the rod came alive and dangerous, bent double, the line tightening, coming out of water, tightening, all in a heavy, dangerous, steady pull. Nick felt the moment when the leader would break if the strain increased and let the line go.

The reel ratcheted into a mechanical shriek as the line went out in a rush. Too fast. Nick could not check it, the line rushing out, the reel note rising as the line ran out.

With the core of the reel showing, his heart feeling stopped with the excitement, leaning back against the current that mounted icily his thighs, Nick thumbed the reel hard with his left hand. It was awkward getting his thumb inside the fly reel frame.

As he put on pressure the line tightened into sudden hardness and beyond the logs a huge trout went high out of water. As he jumped, Nick lowered the tip of the rod. But he felt, as he dropped the tip to ease the strain, the moment when the strain was too great; the hardness too tight. Of course, the leader had broken. There was no mistaking the feeling when all spring left the line and it became dry and hard. Then it went slack.

His mouth dry, his heart down, Nick reeled in. He had never seen so big a trout. There was a heaviness, a power not to be held, and then the bulk of him, as he jumped. He looked as broad as a salmon.

Nick's hand was shaky. He reeled in slowly. The thrill had been too much. He felt, vaguely, a little sick, as though it would be better to sit down.

The leader had broken where the hook was tied to it. Nick

took it in his hand. He thought of the trout somewhere on the bottom, holding himself steady over the gravel, far down below the light, under the logs, with the hook in his jaw. Nick knew the trout's teeth would cut through the snell of the hook. The hook would imbed itself in his jaw. He'd bet the trout was angry. Anything that size would be angry. That was a trout. He had been solidly hooked. Solid as a rock. He felt like a rock, too, before he started off. By God, he was a big one. By God, he was the biggest one I ever heard of.

Nick climbed out onto the meadow and stood, water running down his trousers and out of his shoes, his shoes squelchy. He went over and sat on the logs. He did not want to rush his sensations any.

He wriggled his toes in the water, in his shoes, and got out a cigarette from his breast pocket. He lit it and tossed the match into the fast water below the logs. A tiny trout rose at the match, as it swung around in the fast current. Nick laughed. He would finish the cigarette.

He sat on the logs, smoking, drying in the sun, the sun warm on his back, the river shallow ahead entering the woods, curving into the woods, shallows, light glittering, big water-smooth rocks, cedars along the bank and white birches, the logs warm in the sun, smooth to sit on, without bark, gray to the touch; slowly the feeling of disappointment left him. It went away slowly, the feeling of disappointment that came sharply after the thrill that made his shoulders ache. It was all right now. His rod lying out on the logs, Nick tied a new hook on the leader, pulling the gut tight until it grimped into itself in a hard knot.

He baited up, then picked up the rod and walked to the far end of the logs to get into the water, where it was not too deep. Under and beyond the logs was a deep pool. Nick walked around the shallow shelf near the swamp shore until he came out on the shallow bed of the stream.

On the left, where the meadow ended and the woods began, a great elm tree was uprooted. Gone over in a storm, it lay back into the woods, its roots clotted with dirt, grass growing in them, rising a solid bank beside the stream. The river cut to the edge of the uprooted tree. From where Nick stood he could see deep channels, like ruts, cut in the shallow bed of the stream by the flow of the current. Pebbly where he stood and pebbly and full of boulders beyond; where it curved near the tree roots, the bed of the stream was marly and between the ruts of deep water green weed fronds swung in the current.

Nick swung the rod back over his shoulder and forward, and the line, curving forward, laid the grasshopper down on one of the deep channels in the weeds. A trout struck and Nick hooked him.

Holding the rod far out toward the uprooted tree and sloshing backward in the current, Nick worked the trout, plunging, the rod bending alive, out of the danger of the weeds into the open river. Holding the rod, pumping alive against the current, Nick brought the trout in. He rushed, but always came, the spring of the rod yielding to the rushes, sometimes jerking under water, but always bringing him in. Nick eased downstream with the rushes. The rod above his head he led the trout over the net, then lifted.

The trout hung heavy in the net, mottled trout back and silver sides in the meshes. Nick unhooked him; heavy sides, good to hold, big undershot jaw, and slipped him, heaving and big sliding, into the long sack that hung from his shoulders in the water.

Nick spread the mouth of the sack against the current and it filled, heavy with water. He held it up, the bottom in the stream, and the water poured out through the sides. Inside at the bottom was the big trout, alive in the water.

Nick moved downstream. The sack out ahead of him sunk heavy in the water, pulling from his shoulders.

It was getting hot, the sun hot on the back of his neck.

Nick had one good trout. He did not care about getting many trout. Now the stream was shallow and wide. There were trees along both banks. The trees of the left bank made short shadows on the current in the forenoon sun. Nick knew there were trout in each shadow. In the afternoon, after the sun had crossed toward the hills, the trout would be in the cool shadows on the other side of the stream.

The very biggest ones would lie up close to the bank. You could always pick them up there on the Black. When the sun was down they all moved out into the current. Just when the sun made the water blinding in the glare before it went down, you were liable to strike a big trout anywhere in the current. It was almost impossible to fish then, the surface of the water was blinding as a mirror in the sun. Of course, you could fish upstream, but in a stream like the Black, or this, you had to wallow against the current and in a deep place, the water piled up on you. It was no fun to fish upstream with this much current.

Nick moved along through the shallow stretch watching the banks for deep holes. A beech tree grew close beside the river, so that the branches hung down into the water. The stream went back in under the leaves. There were always trout in a place like that.

Nick did not care about fishing that hole. He was sure he would get hooked in the branches.

It looked deep though. He dropped the grasshopper so the current took it under water, back in under the overhanging branch. The line pulled hard and Nick struck. The trout threshed heavily, half out of water in the leaves and branches. The line was caught. Nick pulled hard and the trout was off. He reeled in and holding the hook in his hand, walked down the stream.

Ahead, close to the left bank, was a big log. Nick saw it was hollow; pointing up river the current entered it smoothly, only a little ripple spread each side of the log. The water was deepening. The top of the hollow log was gray and dry. It was partly in the shadow.

Nick took the cork out of the grasshopper bottle and a hopper clung to it. He picked him off, hooked him and tossed him out. He held the rod far out so that the hopper on the water moved into the current flowing into the hollow log. Nick lowered the rod and the hopper floated in. There was a heavy strike. Nick swung the rod against the pull. It felt as though he were hooked into the log itself, except for the live feeling.

He tried to force the fish out into the current. It came, heavily.

The line went slack and Nick thought the trout was gone. Then he saw him, very near, in the current, shaking his head, trying to get the hook out. His mouth was clamped shut. He was fighting the hook in the clear flowing current.

Looping in the line with his left hand, Nick swung the rod to make the line taut and tried to lead the trout toward the net, but he was gone, out of sight, the line pumping. Nick fought him against the current, letting him thump in the water against the spring of the rod. He shifted the rod to his left hand, worked the trout upstream, holding his weight, fighting on the rod, and then let him down into the net. He lifted him clear of the water, a heavy half circle in the net, the net dripping, unhooked him and slid him into the sack.

He spread the mouth of the sack and looked down in at the two big trout alive in the water.

Through the deepening water, Nick waded over to the hollow log. He took the sack off, over his head, the trout flopping as it came out of water, and hung it so the trout were deep in the water. Then he pulled himself up on the log and sat, the water from his trouser and boots running down into the stream. He laid his rod down, moved along to the shady end of the log and took the sandwiches out of his pocket. He dipped the sandwiches in the cold water. The current carried away the crumbs. He ate the sandwiches and dipped his hat full of water to drink, the water running out through his hat just ahead of his drinking.

It was cool in the shade, sitting on the log. He took a cigarette out and struck a match to light it. The match sunk into the gray wood, making a tiny furrow. Nick leaned over the side of the log, found a hard place and lit the match. He sat smoking and watching the river.

Ahead the river narrowed and went into a swamp. The river became smooth and deep and the swamp looked solid with cedar trees, their trunks close together, their branches solid. It would not be possible to walk through a swamp like that. The branches grew so low. You would have to keep almost level with the ground to move at all. You could not crash through the branches. That must be why the animals that lived in swamps were built the way they were, Nick thought.

He wished he had brought something to read. He felt like reading. He did not feel like going on into the swamp. He looked down the river. A big cedar slanted all the way across the stream. Beyond that the river went into the swamp.

Nick did not want to go in there now. He felt a reaction against deep wading with the water deepening up under his armpits, to hook big trout in places impossible to land them. In the swamp the banks were bare, the big cedars came together overhead, the sun did not come through, except in patches; in the fast deep water, in the half light, the fishing would be tragic. In the swamp fishing was a tragic adventure. Nick did not want it. He did not want to go down the stream any further today.

He took out his knife, opened it and stuck it in the log. Then he pulled up the sack, reached into it and brought out one of the trout. Holding him near the tail, hard to hold, alive, in his hand, he whacked him against the log. The trout quivered, rigid. Nick laid him on the log in the shade and broke the neck of the other fish the same way. He laid them side by side on the log. They were fine trout.

Nick cleaned them, slitting them from the vent to the tip of the jaw. All the insides and the gills and tongue came out in one piece. They were both males; long gray-white strips of milt, smooth and clean. All the insides clean and compact, coming out all together. Nick tossed the offal ashore for the minks to find.

He washed the trout in the stream. When he held them back up in the water they looked like live fish. Their color was not gone yet. He washed his hands and dried them on the log. Then he laid the trout on the sack spread out on the log, rolled them up in it, tied the bundle and put it in the landing net. His knife was still standing, blade stuck in the log. He cleaned it on the wood and put it in his pocket.

Nick stood up on the log, holding his rod, the landing net hanging heavy, then stepped into the water and splashed ashore. He climbed the bank and cut up into the woods, toward the high ground. He was going back to camp. He looked back. The river just showed through the trees. There were plenty of days coming when he could fish the swamp.

8a.

Item 279, Ernest Hemingway Collection, John F. Kennedy Library and Museum, Boston. Untitled handwritten ink manuscript beginning "They got off the train at Seney. . . ." False start of "Big Two-Hearted River" in which Nick is joined by two companions named Jack and Al.

~~We~~ They got off the train at Seney. There was no station. The train stopped, they carried their packs bumping ~~between the~~ down the aisle of the day coach and jumped down. The baggage man opened the door of his car and pitched out the bundle of tenting. The train went on. Nick leaned down and Jack and Al lifted the bundle of tents and bedding out of the cinders alongside the track and onto his back.

The ~~track~~ rails ran straight on, into the burned over pine country. The train was nearly out of sight.

"This was the toughest town in Michigan" Al said.

They all three stood together looking around. The fire had effaced the town. After a winter, the snow melting and the rains of spring and summer, the thirteen saloons had left not a trace. The stone foundations of the Mansion House Hotel were almost level with the ground. The lime stone chipped and split by the fire ~~and~~ was now washed smooth. ~~They~~ Al went over and looked into the ~~basement~~ filled pit where the hotel had been. There was twisted iron work, melted too hard to rust. ~~In a heap beside~~ Thrown together were four gun barrels, pitted and twisted by the heat in one the cartridges had melted into the magazine and formed a ~~swelling~~ bulge of lead and copper

8b.

Item 274, Ernest Hemingway Collection, John F. Kennedy Library and Museum, Boston. Titled handwritten ink manuscript with the first completed draft of "Big Two-Hearted River." The following is the beginning of the story.

Big Two Hearted River

The train went on up the track out of sight around one of the hills of burnt timber. Nick ~~went~~ sat down on the pale bundle of canvas and bedding the baggage man had pitched out of the door of the baggage car. There was no town ~~nor station. The fire~~, nothing but the rails and the burnt over country. The thirteen saloons that had lined the ~~main~~ one street of Seney had not left a trace. The foundations of the Mansion House hotel ~~were still~~ stuck up above the ground. The stone was chipped and ~~cracked~~ split by the fire. It was all there was left of ~~the town of~~ Seney. Even the surface had been burnt off the ground. ~~Nick~~

Nick ~~walked down the~~ looked at the burned over stretch of hill-side where he had expected to find the scattered houses of the town and then walked down the railroad track to the bridge over the river. The river was there. It swirled against the ~~wood~~ log piles of the bridge ~~and looking dow~~. Nick looked down into the clear brown water, ~~brown~~ colored from the pebbly bottom and watched the trout keeping themselves steady in the current with wavering fins. As he watched them they changed their positions by quick angles only to hold steady in the fast water again ~~their fins wavering~~ with ~~the~~ quick, vibrating fins. ~~motion.~~

Nick watched them a long time. [Hemingway wrote in the margin "insert."] ~~He watched them hold themselves steady where the It had been years since he had seen trout. As he watched a big trout shot up stream in a long angle burst through the surface of the water and~~

[Hemingway wrote in the margin "insert page 3—1"]

He watched them holding themselves ~~steady~~ with their noses ~~upstream~~ into the current, many trout in ~~a pool of~~ deep, fast ~~flowing~~ moving water, slightly distorted as he watched far down through the glassy ~~top swell~~ convex surface of the ~~stream~~ pool, ~~as it~~ its surface pushing and swelling smooth against the resistance of the log driven piles of the bridge. At the bottom of the pool were the big trout. Nick did not see them at first. Then he saw them at the bottom of the pool. ~~dim in the water light~~ Big

[Hemingway wrote in the margin "insert page 3 continued—2"]

trout looking to hold themselves on ~~in~~ the gravel bottom in a varying mist of gravel and sand raised in spurts by the current.

Nick looked down into the pool from the bridge. It was a hot day. A kingfisher flew up the stream. It was a long time since Nick had looked into a stream and seen trout. They were very satisfactory. As the shadow of the kingfisher moved up the stream a big trout shot up stream in a long angle, only his shadow marking the

[Hemingway wrote in the margin "insert page 3 continued—3"]

~~shadow~~ angle, then lost his shadow as he came through the surface of the water, caught the sun, and then as he went back into the ~~water~~ stream under the surface his shadow seemed to float ~~back~~ down the stream with the current, unresisting, to his post under the bridge where he tightened, facing up stream.

Nick's heart tightened as the trout moved. He felt all the old ~~thrill~~ ~~This remained~~

feeling.

He turned and looked down the stream.

[page 4]

~~curved in the air to re-enter the water and then under the surface~~ ~~in the fast water again then seemed to float back down stream with~~ ~~the current to its post under the bridge. Nick's heart tightened as the~~ ~~trout moved. He felt all the old thrill. This remained at any rate.~~

~~Standing on the railway bridge he looked down the stream.~~ It stretched away, pebbly bottomed with shallows and big boulders and a deep pool as it curved away around the foot of a bluff.

Nick walked back up the ties to ~~the~~ where his pack lay in the cinders beside the railway track. He was happy. He adjusted the pack harness around the bundle, pulling straps tight, slung the pack on his back, got his arms through the shoulder straps and took some of the pull off his shoulders by leaning his forehead against the wide ~~strap~~ band of the tump line. Still it was heavy. It was much too heavy. He had his leather rod case in his hand and leaning forward to keep the weight of the pack high on his shoulders he walked along the road that paralleled the railway track leaving the burned town behind in the heat and then turned off around a hill ~~into a mountain valley~~ with a high fire scarred hill on either side, ~~to go back~~ on a road that went back into the country. He walked along the road, feeling the ache ~~of~~ from the pull of the heavy pack. The road climbed steadily. It was hard work walking up hill. ~~Although~~ His muscles ached and the day was hot but Nick ~~was~~ felt happy. He felt ~~as though~~ he had left everything behind, the ~~necessity~~ need for thinking, ~~the necessity~~ the ~~necessity~~ need to write, ~~the need to talk~~ other needs. It was all back of him.

From the time ~~when~~ he had gotten down off the train and the baggage man had thrown his pack out of the open car door at him things had been different. Seney was burnt, the country was burned over and changed, but it did not matter. It could not all be burned. He knew that. He hiked along the road, sweating in the sun, climbing to cross the range of hills that separated the railway from the pine plains ~~and he was very happy.~~

The road ran on, dipping occasionally, but always climbing. ~~until it~~ Nick went on up. Finally the road after going parallel to the burnt high hillside reached the top ~~of the range of hills.~~ Nick ~~dropped the pack off by leaning~~ leaned back against a stump and slipped out of the pack harness. Ahead of him as far as he could see was the pine plain. The burned country stopped off at the left with the range of hills. On ahead islands of dark pine trees rose out of the plain. Far off to the left ~~was the line of the the river made a line of greener~~ was the line of the river. Nick followed it with his eye and caught glints of the water in the sun.

8c.

Item 274, Ernest Hemingway Collection, John F. Kennedy Library and Museum, Boston. Titled handwritten ink manuscript with the first completed draft of "Big Two-Hearted River." The following is the original ending. An edited version of this story was published posthumously as "On Writing" in *The Nick Adams Stories*.

It was getting hot, the sun hot on the back of his neck.

Nick had one good trout. He did not care about getting many trout. Now the stream was shallow and wide ~~with~~. There were trees along both banks. The trees of the left bank made short shadows on the current in the hot forenoon sun. Nick knew there were trout in each shadow. He and Bill Smith had discovered that on the Black River one hot day. In the afternoon after the sun had crossed toward the hills, the trout would be in the cool shadows on the other side of the stream. The very biggest ones would lie up close to the bank. As the You could always pick them up there on the Black. Bill and he had discovered it. In When the sun was down they all moved out into the current. Just when the sun made the water blinding in the glare before it went down you were liable to strike a big trout any-where in the current. It was almost impossible to fish then, the sur-face of the river was blinding like a mirror shooting sun in your eyes. Of course you could fish up stream but in a stream like this you had to wallow against the current and in a deep place the water piled up on you. It was no fun to fish up stream although all the books said it was the only way.

All the books. He and Bill had fun with the books in the old days. They all started with a fake premise. Like fox hunting. Bill Bird's dentist in Paris said in fly fishing you pit your intelligence against that of the trout. That's the way I'd always thought of it Ezra said. That was good for a laugh. There were so many things good for a laugh. In the states they thought bull fighting was a joke. Ezra thought fish-ing was a joke. Lots of people think poetry is a joke. Englishmen are a joke to Frenchmen. Remember when they pushed us over the banera into in front of the bull at Pamplona because they thought we were Frenchmen. Bill's dentist is as bad the other way about fishing. Bill Bird that is. Once Bill meant Bill Smith. Now it was means Bill Bird. Bill Bird was in Paris now. When he married he lost Bill Smith, Odgar, the Ghee, all the old gang. Was it because they were virgins? The Ghee certainly was not. No, he lost them because he admitted by marrying that something was more important than the summers and the fishing. He had built it all up. Bill had never fished before they met. Every place they had been together. The Black, the Stur-geon, the Pine Barrens, all the little streams, the upper Minnie. Most about fishing he and Bill had discovered together. He and Bill wrote to each other almost every day all winter. They worked on the farm and fished and took trips in the woods from June to October. Bill always quit his job every Spring, so did he. Ezra thought fishing was a joke. ~~Fat chance. Ezra didn't know anything. Really. Not a damn thing. How could he write like that and not know anything? Joyce didn't know anything either. Jesuits. Hell.~~

Bill forgave him the fishing he had done before they met. He forgave him all the rivers. He was really proud of them. It was like a girl about other girls. If they were before they didn't matter. But after was different. That was why he lost them he guessed. They were all married to fishing. Ezra thought fishing was a joke. So did most everybody. He'd been married to it before he married Hadley. Really married to it. It ~~was not~~ wasn't any joke. So he lost them all. Hadley thought it was because they didn't like her.

Nick sat down on a big boulder in the shade and hung his sack down into the river. He might as well be out of the heat. The rock was dry and cool. He sat letting the water run out of his boots down the side of the rock. Hadley thought it was because they did not like her. She really did. Gosh he remembered the horror he ~~had had~~ used to have of people getting married. It was funny. It was probably because he had always been with older people, non marrying people. Ogdar always wanted to marry Kate. Kate wouldn't ever marry anybody. She and Odgar always quarreled about it but Ogdar did not want anybody else and Kate wouldn't have anybody. She wanted them to be just as good friends and they were always ~~miserable~~ miserable and quarreling trying to be. It was the Madame planted all that asceticism. The Ghee went with girls in houses in Chicago but he had it too. Nick had had it too. It was all a fake ~~premise~~. You had this fake ideal and then you lived your life to it. All the love went into fishing and the summer. He had loved it more than anything. He had loved digging potatoes with Bill in the fall, the long trips in the car, fishing on the bay, reading in the hammock on the front porch, swimming off the dock, playing baseball at Charlevoix and Petoskey, living at the Bay, the Madame's cooking, the way she ~~served~~ had servants serve the food, eating in the dining room looking down across the long fields and the point to the lake, talking with her, the ~~long~~ fishing trips away from the farm, just lying around. He loved the long summer. It used to be so that he felt sick when the first of August came and he realized that there was only four weeks more of trout fishing. Now sometimes he had it that way in dreams. He would dream that the summer was nearly gone and he hadn't been fishing. It made him feel sick in the dream. As though he had been in jail. The hills at the foot of Walloon Lake. Storms on the lake coming up in the motor boat, holding an umbrella over the engine to keep the ~~water slapped~~ waves that came in off the spark plug. Pumping out. Running ~~in the trough of the wave. Drying~~ the boat in big storms, climbing up, sliding down the wave following behind, coming up from the foot of the lake with the groceries the mail and the Chicago paper under a tarpaulin, everything wet, too rough to land, drying out in front of the open fire place. The wind in the hemlocks and the wet pine needles under foot when he was barefoot going for the milk. Coming back the way the water washed down the roads. Getting up at daylight to hike over the hills after a rain to fish in Horton's Creek. Hortons always needed a rain—Shultz's was no good if it rained, running brown and overflowing. The time a bull chased him over a fence and he lost his hook book out of his pocket. If he knew then what he knew about bulls now. Where were Maera and Algabeno now? August the feria at Valencia. Sanchez Mejias in all six corridas. The way phrases from bull fight papers kept coming into his head all the time until he had to quit reading them. The corrida of the Miuras. His notorious defects in the execution of the pase natural. The flower of Andalucia. Chiquelin el camelista.

His whole inner life had been bull fights all one year. Chink pale and miserable about the horses. Don never minded them, he said "And then suddenly I knew I was going to <u>love</u> bull fighting". That must have been Maera. Maera was the greatest man he'd ever known. Chink knew it too. He followed him around in the lucieno. He Nick was the friend of Maera and Maera waved his hand down from box 87 above their <u>sobrepuerto</u> and waited for Hadley to see him and waved again and Hadley worshiped him and there were three picadors in the box and all the other picadors did their stuff right down in front of the box and looked up before and after and he said to Hadley that picadors only worked for each other and of course it was true. And it was the best pic-ing he ever saw and the three pics in the boxes in their Cordoba hats nodded at each good vara and the other pics waved up at them and did their stuff. Like the time the Portuguese were in and the old pic threw his hat in ~~and nearly~~ hanging on over the banera watching young Da Veiga. That was the saddest thing he'd ever seen. That was what that fat pic wanted to be, a caballero in Plaza. ~~That~~ God how that ~~Da Viega~~ kid could ride. That was riding. It didn't show well in the movies. The movies ruined everything. Like talking about something good. That was what had made the war unreal. Too much talking. Talking about anything was bad. Writing about anything actual was bad. It always killed it. The only writing that was any good was what you made up, what you imagined, that made everything come true. Like when he wrote My Old Man he'd never seen a jockey killed and the next week Georges Parfrement was killed at that very jump. Everything good he'd ever written he'd made up. None of it had ever happened. That was what the family couldn't understand. They thought it all was experience. That was the weakness of Joyce. The main one, except Jesuits. Daedalus in Ulysses was Joyce himself so he was terrible. Joyce was so damn romantic and intellectual about him. He'd made Bloom up. Bloom was wonderful. He'd made Mrs. Bloom up. She was the greatest in the world. That was the way with Mac. Mac worked too close to life. You had to digest life and then create your own people. Nick in the stories was never himself. He made him up. Of course he'd never seen an Indian woman having a baby. That was what made it so good.

It was as good a story as anybody ever wrote in lots of ways. He wished he could always write like that. He would sometime. He wanted to be a great writer. He was pretty sure he would be. He knew it in lots of ways. He would in spite of everything. It was hard though. It was hard to be a great writer if you loved the world and living in it and special people. It was hard when you loved so many places. Then you were healthy and felt good and were having a good time and what the hell. He always worked best when Hadley was unwell. Just that much friction. Then there were times when you had to write. Conscience maybe. Peristaltic actions. Then you felt like you could never write but after a while you knew that sooner or later you would write another great story. It was really more fun than anything. That was really why you did it. He had never realized that before. It wasn't conscience. It was simply that it was the greatest pleasure. It had more kick to it than anything else. It was so damned hard to write well too. There were so many tricks. It was easy to write if you used the tricks. ~~Nearly~~ Everybody used them. Joyce had invented hundreds of new ones. Just because they were new didn't make them any better.

He wanted to write like Cezanne painted. Cezanne started with all the tricks. Then he broke the whole thing down and built ~~clearly and slowly~~ the real thing. It was hell to do. He was the greatest. It wasn't a cult. He, Nick, wanted to be able to write about country so that ~~you could have it~~ it would be there like Cezanne had done it. Nobody had ever written about country like that. He felt almost holy about it. Like Uncle Bill about helping the Chinese. It was practical but it was really serious. It was deadly serious. You could do it if you would fight it out. It was a thing you wouldn't talk about. He was going to work on it until he got it. Maybe never, but he would know as he got near it. It was a job. Maybe for all his life. People were easy. All this smart stuff was easy. Against This Age. Sky Scraper Primitives. ~~Most of~~ Cummings when he was smart, not The Enormous Room, that was a book, it was one of the great books, Cummings worked hard to get it, maybe he was right. Was there anybody else? Young Asch had something but you couldn't tell, Jews go bad quickly. They all start with something. Mac had something, Don Stewart had the most next to Cummings. Sometimes in the Haddocks, was there anybody else? Young guys maybe. Great unknowns. There are never any unknowns though. ~~Unknowns to the public maybe.~~ They weren't after what he was after. He could see the Cezannes. The portrait at Gertrude Steins. She'd know it if he ever got things right. The one good one in the Luxembourg. The ones he'd seen at Bernheim's. The soldiers undressing to swim, the house through the trees, the ~~portrait~~ one of the trees with a house beyond, the portrait of the boy, ~~he~~ Cezanne could do people too, but that was easier, he used what he got from the country to do people with. Nick could do that too. He knew just how Cezanne would paint this stretch of the river. God if he were only here to do it. They died and that was the hell of it.

Nick, seeing how Cezanne would do ~~that~~ the stretch of country, stood up. The water was cold and actual. He waded across the stream, moving in the picture. It was good. He kneeled down in the gravel at the edge of the stream and ~~slipped the trout sock over his~~ reached down into the trout sack. The old boy was alive. Nick opened the mouth of the sack and skimmed it back. He slid the trout into the shallow water and watched him move off through the shallows, his back out of the water, threading toward the deep current ~~of~~ at the center of the stream.

"He was too big to eat" Nick said. "I'll get a couple of little ones in front of the camp for supper."

He reeled up the line and started through the brush as fast as he could go ~~carrying~~ managing the rod. He ate a sandwitch as he hurried. ~~He was in a great hurry to get back.~~ He wasn't thinking. He was holding something in his head. He was in a great hurry to get back to camp and get to work.

~~(The End)~~

He moved through the brush holding the rod close to him. The line caught ~~in the~~ on a branch. Nick stopped and cut the leader and reeled the line up. He ~~moved now~~ went through the brush now easily, holding the rod out before him.

~~The End.~~

Ahead of him he saw a rabbit flat out on the trail. He stopped, grudging. There were three ticks on the rabbit's head. ~~One beside each~~ Two behind one ear and one behind the other. They were gray like the rabbit's ear skin, ~~and~~ tight with blood, as big as grapes. Nick pulled them off ~~a~~, their heads tiny and hard with moving feet. He stepped on them all three on the trail. Nick ~~put the~~ picked up the rabbit, limp, with button eyes, and put it ~~in the brush beside~~ under a sweet fern bush beside the trail. It's heart was beating as he laid it down. He went on up the trail. He was holding something in his head.

The End.

8d.

Item 277, Ernest Hemingway Collection, John F. Kennedy Library and Museum, Boston. Handwritten pencil manuscript with the revised ending for "Big Two-Hearted River."

Nick moved along through the shallow stretch watching the banks for deep holes. ~~Sometimes~~ A beech tree grew close beside the ~~stream~~ river, so that the branches hung down into the water. The stream went back in under the leaves. There were always trout ~~there~~ in a place like that.

Nick did not care about fishing that hole. He was sure he would get hooked in the branches.

It looked deep though. He chopped the grasshopper so the current took it under water, back in under the overhanging branch. ~~A trout struck and Nick~~ The line pulled hard and Nick struck. The trout thrashed heavily, half out of the water in the leaves. The line was caught. Nick pulled hard and the trout was off. He reeled in and holding the hook in his hand walked down the stream. ~~It was~~ Ahead, ~~against~~ near the left bank was a big log. Nick saw it was hollow; pointing up river the current entered it smoothly, only a little ripple spread each ~~way~~ side of the log. The water was deepening. The top of the hollow log was grey and dry. It was partly in the shadow.

Nick took the cork out of the hopper bottle and a grasshopper clung to it. He picked him off, hooked him and tossed him out. He held the rod far out so the hopper on the water moved toward the current going into the hollow log. Nick lowered the rod and let the hopper float in. There was a heavy strike. Nick did not need to strike. It felt as though he were hooked into the log itself except for the live feeling. He tried to force fish out into the current. It came, heavily. The line went slack and Nick thought the trout was gone. Then he saw him ~~close~~ very near, in the current, shaking his head, trying to get the hook out. His mouth was clamped shut. He was fighting the hook.

Bringing the line in with his left hand Nick tightened the line with the rod and tried to lead the trout toward the net but he was gone. Nick fought him against the current, letting him thump in the water against the spring of the rod. He shifted the rod to his left hand, worked the trout up stream and then let him down into the net. He lifted him clear of the water, the net dripping, unhooked him and slid him into the sack. He spread the mouth of the sack and looked at the two trout alive in the water. ~~They were taking it very quietly.~~

Through the deepening water Nick waded over to the hollow log. He took the sack off over his head and hung it on the log so the trout were ~~well~~ deep in the water. Then he pulled himself up on the log and sat, the water from his trousers and boots running down into the stream. He laid his rod down, moved to the shady end of the log and took the sandwitches out of his pockets. He dipped the sand-witches in the cold water and ate them; dipping his hat full of water to drink he drank, the water running out through his hat just ahead of his drinking.

It was cool in the shade sitting on the log. He took a cigarette out and lit it. The match struck a match to light it. The match sunk into the grey wood, making a very tiny furrow of crushed wood. Nick leaned over the side and found a hard place and lit the match. He sat smoking and watching the river.

Ahead the river narrowed and went into a swamp. The river became smooth and deep and the swamp looked solid with cedar trees, their trunks close together, their tops branches solid. It would not be possible to walk through a swamp like that. The branches grew so low. You had to keep almost level with the ground to move at all. That was why the animals that lived in swamps were all built the way they were, Nick thought.

He wished he had brought something to read. He felt like read-ing. He did not feel like going on into the dark swamp. He looked down the river. One A big cedar slanted all the way across the stream. Beyond that the stream went into the swamp.

Nick did not want to go in there now. He felt a reaction against deep wading with the water deepening up under his armpits, hooking big trout in impossible places to land them. In the swamp with the naked banks, the big cedars coming together over head, the sun hardly ever coming through, the fast deep water, the fishing would be tragic. In the swamp it was a tragic adventure. Nick did not want it. He did not want to go down the stream any further today.

He took out his knife, opened it and stuck it in the log. Then he reached pulled up the sack reached into it and brought out one of the trout. Holding him near the tail, belly up, he whacked him against the log. The trout quivered rigid. Nick laid him on the log in the shade and broke the neck of the other fish the same way. He laid them side by side on the log. They were fine trout.

Nick cleaned them, slitting them from the vent to the tip of the jaw. All the insides and the gills came out in one piece. They were both males, long grey white strips of milt, smooth and clean. All the insides clean and compact, coming out all together. Nick tossed them ashore for the minks to find.

He washed the trout in the stream, when he held them back up in the water they looked like live fish. Their color was not gone yet. He washed his hands and dried them on the log. Then he laid the trout on the sack, ~~spread flat and~~ rolled them up in it ~~and put the sack~~, tied the bundle and put it in the landing net.

He stood up on the log, holding his rod, the landing net hanging heavy, then stepped into the water and splashed ashore. He climbed the bank and cut up into the woods toward the high ground. He was going back to camp to read. He looked back, the river just showed through the trees. There ~~was~~ were plenty of days coming when he could fish the swamp.

The End

9.

The Killers

1927

The door of Henry's lunch-room opened and two men came in. They sat down at the counter.

"What's yours?" George asked them.

"I don't know," one of the men said. "What do you want to eat, Al?"

"I don't know," said Al. "I don't know what I want to eat."

Outside it was getting dark. The street-light came on outside the window. The two men at the counter read the menu. From the other end of the counter Nick Adams watched them. He had been talking to George when they came in.

"I'll have a roast pork tenderloin with apple sauce and mashed potatoes," the first man said.

"It isn't ready yet."

"What the hell do you put it on the card for?"

"That's the dinner," George explained. "You can get that at six o'clock."

George looked at the clock on the wall behind the counter.

"It's five o'clock."

"The clock says twenty minutes past five," the second man said.

"It's twenty minutes fast."

"Oh, to hell with the clock," the first man said. "What have you got to eat?"

"I can give you any kind of sandwiches," George said. "You can have ham and eggs, bacon and eggs, liver and bacon, or a steak."

"Give me chicken croquettes with green peas and cream sauce and mashed potatoes."

"That's the dinner."

"Everything we want's the dinner, eh? That's the way you work it."

"I can give you ham and eggs, bacon and eggs, liver—"

"I'll take ham and eggs," the man called Al said. He wore a derby hat and a black overcoat buttoned across the chest. His face was small and white and he had tight lips. He wore a silk muffler and gloves.

"Give me bacon and eggs," said the other man. He was about the same size as Al. Their faces were different, but they were dressed like twins. Both wore overcoats too tight for them. They sat leaning forward, their elbows on the counter.

"Got anything to drink?" Al asked.

"Silver beer, bevo, ginger-ale," George said.

"I mean you got anything to *drink?*"

"Just those I said."

"This is a hot town," said the other. "What do they call it?"

"Summit."

"Ever hear of it?" Al asked his friend.

"No," said the friend.

"What do you do here nights?" Al asked.

"They eat the dinner," his friend said. "They all come here and eat the big dinner."

"That's right," George said.

"So you think that's right?" Al asked George.

"Sure."

"You're a pretty bright boy, aren't you?"

"Sure," said George.

"Well, you're not," said the other little man. "Is he, Al?"

"He's dumb," said Al. He turned to Nick. "What's your name?"

"Adams."

"Another bright boy," Al said. "Ain't he a bright boy, Max?"

"The town's full of bright boys," Max said.

George put the two platters, one of ham and eggs, the other of bacon and eggs, on the counter. He set down two side-dishes of fried potatoes and closed the wicket into the kitchen.

"Which is yours?" he asked Al.

"Don't you remember?"

"Ham and eggs."

"Just a bright boy," Max said. He leaned forward and took the ham and eggs. Both men ate with their gloves on. George watched them eat.

"What are *you* looking it?" Max looked at George.

"Nothing."

"The hell you were. You were looking at me."

"Maybe the boy meant it for a joke, Max," Al said.

George laughed.

"*You* don't have to laugh," Max said to him. "*You* don't have to laugh at all, see?"

"All right," said George.

"So he thinks it's all right." Max turned to Al. "He thinks it's all right. That's a good one."

"Oh, he's a thinker," Al said. They went on eating.

"What's the bright boy's name down the counter?" Al asked Max.

"Hey, bright boy," Max said to Nick. "You go around on the other side of the counter with your boy friend."

"What's the idea?" Nick asked.

"There isn't any idea."

"You better go around, bright boy," Al said. Nick went around behind the counter.

"What's the idea?" George asked.

"None of your damn business," Al said. "Who's out in the kitchen?"

"The nigger."

"What do you mean the nigger?"

"The nigger that cooks."

"Tell him to come in."

"What's the idea?"

"Tell him to come in."

"Where do you think you are?"

"We know damn well where we are," the man called Max said. "Do we look silly?"

"You talk silly," Al said to him. "What the hell do you argue with this kid for? Listen," he said to George, "tell the nigger to come out here."

"What are you going to do to him?"

"Nothing. Use your head, bright boy. What would we do to a nigger?"

George opened the slit that opened back into the kitchen. "Sam," he called. "Come in here a minute."

The door to the kitchen opened and the nigger came in. "What was it?" he asked. The two men at the counter took a look at him.

"All right, nigger. You stand right there," Al said.

Sam, the nigger, standing in his apron, looked at the two men sitting at the counter. "Yes, sir," he said. Al got down from his stool.

"I'm going back to the kitchen with the nigger and bright boy," he said. "Go on back to the kitchen, nigger. You go with him, bright boy." The little man walked after Nick and Sam, the cook, back into the kitchen. The door shut after them. The man called Max sat at the counter opposite George. He didn't look at George but looked in the mirror that ran along back of the counter. Henry's had been made over from a saloon into a lunch-counter.

"Well, bright boy," Max said, looking into the mirror, "why don't you say something?"

"What's it all about?"

"Hey, Al," Max called, "bright boy wants to know what it's all about."

"Why don't you tell him?" Al's voice came from the kitchen.

"What do you think it's all about?"

"I don't know."

"What do you think?"

Max looked into the mirror all the time he was talking.

"I wouldn't say."

"Hey, Al, bright boy says he wouldn't say what he thinks it's all about."

"I can hear you, all right," Al said from the kitchen. He had propped open the slit that dishes passed through into the kitchen with a catsup bottle. "Listen, bright boy," he said from the kitchen to George. "Stand a little further along the bar. You move a little to the left, Max." He was like a photographer arranging for a group picture.

"Talk to me, bright boy," Max said. "What do you think's going to happen?"

George did not say anything.

"I'll tell you," Max said. "We're going to kill a Swede. Do you know a big Swede named Ole Andreson?"

"Yes."

"He comes here to eat every night, don't he?"

"Sometimes he comes here."

"He comes here at six o'clock, don't he?"

"If he comes."

"We know all that, bright boy," Max said. "Talk about something else. Ever go to the movies?"

"Once in a while."

"You ought to go to the movies more. The movies are fine for a bright boy like you."

"What are you going to kill Ole Andreson for? What did he ever do to you?"

"He never had a chance to do anything to us. He never even seen us."

"And he's only going to see us once," Al said from the kitchen.

"What are you going to kill him for, then?" George asked.

"We're killing him for a friend. Just to oblige a friend, bright boy."

"Shut up," said Al from the kitchen. "You talk too goddam much."

"Well, I got to keep bright boy amused. Don't I, bright boy?"

"You talk too damn much," Al said. "The nigger and my bright boy are amused by themselves. I got them tied up like a couple of girl friends in the convent."

"I suppose you were in a convent?"

"You never know."

"You were in a kosher convent. That's where you were."

George looked up at the clock.

"If anybody comes in you tell them the cook is off, and if they keep after it, you tell them you'll go back and cook yourself. Do you get that, bright boy?"

"All right," George said. "What you going to do with us afterward?"

"That'll depend," Max said. "That's one of those things you never know at the time."

George looked up at the clock. It was a quarter past six. The door from the street opened. A street-car motorman came in.

"Hello, George," he said. "Can I get supper?"

"Sam's gone out," George said. "He'll be back in about half an hour."

"I'd better go up the street," the motorman said. George looked at the clock. It was twenty minutes past six.

"That was nice, bright boy," Max said. "You're a regular little gentleman."

"He knew I'd blow his head off," Al said from the kitchen.

"No," said Max. "It ain't that. Bright boy is nice. He's a nice boy. I like him."

At six-fifty-five George said: "He's not coming."

Two other people had been in the lunch-room. Once George had gone out to the kitchen and made a ham-and-egg sandwich "to go" that a man wanted to take with him. Inside the kitchen he saw Al, his derby hat tipped back, sitting on a stool beside the wicket with the muzzle of a sawed-off shotgun resting on the ledge. Nick and the cook were back to back in the corner, a towel tied in each of their mouths. George had cooked the sandwich, wrapped it up in oiled paper, put it in a bag, brought it in, and the man had paid for it and gone out.

"Bright boy can do everything," Max said. "He can cook and everything. You'd make some girl a nice wife, bright boy."

"Yes?" George said. "Your friend, Ole Andreson, isn't going to come."

"We'll give him ten minutes," Max said.

Max watched the mirror and the clock. The hands of the clock marked seven o'clock, and then five minutes past seven.

"Come on, Al," said Max. "We better go. He's not coming."

"Better give him five minutes," Al said from the kitchen.

In the five minutes a man came in, and George explained that the cook was sick.

"Why the hell don't you get another cook?" the man asked. "Aren't you running a lunch-counter?" He went out.

"Come on, Al," Max said.

"What about the two bright boys and the nigger?"

"They're all right."

"You think so?"

"Sure. We're through with it."

"I don't like it," said Al. "It's sloppy. You talk too much."

"Oh, what the hell," said Max. "We got to keep amused, haven't we?"

"You talk too much, all the same," Al said. He came out from the kitchen. The cutoff barrels of the shotgun made a slight bulge under the waist of his too tight-fitting overcoat. He straightened his coat with his gloved hands.

"So long, bright boy," he said to George. "You got a lot of luck."

"That's the truth," Max said. "You ought to play the races, bright boy."

The two of them went out the door. George watched them, through the window, pass under the arc-light and cross the street. In their tight overcoats and derby hats they looked like a vaudeville team. George went back through the swinging-door into the kitchen and untied Nick and the cook.

"I don't want any more of that," said Sam, the cook. "I don't want any more of that."

Nick stood up. He had never had a towel in his mouth before.

"Say," he said. "What the hell?" He was trying to swagger it off.

"They were going to kill Ole Andreson," George said. "They were going to shoot him when he came in to eat."

"Ole Andreson?"

"Sure."

The cook felt the corners of his mouth with his thumbs.

"They all gone?" he asked.

"Yeah," said George. "They're gone now."

"I don't like it," said the cook. "I don't like any of it at all."

"Listen," George said to Nick. "You better go see Ole Andreson."

"All right."

"You better not have anything to do with it at all," Sam, the cook, said. "You better stay way out of it."

"Don't go if you don't want to," George said.

"Mixing up in this ain't going to get you anywhere," the cook said. "You stay out of it."

"I'll go see him," Nick said to George. "Where does he live?"

The cook turned away.

"Little boys always know what they want to do," he said.

"He lives up at Hirsch's rooming-house," George said to Nick.

"I'll go up there."

Outside the arc-light shone through the bare branches of a tree. Nick walked up the street beside the car-tracks and turned at the next arc-light down a side-street. Three houses up the street was Hirsch's rooming-house. Nick walked up the two steps and pushed the bell. A woman came to the door.

"Is Ole Andreson here?"

"Do you want to see him?"

"Yes, if he's in."

Nick followed the woman up a flight of stairs and back to the end of a corridor. She knocked on the door.

"Who is it?"

"It's somebody to see you, Mr. Andreson," the woman said.

"It's Nick Adams."

"Come in."

Nick opened the door and went into the room. Ole Andreson was lying on the bed with all his clothes on. He had been a heavy-weight prizefighter and he was too long for the bed. He lay with his head on two pillows. He did not look at Nick.

"What was it?" he asked.

"I was up at Henry's," Nick said, "and two fellows came in and tied up me and the cook, and they said they were going to kill you."

It sounded silly when he said it. Ole Andreson said nothing.

"They put us out in the kitchen," Nick went on. "They were going to shoot you when you came in to supper."

Ole Andreson looked at the wall and did not say anything.

"George thought I better come and tell you about it."

"There isn't anything I can do about it," Ole Andreson said.

"I'll tell you what they were like."

"I don't want to know what they were like," Ole Andreson said. He looked at the wall. "Thanks for coming to tell me about it."

"That's all right."

Nick looked at the big man lying on the bed.

"Don't you want me to go and see the police?"

"No," Ole Andreson said. "That wouldn't do any good."

"Isn't there something I could do?"

"No. There ain't anything to do."

"Maybe it was just a bluff."

"No. It ain't just a bluff."

Ole Andreson rolled over toward the wall.

"The only thing is," he said, talking toward the wall, "I just can't make up my mind to go out. I been in here all day."

"Couldn't you get out of town?"

"No," Ole Andreson said. "I'm through with all that running around."

He looked at the wall.

"There ain't anything to do now."

"Couldn't you fix it up some way?"

"No. I got in wrong." He talked in the same flat voice. "There ain't anything to do. After a while I'll make up my mind to go out."

"I better go back and see George," Nick said.

"So long," said Ole Andreson. He did not look toward Nick. "Thanks for coming around."

Nick went out. As he shut the door he saw Ole Andreson with all his clothes on, lying on the bed looking at the wall.

"He's been in his room all day," the landlady said downstairs. "I guess he don't feel well. I said to him: 'Mr. Andreson, you ought to go out and take a walk on a nice fall day like this,' but he didn't feel like it."

"He doesn't want to go out."

"I'm sorry he don't feel well," the woman said. "He's an awfully nice man. He was in the ring, you know."

"I know it."

"You'd never know it except from the way his face is," the woman said. They stood talking just inside the street door. "He's just as gentle."

"Well, good-night, Mrs. Hirsch," Nick said.

"I'm not Mrs. Hirsch," the woman said. "She owns the place. I just look after it for her. I'm Mrs. Bell."

"Well, good-night, Mrs. Bell," Nick said.

"Good-night," the woman said.

Nick walked up the dark street to the corner under the arc-light, and then along the car-tracks to Henry's eating-house. George was inside, back of the counter.

"Did you see Ole?"

"Yes," said Nick. "He's in his room and he won't go out."

The cook opened the door from the kitchen when he heard Nick's voice.

"I don't even listen to it," he said and shut the door.

"Did you tell him about it?" George asked.

"Sure. I told him but he knows what it's all about."

"What's he going to do?"

"Nothing."

"They'll kill him."

"I guess they will."

"He must have got mixed up in something in Chicago."

"I guess so," said Nick.

"It's a hell of a thing."

"It's an awful thing," Nick said.

They did not say anything. George reached down for a towel and wiped the counter.

"I wonder what he did?" Nick said.

"Double-crossed somebody. That's what they kill them for."

"I'm going to get out of this town," Nick said.

"Yes," said George. "That's a good thing to do."

"I can't stand to think about him waiting in the room and knowing he's going to get it. It's too damned awful."

"Well," said George, "you better not think about it."

9a.

Item 535, Ernest Hemingway Collection, John F. Kennedy Library and Museum, Boston. Handwritten ink manuscript with first page in typescript with ink corrections. Alternate beginning to "The Killers."

~~Sometime~~

~~When~~ Iit was very cold ~~in the~~ that winter and Little Traverse Bay ~~froze right across~~ was frozen across from Petoskey to Harbor Springs. ~~As~~ Nick turned the corner around the cigar store with the wind blowing snow into his eyes. ~~Hh~~e stopped and looking down the street saw the ice smooth inside the breakwater and piled high and white outside with sun on it ~~and way~~ and way across the bay the hills ~~back of the~~ between H~~h~~arbor Springs ~~high and snowy~~ were high snow covered with dark pine trees. The wind blew the snow off the drifts in a steady sifting against his face but he stood ~~looking~~ and looked at the frozen bay in the sunlight and watched the sun on the high hills on the other side.

He ~~looked away and~~ turned up the street toward the railway station. The snow was ~~so~~ dry ~~it~~ and creaked under his shoes as he walked. This was real winter. There was no one on street he knew. Every~~body~~one was inside in this ~~sort of~~ weather. ~~Coming~~ As he came out on the high ground by the railway tracks ~~the wind caught him again~~ he came into the wind and as it struck him he sunk his face down in the collar of his Mackinaw coat. Inside the station the Chicago papers had just come. The train had come in from the south while ~~he was~~ Nick had been in the pool room ~~and gone on up toward the Straits~~. Nick bought a Tribune and hurried across the ~~windy open space~~ snow blowing station park into the side door of ~~O'Neal's Hotel~~ the Parker House.

George O'Neal stood back of the lunch counter.

"Hello, Kid," he said.

~~Nick~~ "Hello, George," said Nick. He sat down on a stool and opened the paper.

"Do you want to eat?"

"~~Yes.~~ I'm pretty hungry."

"Ham and egg sandwich?"

"Put some onion in it."

When the sandwich came Nick opened it and spread tomato catsup over the slice of onion.

"Want a shot?" George O'Neal asked.

"I'll take a glass of milk."

"No," said George. "I meant really. Do you want a shot?"

"Sure."

George leaned down behind the counter and ~~poured~~ handed Nick a ~~heavy~~ coffe[e] cup.

"It's the real stuff."

Nick swallowed the whiskey. "It's swell," he said. The milk tasted cool and smooth. He finished the sandwitch and washed it down with milk.

"How about another?" George asked.

"Swell," said Nick. "Have you got plenty."

"I've got a case." ~~George said.~~

Nick drank the whiskey from the coffee cup. George took the cup and put it under the counter. He watched Nick. "How does it go?"

"It's great."

"It's cold as hell outside," George said.

"It's blowing."

"What's in the paper?"

"Not a thing."

Nick folded up the paper. George leaned down behind the counter and brought up the cup.

"I'll get tight," Nick said.

"No you won't."

Nick handed back the cup.

"What about yourself?"

"~~I don't want to drink in here.~~ All right." George said, "I'll have one with you ~~as soon as I'm off~~. I'm all alone here."

"~~It's nice stuff.~~ Where's your brother," Nick said.

"He's ~~over at the harbour~~ gone to Peelston." ~~"Have another."~~

"~~Sure~~ It's nice stuff," Nick said. ~~Nick~~ He handed back the empty coffee cup. The street door opened and ~~a man~~ two men came in. They sat down at the counter.

"What's yours?" George asked them.

"I don't know," one of the men said. "What do you want to eat, Al?"

"I don't know," said Al. "I don't know what I want to eat."

Outside it was getting dark. The street light came on outside the window. The two men at the counter read the menu.

"I'll have a roast pork tenderloin with apple sauce and mashed potato," the first man said.

"It isn't ready yet."

"What the hell do you put it on the card for?"

"That's the dinner," George said. "You can get that at six o'clock."

"What time is it now?"

George looked at the clock on the wall behind the counter.

"It's five o'clock."

"The clock says twenty minutes past five," the second man said.

"It's twenty minutes fast," George said.

"Oh, to hell with the clock," the first man said. "What have you got to eat?"

"I can give you any kind of sandwitches," George said. "You can get ham and eggs, bacon and eggs, or a steak."

"Give me chicken croquettes with green peas with cream sauce and mashed potatoes."

"That's the dinner."

"Everything we want's the dinner, eh? That's the way you work it."

"I can give you ham and eggs, bacon and eggs or a steak."

"I'll take ham and eggs," the man called Al said. He wore a derby hat and a black overcoat with a silk muffler and he wore gloves. His face was small and ~~white~~ he had tight lips.

"Give me bacon and eggs," said the other man. He was about the same size. They looked as though they might be brothers. Both wore overcoats that were too tight for them. They sat leaning forward on the counter.

"Got anything to drink?" Al asked.

"Silver beer, bevo, ginger ale," George said.

"I mean you got anything to drink."

"Just those I said."

"This is a ~~swell~~ hot town," said the other. "What do they call it?"

"Petoskey," said George.

"Ever hear of it?" Al asked his friend.

"No," said Al.

Neither of them took off their gloves.

"What do you do here nights?" Al said.

"They eat the dinner," his friend said. "They all come here and eat the big dinner."

~~Georg~~ "That's it," said George.

"You think that's it?" the man called Al asked.

"~~Yes~~ Sure."

"You're a pretty bright boy aren't you?"

"Sure," said George.

"Well you're not," said the other little man. "Is he, Al?"

"He's dumb," said Al. He turned to Nick. "What's your name?"

"~~Nick~~ Adams."

"Another bright boy," Al said. "Ain't he a bright boy Max?"

"He's dumb," said Max[.]

George put the two platters, one of ham and eggs, the other of bacon and eggs on the counter. He set down two side dishes of fried potatoes.

"Which is yours?" he asked Al.

"Don't you remember?"

"Ham and eggs," George said.

"Just a bright boy," Max said.

He leaned forward and took the ham and eggs. ~~The~~ Both men ate with their gloves on.

George watched them eat.

9b.

Item 536, Ernest Hemingway Collection, John F. Kennedy Library and Museum, Boston. Pencil corrected draft in typescript and pencil manuscript of "The Killers" dated "Madrid— May 1926/Ernest Hemingway" in pencil on the first page.

[In upper right margin in pencil in the author's hand:] Madrid—May 1926 Ernest Hemingway [Along the right

margin handwritten in pencil:] For uncle Gus! written between 2:15 and 8 pm

The ~~Matadors~~ Killers

The door of Henry's lunch room opened and two men came in. They sat down at the counter.

"What's yours?" George asked them.

"I don't know," one of the men said. "What do you want to eat, Al?"

"I don't know," one of the men said. "I don't know what I want to eat."

Outside it was getting dark. The streetlight came on outside the window. The two men at the counter read the menu. At the other end of the counter Nick Adams watched them. He had been talking to George when they came in.

"I'll have a roast pork tenderloin with apple sauce and mashed potato," the first man said.

"It isn't ready yet."

"What the hell do you put it on the card for?"

"That's the dinner," George explained. "You can get that at six o'clock."

"What time is it now?"

George looked at the clock on the wall behind the counter.

"It's five o'clock."

"The clock says twenty minutes past five," the second man said.

"It's twenty minutes fast."

"Oh to hell with the clock," the first man said. "What have you got to eat?"

"I can give you any kind of sandwitches," George said. "You can have ham and eggs, bacon and eggs, liver and bacon or a steak."

"Give me chicken croquettes with green peas and cream sauce and mashed potatoes."

"That's the dinner."

"Everything we want's the dinner, eh? That's the way you work it."

"I can give you ham and eggs, bacon and eggs, liver—"

"I'll take ham and eggs," the man called Al said.

He wore a derby hat and a black overcoat. His face was small and white and he had ~~tight~~ no lips. He wore a silk muffler and gloves.

"Give me bacon and eggs," said the other man.

He was about the same size as Al. They looked as though they might be brothers. Both wore overcoats too tight for them. They sat leaning forward on the counter.

"Got anything to drink?" Al asked.

"Silver beer, Bevo, ginger ale," George said.

"I mean you got anything to drink?"

"Just those I said."

"This is a hot town," said the other. "What do they call it?"

"~~Petoskey~~ Summit," said George.

"Ever hear of it?" Al asked his friend.

"No," said the friend.

"What do you do here nights?" Al asked.

"They eat the dinner," his friend said. "They all come here and eat the big dinner."

"Sure," George said.

"So you think that's it?" Al asked George.

"Sure."

~~"So you're a thinker."~~ "You're a pretty bright boy ~~ain't~~ aren't you?"

"Sure," said George.

"Well you're not," said the other little man. "Is he Al?"

"He's dumb," said Al. He turned to Nick. "What's your name?"

"Adams."

"Another bright boy," Al said. "Ain't he a bright boy, Max."

"The town's full of bright boys," Max said.

George put the two platters, one of ham and eggs, the other of bacon and eggs, on the counter. He set down two side dishes of fried potatoes.

"Which is yours?" he asked Al.

"Don't you remember?"

"Ham and eggs."

"Just a bright boy," Max said. He leaned forward and took the ham and eggs. Both men ate with their gloves on. George watched them eat.

"What are <u>you</u> looking at" Max ~~turned to Nick~~ looked up at George.

"Nothing," said ~~Nick~~ George.

"The hell you were. You were looking at me."

"Maybe the boy meant it for a joke, Max," Al said.

George laughed.

"You don't have to laugh," Max said to him. "You don't have to laugh at all see?"

"All right," said George.

"So you think it's all right," ~~he~~ Max turned to Al. "He thinks it's all right. That's a good one."

"Oh, he's a thinker," Al said. They went on eating.

"What's the bright boy's name down the counter?" Al asked Max.

"Hey bright boy," Max said to Nick. "You go around to the other side of the counter with your boy friend."

"What's the idea ~~Max~~?" Nick asked.

"There isn't any idea."

"You better go around, bright boy," Al said. Nick went around behind the counter.

"What's the idea" George asked.

"None of your damn business," Al said. "Who's out in the kitchen?"

"The nigger."

"What do you mean the nigger?"

"The nigger that cooks."

"Tell him to come in."

"What's the idea?"

"Tell him to come in."

"Where do you think you are?"

"We know damn well where we are," the man called Max said. "Do we look silly?"

"You talk silly," Al said. "What the hell do you argue with this kid for. Listen," he said to George. "Tell the nigger to come out here."

"What you going to do to him?"

"Nothing. Use your head bright boy. What would we do to a nigger?"

George opened the slit that went back into the kitchen. "Sam," he called. "Come in here a minute."

The door to the kitchen opened and the nigger came in. "What was it?" he asked. The two men at the counter took a look at him.

"All right, nigger. You stand right there," Al said.

Sam ~~in his apron~~ looked at the two men sitting at the counter. "Yes sir," he said. Al got down from his stool.

"I'm going back in the kitchen with the nigger and brightboy," he said. "Go on back to the kitchen nigger. You go with him bright-boy." The little man followed Nick and the cook back into the kitchen. The door shut on them. The man called ~~George~~ Max sat at the counter opposite George. He didn't look at George but looked in the mirror that ran along back of the counter. Henry's had been a bar before it was a lunch counter.

"Well bright boy," Max said looking into the mirror. "Why don't you say something?"

"What's it all about?"

"Hey, Al," Max called. "Bright boy wants to know what it's all about."

"Why don't you tell him."

"What do you think it's all about?"

"I don't know."

"What do you think?"

Max looked into the mirror all the time he was talking.

"I wouldn't say."

"Hey, Al. Bright boy wouldn't say what he thinks it's all about."

"I can hear you all right," Al said from the kitchen. He had propped open the slit that dishes passed through into the kitchen. "Listen bright boy," he said from the kitchen to George. "Stand a lit-tle further along the bar. You move a little to the left, Max." He was like a photographer arranging for a group picture.

"Talk to me bright boy," Max said. "What do you think's going to happen?"

George did not say anything.

"I'll tell you," Max said. "We're going to kill a ~~wop~~ Swede. Do you know a ~~wop~~ big Swede named ~~Dominick Nerone~~ Ole Anderson?"

"Yes."

"He comes here to eat every night don't he?"

"Sometimes he comes here."

"He comes here at six o'clock ~~doesn't~~ don't he?"

"If he comes."

"We know all that bright boy," Max said. "Talk about something else. Ever go to the movies?"

"Once in a while."

"You ought to go to the movies more. The movies are fine for a bright boy like you."

"What are you going to kill ~~this wop~~ Ole Anderson for? What did he ever do to you?"

"He never had a chance to do anything to us. He never even seen us."

"What are you going to kill him for then?"

"We're killing him for a friend. Just to oblige a friend bright boy."

"Shut up," said Al from the kitchen. "You talk too goddam much."

"Well I got to keep bright boy amused. Don't I bright boy?"

"You talk too damn much," Al said. "The nigger and my bright boy are amused by themselves. I got em tied up like a couple of girl friends at a convent."

"I suppose you were in a convent."

"You never know."

"You were in a kosher convent. That's where you were."

George ~~looked out the door. He~~ standing behind the counter looked up at the clock.

"If anybody comes in tell em the cook is off and if they keep after it you tell them you'll go back and cook yourself. Do you get that bright boy?"

"All right," George said. "What you going to do with us afterwards?"

"That'll depend," Max said. "That's one of those things you never know at the time."

George looked up at the clock. It was ~~fifteen minutes~~ a quarter past six. The door opened. A ~~man~~ streetcar motorman came in.

"Hello, George," he said. "Can I get supper?"

"Sam's gone out," George said. "He'll be back in about half an hour."

"I'd better go up the street," the motorman said. George looked at the clock. It was twenty minutes past six.

"That was a very nice, bright boy," Max said. "You're a regular little gentleman."

"He knew I'd blow his head off," Al said from the kitchen.

"No," said Max. "It ain't that. Bright boy is nice. He's a nice boy. I like him."

At six ~~forty-five~~ fifty-five George said, "He isn't coming."

Two other people had been in the lunchroom. Once ~~he~~ George had gone out to the kitchen and made a ham and egg sandwich to go that a man wanted to take with him. Inside the kitchen he saw Al ~~was~~ sitting by the wicket with ~~a sawed-~~ the muzzle of a cut-off shotgun resting on the ledge. Nick and the cook ~~sat~~ were back to back in the corner a towel tied in each of their mouths. George had cooked the sandwich, wrapped it up, put it in a bag, brought it in and the man had paid for it and gone out.

"Bright boy can do everything," Max said. "He can cook and everything. You'd make some~~body~~ girl a nice wife, bright boy."

George said, "Yes? Your boyfriend ~~"He~~ isn't going to come." ~~George said.~~

"We'll give him ten minutes," Max said.

Max wa[t]ched the mirror and the clock. The hands of the clock marked seven o'clock, then five minutes past seven.

"Come on, Al," said Max. "We better go. He's not coming."

"Better give him five minutes," Al said.

In the five minutes a man came in and George explained that the cook was sick. "Why the hell don't you get another cook?" ~~he~~ the man asked. "Aren't you running a lunch counter?" He went out.

"Come on, Al," Max said.

"What about the two bright boys and the nigger?" Al asked.

"They're all right."

"You think so?"

"Sure. We're through with it." ~~We're not in it anymore. Somebody else has got to do it."~~

"I don't like it," said Al. "It's sloppy. You talk too much."

"Oh what the hell," said Max. "We got to keep amused haven't we?"

"You talk too much all the same," Al said. He came out from the kitchen. The cut off barrels of the shotgun made ~~only~~ a slight bulge under ~~his~~ the waist of his too tight fitting overcoat. He straightened his coat with his gloved hands.

"So long bright boy," he said to George. "You got a lot of luck."

"That's the truth," Max said. "You ought to play the races bright boy."

The two of them went out the door. George watched them go out the door. He saw them pass the window under the ~~street~~ arc light and cross the street. In their tight overcoats and derby hats they looked like a vaudeville team. George went back through the swinging door into the kitchen to untie Nick and the cook.

"I don't want any more of that," said Sam the cook. "I don't want any more of that."

[Page is torn and text is missing.]

[". . .] anyway nothing really happened. How do you feel, Sam?"

"Oh I'm all right," Sam said. "I just don't like it. That's all."

"I don't like it either," said George. "Nobody likes it."

"It's a tough place all right," Nick said. He was very excited about it all.

"Everywhere's tough if you happen to hit it when it's that way," George said.

"But I don't want any of it," Sam said. "I don't want any of it at all."

"Well you don't get much of it," George said.

"No and I don't want any of it either," Sam said.

"Want something to eat, Nick?" George asked.

"I'm hungry," Nick said.

"Make us a couple of ham and egg sandwiches, Sam," George said. He felt under his arm. His shirt and his apron were soaked through with ~~sweat~~ perspiration.

"Those were a couple of tough birds," he said to Nick.

"I wonder what would have happened," Nick said.

"I don't know," said George. "But I sweat a lot; while it was going on."

[In the margin top left corner of the page] add The Killers

Nick straightened up.

"Say," he said. "What the hell?"

He was trying to swagger it off.

"They were going to kill ~~Olaf~~ Ole Anderson," George said. "They were going to shoot him when he came in to eat."

"Ole Anderson?"

"Sure."

The cook was feeling of the corners of his mouth.

"They all gone?" he asked.

"Yeah," said George. "They're gone now."

"I don't like it," said the cook. "I don't like it at all."

"Listen," George said to Nick. "You better go see Ole Anderson."

"All right."

"You better not have anything to do with it at all," the cook said.

"Don't go if you don't want to," George said.

"Mixing up in this ain't going to get you anywhere," the cook said. "You stay out of it."

"I'll go see him," Nick said to George. "Where does he live?"

"He lives up at Hisch's ~~boarding~~ Rooming house."

"I'll go up there," Nick said.

Outside ~~the on the street it was dark~~ Nick walked up the street. ~~At the corner The arclight shone through the leaves of the big tree. Nick turned~~ He walked along beside the car tracks and turned ~~the corner~~ at the arc light on the corner down a side street. Three houses up the street was Hisch's ~~Boarding~~ Rooming house. He went up the two steps and pushed the bell. A woman came to the door.

~~"Did you wan~~

"Is Ole Anderson here?"

~~"He's the second floor front~~

"Do you want to see him?"

"Yes."

Nick followed the woman up ~~a~~ one flight of stairs and back to the end of a corridor. She knocked on the door.

"Who is it?"

"It's ~~a m~~ somebody to see you Mr. Anderson," the woman said.

"It's Nick Adams."

~~The~~

"Come in."

Nick opened the door and went in. Ole Anderson was lying on the bed with all his clothes on. ~~He was very tall and his feet reached all the way to the end of the bed.~~ He had been a heavy weight prize-fighter and he was almost too long for the bed. He was lying back with his head on the pillows. He didn't look at Nick.

"I was up at Henry's," Nick said. "And two fellows came in and tied up me and the cook and they said they were going to kill you."

It sounded silly when he said it. Ole Anderson said nothing.

"They put us out in the kitchen," Nick went on. "They were going to shoot you when you came in to supper."

Ole Anderson did not say anything.

"George thought I better come and tell you about it."

"There isn't anything I can do about it," Ole Anderson said.

"I'll tell you what they were like," Nick said.

"I don't want to know what they were like," Ole Anderson said. He looked at the wall. "Thanks for coming to tell me about it."

"That's all right."

Nick looked at the big man lying on the bed.

"Don't you want me to go and see the police?"

"No. That wouldn't do any good."

"Isn't there something I could do?"

"No. There ain't anything to do."

"Maybe it was just a bluff."

"No. It ain't just a bluff."

Ole Anderson turned toward the wall.

"The only thing is," he said. "I just can't make up my mind to go out. I been in here all day."

"Couldn't you get out of town?"

"No," Ole Anderson said. "I'm through with all that moving around."

He looked at the wall.

"There ain't anything to do now."

"Couldn't you fix it up someway?"

"No. I got in wrong."

He talked in the same flat voice. "There ain't anything to do. After a while I'll make up my mind to go out."

"I better go back and see George," Nick said.

"So long," said ~~Ander~~ Ole Anderson. He didn't look toward Nick. "Thanks for coming around."

Nick went out. As he shut the door he saw Ole Anderson with all his clothes on lying on the bed looking at the wall.

"He's been in his room all day," the woman said downstairs. "I guess he don't feel well."

"He feels rotten."

"I'm sorry he don't feel well," the woman said. "He's an awfully nice man, Mr. Anderson. He was in the ring you know."

"I know it."

"You'd never know it except from the way his face is," the woman said. They just stood inside the street door. "He's just as gentle."

"Well good night," Nick said.

"Good night," said the woman.

Nick walked back along the street, ~~down~~ under the arclight and down along the car tracks to Henry's eating house. George was inside back of the counter.

"Did you see Ole?"

"Yes," said Nick. "He's in his room and he won't go out."

The cook had opened the door from the kitchen when he heard Nick's voice.

"I don't even listen to it," he said. He ~~went into~~ shut the door.

"Did you tell him about it?"

"Sure. He knows what it's all about."

"What's he going to do?"

"Nothing."

"They'll kill him."

"I guess they will."

"He must have got mixed up in something in Chicago."

"I guess so," said Nick.

"It's a hell of a thing," George said.

"It's an awful thing," Nick said.

~~"I wonder~~

They did not say anything.

"I wonder what he did?" Nick said.

"Double crossed somebody," George said. "That's what they kill them for."

"I'm going to get out of this town," Nick said.

"Yes," said George. "That's a good thing to do."

"I can't stand to think about Ole Anderson," Nick said. "It's too damned awful."

"Well," said George. "You better not think about it."

10.

In Another Country

1927

In the fall the war was always there, but we did not go to it any more. It was cold in the fall in Milan and the dark came very early. Then the electric lights came on, and it was pleasant along the streets looking in the windows. There was much game hanging outside the shops, and the snow powdered in the fur of the foxes and the wind blew their tails. The deer hung stiff and heavy and empty, and small birds blew in the wind and the wind turned their feathers. It was a cold fall and the wind came down from the mountains.

We were all at the hospital every afternoon, and there were different ways of walking across the town through the dusk to the hospital. Two of the ways were alongside canals, but they were long. Always, though, you crossed a bridge across a canal to enter the hospital. There was a choice of three bridges. On one of them a woman sold roasted chestnuts. It was warm, standing in front of her charcoal fire, and the chestnuts were warm afterward in your pocket. The hospital was very old and very beautiful, and you entered through a gate and walked across a courtyard and out a gate on the other side. There were usually funerals starting from the courtyard. Beyond the old hospital were the new brick pavilions, and there we met every afternoon and were all very polite and interested in what was the matter, and sat in the machines that were to make so much difference.

The doctor came up to the machine where I was sitting and said: "What did you like best to do before the war? Did you practice a sport?"

I said: "Yes, football."

"Good" he said. "You will be able to play football again better than ever."

My knee did not bend and the leg dropped straight from the knee to the ankle without a calf, and the machine was to bend the knee and make it move as in riding a tricycle. But it did not bend yet, and instead the machine lurched when it came to the bending part. The doctor said: "That will all pass. You are a fortunate young man. You will play football again like a champion."

In the next machine was a major who had a little hand like a baby's. He winked at me when the doctor examined his hand, which was between two leather straps that bounced up and down and flapped the stiff fingers, and said: "And will I too play football, captain-doctor?" He had been a very great fencer, and before the war the greatest fencer in Italy.

The doctor went to his office in a back room and brought a photograph which showed a hand that had been withered almost as small as the major's, before it had taken a machine course, and after was a little larger. The major held the photograph with his good hand and looked at it very carefully. "A wound?" he asked.

"An industrial accident," the doctor said.

"Very interesting, very interesting," the major said, and handed it back to the doctor.

"You have confidence?"

"No," said the major.

There were three boys who came each day who were about the same age I was. They were all three from Milan, and one of them was to be a lawyer, and one was to be a painter, and one had intended to be a soldier, and after we were finished with the machines, sometimes we walked back together to the Café Cova, which was next door to the Scala. We walked the short way through the communist quarter because we were four together. The people hated us because we were officers, and from a wineshop some one would call out, *"A basso gli ufficiali!"* as we passed. Another boy who walked with us sometimes and made us five wore a black silk handkerchief across his face because he had no nose then and his face was to be rebuilt. He had gone out to the front from the military academy and been wounded within an hour after he had gone into the front line for the first time. They rebuilt his face, but he came from a very old family and they could never get the nose exactly right. He went to South America and worked in a bank. But this was a long time ago, and then we did not any of us know how it was going to be afterward. We only knew then that there was always the war, but that we were not going to it any more.

We all had the same medals, except the boy with the black silk bandage across his face, and he had not been at the front long enough to get any medals. The tall boy with a very pale face who was to be a lawyer had been a lieutenant of *Arditi* and had three medals of the sort we each had only one of. He had lived a very long time with death and was a little detached. We were all a little detached, and there was nothing that held us together except that we met every afternoon at the hospital. Although, as we walked to the Cova through the tough part of town, walking in the dark, with light and singing coming out of the wine-shops, and sometimes having to walk into the street when the men and women would crowd together on the sidewalk so that we would have had to jostle them to get by, we felt held together by there being something that had happened that they, the people who disliked us, did not understand.

We ourselves all understood the Cova, where it was rich and warm and not too brightly lighted, and noisy and smoky at certain hours, and there were always girls at the tables and the illustrated papers on a rack on the wall. The girls at the Cova were very patriotic, and I found that the most patriotic people in Italy were the café girls—and I believe they are still patriotic.

The boys at first were very polite about my medals and asked me what I had done to get them. I showed them the papers, which were written in very beautiful language and full of *fratellanza* and *abnegazione*, but which really said, with the adjectives removed, that I had been given the medals because I was an American. After that their manner changed a little toward me, although I was their friend against outsiders. I was a friend, but I was never really one of them after they had read the citations, because it had been different with them and they had done very different things to get their medals. I had been wounded, it was true; but we all knew that being wounded, after all, was really an accident. I was never ashamed of the ribbons, though, and sometimes, after the cocktail hour, I would imagine myself having done all the things they had done to get their medals; but walking home at night through the empty streets with the cold wind and all the shops closed, trying to keep near the street lights, I knew that I would never have done such things, and I was very much afraid to die, and often lay in bed at night by myself, afraid to die and wondering how I would be when I went back to the front again.

The three with the medals were like hunting-hawks; and I was not a hawk, although I might seem a hawk to those who had never hunted; they, the three, knew better and so we drifted apart. But I stayed good friends with the boy who had been wounded his first day at the front, because he would never know now how he would have turned out; so he could never be accepted either, and I liked him because I thought perhaps he would not have turned out to be a hawk either.

The major, who had been the great fencer, did not believe in bravery, and spent much time while we sat in the machines correcting my grammar. He had complimented me on how I spoke Italian, and we talked together very easily. One day I had said that Italian seemed such an easy language to me that I could not take a great interest in it; everything was so easy to say. "Ah, yes," the major said. "Why, then, do you not take up the use of grammar?" So we took up the use of grammar, and soon Italian was such a difficult language that I was afraid to talk to him until I had the grammar straight in my mind.

The major came very regularly to the hospital. I do not think he ever missed a day, although I am sure he did not believe in the machines. There was a time when none of us believed in the machines, and one day the major said it was all nonsense. The machines were new then and it was we who were to prove them. It was an idiotic idea, he said, "a theory, like another." I had not learned my grammar, and he said I was a stupid impossible disgrace, and he was a fool to have bothered with me. He was a small man and he sat straight up in his chair with his right hand thrust into the machine and looked straight ahead at the wall while the straps thumped up and down with his fingers in them.

"What will you do when the war is over if it is over?" he asked me. "Speak grammatically!"

"I will go to the States."

"Are you married?"

"No, but I hope to be."

"The more of a fool you are," he said. He seemed very angry. "A man must not marry."

"Why, Signor Maggiore?"

"Don't call me 'Signor Maggiore.'"

"Why must not a man marry?"

"He cannot marry. He cannot marry," he said angrily. "If he is to lose everything, he should not place himself in a position to lose that. He should not place himself in a position to lose. He should find things he cannot lose."

He spoke very angrily and bitterly, and looked straight ahead while he talked.

"But why should he necessarily lose it?"

"He'll lose it," the major said. He was looking at the wall. Then he looked down at the machine and jerked his little hand out from between the straps and slapped it hard against his thigh. "He'll lose it," he almost shouted. "Don't argue with me!" Then he called to the attendant who ran the machines. "Come and turn this damned thing off."

He went back into the other room for the light treatment and the massage. Then I heard him ask the doctor if he might use his telephone and he shut the door. When he came back into the room, I was sitting in another machine. He was wearing his cape and had his cap on, and he came directly toward my machine and put his arm on my shoulder.

"I am so sorry," he said, and patted me on the shoulder with his good hand. "I would not be rude. My wife has just died. You must forgive me."

"Oh—" I said, feeling sick for him. "I am *so* sorry."

He stood there biting his lower lip. "It is very difficult," he said. "I cannot resign myself."

He looked straight past me and out through the window. Then he began to cry. "I am utterly unable to resign myself," he said and choked. And then crying, his head up looking at nothing, carrying himself straight and soldierly, with tears on both his cheeks and biting his lips, he walked past the machines and out the door.

The doctor told me that the major's wife, who was very young and whom he had not married until he was definitely invalided out of the war, had died of pneumonia. She had been sick only a few days. No one expected her to die. The major did not come to the hospital for three days. Then he came at the usual hour, wearing a black band on the sleeve of his uniform. When he came back, there were large framed photographs around the wall, of all sorts of wounds before and after they had been cured by the machines. In front of the machine the major used were three photographs of hands like his that were completely restored. I do not know where the doctor got them. I always understood we were the first to use the machines. The photographs did not make much difference to the major because he only looked out of the window.

10a.

Item 492, Ernest Hemingway Collection, John F. Kennedy Library and Museum, Boston. Typescript of "In Another Country," titled in pencil with pencil corrections.

In Another Country

In the fall the war was always there but we did not go to it anymore. It was cold ~~and the streets were gray~~ in the fall and gray in Milan and the dark came very early. Then the electric lights came on and it was pleasant to walk along and look in the windows. There was much game hanging outside the shops and the snow powdered in the fur of the foxes and the wind blew their tails. The deer hung stiff and heavy and empty ~~in the wind. The~~ and small birds blew in the wind and the wind turned their feathers. It was cold and the wind came down from the mountains.

We were all at the hospital every afternoon and there were ~~new~~ different ways of walking across the town through the dusk to the hospital. Two of the ways were alongside canals. Always you crossed a bridge across a canal to enter the hospital. There was a choice of three bridges. The hospital was very old and very beautiful and you entered through a gate and walked across a courtyard and out a gate on the other side. There were ~~usually often~~ funerals starting from the courtyard. Beyond the old hospital were the new brick pavillions and there we met every afternoon and were all very polite and interested in what was the matter and sat in the machines that were to make so much difference.

The doctor came up and said, "What did you like best to do before the war? Did you practice a sport?"

I said, "Yes, football."

"Good," he said. "You will be able to play foot-ball again better than ever."

My knee did not bend and the leg dropped straight to the ankle without a calf and the machine was to bend the knee and make it move as in riding a tricycle. But it did not bend yet and instead the machine lurched when it came to the bending part. The doctor said, "That will all pass. You are a fortunate young man. You will play football ~~again~~ like a champion."

In the next machine was a major who had a little hand like a baby's. He winked at me and when the doctor examined his hand which was between two leather straps that bounced up and down and flapped the stiff fingers he said, "And will I too play foot-ball, Captain Doctor?" He had been ~~the~~ a very ~~greatest~~ fencer ~~in Italy.~~ and ~~the greatest~~ before the war the greatest fencer in Italy.

The doctor went to his office in a back room and brought back a photograph which showed a hand which had been withered almost as small as the major's before it had taken the machine course and after was a little larger. The major held the photograph with his good hand, ~~which was very white and larger with long fingers.~~ and looked at it very carefully and said, "Very interesting, very interesting," and handed it back to the doctor.

~~"Don't y~~ "You have confidence?"

"No," said the major.

There were three ~~other~~ boys that came every day who were about the same age I was. They were all three from Milan and one of them was to be a lawyer and one was to be a painter and one had intended to be a soldier and after we were finished with the machines sometimes we walked back together to the cafe and restaurant Cova next door to the Scala. We walked the short way through the communist quarter because we were four together. The people hated us because we were officers. And ~~some one~~ they would call out from a wine shop, "A bacco gli ufficialli" as we went by. One of the boys who walked with us sometimes and made us five wore a black silk bandage across his face because he had no nose then and his face was to be rebuilt. He had gone out to the front from the military academy and been wounded ~~an~~ within an hour after he had gone into the line for the first time. They rebuilt his face, but he came from a very old family and they could never get the nose exactly right. He went to South America and worked in a bank. But that was a long time ago and then we did not know how it was going to be afterward. We only knew then that there was always the war but that we were not going to it any more.

We all had the same medals except the boy with the black bandage across his face and he had not been at the front long enough to get any medals. The tall boy who was to be a lawyer and had been a lieutenant of Arditi had three medals of the sort we each ~~only~~ had only one of and he had lived a very long time with death and was a little detached. We were all a little detached and there was nothing that held us together except that we met every afternoon at the hospital. Although as we walked to the Cova through the tough part of town, walking in the dark with light coming out of the wineshops and sometimes having to walk into the street when the men and women would crowd together on the sidewalk so that we would have had to jostle them to get by, we felt held together by there being something that had happened that ~~they~~ the people who ~~cursed~~ disliked us did not understand.

We all understood the Cova where it was rich and warm and not too brightly lighted, and noisy and smoky at certain hours, and there were always girls at the tables and the illustrated papers on a rack on the wall. The girls at the Cova were very patriotic and I found that the most patriotic people in Italy were the whores—and I believe they are still patriotic.

The boys at first were very polite about my medals and asked me what I had done to get them. I showed them the papers, which were written in very beautiful language and full of <u>fratellanza</u> and <u>abnegazione</u>, but which really said, with the adjectives removed, that I had been given the medals because I was an American and after that their manner changed a little toward me although I was their friend against outsiders. I was a friend but I was never really one of them after they had read the citations because it had been different with them and ~~very different about their~~ they had done more than that to get their medals. ~~So while~~ I had been wounded but we all knew that being wounded after all was really an accident. ~~But~~ I was never ashamed of the ribbons though and sometimes, after I had had two or three aperitifs, I would imagine myself having done all the things they had done to get their medals; but walking home at night through the empty streets with the cold wind and all the shops closed and trying to keep near the street lights I knew that I would not have done such things and I was very much afraid to die and often lay in bed at night by myself afraid to die and wondering how I would be when I got back to the front again.

The three with the medals were like hunting hawks and I was not a hawk, and although I I might seem a hawk to those who had never hunted; they, the three, knew better and so we drifted apart. But I stayed good friends with the boy who had been wounded his first day at the front because he ~~he~~ would never know now how he would have turned out and so he could never be accepted either and I liked him because I thought perhaps he would not have turned out to be a hawk either.

The major who had been the great fencer did not believe in bravery and spent much time while we sat in the machines correcting my grammar. He had complimented me on how I spoke Italian and we talked together very easily. One day I had said that Italian seemed such an easy language to me that I could not take great interest in it, everything was so easy to say. "Ah yes," the major said. "Why then do you not take up the study of grammar?" So we took up the study of grammar and soon Italian was such a difficult language that I was afraid to talk to him until I had the grammar straight in my mind.

The major came very regularly to the hospital. I do not think he ever missed a day although I am sure he did not believe in the machines. There was a time when we none of us believed in the machines and one day the major said it was all nonsense. The machines were new then and it was we who were to prove them. It was an idiotic idea he said, "A theory, like another." I had not learned my grammar and he said I was a disgrace and he was a fool to have bothered with me. He was a small man and he sat straight up in his chair with his right hand thrust into the machine and looked straight ahead at the wall and the straps thumped up and down with his fingers in them.

"What ~~would I~~ will you do when the war ~~were~~ is over if it ~~were~~ is over?" he asked.

"I will go to the States."

"Are you married?"

"No, but I hope to be."

"The more of a fool you are," he said. "A man must not marry."

"Why, Signor Maggiore?"

"Don't call me Signor Maggiore."

"Why must not a man marry?"

"He cannot marry. He cannot marry. If he is to lose everything he should not place himself in a position to lose that. He should not place himself in a position to lose. He should find things he can not lose."

He seemed very angry and bitter and looked straight ahead while he talked.

"But why should he lose it?"

"He'll lose it," the major said. He looked straight at the wall. Then he jerked his little hand out of the machine and slapped it against his thigh. "He'll lose it I tell you. Don't argue with me." Then he called to the attendant who ran the machines, "Come and turn this damned thing off."

He went back into the other room for the light treatment and the massage. ~~and~~ Then he used the doctor's telephone and when he came back I was sitting at another machine. He was wearing ~~his cap and~~ his cape and had his cap on and he came up and put his arm on my shoulder.

"I am so sorry," he said. "I would not be rude. My wife has just died ~~today~~. You must forgive me."

~~"Oh –" I could not say anything. I felt a fool. There was nothing~~
~~"Oh –. I am so sorry."~~

"Oh—" I could not say anything. Then "I am _so_ sorry."

He stood there biting his lower lip, "It is very difficult," he said. "I cannot resign myself."

~~We shook hands with his good hand.~~ He looked straight past me and out through the window. Then he began to cry, "I am utterly unable to resign myself," he said and choked. And ~~T~~then crying, his head up, ~~looking~~ carrying himself very ~~military~~ straight and soldierly ~~but~~ with tears on ~~his face~~ both his cheeks, and biting his lip, he walked past the machines and out the door.

The doctor told me that the major's wife, who was very young and lovely, whom he had not married until after he had been definitely invalided out of the war, had died of pneumonia. She had been sick only a few days. The major did not come to the hospital for three days and then he ~~wore~~ came in ~~wearing~~ at the usual hour wearing a black band on his uniform sleeve. When he came back there were big framed photographs around the wall of all sorts of wounds before and after they had been cured by the machines. In front of the machine the major used were three photographs of hands like his that were completely restored. I do not know where the doctor got them. I always understood we were the first to use the machines. They did not make much difference to the major because he only looked out of the window.

End

11.

Hills Like White Elephants

1927

The hills across the valley of the Ebro were long and white. On this side there was no shade and no trees and the station was between two lines of rails in the sun. Close against the side of the station there was the warm shadow of the building and a curtain, made of strings of bamboo beads, hung across the open door into the bar, to keep out flies. The American and the girl with him sat at a table in the shade, outside the building. It was very hot and the express from Barcelona would come in forty minutes. It stopped at this junction for two minutes and went on to Madrid.

"What should we drink?" the girl asked. She had taken off her hat and put it on the table.

"It's pretty hot," the man said.

"Let's drink beer."

"*Dos cervezas,*" the man said into the curtain.

"Big ones?" a woman asked from the doorway.

"Yes. Two big ones."

The woman brought two glasses of beer and two felt pads. She put the felt pads and the beer glasses on the table and looked at the man and the girl. The girl was looking off at the line of hills. They were white in the sun and the country was brown and dry.

"They look like white elephants," she said.

"I've never seen one," the man drank his beer.

"No, you wouldn't have."

"I might have," the man said. "Just because you say I wouldn't have doesn't prove anything."

The girl looked at the bead curtain. "They've painted something on it," she said. "What does it say?"

"Anis del Toro. It's a drink."

"Could we try it?"

The man called "Listen" through the curtain. The woman came out from the bar.

"Four reales."

"We want two Anis del Toro."

"With water?"

"Do you want it with water?"

"I don't know," the girl said. "Is it good with water?"

"It's all right."

"You want them with water?" asked the woman.

"Yes, with water."

"It tastes like licorice," the girl said and put the glass down.

"That's the way with everything."

"Yes," said the girl. "Everything tastes of licorice. Especially all the things you've waited so long for, like absinthe."

"Oh, cut it out."

"You started it," the girl said. "I was being amused. I was having a fine time."

"Well, let's try and have a fine time."

"All right. I was trying. I said the mountains looked like white elephants. Wasn't that bright?"

"That was bright."

"I wanted to try this new drink: That's all we do, isn't it—look at things and try new drinks?"

"I guess so."

The girl looked across at the hills.

"They're lovely hills," she said. "They don't really look like white elephants. I just meant the coloring of their skin through the trees."

"Should we have another drink?"

"All right."

The warm wind blew the bead curtain against the table.

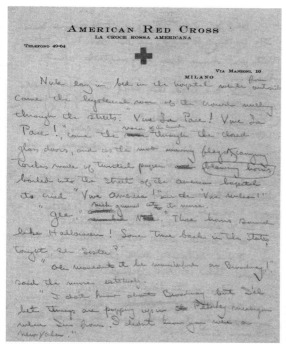

Figure 1. First page of
an untitled handwritten
manuscript on Red Cross
Hospital stationery about a
wounded American.
Ernest Hemingway Collection,
Manuscripts, Stories and Fragments,
Item 604, page 1, at the John F.
Kennedy Presidential Library and
Museum, Boston, MA.

Figure 2. Ernest Hemingway, American
Red Cross (ARC) volunteer, recuperates
from wounds at the ARC Hospital in
Milan, Italy, 1918.   Ernest Hemingway
Collection, John F. Kennedy Presidential Library
and Museum, Boston, MA.

Figure 3. Ernest Hemingway's personal copy of the *Kansas City Star* style book. Ernest Hemingway Collection, John F. Kennedy Presidential Library and Museum, Boston, MA.

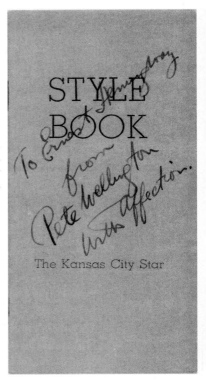

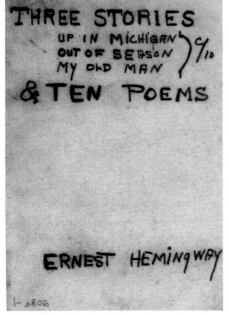

Figure 4. Ernest Hemingway's own mock-up for the cover of *Three Stories and Ten Poems*. Ernest Hemingway Collection, Manuscripts, *Three Stories and Ten Poems*, Item 203a, page 1, at the John F. Kennedy Presidential Library and Museum, Boston, MA.

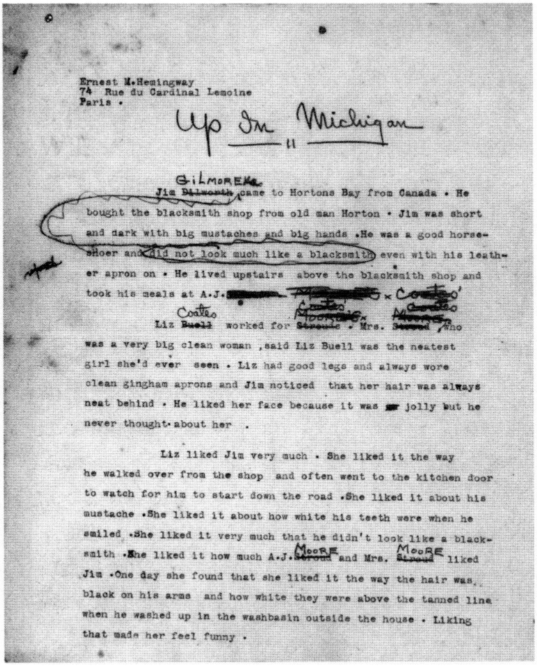

Ernest M. Hemingway
74 Rue du Cardinal Lemoine
Paris.

Up In Michigan

Jim Gilmore came to Hortons Bay from Canada. He bought the blacksmith shop from old man Horton. Jim was short and dark with big mustaches and big hands. He was a good horseshoer and did not look much like a blacksmith even with his leather apron on. He lived upstairs above the blacksmith shop and took his meals at A.J. Coates'.

Liz Coates worked for Coates. Mrs. Coates, who was a very big clean woman, said Liz Buell was the neatest girl she'd ever seen. Liz had good legs and always wore clean gingham aprons and Jim noticed that her hair was always neat behind. He liked her face because it was jolly but he never thought about her.

Liz liked Jim very much. She liked it the way he walked over from the shop and often went to the kitchen door to watch for him to start down the road. She liked it about his mustache. She liked it about how white his teeth were when he smiled. She liked it very much that he didn't look like a blacksmith. She liked it how much A.J. Moore and Mrs. Moore liked Jim. One day she found that she liked it the way the hair was black on his arms and how white they were above the tanned line when he washed up in the washbasin outside the house. Liking that made her feel funny.

Figure 5. First page, titled typescript of "Up in Michigan" with corrections in pen and ink. Ernest Hemingway Collection, Manuscripts, Stories and Fragments, Item 799, page 1, at the John F. Kennedy Presidential Library and Museum, Boston, MA.

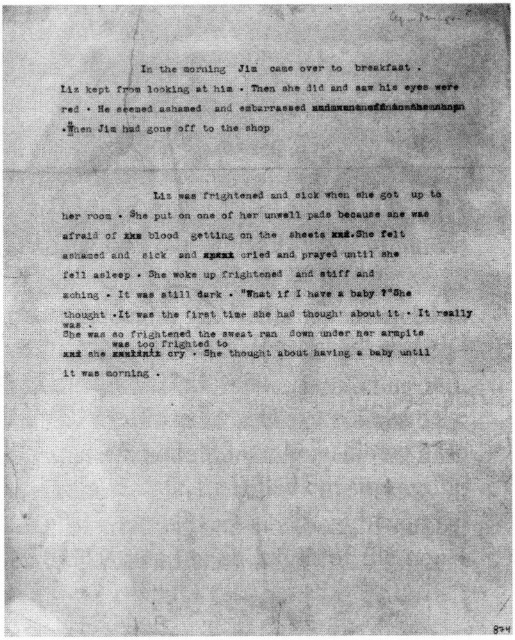

In the morning Jim came over to breakfast. Liz kept from looking at him. Then she did and saw his eyes were red. He seemed ashamed and embarrassed. When Jim had gone off to the shop

Liz was frightened and sick when she got up to her room. She put on one of her unwell pads because she was afraid of blood getting on the sheets. She felt ashamed and sick and cried and prayed until she fell asleep. She woke up frightened and stiff and aching. It was still dark. "What if I have a baby?" She thought. It was the first time she had thought about it. It really was. She was so frightened the sweat ran down under her armpits she was too frighted to cry. She thought about having a baby until it was morning.

874

Figure 6. Untitled typescript fragment with an alternate ending for "Up in Michigan." Ernest Hemingway Collection, Manuscripts, Stories and Fragments, Item 801, at the John F. Kennedy Presidential Library and Museum, Boston, MA.

Personal

One hot evening in Milan there were flocks of chimney swifts in the sky. The searchlights came out and they carried me out onto the roof.

Love

One hot evening in Milan they (Three) carried me up onto the roof and could look out over the tops of the town. There were chimney swifts in the sky. After a while it got dark and the searchlights came out. The others went down and took the bottles with them. We could hear them on the balcony. Ag sat on the bed. She stayed on night duty for three months. They were glad to let her. When I had

the big operation she prepared me for the operating table and we had a joke about friend or enema. When I got on crutches I used to take the temperatures so she wouldn't have to get up from the bed. Before I went back to the front we went into the Duomo and prayed. It was dim and quiet.

We wanted to get married but there wasn't enough time for publishing the banns and we didn't either have birth certificates. We loved each other very much. After the Armistice I went home to get a job so we could get married and Ag

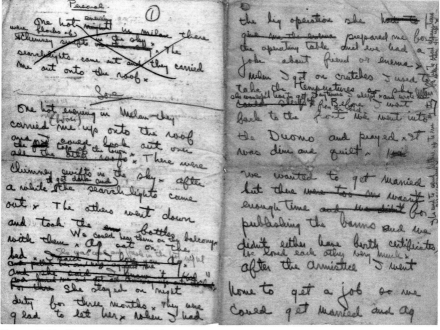

Figure 7. Earliest preserved draft of "A Very Short Story," which Hemingway was writing as a vignette for inclusion in his book *In Our Time*. Ernest Hemingway Collection, Manuscripts, Stories and Fragments, Item 633, page 1, at the John F. Kennedy Presidential Library and Museum, Boston, MA.

It was a long time after supper. Nick had started to undress in the tent. He could see the shadows of his father and his uncle Joe on the wall of the tent. He did not feel very happy.

Nick was undressing. He could see the shadows of his father and uncle George cast by the fire on the canvas wall. He felt very uncomfortable and ashamed and undressed as fast as he could, piling his clothes neatly. He was ashamed because undressing reminded him of the night before. He had kept it out of his mind all day.

Figure 8. The original beginning of "Indian Camp." Untitled ink manuscript page. Ernest Hemingway Collection, Manuscripts, Stories and Fragments, Item 493, page 1, at the John F. Kennedy Presidential Library and Museum, Boston, MA.

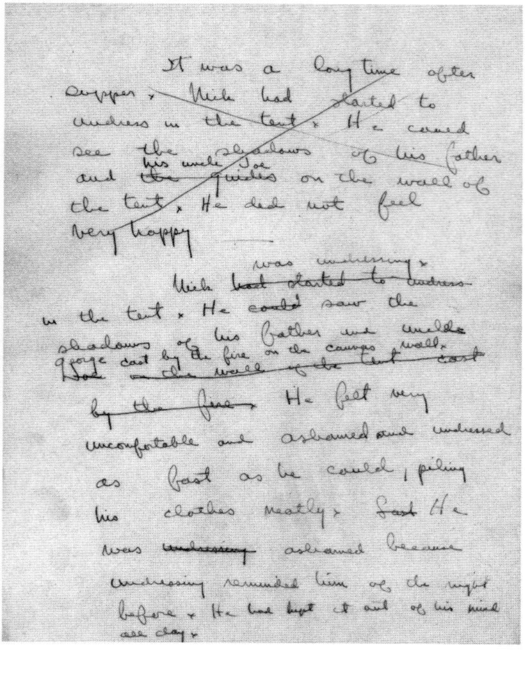

(2)
pocket of his Mackinaw coat.
The road came out of
the orchard on to the top
of the hill. There was
the house, the porch bare,
smoke coming from the
chimney.
As Nick crossed the
open field above the
orchard the door opened
and Bill came out.
He stood on the porch
looking out.
"Well, Wemedge" he

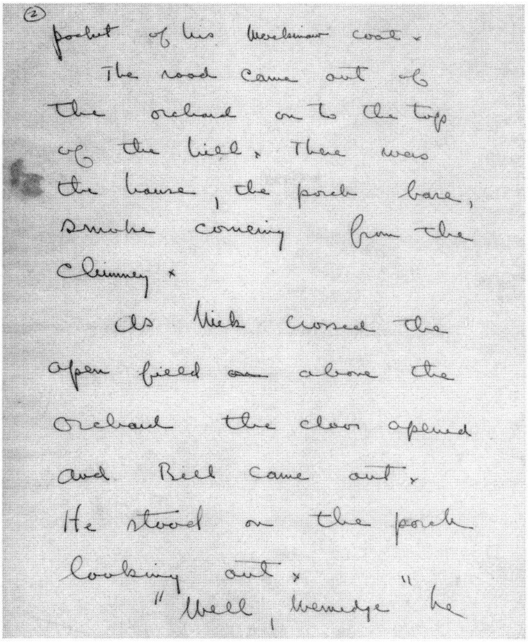

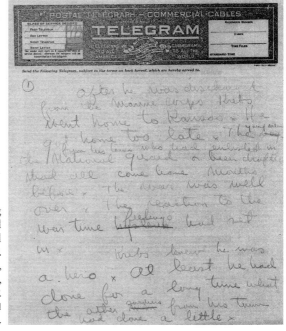

Figure 9. Ink manuscript page from the beginning of "The Three-Day Blow."
Ernest Hemingway Collection, Manuscripts, Stories and Fragments, Item 762, page 2, at the John F. Kennedy Presidential Library and Museum, Boston, MA.

POSTAL TELEGRAPH — COMMERCIAL CABLES
TELEGRAM
TELEGRAMS TO ALL AMERICA
CABLEGRAMS TO ALL THE WORLD
Send the following Telegram, subject to the terms on back hereof, which are hereby agreed to.

(1)
After he was discharged
from the Marine Corps Krebs
went home to Kansas. He
got home too late. The young men
from his town who had enlisted in
the National Guard or been drafted
had all come home months
before. The war was well
over. The reaction to the
war time ~~hysteria~~ feeling had set
in.
Krebs knew he was
a hero. At least he had
done for a long time what
the other ~~fellows~~ from his town
had done a little.

Figure 10. The first beginning of "Soldier's Home." Untitled pencil manuscript on postal telegraph paper.
Ernest Hemingway Collection, Manuscripts, Stories and Fragments, Item 708, page 1, at the John F. Kennedy Presidential Library and Museum, Boston, MA.

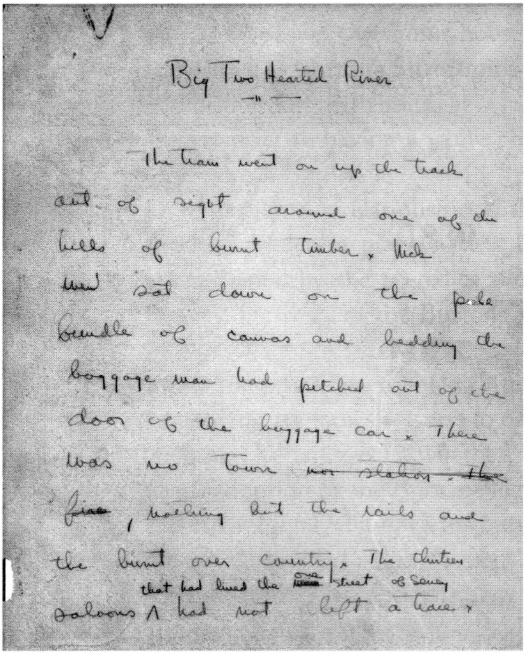

Big Two Hearted River

The train went on up the track out of sight around one of the hills of burnt timber. Nick sat down on the pile bundle of canvas and bedding the baggage man had pitched out of the door of the baggage car. There was no town ~~nor station. The fire~~, nothing but the rails and the burnt over country. The thirteen saloons that had lined the one street of Seney had not left a trace.

Figure 11. Titled ink manuscript of "Big Two-Hearted River."
Ernest Hemingway Collection, Manuscripts, Stories and Fragments, Item 274, page 1, at the John F. Kennedy Presidential Library and Museum, Boston, MA.

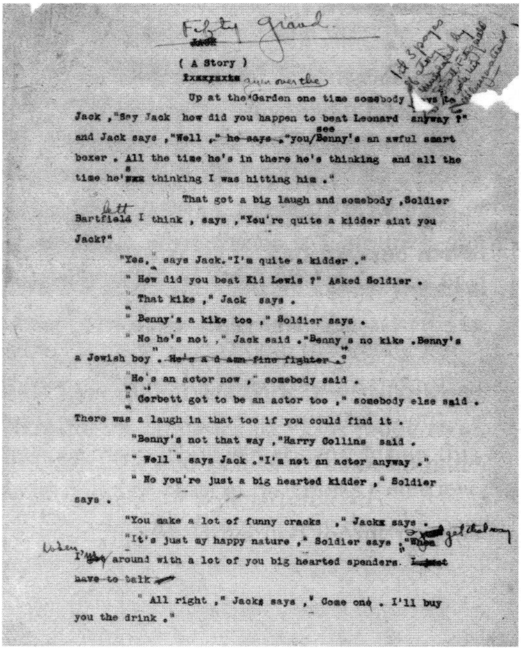

Fifty Grand
~~JACK~~

(A Story)

Up at the Garden one time somebody says to Jack ,"Say Jack how did you happen to beat Leonard anyway ?" and Jack says ,"Well ," ~~he says~~ ,"you see Benny's an awful smart boxer . All the time he's in there he's thinking and all the time he's thinking I was hitting him ."

That got a big laugh and somebody ,Soldier Bartfield I think , says ,"You're quite a kidder aint you Jack?"

"Yes," says Jack."I'm quite a kidder ."

" How did you beat Kid Lewis ?" Asked Soldier .

" That kike ," Jack says .

" Benny's a kike too ," Soldier says .

" No he's not ," Jack said ."Benny's no kike .Benny's a Jewish boy" . ~~He's a d amn fine fighter .~~"

"He's an actor now ," somebody said .

" Corbett got to be an actor too ," somebody else said . There was a laugh in that too if you could find it .

"Benny's not that way ,"Harry Collins said .

" Well " says Jack ."I'm not an actor anyway ."

" No you're just a big hearted kidder ," Soldier says .

"You make a lot of funny cracks ," Jack says .

"It's just my happy nature ," Soldier says ," I got that way when I'm around with a lot of you big hearted spenders. ~~I just have to talk~~ ."

" All right ," Jack says ," Come on . I'll buy you the drink ."

Figure 12. The original beginning of "Fifty Grand" that Hemingway cut on F. Scott Fitzgerald's recommendation.
Ernest Hemingway Collection, Manuscripts, Stories and Fragments, Item 388, page 1, at the John F. Kennedy Presidential Library and Museum, Boston, MA.

A Marriage Has Been Arranged.
The Coming Man.
The New Man
The Short Life of Francis Macomber.
The End of The Marriage
Marriage is a Dangerous Game
The More Dangerous Game.
To lookups
Man
Marriage
Fear
Courage.
A Marriage Has Been Terminated.
The Ruling Classes.
The Fear of Courage.
Brief Mastery
The Master Passion
The Cult of Violence.
The Struggle for Power.

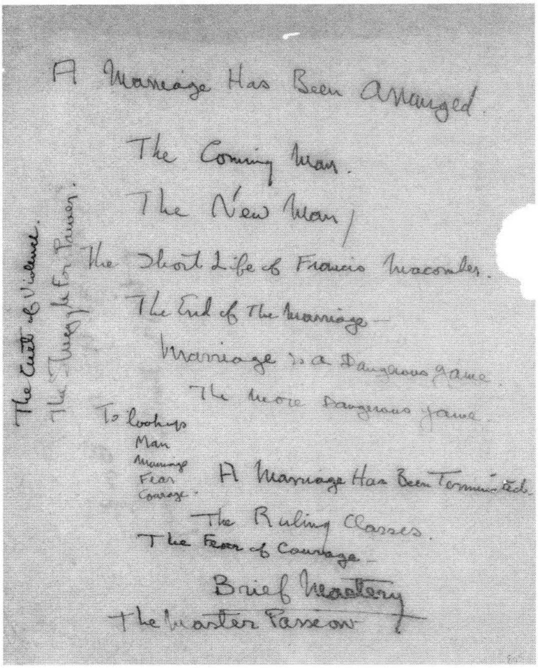

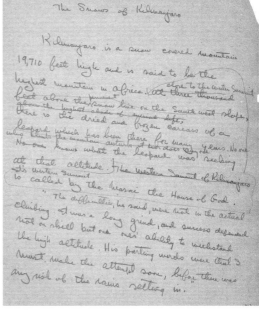

Figure 15. Hemingway's list of possible titles for "The Short Happy Life of Francis Macomber." Ernest Hemingway Collection, Manuscripts, Stories and Fragments, Item 692, page 1, at the John F. Kennedy Presidential Library and Museum, Boston, MA.

The Snows of Kilimanjaro

Kilimanjaro is a snow covered mountain 19,710 feet high and is said to be the highest mountain in Africa. Close to the western summit there is the dried and frozen carcass of a leopard. No one knows what the leopard was seeking at that altitude. Its western summit is called by the Masai the House of God.

"The difficulties, he said, were not in the actual climbing. It was a long grind, and success depended not on skill but on one's ability to withstand the high altitude. His parting words were that I must make the attempt soon, before there was any risk of the rains setting in."

Figure 16. Pencil manuscript draft of the epigraph for "The Snows of Kilimanjaro." Ernest Hemingway Collection, Manuscripts, Stories and Fragments, Item 704, page 1, at the John F. Kennedy Presidential Library and Museum, Boston, MA.

"The beer's nice and cool," the man said.

"It's lovely," the girl said.

"It's really an awfully simple operation, Jig," the man said. "It's not really an operation at all."

The girl looked at the ground the table legs rested on.

"I know you wouldn't mind it, Jig. It's really not anything. It's just to let the air in."

The girl did not say anything.

"I'll go with you and I'll stay with you all the time. They just let the air in and then it's all perfectly natural."

"Then what will we do afterward?"

"We'll be fine afterward. Just like we were before."

"What makes you think so?"

"That's the only thing that bothers us. It's the only thing that's made us unhappy."

The girl looked at the bead curtain, put her hand out and took hold of two of the strings of beads.

"And you think then we'll be all right and be happy."

"I know we will. You don't have to be afraid. I've known lots of people that have done it."

"So have I," said the girl. "And afterward they were all so happy."

"Well," the man said, "if you don't want to you don't have to. I wouldn't have you do it if you didn't want to. But I know it's perfectly simple."

"And you really want to?"

"I think it's the best thing to do. But I don't want you to do it if you don't really want to."

"And if I do it you'll be happy and things will be like they were and you'll love me?"

"I love you now. You know I love you."

"I know. But if I do it, then it will be nice again if I say things are like white elephants, and you'll like it?"

"I'll love it. I love it now but I just can't think about it. You know how I get when I worry."

"If I do it you won't ever worry?"

"I won't worry about that because it's perfectly simple."

"Then I'll do it. Because I don't care about me."

"What do you mean?"

"I don't care about me."

"Well, I care about you."

"Oh, yes. But I don't care about me. And I'll do it and then everything will be fine."

"I don't want you to do it if you feel that way."

The girl stood up and walked to the end of the station. Across, on the other side, were fields of grain and trees along the banks of the Ebro. Far away, beyond the river, were mountains. The shadow of a cloud moved across the field of grain and she saw the river through the trees.

"And we could have all this," she said. "And we could have everything and every day we make it more impossible."

"What did you say?"

"I said we could have everything."

"We can have everything."

"No, we can't."

"We can have the whole world."

"No, we can't."

"We can go everywhere."

"No, we can't. It isn't ours any more."

"It's ours."

"No, it isn't. And once they take it away, you never get it back."

"But they haven't taken it away."

"We'll wait and see."

"Come on back in the shade," he said. "You mustn't feel that way."

"I don't feel any way," the girl said. "I just know things."

"I don't want you to do anything that you don't want to do—"

"Nor that isn't good for me," she said. "I know. Could we have another beer?"

"All right. But you've got to realize—"

"I realize," the girl said. "Can't we maybe stop talking?"

They sat down at the table and the girl looked across at the hills on the dry side of the valley and the man looked at her and at the table.

"You've got to realize," he said, "that I don't want you to do it if you don't want to. I'm perfectly willing to go through with it if it means anything to you."

"Doesn't it mean anything to you? We could get along."

"Of course it does. But I don't want anybody but you. I don't want any one else. And I know it's perfectly simple."

"Yes, you know it's perfectly simple."

"It's all right for you to say that, but I do know it."

"Would you do something for me now?"

"I'd do anything for you."

"Would you please please please please please please please stop talking?"

He did not say anything but looked at the bags against the wall of the station. There were labels on them from all the hotels where they had spent nights.

"But I don't want you to," he said, "I don't care anything about it."

"I'll scream," the girl said.

The woman came out through the curtains with two glasses of beer and put them down on the damp felt pads. "The train comes in five minutes," she said.

"What did she say?" asked the girl.

"That the train is coming in five minutes."

The girl smiled brightly at the woman, to thank her.

"I'd better take the bags over to the other side of the station," the man said. She smiled at him.

"All right. Then come back and we'll finish the beer."

He picked up the two heavy bags and carried them around the station to the other tracks. He looked up the tracks but could not see the train. Coming back, he walked through the barroom, where people waiting for the train were drinking. He drank an Anis at the bar and looked at the people. They were all waiting reasonably for the train. He went out through the bead curtain. She was sitting at the table and smiled at him.

"Do you feel better?" he asked.

"I feel fine," she said. "There's nothing wrong with me. I feel fine."

11a.

Item 472, Ernest Hemingway Collection, John F. Kennedy Library and Museum, Boston. Untitled ink manuscript on a theme similar to "Hills Like White Elephants." Begins "The train moved through the hot valley. . . ."

The train moved through the hot valley. ~~Heads were out the open windows. Ripe grain grew~~ Fields of ripe grain started at the rails to stretch across the valley. Far off beyond the brown ~~grain~~ fields a line of trees ~~marked~~ grew along the course of the Ebro and beyond the river rose abruptly the ~~white~~ mysterious White Mountains.

We had called them that as soon as we saw them. To be disgustingly accurate I had said, "Look at those goddamn White Mountains."

Hadley said, "They are the most mysterious things I have ever seen."

They were white mountains, not white with snow or any ~~other~~ artificial aid but white themselves ~~of white clay~~ furrowed and wrinkled by the rains. ~~like all good mountains and~~ They were very ~~wonderful~~ strange shapes and there were two ranges of them, one on each side of the broad brown and green valley of the Ebro. On a cloudy dark day they might have been gray ~~but in~~ as a white elephant is gray in a circus ~~side show~~ tent, but in the ~~July sun~~ heat they shown white as white elephants in the sun.

Heads stuck out of all the ~~windows~~ car windows. Up ahead I saw a mud built town.

"That's Caseta," the man at the next window said, "Where you get off."

We jumped down with the bags ~~into~~ onto the cindered switching yard and walked over rails and ~~turn tables~~ ties to tables set in the shade of the ~~rows~~ squat adobe railway restaurant. ~~building~~ There was a half hour until the express from Barcelona came through. The waitress came out with two tall beers through a great swinging rattan curtain and we sat and looked across at the mountains. The beers

were cool and there were beads of moisture on the glasses that grad-
ually slipped down and were absorbed by the felt saucers.

It had been a long hot trip from Pamplona. Saragossa was only
a half hour down the line and it seemed ~~it would have been~~ much
better sense ~~to stop over~~ to have gone on and stayed the night in
Saragossa ~~and then~~. Then we could go on to Madrid the next day.

While we talked the curtain blew out from the door, neatly
cleared the table, and on its return swing swept the beers ~~out~~ off their
felt pedestals onto the ground. It must have happened before because
the waitress was not astonished. She came out in her own good time,
listened to the explanation, reinforced and clarified as always in
Spain by all the occupants of nearby tables, witnesses volunteer inter-
preters and innocent bystanders, listened impassively ~~and~~ with her
hands in her apron and brought more beer.

The Barcelona express whistled, we picked up our bags and
made for the track. It came to a stop and we had that feeling of success that comes when in a crowd of people all waiting to mount you
are the ones before whom the door of the carriage halts. We got in at
the head of the crowd. The third class carriage was hot and full. People were standing in the aisle on the side away from the sun. Curtains
were pulled down ~~on~~ against the sun. There looked to be no places.
Next to the window on the sunbaking side were two empty places
but ~~the~~ a woman sitting opposite said they belonged to the Guardia
Civil. There was a soldier of the Guard sitting opposite. He waved
Hadley to the places. "Take them," he said. "Take them. We can
always make room."

We piled the two bags on the rack above our heads and sat down
making two of people who sat on each wooden bench facing in two
upright sweltering lines. There were two priests on our side and a
~~young~~ boy of about fifteen reading a dime novel ~~book~~ entitled "More
Man Than Curate," holding it carefully shielded so the fat boyish
faced priest next to him would not see the title. The priests both read
their breviaries.

The boy wore a straw hat was just beginning to shave and came
from Minorca. This came out later when his father came in from the
aisle and the boy acted as interpreter for him. The father could speak
only a very little Spanish. This was all later though. At the start there
was only the baking hot compartment, the boy and the Guardia Civil

soldier reading their ten centime Anema novels the priests the lady traveller from Saragossa who aimed a cup

11b.

Item 473, Ernest Hemingway Collection, John F. Kennedy Library and Museum, Boston. Titled pencil manuscript of "Hills Like White Elelphants" with pencil note by Ernest Hemingway at end: "Mss for Pauline—well, well, well." Signed with Paris address.

Ernest Hemingway
Guaranty Trust Co. of N.Y.
11 rue des Italiens
Paris

Hills Like White Elephants
A Story

The hills across the valley of the Ebro were long and white. ~~The station was~~ On this side there was no shade ~~in the country sight~~ and no trees and the station was between two ~~lines of railway tracks~~ lines of rails in the sun. Close against the side of the station there was the ~~shade~~ warm shadow of the building and ~~a door~~ a curtain ~~opened into the bar~~ made of ~~heavy~~ strings of bamboo beads hung across the open door into the bar to keep out flies. The American and the girl with him sat at a table in the shade outside the building.

It was very hot and the Express from Barcelona ~~train did not~~ would come ~~from Zaragosa for an hour forty minutes~~ in forty minutes. It stopped at this junction for two minutes and went on to Madrid.

"What should we drink?" the girl asked. She had taken off her hat and put it on the table.

"It's pretty hot," the man said.

"Let's drink beer."

"Dos cervezas," the man said into the curtain. ~~A girl came out with two.~~

"Big ones?" ~~Some one~~ a ~~girl~~ woman asked from the doorway.

"Yes. Two big ones."

The ~~girl~~ woman brought two glasses of beer and ~~set them on~~ two felt pads. She ~~put the beer glasses on the felt pads and~~ put the felt pads and the beer glasses on the table and looked at the man and the girl. The girl was looking off at the line of hills. They were white ~~and~~ in the sun and the country was brown and dry.

"They look like white elephants," she said.

"I've never seen one," the man drank his beer.

"No you wouldn't have."

"I might have," the man said. "Just because you say I wouldn't have doesn't prove anything."

The girl looked at the bead curtain. "They've painted something on it," she said. "What does it say?"

"Anis del Toro. It's a drink."

"Could we try it?"

The man called "Listen!" through the curtain ~~to.~~ The ~~girl~~ woman came out from the bar.

"Four reales ~~Sixty centimes~~," she said.

"We want two Anis del Toro."

"With water?"

"Do you want it with water?"

"I don't know," the girl said. "Is it good with water?"

"Its ~~about~~ all right."

"You want them with water?" asked the woman.

"Yes, with water."

"It tastes like licorice," the girl said.

"That's the way with everything."

"Yes," said the girl. "Everything tastes of licorice. Especially all the things you've waited so long for like absinthe."

"Oh cut it out."

"You started it," the girl said. "I was being amused. I was having a fine time."

"Well let's try and have a fine time."

"All right. I was trying. I said the mountains looked like white elephants. Wasn't that bright?"

~~The man did not say~~

"That was bright."

"I wanted to try this new drink. That's all we do isn't it? Look at things and try new drinks."

"I guess so."

The girl looked across at the hills.

"They're lovely hills," she said. "The don't really look like white elephants. I just meant the coloring of their skin through the trees."

"Should we have another beer?"

"All right." ~~Its nice and cool.~~"

The warm wind ~~came through the~~ blew the bead curtain against the table.

~~"It's good."~~

"~~It's~~ The beer's nice and cool," the man said.

"It's lovely," the girl said.

"It's really an awfully simple operation," the man said. "It's not really an operation at all."

The girl looked ~~away~~ at the ground the table legs rested on.

"I know you wouldn't mind it, Jig. It's really ~~is~~ not anything. It's just to let the air in."

The girl did not say anything.

"I'll go with you and I'll stay with you all the time. They just let the air in and then it's all perfectly natural.["]

"Then what will we do afterwards?"

"We'll be fine afterwards. Just like we were before."

"~~Why do~~ What makes you think so?"

"That's the only thing that bothers us. It's the only thing that's made us unhappy."

The girl looked ~~away~~ at the bead curtains, ~~and~~ put her hand out and took hold of two of the strings of beads.

"And you think then we'll be all right and be happy?"

"I know we will. You don't have to be afraid. I've known lots of people that have done it."

"So have I," said the girl. "And afterwards they were all so happy."

"Well," the man said. "If you don't want to you don't have to. I wouldn't have you do it if you didn't want to. But I know it's perfectly simple."

"And you really want to?"

"I think it's the best thing to do. But I don't want you to do it if you don't really want to."

"And if I do it you'll be happy and things will be like they were and you'll love me?"

"I love you now. You know I love you."

"I know. But if I do it then it will be nice again if I say things are like white elephants and you'll like it?"

"I'll love it. I love it now but I just can't think about it. You know how I get when I worry."

"If I do it you won't ever worry?"

"I won't worry about that because it's perfectly simple."

"Then I'll do it. Because I don't care about me."

"What do you mean?"

"I don't care about me."

"~~But~~ Well I care about you."

"Oh yes. But I don't care about me. And I'll do it and then everything will be fine."

"I don't want you to do it if you feel that way."

The girl stood up and walked to the end of the station. Across on the other side ~~was the~~ were fields of grain and trees along the banks of the Ebro. Far away beyond the river were mountains. The shadow of a cloud moved across the field of grain and she saw the river through the trees. "We could have all this," she said. "And we could have everything and every day we make it more impossible."

"What did you say?"

"I said we could have everything."

"We can have everything."

"No we can't."

"We can have the whole world."

"No we can't."

"We can go everywhere."

"No we can't. It isn't ours anymore."

"It is ours."

"No it isn't and once they take it away you never get it back."

"But they haven't taken it away."

"We'll wait and see."

"Come on back in the shade," he said. "You mustn't feel that way."

"I don't feel any way," the girl said. "I just know things."

"I don't want you to do anything that you don't want to do—"

"No that isn't good for me," she said. "I know. Could we have another beer?"

"All right. But you've got to ~~must~~ realize—"

"I realize," the girl said. "Can't we maybe stop talking?"

They sat down at the table and the girl looked across at the hills on the dry side of the valley and the man looked at her and at the table.

"You've got to realize," he said, "that I don't want you to do it if you don't want to. I'm perfectly willing to go through with it if it means anything to you."

"Doesn't it mean anything to you? ~~Three of us~~ We could get along."

"Of course it does. ~~But it's just a question of expediency~~ But I don't want anybody but you. I don't want anyone else. ~~I know how the other thing is~~. And I know it's perfectly simple."

"Yes you know it's perfectly simple."

"It's all right for you to say that but I do know it."

"Would you do something for me now?"

"I'd do anything for you."

"Would you please please please please please please please stop talking?"

He did not say anything but looked at ~~her~~ the bags against the wall of the station. There were ~~stickers~~ labels on them from all the hotels where they had ~~spent nights~~ stayed.

"But I don't want you to," he said. "I don't care anything about it—" ~~Three of us could get~~

"I'll scream," the girl said.

The woman came out through the curtain with two glasses of beer and put them on the damp felt pads. "The train comes in five minutes," she said.

"What did she say?" asked the girl.

"That the train is coming in ~~ten~~ five minutes."

The girl smiled brightly at the woman to thank her.

"I'd better take the bags over to the other side of the station," the man said. She smiled at him.

"All right. Then come back and we'll finish the beer."

He picked up the two heavy bags and carried them around the station to the other tracks. He looked up the tracks but could not see the train. Coming back he walked through the bar room where people waiting for the train were drinking. He drank an anis at the bar and looked at the people. ~~There must be some actual world. There must be some place you could touch where people were calm and reasonable.~~ They were all waiting reasonably for the train. ~~Once it had all been as simple as this bar~~. He went out through the bead curtain. She was sitting at the table and smiled at him.

"Do you feel better?" he asked.

"I feel fine," she said. "There's nothing wrong with me. I feel fine."

Mss. For Pauline—
<u>well, well, well,</u>

III

12.

The Sea Change

1931

"All right," said the man. "What about it?"

"No," said the girl, "I can't."

"You mean you won't."

"I can't," said the girl. "That's all that I mean."

"You mean that you won't."

"All right," said the girl. "You have it your own way."

"I don't have it my own way. I wish to God I did."

"You did for a long time," the girl said.

It was early, and there was no one in the café except the barman and these two who sat together at a table in the corner. It was the end of the summer and they were both tanned, so that they looked out of place in Paris. The girl wore a tweed suit, her skin was a smooth golden brown, her blonde hair was cut short and grew beautifully away from her forehead. The man looked at her.

"I'll kill her," he said.

"Please don't," the girl said. She had very fine hands and the man looked at them. They were slim and brown and very beautiful.

"I will. I swear to God I will."

"It won't make you happy."

"Couldn't you have gotten into something else? Couldn't you have gotten into some other jam?"

"It seems not," the girl said. "What are you going to do about it?"

"I told you."

"No; I mean really."

"I don't know," he said. She looked at him and put out her hand. "Poor old Phil," she said. He looked at her hands, but he did not touch her hand with his.

"No, thanks," he said.

"It doesn't do any good to say I'm sorry?"

"No."

"Nor to tell you how it is?"

"I'd rather not hear."

"I love you very much."

"Yes, this proves it."

"I'm sorry," she said, "if you don't understand."

"I understand. That's the trouble. I understand."

"You do," she said. "That makes it worse, of course."

"Sure," he said, looking at her. "I'll understand all the time. All day and all night. Especially all night. I'll understand. You don't have to worry about that."

"I'm sorry," she said.

"If it was a man—"

"Don't say that. It wouldn't be a man. You know that. Don't you trust me?"

"That's funny," he said. "Trust you. That's really funny."

"I'm sorry," she said. "That's all I seem to say. But when we do understand each other there's no use to pretend we don't."

"No," he said. "I suppose not."

"I'll come back if you want me."

"No. I don't want you."

Then they did not say anything for a while.

"You don't believe I love you, do you?" the girl asked.

"Let's not talk rot," the man said.

"Don't you really believe I love you?"

"Why don't you prove it?"

"You didn't use to be that way. You never asked me to prove anything. That isn't polite."

"You're a funny girl."

"You're not. You're a fine man and it breaks my heart to go off and leave you—"

"You have to, of course."

"Yes," she said. "I have to and you know it."

He did not say anything and she looked at him and put her hand out again. The barman was at the far end of the bar. His face was white and so was his jacket. He knew these two and thought them a handsome young couple. He had seen many handsome young couples break up and new couples form that were never so handsome long. He was not thinking about this, but about a horse. In half an hour he could send across the street to find if the horse had won.

"Couldn't you just be good to me and let me go?" the girl asked.

"What do you think I'm going to do?"

Two people came in the door and went up to the bar.

"Yes, sir," the barman took the orders.

"You can't forgive me? When you know about it?" the girl asked.

"No."

"You don't think things we've had and done should make any difference in understanding?"

"'Vice is a monster of such fearful mien,'" the young man said bitterly, "that to be something or other needs but to be seen. Then we something, something, then embrace." He could not remember the words. "I can't quote," he said.

"Let's not say vice," she said. "That's not very polite."

"Perversion," he said.

"James," one of the clients addressed the barman, "you're looking very well."

"You're looking very well yourself," the barman said.

"Old James," the other client said. "You're fatter, James."

"It's terrible," the barman said, "the way I put it on."

"Don't neglect to insert the brandy, James," the first client said.

"No, sir," said the barman. "Trust me."

The two at the bar looked over at the two at the table, then looked back at the barman again. Towards the barman was the comfortable direction.

"I'd like it better if you didn't use words like that," the girl said. "There's no necessity to use a word like that."

"What do you want me to call it?"

"You don't have to call it. You don't have to put any name to it."

"That's the name for it."

"No," she said. "We're made up of all sorts of things. You've known that. You've used it well enough."

"You don't have to say that again."

"Because that explains it to you."

"All right," he said. "All right."

"You mean all wrong. I know. It's all wrong. But I'll come back. I told you I'd come back. I'll come back right away."

"No, you won't."

"I'll come back."

"No, you won't. Not to me."

"You'll see."

"Yes," he said. "That's the hell of it. You probably will."

"Of course I will."

"Go on, then."

"Really?" She could not believe him, but her voice was happy.

"Go on," his voice sounded strange to him. He was looking at her, at the way her mouth went and the curve of her cheek bones, at her eyes and at the way her hair grew on her forehead and at the edge of her ear and at her neck.

"Not really. Oh, you're too sweet," she said. "You're too good to me."

"And when you come back tell me all about it." His voice sounded very strange. He did not recognize it. She looked at him quickly. He was settled into something.

"You want me to go?" she asked seriously.

"Yes," he said seriously. "Right away." His voice was not the same, and his mouth was very dry. "Now," he said.

She stood up and went out quickly. She did not look back at him. He watched her go. He was not the same-looking man as he had been before he had told her to go. He got up from the table, picked up the two checks and went over to the bar with them.

"I'm a different man, James," he said to the barman. "You see in me quite a different man."

"Yes, sir?" said James.

"Vice," said the brown young man, "is a very strange thing, James." He looked out the door. He saw her going down the street. As he looked in the glass, he saw he was really quite a different-looking man. The other two at the bar moved down to make room for him.

"You're right there, sir," James said.

The other two moved down a little more, so that he would be quite comfortable. The young man saw himself in the mirror behind the bar. "I said I was a different man, James," he said. Looking into the mirror he saw that this was quite true.

"You look very well, sir," James said. "You must have had a very good summer."

12a.

Item 679, Ernest Hemingway Collection, John F. Kennedy Library and Museum, Boston. Titled handwritten pencil manuscript with ink corrections. Signed at top of the first page "Ernest Hemingway".
[in the upper left corner:] Ernest Hemingway

~~a man and a girl sat together~~
~~Two people sat together at a table in a café in the rue Delambre.~~
~~The café was~~

The Sea Change

It was early and there was no one in the café except the barman and these two who sat together at a table in the corner.

"All right," said the man. "What about it?"

"No," said the girl. "I can't."

"You mean you won't."

"~~If you~~ can't," said the girl. "That's ~~what I said and that's what I mean.~~ all that I mean."

"You mean you won't."

"All right," said the girl "you have it your way."

"I don't have it my own way. I wish to God I did."

"You did for a long time," the girl said.

It was the end of the summer and they were both tanned so that they looked out of place in Paris. The girl wore a tweed suit, her skin was a smooth gold brown, her blonde hair was cut short and ~~the sun had varied the color~~ grew beautifully away from her forehead. She had beautiful hands and her face and throat were tanned, her mouth was a little wide but a lovely shape and her cheek bones a little high but her face very handsome and her body slim. The man was very browned by the sun at the seashore. He was good looking too and he looked across the table at the girl.

~~She leaned forward, her hands~~

~~They were both tanned from the~~
~~It was the end of the summer and they were both tanned. The~~
~~girl's skin was an even gold brown, her hair was lightened by the sun~~
~~and she was slim in a tweed suit.~~

It was the end of the summer and they were both tanned so that they looked out of place in Paris. The barman's face was white and so was his jacket. The girl was nice to look at, her skin smooth gold brown ~~skin, tweed suit, slim, fine hands, fine profile the mouth a little wide but with a lovely shape and the cheek bones a little high but very handsome and~~ her hair, cut short, colored too by the sun.

The man tanned darker from the seashore very handsome too. Too handsome very. He looked across the table at the girl.

In one year Charles Fiske came of age. [Circled on back of page.]

~~In the fall of the year the~~

~~The summer was ended by~~

~~They were a brother and sister who lived together and loved each other very much. This was considered admirable in the old days.~~

~~She was good looking, with a gold tanned skin her skin was tanned a gold that meant that care had been taken in the tanning and her hair was becomingly streaked by the sun. She wore a tweed suit, her body was slim and as she leaned forward her profile was face was handsome. The man was good looking too. He was tanned brown from the sea shore. Together they made what used to be called a handsome young couple. The man looked at her.~~

"I'll kill her," he said.

"Please don't," the girl said. She had very fine hands and the man looked at them. They were slim and brown and very beautiful.

"I will. I swear to God I will."

"It won't make you happy."

"Couldn't you have gotten into something else? Couldn't you have gotten into some other jam?"

"It seems not," the girl said. "What are you going to do about it?"

"I told you."

"No. I mean really."

"I don't know," he said. She looked at him and put out her hand.

"Poor old boy," she said. He looked at her and at her hand but he did not touch her hand with his.

"No thanks," he said. ~~"I'd better not have that."~~

"It doesn't do any good to say I'm sorry?"

"No," he said.

"Nor to tell you how it is?"

"I'd rather not hear."

"I love you very much."

"Yes, this proves it."

"I'm sorry," she said, "if you don't understand."

"I understand. That's the trouble. I understand."

"You do," she said. "That makes it worse of course."

"Sure," he said looking at her. ~~He still ate [fed on] her up with his eyes when he looked at her.~~ "I'll understand all the time. All day and all night. Especially all night. I'll understand. You don't have to worry about that."

"I'm sorry," she said.

"If it was a man—"

"Don't say that. It wouldn't be a man. You know that. Don't you trust me?"

"That's funny," he said. "Trust you. That's really funny."

"I'm sorry," she said. "That's all I seem to say. But when we do understand each other there's no use to pretend we don't."

"No," he said. "I suppose not."

"I'll come back if you want me."

"No. I don't want you."

Then they did not say anything for a long while.

"You don't believe I love you do you?" ~~she said~~ the girl asked.

"Let's not talk rot." The man said. His face was dark from the sun and his hair was dark but streaked by the sun a little too. He looked very healthy and you could not tell anything that went on inside from looking at him.

"Don't you really believe I love you?"

"Why don't you prove it?"

"You didn't use to be that way. You never asked me to prove anything. That isn't polite."

"You're a funny girl."

"You're not. You're a fine man and it breaks my heart to go off and leave you—"

"You have to of course."

"Yes," she said, "I have to and you know it."

He did not say anything and she looked at him and put her hand out again. The barman was at the far end of the bar. His face was white and so was his jacket. He knew these two and thought them a handsome young couple. He had seen many handsome young couples break up and ~~they never formed such~~ new couples formed that were never so handsome. He was not thinking about this though but about a horse or rather, he was thinking of a horse he had a bet on. In half an hour he could send across the street and find out if the horse had won.

"Couldn't you just be good to me and let me go?" the girl asked.

"What do you think I'm going to do?"

Two people came in the door of the café and went up to the bar.

"Yes, sir," the barman took the orders.

"You can't forgive me? When you know about it?" the girl asked him.

"No."

"You don't think things we've had and done should make any difference in understanding?"

"Vice is a monster of such fearful mien," the young man said very bitterly, "that to be something or other needs but to be seen. Then we something ~~or other~~ something ~~or other~~ then embrace" he ~~tried to quote~~ could not remember the words. "I can't quote," he said.

"Let's not say vice," she said. "That's not very polite."

"Perversion," he said.

"James," one of the clients addressed the barman~~tender~~. "You're looking very well."

"Thank you sir," said the barman~~tender~~. "You're looking very well yourself."

"Old James," said the other client said. "You're fatter, James."

"It's terrible," the barman said, "the way I put it on."

"Don't neglect to insert the brandy, James," the first client said.

"No, sir," said the barman. "Trust me."

The two at the bar looked over at the two at the table then

looked ~~at each other and~~ back at the barman again. ~~It~~ Toward the barman was the comfortable direction.

"I'd like it better if you didn't use words like that," the girl said. "There's no necessity to use a word like that."

"What do you want me to call it?"

"You don't have to call it. You don't have to put any name to it."

"That's the name for it."

"No," she said. "We're made up of all sorts of things. You've known that. You've used it well enough."

"You don't have to say that again."

"Because that explains it to you."

"All right," he said. "All right."

"You mean all wrong. ~~you mean. Poor old~~ I know. It's all wrong. But I'll come back. I told you I'd come back. I'll come back right away."

"No you won't."

"I'll come back."

"No you won't. Not to me."

"You'll see."

"Yes," he said. "That's the hell of it. You probably will."

"Of course I will."

"Go on then."

"Really?"

"Go on." His voice sounded strange to him. He was looking at her at the way her mouth went and the curve of her cheek bones, at her eyes and at the way her hair went on her forehead.

"Not really," she said. "Oh you're too sweet. You're too good to me."

"And when you come back tell me all about it." His voice sounded very strange.

She looked at him quickly. He was settled into something.

"You want me to go?" she asked seriously.

"Yes," he said seriously. "Right away." His voice was not the same and his mouth was very dry. "Now," he said.

She stood up and went out quickly. She did not look back at him. He watched her go. He was not the same looking man as before he had told her to go. He got up from the table and picked up the two checks and went over to the bar with them.

"I'm a different man, James," he said to the barman. "You see in me quite a different man."

"Yes sir?" said James.

"Vice," said the brown young man, "is a very strange thing James." He looked out the door. ~~He couldn't see her.~~ She was going down the street. He was really quite a different looking man. The other two at the bar moved down to make room for him.

"You're right there, Sir," James said.

The other two moved down a little more so that he would be quite comfortable. The young man saw himself in the mirror behind the bar. ~~He saw there that what he had said was quite true.~~

"I said I was a different man, James," he said. Looking into the mirror he saw that this was quite true.

"You look very well Sir," James said. "You must have had a very good summer."

12b.

Item 681, Ernest Hemingway Collection, John F. Kennedy Library and Museum, Boston. Untitled handwritten ink manuscript fragment with an alternate ending to "The Sea Change." The fragment appears at the end of a four-page manuscript that contains other story fragments.

"What do the punks drink James? What can you recommend to a recent convert?"

~~"Do you want a~~

~~"What were you drinking?"~~ "Do you want another whiskey-soda?"

"Whatever they ~~punks~~ drink, James. Take a look at me and mix whatever you like."

"You look ~~good fine~~ very good," James said. "You have a fine tan."

"I can see in the glass, James," the young man said. "I can see in the glass very clearly."

13.

A Way You'll Never Be

1933

The attack had gone across the field, been held up by machine-gun fire from the sunken road and from the group of farm houses, encountered no resistance in the town, and reached the bank of the river. Coming along the road on a bicycle, getting off to push the machine when the surface of the road became too broken, Nicholas Adams saw what had happened by the position of the dead.

They lay alone or in clumps in the high grass of the field and along the road, their pockets out, and over them were flies and around each body or group of bodies were the scattered papers.

In the grass and the grain, beside the road, and in some places scattered over the road, there was much material: a field kitchen, it must have come over when things were going well; many of the calf-skin-covered haversacks, stick bombs, helmets, rifles, sometimes one butt-up, the bayonet stuck in the dirt, they had dug quite a little at the last; stick bombs, helmets, rifles, intrenching tools, ammunition boxes, star-shell pistols, their shells scattered about, medical kits, gas masks, empty gas-mask cans, a squat, tripodded machine gun in a nest of empty shells, full belts protruding from the boxes, the water-cooling can empty and on its side, the breech block gone, the crew in odd positions, and around them, in the grass, more of the typical papers.

There were mass prayer books, group postcards showing the machine-gun unit standing in ranked and ruddy cheerfulness as in a football picture for a college annual; now they were humped and swollen in the grass; propaganda postcards showing a soldier in Austrian uniform bending a woman backward over a bed; the figures were impressionistically drawn; very attractively depicted and had nothing in common with actual rape in which the woman's skirts are pulled over her head to smother her, one comrade sometimes sitting upon the head. There were many of these inciting cards which had evidently been issued just before the offensive. Now they were scattered with the smutty postcards, photographic; the small photographs of village girls by village photographers, the occasional pictures of children, and the letters, letters, letters. There was always much paper about the dead and the débris of this attack was no exception.

These were new dead and no one had bothered with anything but their pockets. Our own dead, or what he thought of, still, as our own dead, were surprisingly few, Nick noticed. Their coats had been opened too and their pockets were out, and they showed, by their positions, the manner and the skill of the attack. The hot weather had swollen them all alike regardless of nationality.

The town had evidently been defended, at the last, from the line of the sunken road and there had been few or no Austrians to fall back into it. There were only three bodies in the street and they looked to have been killed running. The houses of the town were broken by the shelling and the street had much rubble of plaster and mortar and there were broken beams, broken tiles, and many holes, some of them yellow-edged from the mustard gas. There were many pieces of shell, and shrapnel balls were scattered in the rubble. There was no one in the town at all.

Nick Adams had seen no one since he had left Fornaci, although, riding along the road through the over-foliaged country, he had seen guns hidden under screens of mulberry leaves to the left of the road, noticing them by the heat-waves in the air above the leaves where the sun hit the metal. Now he went on through the town, surprised to find it deserted, and came out on the low road beneath the bank of the river. Leaving the town there was a bare open space where the road slanted down and he could see the placid reach of the river and the low curve of the opposite bank and the whitened, sun-baked mud where the Austrians had dug.

It was all very lush and over-green since he had seen it last and becoming historical had made no change in this, the lower river.

The battalion was along the bank to the left. There was a series of holes in the top of the bank with a few men in them. Nick noticed where the machine guns were posted and the signal rockets in their racks. The men in the holes in the side of the bank were sleeping. No one challenged. He went on and as he came around a turn in the mud bank a young second lieutenant with a stubble of beard and red-rimmed, very blood-shot eyes pointed a pistol at him.

"Who are you?"

Nick told him.

"How do I know this?"

Nick showed him the tessera with photograph and identification and the seal of the third army. He took hold of it.

"I will keep this."

"You will not," Nick said. "Give me back the card and put your gun away. There. In the holster."

"How am I to know who you are?"

"The tessera tells you."

"And if the tessera is false? Give me that card."

"Don't be a fool," Nick said cheerfully. "Take me to your company commander."

"I should send you to battalion headquarters."

"All right," said Nick. "Listen, do you know the Captain Paravicini? The tall one with the small mustache who was an architect and speaks English?"

"You know him?"

"A little."

"What company does he command?"

"The second."

"He is commanding the battalion."

"Good," said Nick. He was relieved to know that Para was all right. "Let us go to the battalion."

As Nick had left the edge of the town three shrapnel had burst high and to the right over one of the wrecked houses and since then there had been no shelling. But the face of this officer looked like the face of a man during a bombardment. There was the same tightness and the voice did not sound natural. His pistol made Nick nervous.

"Put it away," he said. "There's the whole river between them and you."

"If I thought you were a spy I would shoot you now," the second lieutenant said.

"Come on," said Nick. "Let us go to the battalion." This officer made him very nervous.

The Captain Paravicini, acting major, thinner and more English-looking than ever, rose when Nick saluted from behind the table in the dugout that was battalion headquarters.

"Hello," he said. "I didn't know you. What are you doing in that uniform?"

"They've put me in it."

"I am very glad to see you, Nicolo."

"Right. You look well. How was the show?"

"We made a very fine attack. Truly. A very fine attack. I will show you. Look."

He showed on the map how the attack had gone.

"I came from Fornaci," Nick said. "I could see how it had been. It was very good."

"It was extraordinary. Altogether extraordinary. Are you attached to the regiment?"

"No. I am supposed to move around and let them see the uniform."

"How odd."

"If they see one American uniform that is supposed to make them believe others are coming."

"But how will they know it is an American uniform?"

"You will tell them."

"Oh. Yes, I see. I will send a corporal with you to show you about and you will make a tour of the lines."

"Like a bloody politician," Nick said.

"You would be much more distinguished in civilian clothes. They are what is really distinguished."

"With a homburg hat," said Nick.

"Or with a very furry fedora."

"I'm supposed to have my pockets full of cigarettes and

postal cards and such things," Nick said. "I should have a musette full of chocolate. These I should distribute with a kind word and a pat on the back. But there weren't any cigarettes and postcards and no chocolate. So they said to circulate around anyway."

"I'm sure your appearance will be very heartening to the troops."

"I wish you wouldn't," Nick said. "I feel badly enough about it as it is. In principle, I would have brought you a bottle of brandy."

"In principle," Para said and smiled, for the first time, showing yellowed teeth. "Such a beautiful expression. Would you like some grappa?"

"No, thank you," Nick said.

"It hasn't any ether in it."

"I can taste that still," Nick remembered suddenly and completely.

"You know I never knew you were drunk until you started talking coming back in the camions."

"I was stinking in every attack," Nick said.

"I can't do it," Para said. "I took it in the first show, the very first show, and it only made me very upset and then frightfully thirsty."

"You don't need it."

"You're much braver in an attack than I am."

"No," Nick said. "I know how I am and I prefer to get stinking. I'm not ashamed of it."

"I've never seen you drunk."

"No?" said Nick. "Never? Not when we rode from Mestre to Portogrande that night and I wanted to go to sleep and used the bicycle for a blanket and pulled it up under my chin?"

"That wasn't in the lines."

"Let's not talk about how I am," Nick said. "It's a subject I know too much about to want to think about it any more."

"You might as well stay here a while," Paravicini said. "You can take a nap if you like. They didn't do much to this in the bombardment. It's too hot to go out yet."

"I suppose there is no hurry."

"How are you really?"

"I'm fine. I'm perfectly all right."

"No. I mean really."

"I'm all right. I can't sleep without a light of some sort. That's all I have now."

"I said it should have been trepanned. I'm no doctor but I know that."

"Well, they thought it was better to have it absorb, and that's what I got. What's the matter? I don't seem crazy to you, do I?"

"You seem in top-hole shape."

"It's a hell of a nuisance once they've had you certified as nutty," Nick said. "No one ever has any confidence in you again."

"I would take a nap, Nicolo," Paravicini said. "This isn't battalion headquarters as we used to know it. We're just waiting to be pulled out. You oughtn't to go out in the heat now—it's silly. Use that bunk."

"I might just lie down," Nick said.

Nick lay on the bunk. He was very disappointed that he felt this way and more disappointed, even, that it was so obvious to Captain Paravicini. This was not as large a dugout as the one where that platoon of the class of 1899, just out at the front, got hysterics during the bombardment before the attack, and Para had had him walk them two at a time outside to show them nothing would happen, he wearing his own chin strap tight across his mouth to keep his lips quiet. Knowing they could not hold it when they took it. Knowing it was all a bloody balls—if he can't stop crying, break his nose to give him something else to think about. I'd shoot one but it's too late now. They'd all be worse. Break his nose. They've put it back to five-twenty. We've only got four minutes more. Break that other silly bugger's nose and kick his silly ass out of here. Do you think they'll go over? If they don't, shoot two and try to scoop the others out some way. Keep behind them, sergeant. It's no use to walk ahead and find there's nothing coming behind you. Bail them out as you go. What a bloody balls. All right. That's right. Then, looking at the watch, in that quiet tone, that valuable quiet tone, "Savoia." Making it cold, no time to get it, he couldn't find his own after the cave-in, one whole end had caved in; it was that started them; making it cold up that slope the only time he hadn't done it stinking. And after they came back the *teleferica* house burned, it seemed, and some of the wounded got down four days later and some did not get down, but we went up and we went back and we came down—we always came down. And there was Gaby Delys, oddly enough, with feathers on; you called me baby doll a year ago tadada you said that I was rather nice to know tadada with feathers on, with feathers off, the great Gaby, and my name's Harry Pilcer, too, we used to step out of the far side of the taxis when it got steep going up the hill and he could see that hill every night when he dreamed with Sacré Coeur, blown white, like a soap bubble. Sometimes his girl was there and sometimes she was with some one else and he could not understand that, but those were the nights the river ran so much wider and stiller than it should and outside of Fossalta there was a low house painted yellow with willows all around it and a low stable and there was a canal, and he had been there a thousand times and never seen it, but there it was every night as plain as the hill, only it frightened him. That house meant more than anything and every night he had it. That was what he needed but it frightened him especially when the boat lay there quietly in the willows on the canal, but the banks weren't like this river. It was all lower, as it was at Portogrande, where they had seen them come wallowing across the flooded ground holding the rifles high until they fell with them in the water. Who ordered that one? If it didn't get so damned mixed up he could follow it all right. That was why he noticed everything in such detail to keep it all straight so he would know just where he was, but suddenly it confused without reason as now, he lying in a bunk at battalion headquarters, with Para commanding a battalion and he in a bloody American uniform. He sat up and looked around; they all watching him. Para was gone out. He lay down again.

The Paris part came earlier and he was not frightened of it except when she had gone off with some one else and the fear that they might take the same driver twice. That was what frightened about that. Never about the front. He never dreamed about the front now any more but what frightened him so that he could not get rid of it was that long yellow house and the different width of the river. Now he was back here at the river, he had gone through that same town, and there was no house. Nor was the river that way. Then where did he go each night and what was the peril, and why would he wake, soaking wet, more frightened than he had ever been in a bombardment, because of a house and a long stable and a canal?

He sat up; swung his legs carefully down; they stiffened any time they were out straight for long; returned the stares of the adjutant, the signallers and the two runners by the door and put on his cloth-covered trench helmet.

"I regret the absence of the chocolate, the postal cards and cigarettes," he said. "I am, however, wearing the uniform."

"The major is coming back at once," the adjutant said. In that army an adjutant is not a commissioned officer.

"The uniform is not very correct," Nick told them. "But it gives you the idea. There will be several millions of Americans here shortly."

"Do you think they will send Americans down here?" asked the adjutant.

"Oh, absolutely. Americans twice as large as myself, healthy, with clean hearts, sleep at night, never been wounded, never been blown up, never had their heads caved in, never been scared, don't drink, faithful to the girls they left behind them, many of them never had crabs, wonderful chaps. You'll see."

"Are you an Italian?" asked the adjutant.

"No, American. Look at the uniform. Spagnolini made it but it's not quite correct."

"A North or South American?"

"North," said Nick. He felt it coming on now. He would quiet down.

"But you speak Italian."

"Why not? Do you mind if I speak Italian? Haven't I a right to speak Italian?"

"You have Italian medals."

"Just the ribbons and the papers. The medals come later. Or you give them to people to keep and the people go away; or they are lost with your baggage. You can purchase others in Milan. It is the papers that are of importance. You must not feel badly about them. You will have some yourself if you stay at the front long enough."

"I am a veteran of the Eritrea campaign," said the adjutant stiffly. "I fought in Tripoli."

"It's quite something to have met you," Nick put out his hand. "Those must have been trying days. I noticed the ribbons. Were you, by any chance, on the Carso?"

"I have just been called up for this war. My class was too old."

"At one time I was under the age limit," Nick said. "But now I am reformed out of the war."

"But why are you here now?"

"I am demonstrating the American uniform," Nick said. "Don't you think it is very significant? It is a little tight in the collar but soon you will see untold millions wearing this uniform swarming like locusts. The grasshopper, you know, what we call the grasshopper in America, is really a locust. The true grasshopper is small and green and comparatively feeble. You must not, however, make a confusion with the seven-year locust or cicada which emits a peculiar sustained sound which at the moment I cannot recall. I try to recall it but I cannot. I can almost hear it and then it is quite gone. You will pardon me if I break off our conversation?"

"See if you can find the major," the adjutant said to one of the two runners. "I can see you have been wounded," he said to Nick.

"In various places," Nick said. "If you are interested in scars I can show you some very interesting ones but I would rather talk about grasshoppers. What we call grasshoppers that is; and what are, really, locusts. These insects at one time played a very important part in my life. It might interest you and you can look at the uniform while I am talking."

The adjutant made a motion with his hand to the second runner who went out.

"Fix your eyes on the uniform. Spagnolini made it, you know. You might as well look, too," Nick said to the signallers. "I really have no rank. We're under the American consul. It's perfectly all right for you to look. You can stare, if you like. I will tell you about the American locust. We always preferred one that we called the medium-brown. They last the best in the water and fish prefer them. The larger ones that fly making a noise somewhat similar to that produced by a rattlesnake rattling his rattlers, a very dry sound, have vivid colored wings, some are bright red, others yellow barred with black, but their wings go to pieces in the water and they make a very blowsy bait, while the medium-brown is a plump, compact, succulent hopper that I can recommend as far as one may well recommend something you gentlemen will probably never encounter. But I must insist that you will never gather a sufficient supply of these insects for a day's fishing by pursuing them with your hands or trying to hit them with a bat. That is sheer nonsense and a useless waste of time. I repeat, gentlemen, that you will get nowhere at it. The correct procedure, and one which should be taught all young officers at every small-arms course if I had anything to say about it, and who knows but what I will have, is the employment of a seine or net made of common mosquito netting. Two officers holding this length of netting at alternate ends, or let us say one at each end, stoop, hold the bottom extremity of the net in one hand and the top extremity in the other and run into the wind. The hoppers, flying with the wind, fly against the length of netting and are imprisoned in its folds. It is no trick at all to catch a very great quantity indeed, and no officer, in my opinion, should be without a length of mosquito netting suitable for the improvisation of one of these grasshopper seines. I hope I have made myself clear, gentlemen. Are there any questions? If there is anything in the course you do not understand please ask questions. Speak up. None? Then I would like to close on this note. In the words of that great soldier and gentleman, Sir Henry Wilson: Gentlemen, either you must govern or you must be governed. Let me repeat it. Gentlemen, there is one thing I would like to have you remember. One thing I would like you to take with you as you leave this room. Gentlemen, either you must govern—or you must be governed. That is all, gentlemen. Good-day."

He removed his cloth-covered helmet, put it on again and, stooping, went out the low entrance of the dugout. Para, accompanied by the two runners, was coming down the line of the sunken road. It was very hot in the sun and Nick removed the helmet.

"There ought to be a system for wetting these things," he said. "I shall wet this one in the river." He started up the bank.

"Nicolo," Paravicini called. "Nicolo. Where are you going?"

"I don't really have to go." Nick came down the slope, holding the helmet in his hands. "They're a damned nuisance wet or dry. Do you wear yours all the time?"

"All the time," said Para. "It's making me bald. Come inside." Inside Para told him to sit down.

"You know they're absolutely no damned good," Nick said. "I remember when they were a comfort when we first had them, but I've seen them full of brains too many times."

"Nicolo," Para said. "I think you should go back. I think it would be better if you didn't come up to the line until you had those supplies. There's nothing here for you to do. If you move around, even with something worth giving away, the men will group and that invites shelling. I won't have it."

"I know it's silly," Nick said. "It wasn't my idea. I heard the brigade was here so I thought I would see you or some one else I knew. I could have gone to Zenzon or to San Dona. I'd like to go to San Dona to see the bridge again."

"I won't have you circulating around to no purpose," Captain Paravicini said.

"All right," said Nick. He felt it coming on again.

"You understand?"

"Of course," said Nick. He was trying to hold it in.

"Anything of that sort should be done at night."

"Naturally," said Nick. He knew he could not stop it now.

"You see, I am commanding the battalion," Para said.

"And why shouldn't you be?" Nick said. Here it came. "You can read and write, can't you?"

"Yes," said Para gently.

"The trouble is you have a damned small battalion to command. As soon as it gets to strength again they'll give you back your company. Why don't they bury the dead? I've seen them now. I don't care about seeing them again. They can bury them any time as far as I'm concerned and it would be much better for you. You'll all get bloody sick."

"Where did you leave your bicycle?"

"Inside the last house."

"Do you think it will be all right?"

"Don't worry," Nick said. "I'll go in a little while."

"Lie down a little while, Nicolo."

"All right."

He shut his eyes, and in place of the man with the beard who looked at him over the sights of the rifle, quite calmly before squeezing off, the white flash and clublike impact, on his knees, hot-sweet choking, coughing it onto the rock while they went past him, he saw a long, yellow house with a low stable and the river much wider than it was and stiller. "Christ," he said, "I might as well go."

He stood up.

"I'm going, Para," he said. "I'll ride back now in the afternoon. If any supplies have come I'll bring them down tonight. If not I'll come at night when I have something to bring."

"It is still hot to ride," Captain Paravicini said.

"You don't need to worry," Nick said. "I'm all right now for quite a while. I had one then but it was easy. They're getting much better. I can tell when I'm going to have one because I talk so much."

"I'll send a runner with you."

"I'd rather you didn't. I know the way."

"You'll be back soon?"

"Absolutely."

"Let me send—"

"No," said Nick. "As a mark of confidence."

"Well, *ciao* then."

"*Ciao,*" said Nick. He started back along the sunken road toward where he had left the bicycle. In the afternoon the road would be shady once he had passed the canal. Beyond that there were trees on both sides that had not been shelled at all. It was on that stretch that, marching, they had once passed the Terza Savoia cavalry regiment riding in the snow with their lances. The horses' breath made plumes in the cold air. No, that was somewhere else. Where was that?

"I'd better get to that damned bicycle," Nick said to himself. "I don't want to lose the way to Fornaci."

13a.

Item 746a. Ernest Hemingway Collection, John F. Kennedy Library and Museum, Boston. Early untitled handwritten pencil manuscript for "A Way You'll Never Be," including much material that was cut from the final story.

The attack had gone across the field, been held up by machine gun fire from the sunken road and from the group of farmhouses, encountered no resistance in the town and reached the bank of the river. Coming along the road on a bicycle, getting off to push the machine when the surface of the road became too broken you could see what had happened by the position of the dead. They lay alone or in clumps in the high grass of the field and along the road, their pockets out, and over them were flies and around each body or group of bodies were the scattered papers. In the grass and the grain and beside the road where the dead lay were calfskin covered haversacks, helmets, stick bombs, rifles, ammunition, boxes, star shell pistols, the squat tapered machine guns and scattered all about were letters, mass-prayer books, group postcards showing the machine gun unit, ~~in which now~~ (whose members now lay in odd positions in the field), standing and kneeling in ranked and ruddy cheerfulness as in a ~~college~~ football picture for the college annual, propaganda postcards showing a soldier in Austrian uniform impressionistically drawn bending a woman backward over a bed, (all the figures in it were very attractively depicted); small photographs of girls by village photographers, letters in thin German script, ~~some~~ smutty postcards, official postcards; and letters, letters, letters. There was always much paper around the dead ~~and there were~~.

These were new dead and no one had bothered with anything but their pockets. Our own dead were surprisingly few, their coats had been opened too and their pockets were out. The hot weather had swollen them all regardless of nationality ~~whether they were the winners or losers~~. The town had evidently been defended from the line of the sunken road and there had been few or no Austrians to fall back into it. There were only three bodies in the street and they looked to have been killed running. The houses of the town were broken by the shelling and the street had much rubble, broken tile, many holes, some yellow-edged from the mustard gas. There were many pieces of shell and shrapnel balls ~~lay all about~~ were scattered in the rubble. ~~Like hail stones that had not melted in the heat.~~ There was no one in the town at all ~~although war material was scattered~~.

I had seen no one since I left Fornaci although, riding along the road through the over-foliaged country, I had seen guns hidden under screens of mulberry leaves to the left of the road, noticing them by the heatwaves in the air above the leaves where the sun hit the metal. [Note to "start here".] Now I went on through the town, surprised to find it deserted, and came out on the low road beneath the bank of the river. Leaving the town there was a bare open space where the road slanted down and I could see the placid reach of the river and the low curve of the opposite ~~shore~~ bank and the whitened, sunbaked mud where the Austrians had dug. It was all very lush and over-grown since I had seen it last and ~~history~~ becoming historical had made no change in this the lower river.

The battalion was along the bank to the left. There were a series of holes in the top of the bank with a few men in them. I saw where the machine guns were posted and noticed the rockets in their racks. The men in the holes in the side of the bank were sleeping. No one challenged me.

I came around a turn in the bank and a young second lieutenant with a stubble of beard and his eyes red rimmed and bloodshot pointed a pistol at me. As I had come out of the edge of the town three shrapnel had burst high and to the right over one of the wrecked houses and since then there had been no ~~shells~~ shelling; but the face of this officer looked like that of a man during a bombardment. His face had not recovered since the last shelling.

"Who are you?" he asked.

I told him.

"How do I know this?"

"Because I bloody well tell you so."

"That is not enough."

I showed him my tessera with photograph and identification. He took hold of it.

"I will keep this," he said.

"You will not ~~You're crazy~~," I told him. "Give me back that card and put your gun away. There. In the leather holster."

"How am I to know who you are?"

"The tessera tells you."

"Give me that card."

"Don't be ~~crazy~~ a fool," I said. "Take me to your company commander."

"I should send you to battalion headquarters."

"Take me to the captain Paravicini. The tall one with the little mustache who was an architect and speaks English."

"You know him?"

"A little."

"What company does he command?"

"The second."

"He is commanding the battalion."

"All right," I said. "We will go to the battalion. I should go to the battalion in any case."

The captain was sitting at a make shift table in the ~~hole~~ dugout that was battalion headquarters and he rose as I saluted.

"Hello," he said in English. "What are you doing in that uniform?" He was very tall and he drawled when he spoke with a slight affectation of English manner.

"They've put me in it."

"I'm very glad to see you."

"You look well," I said. "How was the show?"

"We made a very fine attack. Truly, a very fine attack. I will show you. Look."

He showed me on the map.

"I came from Fornaci," I said. "I could see how it had been."

"It was extraordinary," he said. "Altogether extraordinary. Are you attached to the regiment?"

"No. I am supposed to move around and let them see the uniform."

"How odd," he said. ~~"I suppose the theory is that if they see one American uniform they will believe others are coming?"~~ "If they see one American uniform that is supposed to make them believe others are coming."

~~"That's it."~~

"But how will they know it is an American uniform?"

"You will tell them."

"Ok," he said. "Yes. I see. I will send a corporal with you to show you about and you will make a tour of the lines?"

"That's it." ~~"It's fairly disgusting. Isn't it?"~~

~~"Rather~~ "You had better stay here a while before you start. It is so hot."

"I'm supposed to have my [part of page is missing and text is lost here] full of cigarettes and postcards and such things," I said. "I should have a musette full of chocolate. I distribute them with a kind word and a slap on the back. But there weren't any ~~supplies~~ cigarettes and postcards and no chocolate, so they said to circulate around anyway."

"I'm sure your appearance will be very heartening to the troops."

"I wish you wouldn't," I said. "I feel bad enough about it as it is. In principle I would have brought you a bottle of brandy."

"In principle," he said and smiled for the first time showing yellow teeth. "Such a beautiful expression. Would you like some grappa?"

"~~It's so hot~~ Don't you think it's too hot?"

"I don't know. I suppose a Campari with seltzer would be better." ~~"Imagine taking a drink of grappa at this time of day if it were not for the war. I tell you the war is really very extraordinary."~~

"An Americano. Why do they call them that?"

~~"What would you take?"~~

"I don't know," he said. "I never cared for them. Too bitter. Waiter bring a Campari with seltzer," he mimicked the young gentleman of the galleria that we had known a long time before. "The grappa is very good really. It was for the Arditi they say. But we never saw any Arditi. All that hysteria of assault troops is so disgusting. You should have seen our attack. Without hysteria we have done it all beautifully."

"I saw it." ~~I said.~~

"You saw it?"

"No I didn't mean that," I said, ashamed. "I meant that coming along you could see it very clearly from the ~~position of the dead~~ way things were left. I saw where it had been and understood how it had gone."

"You should have stayed," he said. "You left just too soon. But you have acquired a taste for these fantastic appointments."

"I didn't ask for this one," I answered, still ashamed. "Do you know who we are under?"

"No."

"The American Consul. I have no commission, only this bloody uniform and a tessera which is completely mis-leading."

"It's too fantastic. How long will you stroll about heartening the troops with invisible postcards and exhibiting the uniform?"

"Indefinitely."

"Where did you get the uniform?"

"Spagnolini made it. It's not quite correct."

"Do you think you will get the cigarettes, the brandy—and the postal cards?"

"I don't know. There's no sign of them yet."

"Do you go on foot?"

"I rode down on a bicycle."

"It is ~~really~~ fantastic really. No one can tell me that this war is not extraordinary." He folded his hands and looked at them and then at me.

"What about the boy who brought me here. He seemed very upset," I said. "Is he a sample of what you have now?"

"He's quite mad, Nicolo. He's gone quite off his head. I would send him back but I've no one for his platoon."

"Have you had no replacements?"

"None."

"How are you yourself, really? Not joking."

"I am very well. I am still so proud of the attack, and of the regiment and of the brigade that I am truly happy. Let me know you again on the map."

He showed me and he was showing me when the second lieutenant came to the open door of the large dugout. ~~He was accompanied by~~ Beside him were two soldiers, young, shamefaced looking solidly built, and he held his pistol in his hand.

"Signor Capitano," he said.

"It is better to say major," the captain who was commanding the battalion, said. "Put away your pistol."

"Signor Maggiore," the lieutenant put his pistol absent-mindedly into its holster.

"Yes Tenente," said the captain. "What is ~~the matter~~ it?"

"Signor Maggiore while making a tour of the first line I found these two soldiers doing this in one of the old dugouts." He illustrated by a gesture what it was they had been doing. "I would have shot them—"

"That would have been unwise," interrupted the acting major.

"Instead I bring them to you to prefer—"

"We will step outside," the major said.

"Get along the bank," the major said to the two soldiers. "Don't stand together." He turned to the lieutenant. "I will not have any groups so that they invite shelling. Nor will I have you corrupting my signallers and my adjutant. What is your story?"

The lieutenant, flushing, told him.

"So," said the captain. "Now listen closely. Your nerves are undone. You are hysterical. From cause. I understand it is from cause. That has nothing to do with what you tell me, of course. I understand that. No. Listen. It is very hot weather. There are all sorts of people. Some of one sort. Some of another. Then too there are vices. Then too there are childishnesses. What they were doing is a childishness. If it were not a childishness it would be a vice. But you must understand also it is such hot weather and a battalion in the line does not carry women. Childishnesses spring up or might spring up if not checked. Man is not a pure animal. There are no pure animals but there is a definite distinction between childishness and vice. Vice implies corruption. Do I make myself clear?"

The lieutenant was listening, his face with its uneven stubble of beard was flushed, his lips were not steady, his eyes were all wrong. "Yes Signor Maggiore," he said.

"Good," the major went on in the tone of a lecturer in a popular course at a university. "So we have the heat, the absence of women, the fact that all are not built alike and the essential childishness. It would be unjust not to mention that those two peasant boys have made their first attack. They were both very good. I saw them."

"Sir, they were committing a disgusting crime which is also a crime by military law," the lieutenant said. "I apprehended them in the act."

"It is technically known as an act of gross indecency," the major said. "Being of the same age and with mutual consent it is not a crime. It is a nastiness. A childish nastiness. ~~Will you please be still~~. I see I have not made myself clear. I must continue. You are at present in a disordered nervous condition yourself. If ~~those two were not~~ there was not a childishness, or shame, or the presence of a vice, which I doubt, it would still be possible to understand the presence of a disordered nervous condition in these two. I doubt if this is the case. I incline to a definite childishness, the hot weather, the absence of women and excitement ~~relief~~ after the attack. Young goats play at that if there are no she-goats. It is a childishness I tell you. A disgusting childishness. Call the two men."

~~"You are not going to punish them?"~~

"Signor Maggiore—" the lieutenant began.

"Call them," the acting major said.

The two soldiers came over. They were about twenty, bulky, looking rather alike, and both very ashamed. They came to attention.

"Don't stand here making a group," the acting major said. "Get back to your squad and no more nasty tricks. Understand? Never. You are disgusting. Never!"

"Si Signor Capitano."

"Maggiore," said the acting major.

"Si, Signor Maggiore," they saluted.

"Get out," he said. They went off.

The lieutenant saluted and went off looking wilder than ever. I could see he hated both of us. I was sorry to have had to hear it.

Back in the dugout the major remarked aloud to me, "There was some mistake. There was no charge inferred." Then to me, in English, "That boy is very upset. He is hysterical now. I cannot lose good men for childishness however, no matter how nasty. We are not in barracks. In addition, I feel very strongly about everyone who behaved well in the attack. Sit down."

"How was that ~~officer~~ boy in the attack?" I asked.

"He was frightful. He is evidently of an hysterical nature. He doesn't know yet what happened. I will have to get rid of him."

"My god it's hot," I said.

"Look you must wait until evening. In the first place I will not have any grouping up or moving around to attract shelling. Secondly if you really are to hearten them you should go about ~~around~~ at night. It is at night that they are frightened."

"As we are." ~~"Like us."~~

"Yes," he said. "As we are." ~~"Like us."~~

"It's a silly business," I said. "But I suppose it will be better at night."

"Yes," he agreed. "And extraordinary though this whole thing is, Nicolo, we must make the best use of everything. Even as such a thing as your postcardless post-carding. Listen, do you think you understand the attack completely."

"Yes," I said. "I understand it. But not completely. Would you like to show it to me again?"

He showed it to me very gladly and told me every detail. I could see that it was the best thing that had happened to him so far as his life had gone.

"Where is your bicycle?" he asked me later.

"In one of the houses at the end of town."

"You think no one will find it? There will be salvage troops and burial parties up soon. I do not know why they are not up now."

"I think it's all right."

"You will need it when you go back to Fornaci."

"I'll wait and get it when I go back."

The dugout was a relic of how the lines had been before the Austrian offensive. Most of it had survived the bombardment of the fifteenth of June and it was quite spacious.

"I wish they would have the sense to relieve us," the acting major said. "Of course if I hold the command of the battalion a few days longer they will have to promote me major with merito di guerra."

"Do you want to be a major?"

"Very much."

"I'd rather be relieved."

"There is no danger now," he said. "Everything is over. Where we are there is almost no shelling. There is no sniping. We leave them alone now and they do the same for us. If you like you can go up and look across the river and see them."

"I looked over as I left the town," I said. "Who is across the river now?"

"Croats. One swam across the night before last ~~and gave to~~ to give himself up, I presume, but we shot him. I sent the tags back."

"How are the Croats?"

"I believe they are all loyal. They're not like the Czechs."

"They hanged all the Czechs they captured from the legion," I said. "They hanged them to stakes with their feet just off the ground."

"They are great hangers," he said. "For such pleasant people in peacetime they have some very nasty traits. Their empire is kept together by the noose. I don't mind killing them at all. I rather like it. Though of course one never kills the right ones. When they pull those drachen [?] down we'll take a stroll around. Don't you think it's cooler now?"

"I hadn't noticed it," I said.

"Come on," he said. "Your spirits are very low. We'll have a drink of grappa."

"All right." ~~"Do you think we'll ever drink grappa in peacetime?"~~

~~"I doubt it. Although it's really quite good with coffee if you've drunk our red wines first."~~

"How do you like it?"

~~"I doubt if I'll ever drink it."~~

"It's the same," I said.

"You are in bad spirits. At least this hasn't ether in it."

"I tasted that for a week. I was stinking through the whole attack."

"I never knew you were drunk until you commenced talking when we were ~~laying there~~ coming back in the camions."

"You have to get the courage from somewhere."

"I only drank in the first attack. It's no good for me."

"We're not the same," I said.

"You are a very brave man, Nicolo."

"Don't lie to me," I said. "I know how I am."

"You know," he said, "there's no need for you to make a tour even."

"Oh for Christ's sake. Do you think I'm afraid to do <u>that</u> now?"

"Don't be offended, Nicolo. It is only that I am against all unnecessary silliness. We could stalk about like the British and mount guard along the top of the road in plain sight if it were not silly."

"Well I'm not that bad."

"I mean that in the best way. After all we know each other very well."

"I don't like to be protected by you from the danger of making a tour of a quiet section of the line. My Christ that's what all the politicians do. You're an old grandmother."

"But you're not a politician, Nicolo. That's what makes it all so extraordinary and so silly. I ~~could not stand~~ cannot accept that you should do something that is purely silly."

"Maybe it's not so silly," I said. "Who were you going to let me take? Why not send for him? I'll make a little tour and then we can talk."

"No," he said. "We'll wait a little while. Wait until it's dark."

"Grandma Paravicini."

"You do not understand," he took a broken cigar and wrapped it carefully in cigarette papers. "A wounded Tuscan," he explained and lit it, very pleased to find it drew. "We have come now to a strange time in the war. To die is not enough."

"That is D'Annunzio. I don't like to hear you talk like D'Annunzio."

"But I mean it in a different way. The sound men, the men who still function, the useful men, if they are not killed, will win. We do not want too much valor. We want the intelligent use of rifle grenades against a machine gun, we want the sage employment of the stokes mortar, we want to advance with small losses. Have you seen the little egg bombs? We will win it and then it will be over. It is no credit to die. It is no honor to be wounded. You must last. That is why I would not expose to the loss of one man from any form of military silliness."

"You're very sound," I said. "But they ought to clean up that mess and bury the dead. You'll all be sick."

"They will clean it up. You see how clean I have everything here?"

A shell came in and burst off to the left.

"There should be seven more," he said. "Unless they have lessened the allowance. We had eight last night."

Two more came in together, then another. Of all sounds they were, to me, the nastiest to hear.

"That's half," he said cheerfully.

I heard a shout for stretcher bearers and we both went out. I climbed up the side of the sunken road and in the end of the ~~twilight~~ sunset could see the ~~big line of~~ dark sausage balloons still up on the far side and the others far off. One was coming down. Four men were clustered ~~and,~~ bent over, around one of the holes. Two others were coming running along below the bank of the road. My back was tight waiting for the next shell. It did not come. Below the river was reflecting the sunset and I looked up it to the bend and down to where it widened below the town. A farmhouse across the river ~~behind the line~~ that had been shelled to the ground looked[?] like a pile of chalk.

"Come off the skyline," he called.

I slid down.

"Two wounded," he said. "Bad luck. But neither one is grave."

"Signor Maggiore," one of the signallers called from the mouth of the big dugout.

"All right," he said. "I'm coming."

"It's good to look around," I said.

~~Toward us came the second liutenant~~ Around the bend of the trench came the 2nd lieutenant with the bloodshot eyes holding his left wrist in his right hand. He was stooped and I could see the blood running down the fingers of his drooping hand.

"So," said the acting major who had ~~lifted the gas blanket~~ stooped to enter the dugout.

"Tenente," he called. The lieutenant was heading for the dressing station dug-out below the road to the left.

"I am wounded," he called back and started to run.

"Halt," said the major. The lieutenant seemed not to hear and ran on.

"I can't shoot him," said the acting major. "I'm too old for that. Let him take it as it comes."

"Signor Maggiore," the signaller spoke from the mouth of the dugout.

"Aspetto," he said after the lieutenant.

I followed him to the dressing station. On the board table the medical officer was working on one of the men who had been hit in the shoulder by a shell fragment. ~~The collar bone stuck, splintered out of the~~ The shoulder blade showed in the gash.

"It's not even broken," the MO said.

The man's face was white as he lay forward and he screamed out when the iodine swab touched him. The other wounded man lay on his face too. He was groaning as the two orderlies loosened his belt and pulled down on his trousers. The shell fragment had gone through the cheeks of both buttocks.

"Let me see your hand," the major said to the lieutenant. He held it out. It was so covered with blood and dirt that you could tell nothing.

"Wash it off," he said to me.

"With permission?" I said, taking up a basin and sponge. Then in English, "It would be much better if I didn't."

"All right. He can wait."

"We'll take the officer," the medical officer said, finishing the dressing of the shoulder wound. "Anti-tetanus," he said to the orderly. "Put the cross on the arm."

"He can wait," the major said.

"Oh ho!" the doctor said. "One of those. One of those! Oh Ho!"

They laid the man wounded in the buttocks on the table. The doctor cleaned ~~it out~~ the wound out, used the iodine, and poked a dressing through. "Anti-tetanus and put the cross on the butt," he said.

"I did not cry out," the soldier, who had groaned steadily, said when the dressing was taped on.

"You're a good brave boy," ~~said~~ the major patted him.

"What do you want? A medal?" asked the doctor. "You would have cried out if it had hit the nerve."

I saw tears in the man's eyes.

"I did not cry out," he said.

"Another hero," said the doctor. "Wash off the officer's hand."

We all looked as it was washed. There was no possible doubt. There could be no doubt and he had not even used any ruse or any finesse. The small hole of entry was in the palm and the ~~egress~~ exit was through the back of the hand smashing the bone of the center finger, [page torn and small part of text lost] of bone and ~~and leaving~~ the severed tendons ~~hanging loose like~~ protruding, ~~like two strands of wet spaghetti~~.

"How were you wounded?" asked the acting major.

"A fragment from the last shell," he answered sullenly.

"In what position was your hand?"

"Out in front of me," he said looking down.

"I gave you a chance when I called to you," the major said. "I would have let you shoot yourself again in some more likely place. I understand you as well as the people you brought in this afternoon. I have compassion. I understand irregularities. But you wouldn't listen to me. You were too hysterical even to obey. Now it is too late. Take his pistol and certify him as self-inflicted."

"So you couldn't stand the dreadful bombardment," the medical officer said. "Our Dirty Lady but war is a terrible thing."

"Shut ~~up~~ your big mouth, Doctor," the major said.

~~"Who are you to judge him?" said the major. "I've seen you shitting in your pants before this."~~

~~"But never afraid, major.~~ "Oh war is so dreadful," the doctor went on. "Young officers from the best families ~~always~~ shooting themselves in the hands with automatic pistols. It is simply hell."

As he put in the swab of iodine the young lieutenant ~~let out a long scream~~ cried out.

"See," said the medical officer. "It touched the nerve. When it touches the nerve they're all the same."

"They may let you off," the major said to the ~~young~~ lieutenant who stood, ~~crying~~ tears coming out of his red rimmed, gas-injured eyes. "There were no witnesses ~~and I'll not press it.~~ you know."

"Oh oh oh," the boy blubbered.

"You'd have a better chance if you were shaved though," the major said. "You look like a bloody brigand."

"Oh my ~~father~~ mother and my ~~mother~~ father," the boy ~~said now~~ sobbed. His tight hysteria was broken and he was all gone now.

"You'll be saying oh myself soon," the medical officer said. "It will be oh myself before long."

"You're an unpleasant bastard," the acting major said to him. "Send these three wounded back. One man to guard the officer."

"Where do I get him?"

~~"I'll send him."~~ "He will be here."

Outside it was quite dark.

"Very unfortunate," said the major. "Very embarrassing. I suppose I can recommend him for a medal for his actions during the attack and that will help him quite a ~~lot~~ bit but that is very unfair. I don't believe in decorations either. They are very unfair. Now you, Nicolo, I will get you a guide and you will make your little tour."

"Yes, Signor Maggiore."

He put his arm around my shoulder. "Stop it," he said. ~~"What if I did drive him to it. I didn't."~~ "You have no right to act as though I made him crazy. It wasn't my fault. I would have helped him. ~~but~~ You know that. But he took it out of my hands. You can't do anything when it's out of your hands. Besides I'm fed up with him."

"Yes, Signor Maggiore."

"You too," he said. "Well que voulez vous? When you come back bring the cigarettes, the postcards, the afternoon papers, and the French letters."

"Good."

"All right. Ciaou."

"Ciaou," I said. He was the first who had taught me to say it many months before when I had embarrassed him by my ungrammatical formalities. It is ~~a vulgar~~ the colloquial form of saying good-bye used between people ~~who are fond of each other on terms~~ of the same position who are on terms of good friendship.

"I'll do what I can for him," he said.

"The hell with him. ~~I said.~~ I wasn't even thinking about him." The night breeze was from the south. "They ought to clean up that damned mess and bury the dead. You'll all be sick. That's a hell of a way to leave things."

"They will you must have patience."

"The hell with patience. I'm sick of the whole damned business. The smell of it, the sound of it, the taste of it."

"Now you're upset yourself. You mustn't be upset."

"The sight of it is all right. I don't mind of the sight of it."

"You're upset. I knew you'd be upset if you started to talk about it."

"I'm not upset. I'm just sick of the damned thing."

"Well be careful not to shoot yourself in the hand."

"Thank you very much."

"Be careful."

"Be careful your damned battalion doesn't buggar its-self to death."

"That's better," he said. "And I have seen you break a man's nose to rouse his valor."

"That was a long time ago."

"Yes a long time ago. Now you better go to make your little tour."

"Very good."

"We talk too damned much."

"My fault."

"No," he said. "I wanted to talk."

"Ciaou," I said.

"Ciaou.["]

14.

A Clean, Well-Lighted Place

1933

It was late and every one had left the café except an old man who sat in the shadow the leaves of the tree made against the electric light. In the day time the street was dusty, but at night the dew settled the dust and the old man liked to sit late because he was deaf and now at night it was quiet and he felt the difference. The two waiters inside the café knew that the old man was a little drunk, and while he was a good client they knew that if he became too drunk he would leave without paying, so they kept watch on him.

"Last week he tried to commit suicide," one waiter said.

"Why?"

"He was in despair."

"What about?"

"Nothing."

"How do you know it was nothing?"

"He has plenty of money."

They sat together at a table that was close against the wall near the door of the café and looked at the terrace where the tables were all empty except where the old man sat in the shadow of the leaves of the tree that moved slightly in the wind. A girl and a soldier went by in the street. The street light shone on the brass number on his collar. The girl wore no head covering and hurried beside him.

"The guard will pick him up," one waiter said.

"What does it matter if he gets what he's after?"

"He had better get off the street now. The guard will get him. They went by five minutes ago."

The old man sitting in the shadow rapped on his saucer with his glass. The younger waiter went over to him.

"What do you want?"

The old man looked at him. "Another brandy," he said.

"You'll be drunk," the waiter said. The old man looked at him. The waiter went away.

"He'll stay all night," he said to his colleague. "I'm sleepy now. I never get into bed before three o'clock. He should have killed himself last week."

The waiter took the brandy bottle and another saucer from the counter inside the café and marched out to the old man's table. He put down the saucer and poured the glass full of brandy.

"You should have killed yourself last week," he said to the deaf man. The old man motioned with his finger. "A little more," he said. The waiter poured on into the glass so that the brandy slopped over and ran down the stem into the top saucer of the pile. "Thank you," the old man said. The waiter took the bottle back inside the café. He sat down at the table with his colleague again.

"He's drunk now," he said.

"He's drunk every night."

"What did he want to kill himself for?"

"How should I know."

"How did he do it?"

"He hung himself with a rope."

"Who cut him down?"

"His niece."

"Why did they do it?"

"Fear for his soul."

"How much money has he got?"

"He's got plenty."

"He must be eighty years old."

"Anyway I should say he was eighty."

"I wish he would go home. I never get to bed before three o'clock. What kind of hour is that to go to bed?"

"He stays up because he likes it."

"He's lonely. I'm not lonely. I have a wife waiting in bed for me."

"He had a wife once too."

"A wife would be no good to him now."

"You can't tell. He might be better with a wife."

"His niece looks after him. You said she cut him down."

"I know."

"I wouldn't want to be that old. An old man is a nasty thing."

"Not always. This old man is clean. He drinks without spilling. Even now, drunk. Look at him."

"I don't want to look at him. I wish he would go home. He has no regard for those who must work."

The old man looked from his glass across the square, then over at the waiters.

"Another brandy," he said, pointing to his glass. The waiter who was in a hurry came over.

"Finished," he said, speaking with that omission of syntax stupid people employ when talking to drunken people or foreigners. "No more tonight. Close now."

"Another," said the old man.

"No. Finished." The waiter wiped the edge of the table with a towel and shook his head.

The old man stood up, slowly counted the saucers, took a leather coin purse from his pocket and paid for the drinks, leaving half a peseta tip.

The waiter watched him go down the street, a very old man walking unsteadily but with dignity.

"Why didn't you let him stay and drink?" the unhurried waiter asked. They were putting up the shutters. "It is not half-past two."

"I want to go home to bed."

"What is an hour?"

"More to me than to him."

"An hour is the same."

"You talk like an old man yourself. He can buy a bottle and drink at home."

"It's not the same."

"No, it is not," agreed the waiter with a wife. He did not wish to be unjust. He was only in a hurry.

"And you? You have no fear of going home before your usual hour?"

"Are you trying to insult me?"

"No, *hombre*, only to make a joke."

"No," the waiter who was in a hurry said, rising from pulling down the metal shutters. "I have confidence. I am all confidence."

"You have youth, confidence, and a job," the older waiter said. "You have everything."

"And what do you lack?"

"Everything but work."

"You have everything I have."

"No. I have never had confidence and I am not young."

"Come on. Stop talking nonsense and lock up."

"I am of those who like to stay late at the café," the older waiter said. "With all those who do not want to go to bed. With all those who need a light for the night."

"I want to go home and into bed."

"We are of two different kinds," the older waiter said. He was now dressed to go home. "It is not only a question of youth and confidence although those things are very beautiful. Each night I am reluctant to close up because there may be some one who needs the café."

"*Hombre*, there are *bodegas* open all night long."

"You do not understand. This is a clean and pleasant café. It is well lighted. The light is very good and also, now, there are shadows of the leaves."

"Good night," said the younger waiter.

"Good night," the other said. Turning off the electric light he continued the conversation with himself. It is the light of course but it is necessary that the place be clean and pleasant. You do not want music. Certainly you do not want music. Nor can you stand before a bar with dignity although that is all that is provided for these hours. What did he fear? It was not fear or dread. It was a nothing that he knew too well. It was all a nothing and a man was nothing too. It was only that and light was all it needed and a certain cleanness and order. Some lived in it and never felt it but he knew it all was *nada y pues nada y nada y pues nada*. Our *nada* who art in *nada*, *nada* be thy name thy kingdom *nada* thy will be *nada* in *nada* as it is in *nada*. Give us this *nada* our daily *nada* and *nada* us our *nada* as we *nada* our *nadas* and *nada* us not into *nada* but deliver us from *nada*; *pues nada*. Hail nothing full of nothing, nothing is with thee. He smiled and stood before a bar with a shining steam pressure coffee machine.

"What's yours?" asked the barman.

"*Nada*."

"*Otro loco más*," said the barman and turned away.

"A little cup," said the waiter.

The barman poured it for him.

"The light is very bright and pleasant but the bar is unpolished," the waiter said.

The barman looked at him but did not answer. It was too late at night for conversation.

"You want another *copita?*" the barman asked.

"No, thank you," said the waiter and went out. He disliked bars and *bodegas*. A clean, well-lighted café was a very different thing. Now, without thinking further, he would go home to his room. He would lie in the bed and finally, with daylight, he would go to sleep. After all, he said to himself, it is probably only insomnia. Many must have it.

14a.

Item 337, Ernest Hemingway Collection, John F. Kennedy Library and Museum, Boston. Titled handwritten pencil manuscript with one false start. This is the earliest preserved draft of "A Clean Well-Lighted Place."

~~In Zaragossa the~~

~~Everyone had left the café except an old man who sat in the shadow the leaves of the trees made against the electric light. It was dusty in the street and the night wind blew the dust but at night you did not notice it. but at night the dew came and the dust did not blow with the night wind~~

A Clean, Well Lighted Place

It was late and everyone had left the café except an old man who sat in the shadow the leaves of the tree made against the electric light. In the daytime the street was dusty but at night the dew settled the dust and the old man liked to sit late because he was deaf and now at night it was quiet and he felt the difference. The two waiters inside the café ~~where~~ knew that the old man was a little drunk and while he was a good client they knew that if he became too drunk he would leave without paying so they kept watch on him.

"Last week he tried to commit suicide," one waiter said.

"Why?"

"He was in despair."

"What about?"

"Nothing."

"How do you know it was nothing?"

"He has plenty of money."

They sat together at a table that was close against the wall near the door of the café and looked at the terrace where the tables were all empty except where the old man sat in the shadow of the leaves of the trees that moved slightly in the wind. A girl and a soldier went by in the street. The ~~light~~ street light shone on the brass number on his collar. The girl wore no head covering and hurried beside him.

"The guard will pick him up," one waiter said.

"What does it matter if he gets ~~his tail~~ what he's after?"

"He had better get off the street now. The guard will get him. They went by five minutes ago."

The old man sitting in the shadow rapped on his saucer with his glass. ~~One of the~~ The younger waiter went over to him.

"What do you want?"

The old man looked at him. "Another brandy," he said.

"You'll be drunk," the waiter said. The old man looked at him. The waiter went away.

"He'll stay all night," he said to his colleague. "I'm sleepy now. I never get into bed before three o'clock. He should have killed himself last week."

The waiter took the brandy bottle and another saucer from the counter inside the cafe and walked out to the old man's table. He put down the saucer and poured the glass full of brandy.

"You should have killed yourself last week," he said to the deaf man. The old man motioned with his finger, "A little more," he said. The waiter poured on into the glass so that the brandy slopped over and ran down the stem into the top saucer of the pile. "Thank you," the old man said. The waiter took the bottle back inside the cafe. He sat down at the table with his colleague again.

"He's drunk now," he said.

"He's drunk every night."

"What did he want to kill himself for?"

"~~Christ~~ How should I know?"

"How did he do it?"

"He ~~hanged~~ hung himself with a rope."

"Who cut him down?"

"His niece."

"Why did they do it?"

"Fear for his soul."

"How much money has he got?"

"He's got plenty."

"He must be eighty years old."

"Anyway, I should say he was eighty."

"I wish he would go home. I never get to bed before three o'clock. What kind of hour is that to go to bed?"

"He stays up because he likes it."

"He's lonely. I'm not lonely. I have a wife waiting in the bed for me."

"He had a wife once too."

"A wife would be no good to him now."

"You can't tell. He might be better with a wife."

"His niece looks after him."

"I know. You said she cut him down."

"I wouldn't want to be that old. An old man is a nasty thing."

"Not always. This old man is clean. He drinks without spilling. Even now, drunk. Look at him."

"I don't want to look at him. I wish he would go home. He has no regard for those who must work."

The old man looked from his glass across the square then over at the waiters.

"Another brandy," he said pointing to his glass. One of The waiter who was in a hurry came over.

"Finished," he said, speaking with that omission of syntax stupid people employ when talking to drunken people or foreigners. "No more tonight. Close now."

"Another," said the old man.

"No. Finished." The waiter wiped the edge of the table with a towel and shook his head.

The old man stood up, slowly counted the saucers, took a leather coin purse from his pocket, opened it, chose coins from among the silver and paid for the drinks, leaving half a peseta tip.

The waiter watched him go down the street, a very old man, walking unsteadily but with dignity.

"Why didn't you let him stay and drink?" the unhurried waiter asked. They were putting up the shutters. "It is not half past two."

"I want to go home to bed."

"What is an hour?"

"More to me than to him."

"An hour is the same."

"You talk like an old man yourself. He can buy a bottle and drink at home."

~~"Perhaps.~~

"It's not the same."

"No it is not," agreed the waiter with a wife. He did not wish to be unjust. He was only in a hurry. ~~Although neither of them had studied the question they knew there was a good reason for cafés~~

"And you? You have no fear of going home before your usual hour?"

"Are you trying to insult me?"

"No, hombre, only to make a joke."

"No," the waiter who was in a hurry said, rising from pulling down the metal shutters. "I have confidence. I am all confidence."

"You have youth, confidence and a job," the older waiter said. "You have everything."

"And what do you lack?"

"Everything but work."

"You have everything I have."

"No. I have never had confidence and I am not young."

"Come on. Stop talking nonsense and lock up."

"I am of those who like to stay late at the café," the older waiter said. "With all those who do not want to go to bed. With all those who need a light for the night."

"I want to get home and into bed."

"We are of two different kinds," the older waiter said. He was now dressed to go home. "It is not only a question of youth and confidence although those things are very beautiful. Each night I am reluctant to close up because there may be someone who needs the café."

"Hombre there are bodegas open all night long."

"You do not understand. This is a clean and pleasant café. It is well lighted. The light is very good and also, now, there are the shadows of the leaves."

"Good night," said the younger waiter.

"Good night," the other said.

Turning off the electric light he continued the conversation with himself. It is the light of course but it ~~makes~~ is necessary that the place be clean and pleasant. You do not want music. Certainly you do not want music. Nor can you stand before a bar with dignity although that is all that is provided for these hours. What did he fear?

He did not fear. It was no fear or dread. It was a nothing that he knew too well. It was all a nothing and a man was nothing. It was only that and light was all it needed and a certain clean-ness and order. Some lived in it and never felt it but he knew it all was nada y pues nada y nada y pues nada. Our nada who art in nada, nada be thy name thy kingdom nada they will be nada in nada as it is in nada. Give us this ~~day~~ nada our daily nada and nada us our nada as we nada our nadas and nada us not into nada but deliver us from nada pues nada. Hail Nothing full of nothing, nothing is with thee. He smiled and stood before a bar with a shining steam pressure coffee machine.

"What's yours?" asked the barman.

"Nada."

"Otro loco mas," said the barman and turned way.

"A little cup," said the waiter.

The barman poured it for him.

"The light is very bright and pleasant but the bar is unpolished," the waiter said.

The barman looked at him but did not answer. It was too late at night for conversation.

"You want another copita?" the barman asked.

"No thank you," said the waiter and went out. He disliked bars and bodegas. A clean well lighted café was a very different thing. Now, without thinking further, he would go home to his room. He would lie in the bed and finally, ~~towards morning~~ with daylight he would go to sleep. After all, he said to himself, it is probably only insomnia. Many must have it. ~~Still one does not know. It would be easier if one knew. One feels certain things but one knows nothing. Certainly there is no one who knows about those.~~

15.

Fathers and Sons

1933

There had been a sign to detour in the center of the main street of this town, but cars had obviously gone through, so, believing it was some repair which had been completed, Nicholas Adams drove on through the town along the empty, brick-paved street, stopped by traffic lights that flashed on and off on this traffic-less Sunday, and would be gone next year when the payments on the system were not met; on under the heavy trees of the small town that are a part of your heart if it is your town and you have walked under them, but that are only too heavy, that shut out the sun and that dampen the houses for a stranger; out past the last house and onto the highway that rose and fell straight away ahead with banks of red dirt sliced cleanly away and the second-growth timber on both sides. It was not his country but it was the middle of fall and all of this country was good to drive through and to see. The cotton was picked and in the clearings there were patches of corn, some cut with streaks of red sorghum, and, driving easily, his son asleep on the seat by his side, the day's run made, knowing the town he would reach for the night, Nick noticed which corn fields had soy beans or peas in them, how the thickets and the cut-over land lay, where the cabins and houses were in relation to the fields and the thickets; hunting the country in his mind as he went by; sizing up each clearing as to feed and cover and figuring where you would find a covey and which way they would fly.

In shooting quail you must not get between them and their habitual cover, once the dogs have found them, or when they flush they will come pouring at you, some rising steep, some skimming by your ears, whirring into a size you have never seen them in the air as they pass, the only way being to turn and take them over your shoulder as they go, before they set their wings and angle down into the thicket. Hunting this country for quail as his father had taught him, Nicholas Adams started thinking about his father. When he first thought about him it was always the eyes. The big frame, the quick movements, the wide shoulders, the hooked, hawk nose, the beard that covered the weak chin, you never thought about—it was always the eyes. They were protected in his head by the formation of the brows; set deep as though a special protection had been devised for some very valuable instrument. They saw much farther and much quicker than the human eye sees and they were the great gift his father had. His father saw as a big-horn ram or as an eagle sees, literally.

He would be standing with his father on one shore of the lake, his own eyes were very good then, and his father would say, "They've run up the flag." Nick could not see the flag or the flag pole. "There," his father would say, "it's your sister Dorothy. She's got the flag up and she's walking out onto the dock."

Nick would look across the lake and he could see the long wooded shore-line, the higher timber behind, the point that guarded the bay, the clear hills of the farm and the white of their cottage in the trees but he could not see any flag pole, or any dock, only the white of the beach and the curve of the shore.

"Can you see the sheep on the hillside toward the point?"

"Yes."

They were a whitish patch on the gray-green of the hill.

"I can count them," his father said.

Like all men with a faculty that surpasses human requirements, his father was very nervous. Then, too, he was sentimental, and, like most sentimental people, he was both cruel and abused. Also, he had much bad luck, and it was not all of it his own. He had died in a trap that he had helped only a little to set, and they had all betrayed him in their various ways before he died. All sentimental people are betrayed so many times. Nick could not write about him yet, although he would, later, but the quail country made him remember him as he was when Nick was a boy and he was very grateful to him for two things: fishing and shooting. His father was as sound on those two things as he was unsound on sex, for instance, and Nick was glad that it had been that way; for some one has to give you your first gun or the opportunity to get it and use it, and you have to live where there is game or fish if you are to learn about them, and now, at thirty-eight, he loved to fish and to shoot exactly as much as when he first had gone with his father. It was a passion that had never slackened and he was very grateful to his father for bringing him to know it.

While for the other, that his father was not sound about, all the equipment you will ever have is provided and each man learns all there is for him to know about it without advice; and it makes no difference where you live. He remembered very clearly the only two pieces of information his father had given him about that. Once when they were out shooting together Nick shot a red squirrel out of a hemlock tree. The squirrel fell, wounded, and when Nick picked him up bit the boy clean through the ball of the thumb.

"The dirty little bugger," Nick said and smacked the squirrel's head against the tree. "Look how he bit me."

His father looked and said, "Suck it out clean and put some iodine on when you get home."

"The little bugger," Nick said.

"Do you know what a bugger is?" his father asked him.

"We call anything a bugger," Nick said.

"A bugger is a man who has intercourse with animals."

"Why?" Nick said.

"I don't know," his father said. "But it is a heinous crime."

Nick's imagination was both stirred and horrified by this and he thought of various animals but none seemed attractive or practical and that was the sum total of direct sexual knowledge bequeathed him by his father except on one other subject. One morning he read in the paper that Enrico Caruso had been arrested for mashing.

"What is mashing?"

"It is one of the most heinous of crimes," his father answered.

Nick's imagination pictured the great tenor doing something strange, bizarre, and heinous with a potato masher to a beautiful lady who looked like the pictures of Anna Held on the inside of cigar boxes. He resolved, with considerable horror, that when he was old enough he would try mashing at least once.

His father had summed up the whole matter by stating that masturbation produced blindness, insanity, and death, while a man who went with prostitutes would contract hideous venereal diseases and that the thing to do was to keep your hands off of people. On the other hand his father had the finest pair of eyes he had ever seen and Nick had loved him very much and for a long time. Now, knowing how it had all been, even remembering the earliest times before things had gone badly was not good remembering. If he wrote it he could get rid of it. He had gotten rid of many things by writing them. But it was still too early for that. There were still too many people. So he decided to think of something else. There was nothing to do about his father and he had thought it all through many times. The handsome job the undertaker had done on his father's face had not blurred in his mind and all the rest of it was quite clear, including the responsibilities. He had complimented the undertaker. The undertaker had been both proud and smugly pleased. But it was not the undertaker that had given him that last face. The undertaker had only made certain dashingly executed repairs of doubtful artistic merit. The face had been making itself and being made for a long time. It had modelled fast in the last three years. It was a good story but there were still too many people alive for him to write it.

Nick's own education in those earlier matters had been acquired in the hemlock woods behind the Indian camp. This was reached by a trail which ran from the cottage through the woods to the farm and then by a road which wound through the slashings to the camp. Now if he could still feel all of that trail with bare feet. First there was the pine-needle loam through the hemlock woods behind the cottage where the fallen logs crumbled into wood dust and long splintered pieces of wood hung like javelins in the tree that had been struck by lightning. You crossed the creek on a log and if you stepped off there was the black muck of the swamp. You climbed a fence out of the woods and the trail was

hard in the sun across the field with cropped grass and sheep sorrel and mullen growing and to the left the quaky bog of the creek
bottom where the killdeer plover fed. The spring house was in that
creek. Below the barn there was fresh warm manure and the other
older manure that was caked dry on top. Then there was another
fence and the hard, hot trail from the barn to the house and the
hot sandy road that ran down to the woods, crossing the creek,
on a bridge this time, where the cat-tails grew that you soaked in
kerosene to make jack-lights with for spearing fish at night.

Then the main road went off to the left, skirting the woods
and climbing the hill, while you went into the woods on the wide
clay and shale road, cool under the trees, and broadened for them
to skid out the hemlock bark the Indians cut. The hemlock bark
was piled in long rows of stacks, roofed over with more bark, like
houses, and the peeled logs lay huge and yellow where the trees
had been felled. They left the logs in the woods to rot, they did
not even clear away or burn the tops. It was only the bark they
wanted for the tannery at Boyne City; hauling it across the lake
on the ice in winter, and each year there was less forest and more
open, hot, shadeless, weed-grown slashing.

But there was still much forest then, virgin forest where the
trees grew high before there were any branches and you walked
on the brown, clean, springy-needled ground with no undergrowth and it was cool on the hottest days and they three lay
against the trunk of a hemlock wider than two beds are long,
with the breeze high in the tops and the cool light that came in
patches, and Billy said:

"You want Trudy again?"

"You want to?"

"Un Huh."

"Come on."

"No, here."

"But Billy—"

"I no mind Billy. He my brother."

Then afterwards they sat, the three of them, listening for a black
squirrel that was in the top branches where they could not see

him. They were waiting for him to bark again because when he barked he would jerk his tail and Nick would shoot where he saw any movement. His father gave him only three cartridges a day to hunt with and he had a single-barrel twenty-gauge shotgun with a very long barrel.

"Son of a bitch never move," Billy said.

"You shoot, Nickie. Scare him. We see him jump. Shoot him again," Trudy said. It was a long speech for her.

"I've only got two shells," Nick said.

"Son of a bitch," said Billy.

They sat against the tree and were quiet. Nick was feeling hollow and happy.

"Eddie says he going to come some night sleep in bed with you sister Dorothy."

"What?"

"He said."

Trudy nodded.

"That's all he want do," she said. Eddie was their older half-brother. He was seventeen.

"If Eddie Gilby ever comes at night and even speaks to Dorothy you know what I'd do to him? I'd kill him like this." Nick cocked the gun and hardly taking aim pulled the trigger, blowing a hole as big as your hand in the head or belly of that half-breed bastard Eddie Gilby. "Like that. I'd kill him like that."

"He better not come then," Trudy said. She put her hand in Nick's pocket.

"He better watch out plenty," said Billy.

"He's big bluff," Trudy was exploring with her hand in Nick's pocket. "But don't you kill him. You get plenty trouble."

"I'd kill him like that," Nick said. Eddie Gilby lay on the ground with all his chest shot away. Nick put his foot on him proudly.

"I'd scalp him," he said happily.

"No," said Trudy. "That's dirty."

"I'd scalp him and send it to his mother."

"His mother dead," Trudy said. "Don't you kill him, Nickie. Don't you kill him for me."

"After I scalped him I'd throw him to the dogs."

Billy was very depressed. "He better watch out," he said gloomily.

"They'd tear him to pieces," Nick said, pleased with the picture. Then, having scalped that half-breed renegade and standing, watching the dogs tear him, his face unchanging, he fell backward against the tree, held tight around the neck, Trudy holding, choking him, and crying, "No kill him! No kill him! No kill him! No. No. No. Nickie. Nickie. Nickie!"

"What's the matter with you?"

"No kill him."

"I got to kill him."

"He just a big bluff."

"All right," Nickie said. "I won't kill him unless he comes around the house. Let go of me."

"That's good," Trudy said. "You want to do anything now? I feel good now."

"If Billy goes away." Nick had killed Eddie Gilby, then pardoned him his life, and he was a man now.

"You go, Billy. You hang around all the time. Go on."

"Son a bitch," Billy said. "I get tired this. What we come? Hunt or what?"

"You can take the gun. There's one shell."

"All right. I get a big black one all right."

"I'll holler," Nick said.

Then, later, it was a long time after and Billy was still away.

"You think we make a baby?" Trudy folded her brown legs together happily and rubbed against him. Something inside Nick had gone a long way away.

"I don't think so," he said.

"Make plenty baby what the hell."

They heard Billy shoot.

"I wonder if he got one."

"Don't care," said Trudy.

Billy came through the trees. He had the gun over his shoulder and he held a black squirrel by the front paws.

"Look," he said. "Bigger than a cat. You all through?"

"Where'd you get him?"

"Over there. Saw him jump first."

"Got to go home," Nick said.

"No," said Trudy.

"I got to get there for supper."

"All right."

"Want to hunt tomorrow?"

"All right."

"You can have the squirrel."

"All right."

"Come out after supper?"

"No."

"How you feel?"

"Good."

"All right."

"Give me kiss on the face," said Trudy.

Now, as he rode along the highway in the car and it was getting dark, Nick was all through thinking about his father. The end of the day never made him think of him. The end of the day had always belonged to Nick alone and he never felt right unless he was alone at it. His father came back to him in the fall of the year, or in the early spring when there had been jacksnipe on the prairie, or when he saw shocks of corn, or when he saw a lake, or if he ever saw a horse and buggy, or when he saw, or heard, wild geese, or in a duck blind; remembering the time an eagle dropped through the whirling snow to strike a canvas-covered decoy, rising, his wings beating, the talons caught in the canvas. His father was with him, suddenly, in deserted orchards and in new-plowed fields, in thickets, on small hills, or when going through dead grass, whenever splitting wood or hauling water, by grist mills, cider mills and dams and always with open fires. The towns he lived in were not towns his father knew. After he was fifteen he had shared nothing with him.

His father had frost in his beard in cold weather and in hot weather he sweated very much. He liked to work in the sun on the farm because he did not have to and he loved manual work, which Nick did not. Nick loved his father but hated the smell of him and once when he had to wear a suit of his father's underwear that had gotten too small for his father it made him feel sick and he took it off and put it under two stones in the creek and said that he had lost it. He had told his father how it was when his father had made him put it on but his father had said it was freshly washed. It had been, too. When Nick had asked him to smell of it his father sniffed at it indignantly and said that it was clean and fresh. When Nick came home from fishing without it and said he lost it he was whipped for lying.

Afterwards he had sat inside the woodshed with the door open, his shotgun loaded and cocked, looking across at his father sitting on the screen porch reading the paper, and thought, "I can blow him to hell. I can kill him." Finally he felt his anger go out of him and he felt a little sick about it being the gun that his father had given him. Then he had gone to the Indian camp, walking there in the dark, to get rid of the smell. There was only one person in his family that he liked the smell of; one sister. All the others he avoided all contact with. That sense blunted when he started to smoke. It was a good thing. It was good for a bird dog but it did not help a man.

"What was it like, Papa, when you were a little boy and used to hunt with the Indians?"

"I don't know," Nick was startled. He had not even noticed the boy was awake. He looked at him sitting beside him on the seat. He had felt quite alone but this boy had been with him. He wondered for how long. "We used to go all day to hunt black squirrels," he said. "My father only gave me three shells a day because he said that would teach me to hunt and it wasn't good for a boy to go banging around. I went with a boy named Billy Gilby and his sister Trudy. We used to go out nearly every day all one summer."

"Those are funny names for Indians."

"Yes, aren't they," Nick said.

"But tell me what they were like."

"They were Ojibways," Nick said. "And they were very nice."

"But what were they like to be with?"

"It's hard to say," Nick Adams said. Could you say she did first what no one has ever done better and mention plump brown legs, flat belly, hard little breasts, well holding arms, quick searching tongue, the flat eyes, the good taste of mouth, then uncomfortably, tightly, sweetly, moistly, lovely, tightly, achingly, fully, finally, unendingly, never-endingly, never-to-endingly, suddenly ended,

the great bird flown like an owl in the twilight, only it was daylight in the woods and hemlock needles stuck against your belly.
So that when you go in a place where Indians have lived you smell
them gone and all the empty pain killer bottles and the flies that
buzz do not kill the sweetgrass smell, the smoke smell and that
other like a fresh cased marten skin. Nor any jokes about them
nor old squaws take that away. Nor the sick sweet smell they get
to have. Nor what they did finally. It wasn't how they ended. They
all ended the same. Long time ago good. Now no good.

And about the other. When you have shot one bird flying you
have shot all birds flying. They are all different and they fly in
different ways but the sensation is the same and the last one is as
good as the first. He could thank his father for that.

"You might not like them," Nick said to the boy. "But I think
you would."

"And my grandfather lived with them too when he was a boy,
didn't he?"

"Yes. When I asked him what they were like he said that he
had many friends among them."

"Will I ever live with them?"

"I don't know," Nick said. "That's up to you."

"How old will I be when I get a shotgun and can hunt by
myself?"

"Twelve years old if I see you are careful."

" 'I wish I was twelve now."

"You will be, soon enough."

"What was my grandfather like? I can't remember him except
that he gave me an air rifle and an American flag when I came
over from France that time. What was he like?"

"He's hard to describe. He was a great hunter and fisherman
and he had wonderful eyes."

"Was he greater than you?"

"He was a much better shot and his father was a great wing
shot too."

"I'll bet he wasn't better than you."

"Oh, yes he was. He shot very quickly and beautifully. I'd
rather see him shoot than any man I ever knew. He was always
very disappointed in the way I shot."

"Why do we never go to pray at the tomb of my grandfather?"

"We live in a different part of the country. It's a long way from here."

"In France that wouldn't make any difference. In France we'd go. I think I ought to go to pray at the tomb of my grandfather."

"Sometime we'll go."

"I hope we won't live somewhere so that I can never go to pray at your tomb when you are dead."

"We'll have to arrange it."

"Don't you think we might all be buried at a convenient place? We could all be buried in France. That would be fine."

"I don't want to be buried in France," Nick said.

"Well, then, we'll have to get some convenient place in America. Couldn't we all be buried out at the ranch?"

"That's an idea."

"Then I could stop and pray at the tomb of my grandfather on the way to the ranch."

"You're awfully practical."

"Well, I don't feel good never to have even visited the tomb of my grandfather."

"We'll have to go," Nick said. "I can see we'll have to go."

15a.

Item 382, Ernest Hemingway Collection, John F. Kennedy Library and Museum, Boston. Early handwritten pencil manuscript and false start of "Fathers and Sons," untitled, with writing on both sides of the piece of paper.

My father was etc eyes built like etc but all he ever told me about sexual life was that etc

Now my when my boy asks me "what was it like Papa when you lived with the Indians when you were a boy?" I say I didn't really live with them but ~~well~~ we used to go squirrel hunting all day and take a lunch[.] My father used to give me three shells because he said it was all right for a boy to hunt all day but ~~not to~~ that you'd never learn to hunt if you had lots of shells. There was an Indian girl named Prudy Gilby that I was very fond of[.] We were very good friends.
  "What happened to her?"
  "She went away to be a hooker."
  "What is a hooker?"
  "I'll tell you sometime."
  But I cannot tell him of the thin brown legs, the flat belly and the hard little breasts, nor of the quick searching tongue, the flat eyes nor how she did first what no one has done better[,] nor how I felt when first the great bird flew[,] ~~nor how it was when I came back and found she was a whore, a hooker we said then, w what The smell of sweetgrass~~ nor the hemlock needles stuck against your belly nor the sweet Indian smell like sweetgrass smoke and armpit salt
  "You want?"
  "Uh huh."
  "Like it so much."
  So now if I go in a place where Indians have lived I smell them ~~right away~~ gone and even the empty pain killer bottles and the flies would not turn me against that smell. So when he asks me ["]what were they like Papa?" I say "I always liked them[.] We had good

times then and later on we played a lot of baseball. Her brother Dick was a very good ball player.

And ~~you~~ so I wonder what my father knew beside the nonsense that he told me and how things were with him because when I asked him what the Indians were like when he was a boy he said that ~~they~~ he had very good friends among them, that he was very fond of them and that they called him We-Tek-Ta-La which means Eagle Eye.

15b.

Item 383, Ernest Hemingway Collection, John F. Kennedy Library and Museum, Boston. Handwritten pencil manuscript titled "The Tomb of My Grandfather." Early draft of "Fathers and Sons."

The Tomb of My Grandfather

There had been a sign to detour in the center of the main street of this town but cars had obviously gone through, so, thinking it was some repair which had been completed, we went on through the town along the empty brick paved ~~main~~ street, ~~held up~~ stopped by traffic lights that flashed on and off ~~with the too heavy trees~~ this traffic-less Sunday, and would be gone next year when the payments on the system were not met, on under the too heavy trees of the small town that ~~were~~ are a part of your heart if it is your own town and you have walked under them but are only too heavy, that shut out the sun and dampen the houses for a stranger, and onto the highway that rose and fell straightaway ahead, the banks of red-dirt sliced cleanly away and the forest on both sides. ~~The boy was asleep.~~ It was not my country but it was mid-fall and it was a fine country to see, ~~much~~ with much more forest than I had thought there would be. The cotton was picked and in the clearings there were good patches of corn, some cut with streaks of red sorghum and driving early with the boy asleep on the seat beside me, having made the days run and knowing the town we would reach for the night I watched the country noticing what ~~patches of~~ corn fields had soybeans or peas in them, ~~and~~ how the thickets and the cutover land lay and where they were from the cabins and houses ~~and~~ so that I hunted the country as we went by; sizing up each clearing as to feed and cover and figuring ~~which~~ where you would find a covey and which way they would fly. In shooting quail you must not get between them and their habitual cover once the dogs have found them or they will come pouring at you some rising steep, some skimming by your ears; whirring into a size you have never seen them in the air as they pass and you will ~~miss~~ be shooting at them at the guns muzzle ~~unless you~~ so that the only way is to turn and take them over your shoulder when they are past as they set their wings and angle down into the thicket.

Hunting this country for quail as my father had taught me I thought of him and when you first thought of him it was always the eyes. The nervousness, the quick movements, the big frame, the wide shoulders, the hooked hawk nose, the beard that covered the weak chin you never thought about. It was always the eyes. They were protected in his head by the foremation of the brows; set deep as though a special protection had been devised for some very valuable instrument. They saw much further and much quicker than the human eye sees. As a big horn ram ~~mountain sheep can~~ will see you when you can just make him out with eight power glasses; and you know if you see his eyes looking at you through the glasses that he sees you; while a bear sees no further than a pig and an elk can lift his head and look straight at you at four ~~three~~ hundred yards and never make you out if you keep still (the wind protects them); so my father saw as a big horn or as an eagle sees. Sometimes we would be on the shore of the lake, my eyes were very good then, and he would say "They've run up the flag." I could not see the flag nor the flag pole. "There," he would say. "Its your sister Dorothy. She's got the flag up and now she's walking out onto the dock."

I looked across the lake and saw the long wooded ~~point~~ shoreline, the timber behind, the point that guarded the bay, the clear hills of the farm and the white of our cottage in the trees but I could not see flag pole, nor dock, only the white of the beach and the curve of the shore.

"Can you see the sheep on the hillside toward the point?"

"Yes." They were grey ~~with patch~~ on the grey green of the hill.

"I can count them," he said.

~~As all men with a faculty that surpasses human requirements he was very nervous. He was married to a woman with whom he had no more in common than a coyote has with a white French poodle. For he was no wolf, my father, he was sentimental and like all senti-mental people he was cruel; often he had too many emotions and when everything was gone to pieces he went in for martyrdom, and he went years before he discovered that the injustices~~

~~He had the eyes and the nose of a bird of prey and he was built, then, like the pictures of James J. Jeffries in the police gazette.~~

There are too many people alive for me to write about my father yet. He had much bad luck and it was not all of it his own (we betrayed him in our several ways some more than others) but while you wait for two to die there is no harm in ~~considering~~ speaking well of his eyes. He had the finest eyes that I have ever seen in human, animal or bird ~~and it is now many years since I believed he could have whipped~~
~~on the other~~

and he was built, then, like the pictures of James J. Jeffries in the Police Gazette. I loved him very much and I was fourteen before I knew that however he had made his life I must make mine differently if I was to come through since his ~~own~~ life by then was ruined. That was the ~~thing~~ conviction we all started with and which helped us make some of our ~~bloodiest~~ most lurid mistakes. You could believe nothing your parents told you after a certain age because you had the example of their lives before you and you knew that whatever happened to your own life it should not be like that. So you made a very different life and, at least, it was more fantastic if it will be no more successful.

I have seen him when we used to row in the boat in the evenings, trolling, the lake quiet, the sun down behind the hills, widening cir-cles where the bars rose, ask me to take the oars because it was too uncomfortable.

"It is a combination of the hot weather and the exercise," he said. I would row, not knowing what it was about, trying to please him by my rowing, watching the dark bulk of him sitting in the stern holding the rod and I did not know what it was made him so uncomfortable. I had not started to be uncomfortable that way yet and when I was all he ever told me was that masturbation produced blindness, insan-ity and death while prostitutes gave you gonorrhea and syphilis and that the thing to do was keep your hands off of people. He ~~also~~ gave me only two other pieces of information on such matters. Once when we were hunting I shot a red squirrel in a hemlock tree that squirrel fell, contorting ~~clawing~~ turning and grabbing at the branches and when I held him with my hand he bit me clean through the ball of the thumb.

"The little buggar," I said and smacked his head against the tree. "Look how he bit me!"

"Do you know what a buggar is?" my father asked.

"No. We call anything a buggar."

"A buggar is a man who has intercourse with animals."

"Why?" I asked.

"I don't know," he said. "But it is a heinous crime."

My imagination was stirred by this and I thought of various animals but none seemed very attractive or practical and that is the sum total of sexual knowledge bequeathed me by my father except on one other subject. I read in the papers that Enrico Caruso had been arrested for mashing.

"What is mashing?"

"It is one of the most heinous of crimes," my father answered. My imagination pictured the great tenor doing something strange, bizarre and heinous to a beautiful lady with a potato masher. I resolved with considerable horror that when I was old enough I would try mashing ~~perhaps~~ once at least.

~~My father, when we undressed in the boathouse to go swimming, was built like the pictures of James J. Jeffries in the police gazette.~~

~~Our~~ My own ~~sexual~~ education in these matters was ~~derived from~~ acquired in the Hemlock woods behind the Indian camp which was reached by a trail through the woods behind the cottage to the farm and then by a road which wound through the slashings to the camp. Now I can feel all of that trail with bare feet, the pine needle loam through the first hemlock woods behind the house, the black muck of the creek bottom, the hardened dirt with cropped grass and sheep sorell [sorrel] that ran beside the bog of the creek where killdeer plover always fed, the good fresh manure of the lower barn, then the baked hard trail ~~through~~ from the barn to the farmhouse and the hot sandy road that went down to the woods then clay and shale as it widened and turned in the woods where it had been broadened for them to ~~hand~~ skid out the ~~loads of~~ hemlock bark ~~that was piled~~ the Indians cut. The hemlock bark was ~~piled stacked~~ piled in long rows of ~~piles~~ stacks roofed over with more bark like houses and the peeled logs lay huge and yellow ~~white~~ where the trees had been felled. They left the logs in the woods to rot, they did not clear away or burn the tops. It was only the bark the[y] wanted for the tannery at Boyne City; hauling it across the lake on the ice in winter and each year there was less ~~cool~~ forest and more ~~bare, impassible tangled~~ open, hot, shadeless, weed-grown slashing. But there was still much forest then, virgin forest where the trees grew very high before there were any branches and you walked on the brown, clean, springy-needled ground with no undergrowth and it was cool on the hottest days and we three ~~sat~~ lay against the trunk of a hemlock wider than two beds are long with the ~~wind~~ breeze high in the tops and the cool light that came in patches and Dick said, "You want Prudy again?"

"You want?"

"Uh huh."

"Come on."

"No, here."

"But Dick."

"I no mind Dick. He my brother."

Dick laughed. And thought it was funny.

Then after a while we were sitting, the three of us, listening for a black squirrel that was in the top branches where we could not see him. We were waiting for him to bark again because when~~ever~~ he barked he would jerk his tail and I would shoot where I saw ~~the tail move~~ any movement. My father gave me three cartridges a day to hunt with and I had a single barrel 20 gauge with a very long barrell.

"Son of a bitch never move," Dick said.

"You shoot Nickie. Scare him. We see him jump. Shoot him again," Prudy said.

"We only got two shells," I said.

"Son a bitch," said Dick.

We sat against the tree and were quiet. I was feeling hollow and happy.

"Eddie says he is going to come some night sleep in bed with your sister Dorothy."

"What?" ~~I was outraged.~~

"He said."

Prudy nodded.

"That's all he want to do," she said.

Eddie was their older half-brother. He was seventeen.

"~~Listen~~ If Eddie Gilbey ever comes at night and even speaks to Dorothy you know what I'd do to him. I'd kill him like this." I cocked the gun and pulled the trigger blowing a hole as big as your hand in the head or belly of that half breed bastard Eddie Gilbey. "Like that. I'd kill him like that."

"He better not come then," Prudy said. She put her hand in my pocket.

"He better watch out plenty," ~~Dick~~ said Dick.

"He's big bluff," Prudy put her hand on me. "But don't you kill him. You get plenty trouble."

"I'd kill him like that," I said. Eddie Gilbey lay on the ground with all his chest shot away. I put my foot on him proudly.

"I'd scalp him," I said happily ~~proudly~~.

"No," said Prudy. "That's dirty."

"I'd scalp him and send it to his mother."

"His mother dead." Prudy said. "Don't you kill him Nickie. Don't you kill him for me."

"After I scalped him I'd throw him to the dogs."

Dick was very depressed. "He better watch out," he said gloomily-happily.

"They'd tear him to pieces," I said.

Then ~~while~~ having scalped that half breed renegade and standing watching the dogs tear him, my face not changing, I fell back~~wards~~ against the tree, held tight around the neck Prudy ~~holding, tight~~ squeezing, and crying, "No kill him. No kill him. No kill him. No. No. No. Nickie, Nickie, Nickie."

"What's the matter with you?"

"No kill him."

"I got to kill him."

"He just a big bluff."

"All right," I said. "I won't kill him unless he comes around the house."

"You're good," Prudy said.

"You want to do anything now? I feel good now."

"If Dick goes away." I had killed Eddie Gilbey, then pardoned his life and I was a man now.

"You go Dick. You hang around ~~us~~ all the time. ~~What's a matter?~~ Go on."

"Son a bitch," Dick said. "I get tired this. What we come? Hunt or what?"

"You can take the gun. There's one shell."

"All right. I get ~~that~~ a big black ~~son a bitch~~ one all right."

"I'll holler," I said.

It was a long time and Dick hadn't come back yet.

"You think we make a baby?" Prudy said folding her brown legs together happily and rubbing against me like a kitten.

"I don't think so."

"Make plenty baby what the hell."

We heard Dick shoot.

"I wonder if he got one."

"Don't care," said Prudy. "Feel too good."

Dick came through the trees. He had the gun over his shoulder and he held a black squirrel by the front paws.

"Look," he said. "Bigger than a cat. You all through?"

"Where'd you get him?"

"Over there. I saw him jump first."

"Got to go home," I said.

"No," said Prudy.

"I got to get there for supper."

"All right."

"Want to hunt tomorrow?"

"All right."

"You can have the squirrel."

"All right."

"Come out after supper?"

"No."

"How you feel?"

"Good."

"All right."

"Give me kiss on the face," said Prudy.

Now we rode along the highway in the car and it was getting dark. I was all through thinking about my father.

"What was it like Papa when you were a little boy and used to hunt with the Indians?"

"I don't know Schatz." I said. I was startled. "We used to go all day to hunt black squirrels. My father only gave me three shells a day because he said that would teach me to hunt and it wasn't good for a boy to go banging around. I went with a boy named Dick Gilbey and his sister Prudy. We used to go out nearly every day all one summer."

"Those are funny names for Indians."

"Yes, aren't they," I said.

"But tell me what they were like."

"They were Ojibways," I said. "And they were very nice."

"But what were they like to be with?"

"It's hard to say," I said. I could not tell him of the plump brown legs, the flat belly, the hard little breasts, nor the quick searching tongue nor the flat eyes, nor how she did first what no one ever has done better, nor hemlock needles stuck against your belly, nor the sweet Indian smell of sweetgrass, smoke and arm-pit salt nor good taste of her mouth nor how it was at first when the big bird flew hollowly like an owl in the twilight only it was broad day in the woods.

"You want."

"Uh huh."

"All the way. Like it so much the most."

If you go to a place where Indians have lived you smell them gone and all the empty pain killer bottles and the flies that buzz do not kill the good smell.

"You might not like them but I think you would."

"And my grandfather lived with them when he was a boy too didn't he?"

"Yes. When I asked him what they were like he said that he had many friends among them."

"Will I ever live with them?"

"I don't know," I said. "That's up to you."

"How old will I be when I get a shotgun?"

"Twelve years old if I see you are careful."

"I wish I was twelve now."

"You will be soon enough."

"What was my grandfather like? I can't remember him except that he gave me an American flag."

"He's hard to describe. He was a great hunter and fisherman."

"Greater than you?"

"A much better shot and his father was a great wing shot."

"I'll bet he wasn't better than you."

"Oh yes he was. He shot very quickly and beautifully. I'd rather see him shoot than any man I ever knew."

"Why do we never go to pray at the tomb of my grandfather?"

"We live in a different part of the country. It's a long way from here."

"In France that wouldn't make any difference. In France we'd go. I think I ought to go to pray at the tomb of my grandfather."

"Sometime we'll go."

"I hope we won't live somewhere so that I can never go to pray at your tomb when you are dead."

"We'll have to arrange it."

"Don't you think we might all be buried at a convenient place. We could all be buried in France. That would be fine."

"I don't want to be buried in France."

"Well then we'll have to get some convenient place in America. Couldn't we all be buried out at the ranch?"

"That's an idea."

"Then I could stop and pray at the tomb of my grandfather on the way to the ranch."

"You're awfully practical."

"Well I don't feel good never to have even visited the tomb of my grandfather."

"We'll have to go," I said. "I can see we'll have to go."

15c.

Item 384, Ernest Hemingway Collection, John F. Kennedy Library and Museum, Boston. Discarded pencil manuscript fragment relating to "Fathers and Sons."

a man suffers in his own home are only a proof of his weakness. There is only one thing to do if ~~you are~~ a man is married to a woman with whom he has nothing in common, with whom there can be no question of justice but only a gross fact of utter selfishness and hysterical emotionalism and that is to get rid of her. He might try to whip her first but it would probably be no good. Whoever, in a marriage of that sort, wins the first encounter is in command and, having lost, to continue to appeal to reason, to write letters at night, hysterically logical letters explaining your position, to have it out again before the children—then the inevitable making up, loser received by victor with some magnanimity, everything that had been told the children cancelled, the home full of love, and mother carried you, darling, over her heart all those months and her heart beat in your heart. Oh yes and what about his ~~poor bloody~~ heart and where did it beat and who ~~beats it now and what a hollow sound it makes.~~ I've seen him when we used to row in the boat in the evening, trolling, the lake quiet, the sun down behind the hills, widening circles where the bass rose, ask me to take the oars because it was too uncomfortable. "It's the hot weather," he said. "And the exercise."

I would row, not knowing what it was about, watching him sitting in the stern the ~~big~~ bulk of him, the blackness of him, he was very big and his hair and beard were black, his skin was dark and he had an indian nose and those wonderful eyes and I didn't know what it was that made him so uncomfortable. I had not started to be uncomfortable that way yet and when I was all he ever told me about sex was that masturbation produced blindness, insanity and death while prostitutes gave you gonorrhea and syphilis and once when we were squirrel

15d.

Item 385, Ernest Hemingway Collection, John F. Kennedy Library and Museum, Boston. Sentence fragment written by hand in pencil on the back side of Hotel Ambos Mundos stationery. One page.

I could not tell him of hemlock needles stuck against your belly, nor the flat eyes, brown legs, smooth belly and hard little breasts nor the sweet Indian smell of

15e.

Item 385a, Ernest Hemingway Collection, John F. Kennedy Library and Museum, Boston. Untitled typescript with pencil corrections and a three page pencil insert.

There had been a sign to detour in the center of the main street of this town but cars had obviously gone through, so believing it was some repair which had been completed, Nicholas Adams drove on through the town along the empty, brick-paved street, stopped by traffic lights that flashed on and off on this traffic-less Sunday; and would be gone next year when payments on the system were not met; on under the heavy trees of the small town that are a part of your heart if it is your own town and have walked under them, but that are only too heavy, that shut out the sun and dampen the houses for a stranger; out past the last house and onto the highway that rose and fell straight away ahead with banks of red dirt sliced cleanly away and the second growth timber on both sides. It was not his country but it was ~~mid~~ the middle of fall and all of this country was good to drive through and to see. The cotton was picked and in the clearings there were patches of corn, some cut with streaks of red sorghum, and driving easily, his son asleep on the seat by his side, the days' run made, knowing the town he would reach for the night, ~~he~~ Nick noticed which corn fields had soy beans or peas in them, how the thickets and the cut-over land lay, where the cabins and houses were in relation to the fields and the thickets, hunting the country in his mind as he went by; sizing up each clearing as to feed and cover and figuring where you would find a covey and which way they would fly.

In shooting quail you must not get between them and their habitual cover, once the dogs have found them, or when they flush they will come pouring at you, some rising steep, some skimming by your ears, whirring into a size you have never seen them in the air as they pass; the only way being to turn and take them over your shoulder as they go before they set their wings and angle down into the thicket. Hunting this country for quail as his father had taught him Nicholas Adams ~~thought~~ started thinking about his father. When he first thought about him it was always the eyes. The big frame, the quick movements, the wide shoulders, the hooked hawk nose, the beard that covered the weak chin you never thought about. It was always the eyes. They were protected in his head by the formation of the brows; set deep as though a special protection had been devised for some very valuable instrument. They saw much further and much quicker than the human eyes sees and they were the great gift his father had. His father saw as a big horn ram or as an eagle sees, literally.

He would be standing with his father on one shore of the lake, his own eyes were very good then, and his father would say, "They've run up the flag." Nick could not see the flag nor the flag pole. "There," his father would say. "It's your sister Dorothy. She's got the flag up and now she's walking out onto the dock."

Nick would look across the lake and he could see the long wooded shore-line and the higher timber behind, the point that guarded the bay, the clear hills of the farm and the white of their cottage in the trees but he could not see any flag pole, nor any dock, only the white of the beach and the curve of the shore.

"Can you see the sheep on the hillside toward the point?"

"Yes." They were a whitish patch on the grey, green of the hill.

"I can count them," his father said.

Like all men with a faculty that surpasses human requirements his father was very nervous. Then too he was sentimental and like most sentimental people he was both cruel and abused. Also he had much bad luck and it was not all of it his own. He had died in a trap that he had not helped to set and they had all betrayed him in their various ways before he died. All sentimental people are betrayed so many times. Nick could not write about him yet although he would later truly and fully, but the quail country made him remember him as he was when Nick was a boy, and he was very grateful to him for two things: fishing and shooting. His father was as sound on those things as he was unsound on sex sex for instance and Nick was glad that it had been that way for someone has to give you your first gun or the opportunity to get it and you have to live where there is game or fish if you are to learn about them, and now, at thirty eight, he loved to fish and to shoot exactly as much as when he first had gone with his father. It was a passion that had never slackened and he was very grateful to his father for teaching him about it.

While for the other, that his father was not sound about, all the equipment you will ever have is provided and each man learns all there is for him to know about it without advice and it makes no difference where you live. He remembered very clearly the only two pieces of information his father had given him about that. Once when they were out shooting together Nick shot a red squirrel out of a hemlock tree. The squirrel fell, wounded, and when he picked him up bit the boy clean through the ball of the thumb.

"The dirty little buggar," Nick said and smacked the squirrel's head against the tree. "Look how he bit me."

His father looked and said, "Suck it out clean and put some iodine on when you get home."

"The little buggar," Nick said.

"Do you know what a buggar is?" his father asked.

"We call anything a buggar," Nick said.

"A buggar is a man who has intercourse with animals."

"Why?" Nick asked.

"I don't know," he said. "But it is a heinous crime."

Nick's imagination was stirred by this and he thought of various animals but none seemed ~~either~~ attractive nor practical and that was the sum total of direct sexual knowle[d]ge bequeathed him by his father except on one other subject. One morning he read in the paper that Enrico Caruso had been arrested for mashing.

"What is mashing?"

"It is one of the most heinous of crimes," his father answered. Nick's ~~mind~~ imagination pictured the great tenor doing something strange, bizarre and heinous with a potato masher to a beautiful lady who looked like the pictures of Anna Held on the inside of cigar boxes. He resolved, with considerable horror, that when he was old enough he would try mashing at least once.

His father had summed up the whole matter by stating that masturbation produced blindness, insanity and death while a man who went with prostitutes would contract hideous venereal diseases and that the thing to do was to keep your hands off of people. On the other hand his father had the finest pair of eyes he had ever seen and Nick had loved him very much and when he thought about him it always made him sad. If he wrote it he could get rid of it. But it was still too early for that. He would tell it all or nothing. So he decided to think of something else.

Nick's own education in ~~this~~ these matters was acquired in the hemlock woods behind the Indian camp. This was reached by a trail which ran from the cottage through the woods to the farm and then by a road which wound through the slashings to the camp. Now he could still feel all of that trail with bare feet. First there was the pine needle loam through the hemlock woods behind the cottage where the fallen logs crumbled into wood dust and long splintered pieces of wood hung like javelins in the tree that had been struck by lightening. You crossed the creek on a log and if you stepped off there was the black muck of the swamp. You climbed a fence out of the woods and the trail was hard in the sun across the field with cropped grass and sheep sorrel and mullen growing and to the left the quaky bog of the creek bottom where the killdeer plover fed. The spring house was in that creek. Below the barn there was fresh warm manure and other that was caked dry on top. Then another fence and the hard, hot trail from the barn to the house and the hot sandy road that ran down to the woods, crossing the creek on a bridge this time where the cat tails grew that you soaked in kerosene to make jack-lights with.

Then the main road went off to the left skirting the woods and climbing the hill while you went into the woods on the wide clay and shale road cool under the trees and broadened for them to skid out the hemlock bark the Indians cut. The hemlock bark was piled in long rows of stacks, roofed over with more bark like houses and the peeled logs lay huge and yellow where the trees had been felled. They left the logs in the woods to rot, they did not even clear away or burn the tops. It was only the bark they wanted for the tannery at Boyne City; hauling it across the lake on the ice in winter and each year there was less forest and more open, hot, shadeless, weed-grown slashing.

But there was still much forest then; virgin forest where the trees grew high before there were any branches and you walked on the brown, clean, springy-needled ground with no undergrowth ~~only the tall trunks~~ and it was cool on the hottest days and they three lay against the trunk of a hemlock wider than two beds are long with the breeze high in the tops and the cool light that came in patches and Billy said, "You want Trudy again?"

"You want to?"

"Uh huh."

"Come on."

"No, here."

"But Billy—"

"I no mind Billy. He my brother."

Then ~~they would sit~~ afterwards they sat, the three of them, listening for a black squirrel that was in the top branches where they could not see him. They were waiting for him to bark again because when he barked he would jerk his tail and Nick would shoot where he saw any movement. His father gave him only three cartridges a day to hunt with and he had a single barrel twenty gauge shot gun with a very long barrel.

"Son of a bitch never move," Billy said.

"You shoot, Nickie. Scare him. We see him jump. Shoot him again," Trudy said. It was a long speech for her.

"I've only got two shells," Nick said.

"Son a bitch," said Billy.

They sat against the tree and were quiet. Nick was feeling hollow and happy.

"Eddie says he going to come some night sleep in bed with you sister Dorothy."

"What?"

"He said."

Trudy nodded.

"That's all he want to do," she said. Eddie was their older half-brother. He was seventeen.

"If Eddie Gilbey ever comes at night and even speaks to Dorothy you know what I'd do to him? I'd kill him like this." Nick cocked the gun and hardly taking aim ~~blew~~ pulled the trigger blowing a hole as big as your hand in the head or belly of that half breed bastard Eddie Gilbey. "Like that. I'd kill him like that."

"He better not come then," Trudy said. She put her hand in Nick's pocket.

"He better watch out plenty," said Billy.

"He's big bluff," Trudy was exploring with her hand in Nick's pocket. "But don't you kill him. You get plenty trouble."

"I'd kill him like that," Nick said. Eddie Gilbey lay on the ground with all his chest shot away. Nick put his foot on him proudly.

"I'd scalp him," he said happily.

"No," said Trudy. "That's dirty."

"I'd scalp him and send it to his mother."

"His mother dead," Trudy said. "Don't you kill him Nickie. Don't you kill him for me."

"After I scalped him I'd throw him to the dogs."

Billy was very depressed. "He better watch out," he said gloomily.

"They'd tear him to pieces," Nick said, pleased with the picture. Then, having scalped that half breed renegade and standing watching the dogs tear him, his face unchanging, he fell backward against the tree, held tight around the neck, Trudy holding, choking him and crying, "No kill him! No kill him! No kill him! No. No. No. Nickie. Nickie. Nickie!"

"What's the matter with you?"

"No kill him."

"I got to kill him."

"He just a big bluff."

"All right," Nick said. "I won't kill him unless he comes around the house. Let go of me."

"That's good," Trudy said. "You want to do anything now? I feel good now."

"If Billy goes away," Nick had killed Eddie Gilbey, then pardoned his life, and he was a man now.

"You go Billy. You hang around all the time. Go on."

"Son a bitch," Billy said. "I get tired this. What we come? Hunt or what?"

"You can take the gun. There's one shell."

"All right. I get a big black one all right."

"I'll holler," Nick said.

It was a long time after and Billy was still away.

"You think we make a baby?" Trudy folded her brown legs together happily and rubbed against him. Something inside Nick ~~was feeling~~ had gone a long way ~~off~~ away.

"I don't think so," he said.

"Make plenty baby what the hell."

~~We~~ They heard Billy shoot.

"I wonder if he got one."

"Don't care," said Trudy.

Billy came through the trees. He had the gun over his shoulder and he held a black squirrel by the front paws.

"Look," he said. "Bigger than a cat. You all through?"

"Where'd you get him?"

"Over there. Saw him jump first."

"Got to go home," Nick said.

"No," said Trudy.

"I got to get there for supper."

"All right."

"Want to hunt tomorrow?"

"All right."

"You can have the squirrel."

"All right."

"Come out after supper?"

"No."

"How you feel?"

"Good."

"All right."

"Give me kiss on the face," said Trudy.

Now as he rode along the highway in the car and it was getting dark Nick was all through thinking about his father. (Insert)

(Insert) [handwritten in pencil]

His father came back to him in the fall of the year, or in the early spring when there were jacksnipe on the prairie, or when he saw shocks of corn, or when he saw a lake, ~~any lake, anywhere,~~ or if he ever saw a horse and buggy, or in a duck blind, remembering the time a golden eagle dropped through the whirling snow to strike a canvas covered decoy, rising, his wings beating, the talons caught in the canvas, and in all deserted orchards and in all new plowed fields, in all thickets, in small hills or when going through dead grass, whenever splitting wood or hauling water by grist mills, cider mills and dams and always with open fires. His father had frost in his beard in cold weather and in hot weather he sweated very much. He liked to work in the sun on the farm because he did not have to and he loved manual work which Nick did not. Nick loved his father but hated the smell of him and once when he had to wear a suit of his father's underwear that had gotten too small for his father it made him feel sick all day and he took it off and put it under two stones in the creek and said he had lost it. He had ~~complained~~ told his father how it was when his father had made him put it on but his father had said it was freshly washed. When Nick had asked him to smell of it his father had smelled it indignantly and said it was clean and fresh. When Nick came home from fishing without it and said he had lost it he was whipped for lying. Afterwards he had sat inside the woodshed with the door open, his shotgun cocked, looking across at his father sitting on the screen porch reading the paper, and he thought, "I can blow him to hell. I can kill him." And felt his anger go out of him finally. Then he had gone to the Indian camp, walking there in the dark, to get rid of the smell. There was only one person in his family that he liked the smell of, one sister. All the others Nick avoided personal contact with. . . . sense blunted when he started to smoke . . . a good thing. It was good for a . . . it did not hel[p a] man. [Parts of the page are torn and text is missing.]

"What was it like papa when you were a little boy and used to hunt with the Indians?"

"I don't know," he Nick was startled. He had not even noticed the boy was awake. "We used to go all day to hunt black squirrels. My father only gave me three shells a day because he said that would teach me to hunt and it wasn't good for a boy to go banging around. I went with a boy named Billy Gilbey and his sister Trudy. We used to go out nearly every day all summer."

"Those are funny names for Indians."

"Yes. Aren't they," Nick said.

"But tell me what were they like."

"They were Ojibways," Nick said. "And they were very nice."

"But what were they like to be with?"

"It's hard to say," Nick Adams said. Could you say she did first what no one ever has done better and describe plump brown legs, flat belly, hard little breasts quick searching tongue, nor the flat eyes, good taste of mouth and then uncomfortably, sweetly, moistly, lovely, tightly, achingly, fully, finally, unendingly, never-endingly, never-to-endingly, suddenly ended the great bird flown like an owl in the twilight only it xxxx daylight in the woods and hemlock needles stuck against your belly. So when you go in a place where Indians have lived you smell them gone and all the empty pain killer bottles and the flies that buzz do not kill sweetgrass, smoke and what was that other? Nor any jokes about them nor old squaws take it away. It wasn't how they ended and about the other. When you have shot one bird flying you have shot all birds flying. They are all different and they fly in different ways but the sensation is the same and the last one is as good as the first. His father was very intelligent about shooting and fishing. He could not talk about it either.

"You might not like them," Nick said to the boy. "But I think you would."

"And my grandfather lived with them too when he was a boy didn't he?"

"Yes. When I asked him what they were like he said that he had many friends among them."

"Will I ever live with them?"

"I don't know," Nick said. "That's up to you."

"How old will I be when I get a shotgun and can hunt by myself?"

"Twelve years old if I see you are careful."

"I wish I was twelve now."

"You will be, soon enough."

"What was my grandfather like? I can't remember him except that he gave me an air rifle and an American flag when I came over from France that time. What was he like?"

"He's hard to describe. He was a great hunter and fisherman and he had wonderful eyes."

"Was he greater than you?"

"He was a much better shot and his father was a great wing shot too."

"I'll bet he wasn't better than you."

"Oh yes he was. He shot very quickly and beautifully. I'd rather see him shoot than any man I ever knew. He was always very disappointed in the way I shot."

"Why do we never go to pray at the tomb of my grandfather?"

"We live in a different part of the country. It's a long way from here."

"In France that wouldn't make any difference. In France we'd go. I think I ought to go to pray at the tomb of my grandfather."

"Sometime we'll go."

"I hope we won't live somewhere so that I can never go to pray at your tomb when you are dead."

"We'll have to arrange it."

"Don't you think we might all be buried at a convenient place. We could all be buried in France. That would be fine."

"I don't want to be buried in France," Nick said.

"Well then we'll have to get some convenient place in America. Couldn't we all be buried out at the ranch?"

"That's an idea."

"Then I could stop and pray at the tomb of my grandfather on the way to the ranch."

"You're awfully practical."

"Well I don't feel good never to have even visited the tomb of my grandfather."

"We'll have to go," Nick said. "I can see we'll have to go."

16.

The Short Happy Life of Francis Macomber

1936

It was now lunch time and they were all sitting under the double green fly of the dining tent pretending that nothing had happened.

"Will you have lime juice or lemon squash?" Macomber asked.

"I'll have a gimlet," Robert Wilson told him.

"I'll have a gimlet too. I need something," Macomber's wife said.

"I suppose it's the thing to do," Macomber agreed. "Tell him to make three gimlets."

The mess boy had started them already, lifting the bottles out of the canvas cooling bags that sweated wet in the wind that blew through the trees that shaded the tents.

"What had I ought to give them?" Macomber asked.

"A quid would be plenty," Wilson told him. "You don't want to spoil them."

"Will the headman distribute it?"

"Absolutely."

Francis Macomber had, half an hour before, been carried to his tent from the edge of the camp in triumph on the arms and shoulders of the cook, the personal boys, the skinner and the porters. The gun-bearers had taken no part in the demonstration. When the native boys put him down at the door of his tent, he had shaken all their hands, received their congratulations, and then gone into the tent and sat on the bed until his wife came in. She did not speak to him when she came in and he left the tent at once to wash his face and hands in the portable wash basin outside and go over to the dining tent to sit in a comfortable canvas chair in the breeze and the shade.

"You've got your lion," Robert Wilson said to him, "and a damned fine one too."

Mrs. Macomber looked at Wilson quickly. She was an extremely handsome and well-kept woman of the beauty and social position which had, five years before, commanded five thousand dollars as the price of endorsing, with photographs, a beauty product which she had never used. She had been married to Francis Macomber for eleven years.

"He is a good lion, isn't he?" Macomber said. His wife looked at him now. She looked at both these men as though she had never seen them before.

One, Wilson, the white hunter, she knew she had never truly seen before. He was about middle height with sandy hair, a stubby mustache, a very red face and extremely cold blue eyes with faint white wrinkles at the corners that grooved merrily when he smiled. He smiled at her now and she looked away from his face at the way his shoulders sloped in the loose tunic he wore with the four big cartridges held in loops where the left breast pocket should have been, at his big brown hands, his old slacks, his very dirty boots and back to his red face again. She noticed where the baked red of his face stopped in a white line that marked the circle left by his Stetson hat that hung now from one of the pegs of the tent pole.

"Well, here's to the lion," Robert Wilson said. He smiled at her again and, not smiling, she looked curiously at her husband.

Francis Macomber was very tall, very well built if you did not mind that length of bone, dark, his hair cropped like an oarsman, rather thin-lipped, and was considered handsome. He was dressed in the same sort of safari clothes that Wilson wore except that his were new, he was thirty-five years old, kept himself very fit, was good at court games, had a number of big-game fishing records, and had just shown himself, very publicly, to be a coward.

"Here's to the lion," he said. "I can't ever thank you for what you did."

Margaret, his wife, looked away from him and back to Wilson.

"Let's not talk about the lion," she said.

Wilson looked over at her without smiling and now she smiled at him.

"It's been a very strange day," she said. "Hadn't you ought to put your hat on even under the canvas at noon? You told me that, you know."

"Might put it on," said Wilson.

"You know you have a very red face, Mr. Wilson," she told him and smiled again.

"Drink," said Wilson.

"I don't think so," she said. "Francis drinks a great deal, but his face is never red."

"It's red today," Macomber tried a joke.

"No," said Margaret. "It's mine that's red today. But Mr. Wilson's is always red."

"Must be racial," said Wilson. "I say, you wouldn't like to drop my beauty as a topic, would you?"

"I've just started on it."

"Let's chuck it," said Wilson.

"Conversation is going to be so difficult," Margaret said.

"Don't be silly, Margot," her husband said.

"No difficulty," Wilson said. "Got a damn fine lion."

Margot looked at them both and they both saw that she was going to cry. Wilson had seen it coming for a long time and he dreaded it. Macomber was past dreading it.

"I wish it hadn't happened. Oh, I wish it hadn't happened," she said and started for her tent. She made no noise of crying but they could see that her shoulders were shaking under the rose-colored, sun-proofed shirt she wore.

"Women upset," said Wilson to the tall man. "Amounts to nothing. Strain on the nerves and one thing'n another."

"No," said Macomber. "I suppose that I rate that for the rest of my life now."

"Nonsense. Let's have a spot of the giant killer," said Wilson. "Forget the whole thing. Nothing to it anyway."

"We might try," said Macomber. "I won't forget what you did for me though."

"Nothing," said Wilson. "All nonsense."

So they sat there in the shade where the camp was pitched under some wide-topped acacia trees with a boulder-strewn cliff behind them, and a stretch of grass that ran to the bank of a boulder-filled stream in front with forest beyond it, and drank their just-cool lime drinks and avoided one another's eyes while the boys set the table for lunch. Wilson could tell that the boys all knew about it now and when he saw Macomber's personal boy looking curiously at his master while he was putting dishes on the table he snapped at him in Swahili. The boy turned away with his face blank.

"What were you telling him?" Macomber asked.

"Nothing. Told him to look alive or I'd see he got about fifteen of the best."

"What's that? Lashes?"

"It's quite illegal," Wilson said. "You're supposed to fine them."

"Do you still have them whipped?"

"Oh, yes. They could raise a row if they chose to complain. But they don't. They prefer it to the fines."

"How strange!" said Macomber.

"Not strange, really," Wilson said. "Which would you rather do? Take a good birching or lose your pay?"

Then he felt embarrassed at asking it and before Macomber could answer he went on, "We all take a beating every day, you know, one way or another."

This was no better. "Good God," he thought. "I am a diplomat, aren't I?"

"Yes, we take a beating," said Macomber, still not looking at him. "I'm awfully sorry about that lion business. It doesn't have to go any further, does it? I mean no one will hear about it, will they?"

"You mean will I tell it at the Mathaiga Club?" Wilson looked at him now coldly. He had not expected this. So he's a bloody four-letter man as well as a bloody coward, he thought. I rather liked him too until today. But how is one to know about an American?

"No," said Wilson. "I'm a professional hunter. We never talk about our clients. You can be quite easy on that. It's supposed to be bad form to ask us not to talk though."

He had decided now that to break would be much easier. He would eat, then, by himself and could read a book with his meals. They would eat by themselves. He would see them through the safari on a very formal basis—what was it the French called it? Distinguished consideration—and it would be a damn sight easier than having to go through this emotional trash. He'd insult him and make a good clean break. Then he could read a book with his meals and he'd still be drinking their whisky. That was the phrase for it when a safari went bad. You ran into another white hunter and you asked, "How is everything going?" and he answered, "Oh, I'm still drinking their whisky," and you knew everything had gone to pot.

"I'm sorry," Macomber said and looked at him with his American face that would stay adolescent until it became middle-aged, and Wilson noted his crew-cropped hair, fine eyes only faintly shifty, good nose, thin lips and handsome jaw. "I'm sorry I didn't realize that. There are lots of things I don't know."

So what could he do, Wilson thought. He was all ready to break it off quickly and neatly and here the beggar was apologizing after he had just insulted him. He made one more attempt. "Don't worry about me talking," he said. "I have a living to make. You know in Africa no woman ever misses her lion and no white man ever bolts."

"I bolted like a rabbit," Macomber said.

Now what in hell were you going to do about a man who talked like that, Wilson wondered.

Wilson looked at Macomber with his flat, blue, machine-gunner's eyes and the other smiled back at him. He had a pleasant smile if you did not notice how his eyes showed when he was hurt.

"Maybe I can fix it up on buffalo," he said. "We're after them next, aren't we?"

"In the morning if you like," Wilson told him. Perhaps he had been wrong. This was certainly the way to take it. You most certainly could not tell a damned thing about an American. He was all for Macomber again. If you could forget the morning. But, of course, you couldn't. The morning had been about as bad as they come.

"Here comes the Memsahib," he said. She was walking over from her tent looking refreshed and cheerful and quite lovely. She had a very perfect oval face, so perfect that you expected her to be stupid. But she wasn't stupid, Wilson thought, no, not stupid.

"How is the beautiful red-faced Mr. Wilson? Are you feeling better, Francis, my pearl?"

"Oh, much," said Macomber.

"I've dropped the whole thing," she said, sitting down at the table. "What importance is there to whether Francis is any good at killing lions? That's not his trade. That's Mr. Wilson's trade. Mr. Wilson is really very impressive killing anything. You do kill anything, don't you?"

"Oh, anything," said Wilson. "Simply anything." They are, he thought, the hardest in the world; the hardest, the cruelest, the most predatory and the most attractive and their men have softened or gone to pieces nervously as they have hardened. Or is it that they pick men they can handle? They can't know that much at the age they marry, he thought. He was grateful that he had gone through his education on American women before now because this was a very attractive one.

"We're going after buff in the morning," he told her.

"I'm coming," she said.

"No, you're not."

"Oh, yes, I am. Mayn't I, Francis?"

"Why not stay in camp?"

"Not for anything," she said. "I wouldn't miss something like today for anything."

When she left, Wilson was thinking, when she went off to cry, she seemed a hell of a fine woman. She seemed to understand, to realize, to be hurt for him and for herself and to know how things really stood. She is away for twenty minutes and now she is back, simply enamelled in that American female cruelty. They are the damnedest women. Really the damnedest.

"We'll put on another show for you tomorrow," Francis Macomber said.

"You're not coming," Wilson said.

"You're very mistaken," she told him. "And I want *so* to see you perform again. You were lovely this morning. That is if blowing things' heads off is lovely."

"Here's the lunch," said Wilson. "You're very merry, aren't you?"

"Why not? I didn't come out here to be dull."

"Well, it hasn't been dull," Wilson said. He could see the boulders in the river and the high bank beyond with the trees and he remembered the morning.

"Oh, no," she said. "It's been charming. And tomorrow. You don't know how I look forward to tomorrow."

"That's eland he's offering you," Wilson said.

"They're the big cowy things that jump like hares, aren't they?"

"I suppose that describes them," Wilson said.

"It's very good meat," Macomber said.

"Did you shoot it, Francis?" she asked.

"Yes."

"They're not dangerous, are they?"

"Only if they fall on you," Wilson told her.

"I'm so glad."

"Why not let up on the bitchery just a little, Margot," Macomber said, cutting the eland steak and putting some mashed potato, gravy and carrot on the down-turned fork that tined through the piece of meat.

"I suppose I could," she said, "since you put it so prettily."

"Tonight we'll have champagne for the lion," Wilson said. "It's a bit too hot at noon."

"Oh, the lion," Margot said. "I'd forgotten the lion!"

So, Robert Wilson thought to himself, she *is* giving him a ride, isn't she? Or do you suppose that's her idea of putting up a good show? How should a woman act when she discovers her husband is a bloody coward? She's damn cruel but they're all cruel. They govern, of course, and to govern one has to be cruel sometimes. Still, I've seen enough of their damn terrorism.

"Have some more eland," he said to her politely.

That afternoon, late, Wilson and Macomber went out in the motor car with the native driver and the two gun-bearers. Mrs. Macomber stayed in the camp. It was too hot to go out, she said, and she was going with them in the early morning. As they drove off Wilson saw her standing under the big tree, looking pretty rather than beautiful in her faintly rosy khaki, her dark hair drawn back off her forehead and gathered in a knot low on her neck, her face as fresh, he thought, as though she were in England. She waved to them as the car went off through the swale of high grass and curved around through the trees into the small hills of orchard bush.

In the orchard bush they found a herd of impala, and leaving the car they stalked one old ram with long, wide-spread horns and Macomber killed it with a very creditable shot that knocked the buck down at a good two hundred yards and sent the herd off bounding wildly and leaping over one another's backs in long, leg-drawn-up leaps as unbelievable and as floating as those one makes sometimes in dreams.

"That was a good shot," Wilson said. "They're a small target."

"Is it a worth-while head?" Macomber asked.

"It's excellent," Wilson told him. "You shoot like that and you'll have no trouble."

"Do you think we'll find buffalo tomorrow?"

"There's a good chance of it. They feed out early in the morning and with luck we may catch them in the open."

"I'd like to clear away that lion business," Macomber said. "It's not very pleasant to have your wife see you do something like that."

I should think it would be even more unpleasant to do it, Wilson thought, wife or no wife, or to talk about it having done it. But he said, "I wouldn't think about that any more. Any one could be upset by his first lion. That's all over."

But that night after dinner and a whisky and soda by the fire before going to bed, as Francis Macomber lay on his cot with the mosquito bar over him and listened to the night noises it was not all over. It was neither all over nor was it beginning. It was there exactly as it happened with some parts of it indelibly emphasized and he was miserably ashamed at it. But more than shame he felt cold, hollow fear in him. The fear was still there like a cold slimy hollow in all the emptiness where once his confidence had been and it made him feel sick. It was still there with him now.

It had started the night before when he had wakened and heard the lion roaring somewhere up along the river. It was a deep sound and at the end there were sort of coughing grunts that made him seem just outside the tent, and when Francis Macomber woke in the night to hear it he was afraid. He could hear his wife breathing quietly, asleep. There was no one to tell he was afraid, nor to be afraid with him, and, lying alone, he did not know the Somali proverb that says a brave man is always frightened three times by a lion; when he first sees his track, when he first hears him roar and when he first confronts him. Then while they were eating breakfast by lantern light out in the dining tent, before the sun was up, the lion roared again and Francis thought he was just at the edge of camp.

"Sounds like an old-timer," Robert Wilson said, looking up from his kippers and coffee. "Listen to him cough."

"Is he very close?"

"A mile or so up the stream."

"Will we see him?"

"We'll have a look."

"Does his roaring carry that far? It sounds as though he were right in camp."

"Carries a hell of a long way," said Robert Wilson. "It's strange the way it carries. Hope he's a shootable cat. The boys said there was a very big one about here."

"If I get a shot, where should I hit him," Macomber asked, "to stop him?"

"In the shoulders," Wilson said. "In the neck if you can make it. Shoot for bone. Break him down."

"I hope I can place it properly," Macomber said.

"You shoot very well," Wilson told him. "Take your time. Make sure of him. The first one in is the one that counts."

"What range will it be?"

"Can't tell. Lion has something to say about that. Don't shoot unless it's close enough so you can make sure."

"At under a hundred yards?" Macomber asked.

Wilson looked at him quickly.

"Hundred's about right. Might have to take him a bit under. Shouldn't chance a shot at much over that. A hundred's a decent range. You can hit him wherever you want at that. Here comes the Memsahib."

"Good morning," she said. "Are we going after that lion?"

"As soon as you deal with your breakfast," Wilson said. "How are you feeling?"

"Marvellous," she said. "I'm very excited."

"I'll just go and see that everything is ready." Wilson went off. As he left the lion roared again.

"Noisy beggar," Wilson said. "We'll put a stop to that."

"What's the matter, Francis?" his wife asked him.

"Nothing," Macomber said.

"Yes, there is," she said. "What are you upset about?"

"Nothing," he said.

"Tell me," she looked at him. "Don't you feel well?"

"It's that damned roaring," he said. "It's been going on all night, you know."

"Why didn't you wake me," she said. "I'd love to have heard it."

"I've got to kill the damned thing," Macomber said, miserably.

"Well, that's what you're out here for, isn't it?"

"Yes. But I'm nervous. Hearing the thing roar gets on my nerves."

"Well then, as Wilson said, kill him and stop his roaring."

"Yes, darling," said Francis Macomber. "It sounds easy, doesn't it?"

"You're not afraid, are you?"

"Of course not. But I'm nervous from hearing him roar all night."

"You'll kill him marvellously," she said. "I know you will. I'm awfully anxious to see it."

"Finish your breakfast and we'll be starting."

"It's not light yet," she said. "This is a ridiculous hour."

Just then the lion roared in a deep-chested moaning, suddenly guttural, ascending vibration that seemed to shake the air and ended in a sigh and a heavy, deep-chested grunt.

"He sounds almost here," Macomber's wife said.

"My God," said Macomber. "I hate that damned noise."

"It's very impressive."

"Impressive. It's frightful."

Robert Wilson came up then carrying his short, ugly, shockingly bigbored .505 Gibbs and grinning.

"Come on," he said. "Your gun-bearer has your Springfield and the big gun. Everything's in the car. Have you solids?"

"Yes."

"I'm ready," Mrs. Macomber said.

"Must make him stop that racket," Wilson said. "You get in front. The Memsahib can sit back here with me."

They climbed into the motor car and, in the gray first daylight, moved off up the river through the trees. Macomber opened the breech of his rifle and saw he had metal-cased bullets, shut the bolt and put the rifle on safety. He saw his hand was trembling. He felt in his pocket for more cartridges and moved his fingers over the cartridges in the loops of his tunic front. He turned back to where Wilson sat in the rear seat of the doorless, box-bodied motor car beside his wife, them both grinning with excitement, and Wilson leaned forward and whispered,

"See the birds dropping. Means the old boy has left his kill."

On the far bank of the stream Macomber could see, above the trees, vultures circling and plummeting down.

"Chances are he'll come to drink along here," Wilson whispered. "Before he goes to lay up. Keep an eye out."

They were driving slowly along the high bank of the stream which here cut deeply to its boulder-filled bed, and they wound in and out through big trees as they drove. Macomber was watching the opposite bank when he felt Wilson take hold of his arm. The car stopped.

"There he is," he heard the whisper. "Ahead and to the right. Get out and take him. He's a marvellous lion."

Macomber saw the lion now. He was standing almost broadside, his great head up and turned toward them. The early morning breeze that blew toward them was just stirring his dark mane, and the lion looked huge, silhouetted on the rise of bank in the gray morning light, his shoulders heavy, his barrel of a body bulking smoothly.

"How far is he?" asked Macomber, raising his rifle.

"About seventy-five. Get out and take him."

"Why not shoot from where I am?"

"You don't shoot them from cars," he heard Wilson saying in his ear. "Get out. He's not going to stay there all day."

Macomber stepped out of the curved opening at the side of the front seat, onto the step and down onto the ground. The lion still stood looking majestically and coolly toward this object that his eyes only showed in silhouette, bulking like some super-rhino. There was no man smell carried toward him and he watched the object, moving his great head a little from side to side. Then watching the object, not afraid, but hesitating before going down the bank to drink with such a thing opposite him, he saw a man figure detach itself from it and he turned his heavy head and swung away toward the cover of the trees as he heard a cracking crash and felt the slam of a .30-06 220-grain solid bullet that bit his flank and ripped in sudden hot scalding nausea through his stomach. He trotted, heavy, bigfooted, swinging wounded full-bellied, through the trees toward the tall grass and cover, and the crash came again to go past him ripping the air apart. Then it crashed again and he felt the blow as it hit his lower ribs and ripped on through, blood sudden hot and frothy in his mouth, and he galloped toward the high grass where he could crouch and not be seen and make them bring the crashing thing close enough so he could make a rush and get the man that held it.

Macomber had not thought how the lion felt as he got out of the car. He only knew his hands were shaking and as he walked away from the car it was almost impossible for him to make his legs move. They were stiff in the thighs, but he could feel the muscles fluttering. He raised the rifle, sighted on the junction of the lion's head and shoulders and pulled the trigger. Nothing happened though he pulled until he thought his finger would break. Then he knew he had the safety on and as he lowered the rifle to move the safety over he moved another frozen pace forward, and the lion seeing his silhouette flow clear of the silhouette of the car, turned and started off at a trot, and, as Macomber fired, he heard a whunk that meant that the bullet was home; but the lion kept on going. Macomber shot again and every one saw the bullet throw a spout of dirt beyond the trotting lion. He shot again, remembering to lower his aim, and they all heard the bullet hit, and the lion went into a gallop and was in the tall grass before he had the bolt pushed forward.

Macomber stood there feeling sick at his stomach, his hands that held the Springfield still cocked, shaking, and his wife and Robert Wilson were standing by him. Beside him too were the two gun-bearers chattering in Wakamba.

"I hit him," Macomber said. "I hit him twice."

"You gut-shot him and you hit him somewhere forward," Wilson said without enthusiasm. The gun-bearers looked very grave. They were silent now.

"You may have killed him," Wilson went on. "We'll have to wait a while before we go in to find out."

"What do you mean?"

"Let him get sick before we follow him up."

"Oh," said Macomber.

"He's a hell of a fine lion," Wilson said cheerfully. "He's gotten into a bad place though."

"Why is it bad?"

"Can't see him until you're on him."

"Oh," said Macomber.

"Come on," said Wilson. "The Memsahib can stay here in the car. We'll go to have a look at the blood spoor."

"Stay here, Margot," Macomber said to his wife. His mouth was very dry and it was hard for him to talk.

"Why?" she asked.

"Wilson says to."

"We're going to have a look," Wilson said. "You stay here. You can see even better from here."

"All right."

Wilson spoke in Swahili to the driver. He nodded and said, "Yes, Bwana."

Then they went down the steep bank and across the stream, climbing over and around the boulders and up the other bank, pulling up by some projecting roots, and along it until they found where the lion had been trotting when Macomber first shot. There was dark blood on the short grass that the gun-bearers pointed out with grass stems, and that ran away behind the river bank trees.

"What do we do?" asked Macomber.

"Not much choice," said Wilson. "We can't bring the car over. Bank's too steep. We'll let him stiffen up a bit and then you and I'll go in and have a look for him."

"Can't we set the grass on fire?" Macomber asked.

"Too green."

"Can't we send beaters?"

Wilson looked at him appraisingly. "Of course we can," he said. "But it's just a touch murderous. You see, we know the lion's wounded. You can drive an unwounded lion—he'll move on ahead of a noise—but a wounded lion's going to charge. You can't see him until you're right on him. He'll make himself perfectly flat in cover you wouldn't think would hide a hare. You can't very well send boys in there to that sort of a show. Somebody bound to get mauled."

"What about the gun-bearers?"

"Oh, they'll go with us. It's their *shauri*. You see, they signed on for it. They don't look too happy though, do they?"

"I don't want to go in there," said Macomber. It was out before he knew he'd said it.

"Neither do I," said Wilson very cheerily. "Really no choice though." Then, as an afterthought, he glanced at Macomber and saw suddenly how he was trembling and the pitiful look on his face.

"You don't have to go in, of course," he said. "That's what I'm hired for, you know. That's why I'm so expensive."

"You mean you'd go in by yourself? Why not leave him there?"

Robert Wilson, whose entire occupation had been with the lion and the problem he presented, and who had not been thinking about Macomber except to note that he was rather windy, suddenly felt as though he had opened the wrong door in a hotel and seen something shameful.

"What do you mean?"

"Why not just leave him?"

"You mean pretend to ourselves he hasn't been hit?"

"No. Just drop it."

"It isn't done."

"Why not?"

"For one thing, he's certain to be suffering. For another, some one else might run onto him."

"I see."

"But you don't have to have anything to do with it."

"I'd like to," Macomber said. "I'm just scared, you know."

"I'll go ahead when we go in," Wilson said, "with Kongoni tracking. You keep behind me and a little to one side. Chances are we'll hear him growl. If we see him we'll both shoot. Don't worry about anything. I'll keep you backed up. As a matter of fact, you know, perhaps you'd better not go. It might be much better. Why don't you go over and join the Memsahib while I just get it over with?"

"No, I want to go."

"All right," said Wilson. "But don't go in if you don't want to. This is my *shauri* now, you know."

"I want to go," said Macomber.

They sat under a tree and smoked.

"Want to go back and speak to the Memsahib while we're waiting?" Wilson asked.

"No."

"I'll just step back and tell her to be patient."

"Good," said Macomber. He sat there, sweating under his arms, his mouth dry, his stomach hollow feeling, wanting to find courage to tell Wilson to go on and finish off the lion without him. He could not know that Wilson was furious because he had not noticed the state he was in earlier and sent him back to his wife. While he sat there Wilson came up. "I have your big gun," he said. "Take it. We've given him time, I think. Come on."

Macomber took the big gun and Wilson said:

"Keep behind me and about five yards to the right and do exactly as I tell you." Then he spoke in Swahili to the two gun-bearers who looked the picture of gloom.

"Let's go," he said.

"Could I have a drink of water?" Macomber asked. Wilson spoke to the older gun-bearer, who wore a canteen on his belt, and the man unbuckled it, unscrewed the top and handed it to Macomber, who took it noticing how heavy it seemed and how hairy and shoddy the felt covering was in his hand. He raised it to drink and looked ahead at the high grass with the flat-topped trees behind it. A breeze was blowing toward them and the grass rippled gently in the wind. He looked at the gun-bearer and he could see the gun-bearer was suffering too with fear.

Thirty-five yards into the grass the big lion lay flattened out along the ground. His ears were back and his only movement was a slight twitching up and down of his long, black-tufted tail. He had turned at bay as soon as he had reached this cover and he was sick with the wound through his full belly, and weakening with the wound through his lungs that brought a thin foamy red to his mouth each time he breathed. His flanks were wet and hot and flies were on the little openings the solid bullets had made in his tawny hide, and his big yellow eyes, narrowed with hate, looked straight ahead, only blinking when the pain came as he breathed, and his claws dug in the soft baked earth. All of him, pain, sickness, hatred and all of his remaining strength, was tightening into an absolute concentration for a rush. He could hear the men talking and he waited, gathering all of himself into this preparation for a charge as soon as the men would come into the grass. As he heard their voices his tail stiffened to twitch up and down, and, as they came into the edge of the grass, he made a coughing grunt and charged.

Kongoni, the old gun-bearer, in the lead watching the blood spoor, Wilson watching the grass for any movement, his big gun ready, the second gun-bearer looking ahead and listening, Macomber close to Wilson, his rifle cocked, they had just moved into the grass when Macomber heard the blood-choked coughing grunt, and saw the swishing rush in the grass. The next thing he knew he was running; running wildly, in panic in the open, running toward the stream.

He heard the *ca-ra-wong!* of Wilson's big rifle, and again in a second crashing *carawong!* and turning saw the lion, horrible-looking now, with half his head seeming to be gone, crawling toward Wilson in the edge of the tall grass while the red-faced man worked the bolt on the short ugly rifle and aimed carefully as

another blasting *carawong!* came from the muzzle, and the crawling, heavy, yellow bulk of the lion stiffened and the huge, muti-
lated head slid forward and Macomber, standing by himself in the
clearing where he had run, holding a loaded rifle, while two black
men and a white man looked back at him in contempt, knew the
lion was dead. He came toward Wilson, his tallness all seeming a
naked reproach, and Wilson looked at him and said:

"Want to take pictures?"

"No," he said.

That was all any one had said until they reached the motor
car. Then Wilson had said:

"Hell of a fine lion. Boys will skin him out. We might as well
stay here in the shade."

Macomber's wife had not looked at him nor he at her and he
had sat by her in the back seat with Wilson sitting in the front
seat. Once he had reached over and taken his wife's hand without
looking at her and she had removed her hand from his. Looking
across the stream to where the gun-bearers were skinning out the
lion he could see that she had been able to see the whole thing.
While they sat there his wife had reached forward and put her
hand on Wilson's shoulder. He turned and she had leaned forward over the low seat and kissed him on the mouth.

"Oh, I say," said Wilson, going redder than his natural baked
color.

"Mr. Robert Wilson," she said. "The beautiful red-faced Mr.
Robert Wilson."

Then she sat down beside Macomber again and looked away
across the stream to where the lion lay, with uplifted, white-
muscled, tendon-marked naked forearms, and white bloating belly,
as the black men fleshed away the skin. Finally the gun-bearers
brought the skin over, wet and heavy, and climbed in behind with
it, rolling it up before they got in, and the motor car started. No
one had said anything more until they were back in camp.

That was the story of the lion. Macomber did not know how
the lion had felt before he started his rush, nor during it when the
unbelievable smash of the .505 with a muzzle velocity of two tons
had hit him in the mouth, nor what kept him coming after that,
when the second ripping crash had smashed his hind quarters and

he had come crawling on toward the crashing, blasting thing that had destroyed him. Wilson knew something about it and only expressed it by saying, "Damned fine lion," but Macomber did not know how Wilson felt about things either. He did not know how his wife felt except that she was through with him.

His wife had been through with him before but it never lasted. He was very wealthy, and would be much wealthier, and he knew she would not leave him ever now. That was one of the few things that he really knew. He knew about that, about motor cycles—that was earliest—about motor cars, about duck-shooting, about fishing, trout, salmon and big-sea, about sex in books, many books, too many books, about all court games, about dogs, not much about horses, about hanging on to his money, about most of the other things his world dealt in, and about his wife not leaving him. His wife had been a great beauty and she was still a great beauty in Africa, but she was not a great enough beauty any more at home to be able to leave him and better herself and she knew it and he knew it. She had missed the chance to leave him and he knew it. If he had been better with women she would probably have started to worry about him getting another new, beautiful wife; but she knew too much about him to worry about him either. Also, he had always had a great tolerance which seemed the nicest thing about him if it were not the most sinister.

All in all they were known as a comparatively happily married couple, one of those whose disruption is often rumored but never occurs, and as the society columnist put it, they were adding more than a spice of *adventure* to their much envied and ever-enduring *Romance* by a *Safari* in what was known as *Darkest Africa* until the Martin Johnsons lighted it on so many silver screens where they were pursuing *Old Simba* the lion, the buffalo, *Tembo* the elephant and as well collecting specimens for the Museum of Natural History. This same columnist had reported them *on the verge* at least three times in the past and they had been. But they always made it up. They had a sound basis of union. Margot was too beautiful for Macomber to divorce her and Macomber had too much money for Margot ever to leave him.

It was now about three o'clock in the morning and Francis

Macomber, who had been asleep a little while after he had stopped thinking about the lion, wakened and then slept again, woke suddenly, frightened in a dream of the bloody-headed lion standing over him, and listening while his heart pounded, he realized that his wife was not in the other cot in the tent. He lay awake with that knowledge for two hours.

At the end of that time his wife came into the tent, lifted her mosquito bar and crawled cozily into bed.

"Where have you been?" Macomber asked in the darkness.

"Hello," she said. "Are you awake?"

"Where have you been?"

"I just went out to get a breath of air."

"You did, like hell."

"What do you want me to say, darling?"

"Where have you been?"

"Out to get a breath of air."

"That's a new name for it. You *are* a bitch."

"Well, you're a coward."

"All right," he said. "What of it?"

"Nothing as far as I'm concerned. But please let's not talk, darling, because I'm very sleepy."

"You think that I'll take anything."

"I know you will, sweet."

"Well, I won't."

"Please, darling, let's not talk. I'm so very sleepy."

"There wasn't going to be any of that. You promised there wouldn't be."

"Well, there is now," she said sweetly.

"You said if we made this trip that there would be none of that. You promised."

"Yes, darling. That's the way I meant it to be. But the trip was spoiled yesterday. We don't have to talk about it, do we?"

"You don't wait long when you have an advantage, do you?"

"Please let's not talk. I'm so sleepy, darling."

"I'm going to talk."

"Don't mind me then, because I'm going to sleep." And she did.

At breakfast they were all three at the table before daylight and Francis Macomber found that, of all the many men that he had hated, he hated Robert Wilson the most.

"Sleep well?" Wilson asked in his throaty voice, filling a pipe.

"Did you?"

"Topping," the white hunter told him.

You bastard, thought Macomber, you insolent bastard.

So she woke him when she came in, Wilson thought, looking at them both with his flat, cold eyes. Well, why doesn't he keep his wife where she belongs? What does he think I am, a bloody plaster saint? Let him keep her where she belongs. It's his own fault.

"Do you think we'll find buffalo?" Margot asked, pushing away a dish of apricots.

"Chance of it," Wilson said and smiled at her. "Why don't you stay in camp?"

"Not for anything," she told him.

"Why not order her to stay in camp?" Wilson said to Macomber.

"You order her," said Macomber coldly.

"Let's not have any ordering, nor," turning to Macomber, "any silliness, Francis," Margot said quite pleasantly.

"Are you ready to start?" Macomber asked.

"Any time," Wilson told him. "Do you want the Memsahib to go?"

"Does it make any difference whether I do or not?"

The hell with it, thought Robert Wilson. The utter complete hell with it. So this is what it's going to be like. Well, this is what it's going to be like, then.

"Makes no difference," he said.

"You're sure you wouldn't like to stay in camp with her yourself and let me go out and hunt the buffalo?" Macomber asked.

"Can't do that," said Wilson. "Wouldn't talk rot if I were you."

"I'm not talking rot. I'm disgusted."

"Bad word, disgusted."

"Francis, will you please try to speak sensibly," his wife said.

"I speak too damned sensibly," Macomber said. "Did you ever eat such filthy food?"

"Something wrong with the food?" asked Wilson quietly.

"No more than with everything else."

"I'd pull yourself together, laddybuck," Wilson said very quietly. "There's a boy waits at table that understands a little English."

"The hell with him."

Wilson stood up and puffing on his pipe strolled away, speaking a few words in Swahili to one of the gun-bearers who was standing waiting for him. Macomber and his wife sat on at the table. He was staring at his coffee cup.

"If you make a scene I'll leave you, darling," Margot said quietly.

"No, you won't."

"You can try it and see."

"You won't leave me."

"No," she said. "I won't leave you and you'll behave yourself."

"Behave myself? That's a way to talk. Behave myself."

"Yes. Behave yourself."

"Why don't *you* try behaving?"

"I've tried it so long. So very long."

"I hate that red-faced swine," Macomber said. "I loathe the sight of him."

"He's really *very* nice."

"Oh, *shut up,*" Macomber almost shouted. Just then the car came up and stopped in front of the dining tent and the driver and the two gunbearers got out. Wilson walked over and looked at the husband and wife sitting there at the table.

"Going shooting?" he asked.

"Yes," said Macomber, standing up. "Yes."

"Better bring a woolly. It will be cool in the car," Wilson said.

"I'll get my leather jacket," Margot said.

"The boy has it," Wilson told her. He climbed into the front with the driver and Francis Macomber and his wife sat, not speaking, in the back seat.

Hope the silly beggar doesn't take a notion to blow the back of my head off, Wilson thought to himself. Women *are* a nuisance on safari.

The car was grinding down to cross the river at a pebbly ford in the gray daylight and then climbed, angling up the steep bank, where Wilson had ordered a way shovelled out the day before so they could reach the parklike wooded rolling country on the far side.

It was a good morning, Wilson thought. There was a heavy dew and as the wheels went through the grass and low bushes he could smell the odor of the crushed fronds. It was an odor like verbena and he liked this early morning smell of the dew, the crushed bracken and the look of the tree trunks showing black through the early morning mist, as the car made its way through the untracked, parklike country. He had put the two in the back seat out of his mind now and was thinking about buffalo. The buffalo that he was after stayed in the daytime in a thick swamp where it was impossible to get a shot, but in the night they fed out into an open stretch of country and if he could come between them and their swamp with the car, Macomber would have a good chance at them in the open. He did not want to hunt buff with Macomber in thick cover. He did not want to hunt buff or anything else with Macomber at all, but he was a professional hunter and he had hunted with some rare ones in his time. If they got buff today there would only be rhino to come and the poor man would have gone through his dangerous game and things might pick up. He'd have nothing more to do with the woman and Macomber would get over that too. He must have gone through plenty of that before by the look of things. Poor beggar. He must have a way of getting over it. Well, it was the poor sod's own bloody fault.

He, Robert Wilson, carried a double size cot on safari to accommodate any windfalls he might receive. He had hunted for a certain clientele, the international, fast, sporting set, where the women did not feel they were getting their money's worth unless they had shared that cot with the white hunter. He despised them when he was away from them although he liked some of them well enough at the time, but he made his living by them; and their standards were his standards as long as they were hiring him.

They were his standards in all except the shooting. He had his own standards about the killing and they could live up to them or get some one else to hunt them. He knew, too, that they all respected him for this. This Macomber was an odd one though. Damned if he wasn't. Now the wife. Well, the wife. Yes, the wife. Hm, the wife. Well he'd dropped all that. He looked around at them. Macomber sat grim and furious. Margot smiled at him. She looked younger today, more innocent and fresher and not so professionally beautiful. What's in her heart God knows, Wilson thought. She hadn't talked much last night. At that it was a pleasure to see her.

The motor car climbed up a slight rise and went on through the trees and then out into a grassy prairie-like opening and kept in the shelter of the trees along the edge, the driver going slowly and Wilson looking carefully out across the prairie and all along its far side. He stopped the car and studied the opening with his field glasses. Then he motioned to the driver to go on and the car moved slowly along, the driver avoiding warthog holes and driving around the mud castles ants had built. Then, looking across the opening, Wilson suddenly turned and said, "By God, there they are!"

And looking where he pointed, while the car jumped forward and Wilson spoke in rapid Swahili to the driver, Macomber saw three huge, black animals looking almost cylindrical in their long heaviness, like big black tank cars, moving at a gallop across the far edge of the open prairie. They moved at a stiff-necked, stiff bodied gallop and he could see the upswept wide black horns on their heads as they galloped heads out; the heads not moving.

"They're three old bulls," Wilson said. "We'll cut them off before they get to the swamp."

The car was going a wild forty-five miles an hour across the open and as Macomber watched, the buffalo got bigger and bigger until he could see the gray, hairless, scabby look of one huge bull and how his neck was a part of his shoulders and the shiny black of his horns as he galloped a little behind the others that were strung out in that steady plunging gait; and then, the car swaying as though it had just jumped a road, they drew up close and he could see the plunging hugeness of the bull, and the dust in his sparsely haired hide, the wide boss of horn and his outstretched, wide-nostrilled muzzle, and he was raising his rifle when Wilson shouted, "Not from the car, you fool!" and he had no fear, only hatred of Wilson, while the brakes clamped on and the car skidded, plowing sideways to an almost stop and Wilson was out on one side and he on the other, stumbling as his feet hit the still speeding-by of the earth, and then he was shooting at the bull as he moved away, hearing the bullets whunk into him, emptying his rifle at him as he moved steadily away, finally remembering to get his shots forward into the shoulder, and as he fumbled to re-load, he saw the bull was down. Down on his knees, his big head tossing, and seeing the other two still galloping he shot at the leader and hit him. He shot again and missed and he heard the *carawonging* roar as Wilson shot and saw the leading bull slide forward onto his nose.

"Get that other," Wilson said. "Now you're shooting!"

But the other bull was moving steadily at the same gallop and he missed, throwing a spout of dirt, and Wilson missed and the dust rose in a cloud and Wilson shouted, "Come on. He's too far!" and grabbed his arm and they were in the car again, Macomber and Wilson hanging on the sides and rocketing swayingly over the uneven ground, drawing up on the steady, plunging, heavy-necked, straight-moving gallop of the bull.

They were behind him and Macomber was filling his rifle, dropping shells onto the ground, jamming it, clearing the jam, then they were almost up with the bull when Wilson yelled "Stop," and the car skidded so that it almost swung over and Macomber fell forward onto his feet, slammed his bolt forward and fired as far forward as he could aim into the galloping, rounded black back, aimed and shot again, then again, then again, and the bullets, all of them hitting, had no effect on the buffalo that he could see. Then Wilson shot, the roar deafening him, and he could see the bull stagger. Macomber shot again, aiming carefully, and down he came, onto his knees.

"All right," Wilson said. "Nice work. That's the three."

Macomber felt a drunken elation.

"How many times did you shoot?" he asked.

"Just three," Wilson said. "You killed the first bull. The biggest one. I helped you finish the other two. Afraid they might have got into cover. You had them killed. I was just mopping up a little. You shot damn well."

"Let's go to the car," said Macomber. "I want a drink."

"Got to finish off that buff first," Wilson told him. The buffalo was on his knees and he jerked his head furiously and bellowed in pig-eyed, roaring rage as they came toward him.

"Watch he doesn't get up," Wilson said. Then, "Get a little broadside and take him in the neck just behind the ear."

Macomber aimed carefully at the center of the huge, jerking, rage-driven neck and shot. At the shot the head dropped forward.

"That does it," said Wilson. "Got the spine. They're a hell of a looking thing, aren't they?"

"Let's get the drink," said Macomber. In his life he had never felt so good.

In the car Macomber's wife sat very white-faced. "You were marvellous, darling," she said to Macomber. "What a ride."

"Was it rough?" Wilson asked.

"It was frightful. I've never been more frightened in my life."

"Let's all have a drink," Macomber said.

"By all means," said Wilson. "Give it to the Memsahib." She drank the neat whisky from the flask and shuddered a little when she swallowed. She handed the flask to Macomber who handed it to Wilson.

"It was frightfully exciting," she said. "It's given me a dreadful headache. I didn't know you were allowed to shoot them from cars though."

"No one shot from cars," said Wilson coldly.

"I mean chase them from cars."

"Wouldn't ordinarily," Wilson said. "Seemed sporting enough to me though while we were doing it. Taking more chance driving that way across the plain full of holes and one thing and another than hunting on foot. Buffalo could have charged us each time we shot if he liked. Gave him every chance. Wouldn't mention it to any one though. It's illegal if that's what you mean."

"It seemed very unfair to me," Margot said, "chasing those big helpless things in a motor car."

"Did it?" said Wilson.

"What would happen if they heard about it in Nairobi?"

"I'd lose my licence for one thing. Other unpleasantnesses," Wilson said, taking a drink from the flask. "I'd be out of business."

"Really?"

"Yes, really."

"Well," said Macomber, and he smiled for the first time all day. "Now she has something on you."

"You have such a pretty way of putting things, Francis," Margot Macomber said. Wilson looked at them both. If a four-letter man marries a five-letter woman, he was thinking, what number of letters would their children be? What he said was, "We lost a gun-bearer. Did you notice it?"

"My God, no," Macomber said.

"Here he comes," Wilson said. "He's all right. He must have fallen off when we left the first bull."

Approaching them was the middle-aged gun-bearer, limping along in his knitted cap, khaki tunic, shorts and rubber sandals, gloomy-faced and disgusted looking. As he came up he called out to Wilson in Swahili and they all saw the change in the white hunter's face.

"What does he say?" asked Margot.

"He says the first bull got up and went into the bush," Wilson said with no expression in his voice.

"Oh," said Macomber blankly.

"Then it's going to be just like the lion," said Margot, full of anticipation.

"It's not going to be a damned bit like the lion," Wilson told her. "Did you want another drink, Macomber?"

"Thanks, yes," Macomber said. He expected the feeling he had had about the lion to come back but it did not. For the first time in his life he really felt wholly without fear. Instead of fear he had a feeling of definite elation.

"We'll go and have a look at the second bull," Wilson said. "I'll tell the driver to put the car in the shade."

"What are you going to do?" asked Margaret Macomber.

"Take a look at the buff," Wilson said.

"I'll come."

"Come along."

The three of them walked over to where the second buffalo bulked blackly in the open, head forward on the grass, the massive horns swung wide.

"He's a very good head," Wilson said. "That's close to a fifty-inch spread."

Macomber was looking at him with delight.

"He's hateful looking," said Margot. "Can't we go into the shade?"

"Of course," Wilson said. "Look," he said to Macomber, and pointed. "See that patch of bush?"

"Yes."

"That's where the first bull went in. The gun-bearer said when he fell off the bull was down. He was watching us helling along and the other two buff galloping. When he looked up there was the bull up and looking at him. Gun-bearer ran like hell and the bull went off slowly into that bush."

"Can we go in after him now?" asked Macomber eagerly.

Wilson looked at him appraisingly. Damned if this isn't a strange one, he thought. Yesterday he's scared sick and today he's a ruddy fire eater.

"No, we'll give him a while."

"Let's please go into the shade," Margot said. Her face was white and she looked ill.

They made their way to the car where it stood under a single, widespreading tree and all climbed in.

"Chances are he's dead in there," Wilson remarked. "After a little we'll have a look."

Macomber felt a wild unreasonable happiness that he had never known before.

"By God, that was a chase," he said. "I've never felt any such feeling. Wasn't it marvellous, Margot?"

"I hated it."

"Why?"

"I hated it," she said bitterly. "I loathed it."

"You know I don't think I'd ever be afraid of anything again," Macomber said to Wilson. "Something happened in me after we first saw the buff and started after him. Like a dam bursting. It was pure excitement."

"Cleans out your liver," said Wilson. "Damn funny things happen to people."

Macomber's face was shining. "You know something did happen to me," he said. "I feel absolutely different."

His wife said nothing and eyed him strangely. She was sitting far back in the seat and Macomber was sitting forward talking to Wilson who turned sideways talking over the back of the front seat.

"You know, I'd like to try another lion," Macomber said. "I'm really not afraid of them now. After all, what can they do to you?"

"That's it," said Wilson. "Worst one can do is kill you. How does it go? Shakespeare. Damned good. See if I can remember. Oh, damned good. Used to quote it to myself at one time. Let's see. 'By my troth, I care not; a man can die but once; we owe God a death and let it go which way it will, he that dies this year is quit for the next.' Damned fine, eh?"

He was very embarrassed, having brought out this thing he had lived by, but he had seen men come of age before and it always moved him. It was not a matter of their twenty-first birthday.

It had taken a strange chance of hunting, a sudden precipitation into action without opportunity for worrying beforehand, to bring this about with Macomber, but regardless of how it had happened it had most certainly happened. Look at the beggar now, Wilson thought. It's that some of them stay little boys so long, Wilson thought. Sometimes all their lives. Their figures stay boyish when they're fifty. The great American boy-men. Damned strange people. But he liked this Macomber now. Damned strange fellow. Probably meant the end of cuckoldry too. Well, that would be a damned good thing. Damned good thing. Beggar had probably been afraid all his life. Don't know what started it. But over now. Hadn't had time to be afraid with the buff. That and being angry too. Motor car too. Motor cars made it familiar. Be a damn fire eater now. He'd seen it in the war work the same way. More of a change than any loss of virginity. Fear gone like an operation. Something else grew in its place. Main thing a man had. Made him into a man. Women knew it too. No bloody fear.

From the far corner of the seat Margaret Macomber looked at the two of them. There was no change in Wilson. She saw Wilson as she had seen him the day before when she had first realized what his great talent was. But she saw the change in Francis Macomber now.

"Do you have that feeling of happiness about what's going to happen?" Macomber asked, still exploring his new wealth.

"You're not supposed to mention it," Wilson said, looking in the other's face. "Much more fashionable to say you're scared. Mind you, you'll be scared too, plenty of times."

"But you *have* a feeling of happiness about action to come?"

"Yes," said Wilson. "There's that. Doesn't do to talk too much about all this. Talk the whole thing away. No pleasure in anything if you mouth it up too much."

"You're both talking rot," said Margot. "Just because you've chased some helpless animals in a motor car you talk like heroes."

"Sorry," said Wilson. "I have been gassing too much." She's worried about it already, he thought.

"If you don't know what we're talking about why not keep out of it?" Macomber asked his wife.

"You've gotten awfully brave, awfully suddenly," his wife said contemptuously, but her contempt was not secure. She was very afraid of something.

Macomber laughed, a very natural hearty laugh. "You know I *have*," he said. "I really have."

"Isn't it sort of late?" Margot said bitterly. Because she had done the best she could for many years back and the way they were together now was no one person's fault.

"Not for me," said Macomber.

Margot said nothing but sat back in the corner of the seat.

"Do you think we've given him time enough?" Macomber asked Wilson cheerfully.

"We might have a look," Wilson said. "Have you any solids left?"

"The gun-bearer has some."

Wilson called in Swahili and the older gun-bearer, who was skinning out one of the heads, straightened up, pulled a box of solids out of his pocket and brought them over to Macomber, who filled his magazine and put the remaining shells in his pocket.

"You might as well shoot the Springfield," Wilson said. "You're used to it. We'll leave the Mannlicher in the car with the Memsahib. Your gunbearer can carry your heavy gun. I've this damned cannon. Now let me tell you about them." He had saved this until the last because he did not want to worry Macomber. "When a buff comes he comes with his head high and thrust straight out. The boss of the horns covers any sort of a brain shot. The only shot is straight into the nose. The only other shot is into his chest or, if you're to one side, into the neck or the shoulders. After they've been hit once they take a hell of a lot of killing. Don't try anything fancy. Take the easiest shot there is. They've finished skinning out that head now. Should we get started?"

He called to the gun-bearers, who came up wiping their hands, and the older one got into the back.

"I'll only take Kongoni," Wilson said. "The other can watch to keep the birds away."

As the car moved slowly across the open space toward the island of brushy trees that ran in a tongue of foliage along a dry water course that cut the open swale, Macomber felt his heart pounding and his mouth was dry again, but it was excitement, not fear.

"Here's where he went in," Wilson said. Then to the gun-bearer in Swahili, "Take the blood spoor."

The car was parallel to the patch of bush. Macomber, Wilson and the gun-bearer got down. Macomber, looking back, saw his wife, with the rifle by her side, looking at him. He waved to her and she did not wave back.

The brush was very thick ahead and the ground was dry. The middle-aged gun-bearer was sweating heavily and Wilson had his hat down over his eyes and his red neck showed just ahead of Macomber. Suddenly the gun-bearer said something in Swahili to Wilson and ran forward.

"He's dead in there," Wilson said. "Good work," and he turned to grip Macomber's hand and as they shook hands, grinning at each other, the gun-bearer shouted wildly and they saw him coming out of the bush sideways, fast as a crab, and the bull coming, nose out, mouth tight closed, blood dripping, massive head straight out, coming in a charge, his little pig eyes bloodshot as he looked at them. Wilson, who was ahead, was kneeling shooting, and Macomber, as he fired, unhearing his shot in the roaring of Wilson's gun, saw fragments like slate burst from the huge boss of the horns, and the head jerked, he shot again at the wide nostrils and saw the horns jolt again and fragments fly, and he did not see Wilson now and, aiming carefully, shot again with the buffalo's huge bulk almost on him and his rifle almost level with the on-coming head, nose out, and he could see the little wicked eyes and the head started to lower and he felt a sudden white-hot, blinding flash explode inside his head and that was all he ever felt.

Wilson had ducked to one side to get in a shoulder shot. Macomber had stood solid and shot for the nose, shooting a touch high each time and hitting the heavy horns, splintering and chipping them like hitting a slate roof, and Mrs. Macomber, in the car, had shot at the buffalo with the 6.5 Mannlicher as it seemed about to gore Macomber and had hit her husband about two inches up and a little to one side of the base of his skull.

Francis Macomber lay now, face down, not two yards from where the buffalo lay on his side and his wife knelt over him with Wilson beside her.

"I wouldn't turn him over," Wilson said.

The woman was crying hysterically.

"I'd get back in the car," Wilson said. "Where's the rifle?"

She shook her head, her face contorted. The gun-bearer picked up the rifle.

"Leave it as it is," said Wilson. Then, "Go get Abdulla so that he may witness the manner of the accident."

He knelt down, took a handkerchief from his pocket, and spread it over Francis Macomber's crew-cropped head where it lay. The blood sank into the dry, loose earth.

Wilson stood up and saw the buffalo on his side, his legs out, his thinly-haired belly crawling with ticks. "Hell of a good bull," his brain registered automatically. "A good fifty inches, or better. Better." He called to the driver and told him to spread a blanket over the body and stay by it. Then he walked over to the motor car where the woman sat crying in the corner.

"That was a pretty thing to do," he said in a toneless voice. "He *would* have left you too."

"Stop it," she said.

"Of course it's an accident," he said. "I know that."

"Stop it," she said.

"Don't worry," he said. "There will be a certain amount of unpleasantness but I will have some photographs taken that will be very useful at the inquest. There's the testimony of the gun-bearers and the driver too. You're perfectly all right."

"Stop it," she said.

"There's a hell of a lot to be done," he said. "And I'll have to send a truck off to the lake to wireless for a plane to take the three of us into Nairobi. Why didn't you poison him? That's what they do in England."

"Stop it. Stop it. Stop it," the woman cried.

Wilson looked at her with his flat blue eyes.

"I'm through now," he said. "I was a little angry. I'd begun to like your husband."

"Oh, please stop it," she said. "Please stop it."

"That's better," Wilson said. "Please is much better. Now I'll stop."

16a.

Item 689, Ernest Hemingway Collection, John F. Kennedy Library and Museum, Boston. Untitled pencil manuscript beginning "Of course by the third day . . . " and an early false start for "The Short Happy Life of Francis Macomber."

Of course by the third day the old man was gone about her. He always falls in love with them, or thinks he does, but this time ~~it worked much faster~~ he didn't wait for it to be the ripening of a beautiful friendship or anything else. He was gone before he even knew it. She was ~~dark and smooth and cool and very expensive looking. She didn't mean a thing to me~~ like any of the rest of them, only dark instead of blonde, and cool and smooth and expensive looking. They're the god-damnest women on earth, really. They only have them in two countries, ours and yours, I suppose. ~~They're lovely looking and damned nice if you don't care and they hunt alone, in pairs, and in packs too~~ She was a fine example of how good the best of them can look. ~~and I suppose, though I've never seen them in packs. But they never stop hunting. Well she didn't have to hunt him any. She had him before it ever started. Of course she couldn't be expected to know anything about the old man or what he was about. Of course what she didn't realize was that although that's the one thing they're supposed to really know. The old man difference between what a man~~

    The husband was one of these ~~old Bones~~ Yale old bones men who are so pleasant and such a good fellow and such a fine sportsman that you don't know what it's all about for a long time. The buggar could shoot too. ~~The wife, Dorothy Macomber~~

The O.M. is a strange bird. You would have to have seen him young to know what it's all about because since cars came in he's got himself covered in a perfect disguise made out of his own body that's put on a belly there and thickened up here and filled his face out so you can't see what its about. Now he looks so unlike how he really is that it isn't even a caricature and the only place he shows out of himself is his eyes. I work for him driving cars so I keep pretty good track of his eyes. Now I tell you truly I've been out here a long time and I've been around some other places and I don't spook unless there is something to be spooked of but I tell you truly he can still spook me with his eyes. ~~and I can't look at them when he's angry~~

Now the wife, Dorothy Macomber, was a lovely looking woman and Macomber was a good looking young fellow and they looked nice sitting there by the fire light in the evening with the O.M., all leaning back in the canvas chairs, ~~with it getting~~ she with a gimlet and the two men with whiskeys and sodas and it getting dark and the boys working around their fires.

"There they are," the old man said. "Listen."

Everybody listened and high up above the trees in the dark you could hear a which-a-whicha-whicha sound, like a shell going high over away from you at night, only slower. There was just one. Then the air was full of them.

"They're flamingos," the old man said. "They're flighting from the lake."

"Arent they lovely," ~~Dorothy said~~ the Macomber woman said. "Could we see them?"

"They only fly at night," the O.M. said. "You can see them on the lake in the daytime."

"Are there very many?" Macomber asked.

"Perhaps half a million," the O.M. said.

"It's wonderful," the wife said. "Aren't you glad we came, Denny? Listen to them."

They were flighting in big bunches now and they made that sound like tearing silk.

16b.

Item 690, Ernest Hemingway Collection, John F. Kennedy Library and Museum, Boston. Untitled pencil manuscript beginning "She looked like all those pictures . . ." and an early false start for "The Short Happy Life of Francis Macomber."

She looked like all those pictures of the women who endorse things
in the shiny paper magazines. You know, smooth and cool and very
expensive. The kind you can't imagine being mussed or excited or
breathing hard or up too early in the morning

that never had her hair cut when everybody else had theirs short
and you couldn't imagine her mussed up, or breathing hard or up too
early in the morning. But believe me brother they muss the worst
when one of what we call backgammon bitches but she was no bitch
particularly. She was a nice enough woman. No. And the funny thing
was she didn't play backgammon either.

The husband was one of those old Bones men from Yale that was
so pleasant and nice and obviously such a good fellow that you didn't
know what it was all about for a long time. You started out liking him
and distrusting her and you ended up. God knows how you ended up.

Of course the old man was gone about her by the third day. He
always falls in love with them or thinks he does. It's in the contract
price probably. If the white hunter doesn't fall in love with them or
they with the white hunter they get half their money back. You know
the kind of falling in love; lots of talking about it, a pleasant sort of
joke between three people and really just a compliment to the husband with the old man drinking obviously just a little too much to
drown his sorrow. I've seen it so many times and a man has to ~~pre-~~
~~tend to~~ play at something out alone with them for two months.

Well the old man took them out to Mutu-umbu to see if they
could learn to shoot a little first. We camped there in the big trees and
took them up the valley the next morning. This fellow Macomber, the
husband, was a good shot. He ~~got a wildebeest~~ made a nice shot on a
wildebeest. Then he made a hell of a good shot on quite a good Grant.
That was all the meat we could use and the heads there aren't up to
anything but the old man wanted to see them shoot some more. So he
said, "We might take a Tommy so you can try Tommy chops. Wait till
we see a ram. No that's not a ram. That's a female granti. There's a
ram. You get out and we'll pull off."

So Macomber gets out and sits down and we drive away about
four hundred yards and the Tommys move off too. What he has now
is a hell of a shot, the wind is blowing a big breeze and the light has
started to get that heat haze. It was a long shot and a bad one to

make. I wouldn't have tried it. But we saw him sitting there, comfortable looking, well back on his heels, using the sling to steady himself in the wind and saw the rifle spit and whack the Tommy was down and the rest of them bouncing off over the plain. We drove over and he came walking up.

"Where did you shoot?" the old man asked him.

"At the top of the shoulder," Macomber said. I turned the Tommy over and there was the hole. It was a little further back than he'd figured because of the wind.

"Well you _can_ shoot," the old man said. "That was a damned fine shot."

"How much did you allow for the wind?" I asked him.

"Almost a yard."

"You can shoot" the old man told him. But Macomber didn't seem very pleased and he didn't seem very happy.

The woman could shoot just like any woman. She could hit them fine and miss them just as well and didn't know why she did either, and she was a damned beautiful woman and I didn't give a damn how she shot, but this fellow Macomber was a rifle shot. But there was something funny about him.

In the evening we sat around the fire and had drinks and the old man began to feel good and Dorothy Macomber began to feel good, and give me two and I always feel good, but Macomber was serious as hell and wanted to talk about shock, and penetration and all the rest of it.

16c.

Item 692, Ernest Hemingway Collection, John F. Kennedy Library and Museum, Boston. Handwritten ink manuscript with a list of possible titles for "The Short Happy Life of Francis Macomber."

A Marriage Has Been Arranged
The Coming Man
The New Man

The Short Life of Francis Macomber
The End of The Marriage
Marriage Is a Dangerous Game
The More Dangerous Game
A Marriage Has Been Terminated
The Ruling Classes
The Fear of Courage
Brief Mastery
The Master Passion
The Cult of Violence
The Struggle For Power
To look up
    Man
    Marriage
    Fear
    Courage
[On the verso:] Marriage is a Bond
Thr[ou]gh Darkest Marriage

17.

The Snows of Kilimanjaro

1936

*Kilimanjaro is a snow-covered mountain 19,710 feet high,
and is said to be the highest mountain in Africa. Its western
summit is called the Masai "Ngàje Ngài," the House of God.
Close to the western summit there is the dried and frozen
carcass of a leopard. No one has explained what the leopard
was seeking at that altitude.*

"The marvellous thing is that it's painless," he said. "That's how
you know when it starts."

"Is it really?"

"Absolutely. I'm awfully sorry about the odor though. That
must bother you."

"Don't! Please don't."

"Look at them," he said. "Now is it sight or is it scent that
brings them like that?"

The cot the man lay on was in the wide shade of a mimosa
tree and as he looked out past the shade onto the glare of the
plain there were three of the big birds squatted obscenely, while
in the sky a dozen more sailed, making quick-moving shadows as
they passed.

"They've been there since the day the truck broke down," he
said. "Today's the first time any have lit on the ground. I watched

the way they sailed very carefully at first in case I ever wanted to use them in a story. That's funny now."

"I wish you wouldn't," she said.

"I'm only talking," he said. "It's much easier if I talk. But I don't want to bother you."

"You know it doesn't bother me," she said. "It's that I've gotten so very nervous not being able to do anything. I think we might make it as easy as we can until the plane comes."

"Or until the plane doesn't come."

"Please tell me what I can do. There must be something I can do."

"You can take the leg off and that might stop it, though I doubt it. Or you can shoot me. You're a good shot now. I taught you to shoot, didn't I?"

"Please don't talk that way. Couldn't I read to you?"

"Read what?"

"Anything in the book bag that we haven't read."

"I can't listen to it," he said. "Talking is the easiest. We quarrel and that makes the time pass."

"I don't quarrel. I never want to quarrel. Let's not quarrel any more. No matter how nervous we get. Maybe they will be back with another truck today. Maybe the plane will come."

"I don't want to move," the man said. "There is no sense in moving now except to make it easier for you."

"That's cowardly."

"Can't you let a man die as comfortably as he can without calling him names? What's the use of slanging me?"

"You're not going to die."

"Don't be silly. I'm dying now. Ask those bastards." He looked over to where the huge, filthy birds sat, their naked heads sunk in the hunched feathers. A fourth planed down, to run quick-legged and then waddle slowly toward the others.

"They are around every camp. You never notice them. You can't die if you don't give up."

"Where did you read that? You're such a bloody fool."

"You might think about some one else."

"For Christ's sake," he said, "that's been my trade."

He lay then and was quiet for a while and looked across the

heat shimmer of the plain to the edge of the bush. There were a few Tommies that showed minute and white against the yellow and, far off, he saw a herd of zebra, white against the green of the bush. This was a pleasant camp under big trees against a hill, with good water, and close by, a nearly dry water hole where sand grouse flighted in the mornings.

"Wouldn't you like me to read?" she asked. She was sitting on a canvas chair beside his cot. "There's a breeze coming up."

"No thanks."

"Maybe the truck will come."

"I don't give a damn about the truck."

"I do."

"You give a damn about so many things that I don't."

"Not so many, Harry."

"What about a drink?"

"It's supposed to be bad for you. It said in Black's to avoid all alcohol. You shouldn't drink."

"Molo!" he shouted.

"Yes Bwana."

"Bring whiskey-soda."

"Yes Bwana."

"You shouldn't," she said. "That's what I mean by giving up. It says it's bad for you. I know it's bad for you."

"No," he said. "It's good for me."

So now it was all over, he thought. So now he would never have a chance to finish it. So this was the way it ended, in a bickering over a drink. Since the gangrene started in his right leg he had no pain and with the pain the horror had gone and all he felt now was a great tiredness and anger that this was the end of it. For this, that now was coming, he had very little curiosity. For years it had obsessed him; but now it meant nothing in itself. It was strange how easy being tired enough made it.

Now he would never write the things that he had saved to write until he knew enough to write them well. Well, he would not have to fail at trying to write them either. Maybe you could never write them, and that was why you put them off and delayed the starting. Well he would never know, now.

"I wish we'd never come," the woman said. She was looking

at him, holding the glass and biting her lip. "You never would have gotten anything like this in Paris. You always said you loved Paris. We could have stayed in Paris or gone anywhere. I'd have gone anywhere. I said I'd go anywhere you wanted. If you wanted to shoot we could have gone shooting in Hungary and been comfortable."

"Your bloody money," he said.

"That's not fair," she said. "It was always yours as much as mine. I left everything and I went wherever you wanted to go and I've done what you wanted to do. But I wish we'd never come here."

"You said you loved it."

"I did when you were all right. But now I hate it. I don't see why that had to happen to your leg. What have we done to have that happen to us?"

"I suppose what I did was to forget to put iodine on it when I first scratched it. Then I didn't pay any attention to it because I never infect. Then, later, when it got bad, it was probably using that weak carbolic solution when the other antiseptics ran out that paralyzed the minute blood vessels and started the gangrene." He looked at her, "What else?"

"I don't mean that."

"If we would have hired a good mechanic instead of a half-baked Kikuyu driver, he would have checked the oil and never burned out that bearing in the truck."

"I don't mean that."

"If you hadn't left your own people, your goddamned Old Westbury, Saratoga, Palm Beach people to take me on—"

"Why, I loved you. That's not fair. I love you now. I'll always love you. Don't you love me?"

"No," said the man. "I don't think so. I never have."

"Harry, what are you saying? You're out of your head."

"No. I haven't any head to go out of."

"Don't drink that," she said. "Darling, please don't drink that. We have to do everything we can."

"You do it," he said. "I'm tired."

* * *

Now in his mind he saw a railway station at Karagatch and he was standing with his pack and that was the headlight of the Simplon-Orient cutting the dark now and he was leaving Thrace then after the retreat. That was one of the things he had saved to write, with, in the morning at breakfast, looking out the window and seeing snow on the mountains in Bulgaria and Nansen's Secretary asking the old man if it were snow and the old man looking at it and saying, No, that's not snow. It's too early for snow. And the Secretary repeating to the other girls, No, you see. It's not snow and them all saying, It's not snow we were mistaken. But it was the snow all right and he sent them on into it when he evolved exchange of populations. And it was snow they tramped along in until they died that winter.

It was snow too that fell all Christmas week that year up in the Gauertal, that year they lived in the woodcutter's house with the big square porcelain stove that filled half the room, and they slept on mattresses filled with beech leaves, the time the deserter came with his feet bloody in the snow. He said the police were right behind him and they gave him woolen socks and held the gendarmes talking until the tracks had drifted over.

In Schrunz, on Christmas day, the snow was so bright it hurt your eyes when you looked out from the Weinstube and saw every one coming home from church. That was where they walked up the sleigh-smoothed urine-yellowed road along the river with the steep pine hills, skis heavy on the shoulder, and where they ran that great run down the glacier above the Madlener-haus, the snow as smooth to see as cake frosting and as light as powder and he remembered the noiseless rush the speed made as you dropped down like a bird.

They were snow-bound a week in the Madlener-haus that time in the blizzard playing cards in the smoke by the lantern light and the stakes were higher all the time as Herr Lent lost more. Finally he lost it all. Everything, the Skischule money and all the season's profit and then his capital. He could see him with his long nose, picking up the cards and then opening, "Sans Voir." There was always gambling then. When there was no snow you gambled and when there was too much you gambled. He thought of all the time in his life he had spent gambling.

But he had never written a line of that, nor of that cold, bright Christmas day with the mountains showing across the plain that Barker had flown across the lines to bomb the Austrian officers' leave train, machine-gunning them as they scattered and ran. He remembered Barker afterwards coming into the mess and starting to tell about it. And how quiet it got and then somebody saying, "You bloody murderous bastard."

Those were the same Austrians they killed then that he skied with later. No not the same. Hans, that he skied with all that year, had been in the Kaiser-Jägers and when they went hunting hares together up the little valley above the saw-mill they had talked of the fighting on Pasubio and of the attack on Perticara and Asalone and he had never written a word of that. Nor of Monte Corona, nor the Sette Communi, nor of Arsiero.

How many winters had he lived in the Vorarlberg and the Arlberg? It was four and then he remembered the man who had the fox to sell when they had walked into Bludenz, that time to buy presents, and the cherry-pit taste of good kirsch, the fast-slipping rush of running powder-snow on crust, singing "Hi! Ho! said Rolly!" as you ran down the last stretch to the steep drop, taking it straight, then running the orchard in three turns and out across the ditch and onto the icy road behind the inn. Knocking your bindings loose, kicking the skis free and leaning them up against the wooden wall of the inn, the lamplight coming from the window, where inside, in the smoky, new-wine smelling warmth, they were playing the accordion.

"Where did we stay in Paris?" he asked the woman who was sitting by him in a canvas chair, now, in Africa.

"At the Crillon. You know that."

"Why do I know that?"

"That's where we always stayed."

"No. Not always."

"There and at the Pavillion Henri-Quatre in St. Germain. You said you loved it there."

"Love is a dunghill," said Harry. "And I'm the cock that gets on it to crow."

"If you have to go away," she said, "is it absolutely necessary to kill off everything you leave behind? I mean do you have to take away everything? Do you have to kill your horse, and your wife and burn your saddle and your armour?"

"Yes," he said. "Your damned money was my armour. My Swift and my Armour."

"Don't."

"All right. I'll stop that. I don't want to hurt you."

"It's a little bit late now."

"All right then. I'll go on hurting you. It's more amusing. The only thing I ever really liked to do with you I can't do now."

"No, that's not true. You liked to do many things and everything you wanted to do I did."

"Oh, for Christ sake stop bragging, will you?"

He looked at her and saw her crying.

"Listen," he said. "Do you think that it is fun to do this? I don't know why I'm doing it. It's trying to kill to keep yourself alive, I imagine. I was all right when we started talking. I didn't mean to start this, and now I'm crazy as a coot and being as cruel to you as I can be. Don't pay any attention, darling, to what I say. I love you, really. You know I love you. I've never loved any one else the way I love you."

He slipped into the familiar lie he made his bread and butter by.

"You're sweet to me."

"You bitch," he said. "You rich bitch. That's poetry. I'm full of poetry now. Rot and poetry. Rotten poetry."

"Stop it. Harry, why do you have to turn into a devil now?"

"I don't like to leave anything," the man said. "I don't like to leave things behind."

It was evening now and he had been asleep. The sun was gone behind the hill and there was a shadow all across the plain and the small animals were feeding close to camp; quick dropping heads and switching tails, he watched them keeping well out away from the bush now. The birds no longer waited on the ground. They were all perched heavily in a tree. There were many more of them. His personal boy was sitting by the bed.

"Memsahib's gone to shoot," the boy said. "Does Bwana want?"

"Nothing."

She had gone to kill a piece of meat and, knowing how he liked to watch the game, she had gone well away so she would not disturb this little pocket of the plain that he could see. She was always thoughtful, he thought. On anything she knew about, or had read, or that she had ever heard.

It was not her fault that when he went to her he was already over. How could a woman know that you meant nothing that you said; that you spoke only from habit and to be comfortable? After he no longer meant what he said, his lies were more successful with women than when he had told them the truth.

It was not so much that he lied as that there was no truth to tell. He had had his life and it was over and then he went on living it again with different people and more money, with the best of the same places, and some new ones.

You kept from thinking and it was all marvellous. You were equipped with good insides so that you did not go to pieces that way, the way most of them had, and you made an attitude that you cared nothing for the work you used to do, now that you could no longer do it. But, in yourself, you said that you would write about these people; about the very rich; that you were really not of them but a spy in their country; that you would leave it and write of it and for once it would be written by some one who knew what he was writing of. But he would never do it, because each day of not writing, of comfort, of being that which he despised, dulled his ability and softened his will to work so that, finally, he did no work at all. The people he knew now were all much more comfortable when he did not work. Africa was where he had been happiest in the good time of his life, so he had come out here to start again. They had made this safari with the minimum of comfort. There was no hardship; but there was no luxury and he had thought that he could get back into training that way. That in some way he could work the fat off his soul the way a fighter went into the mountains to work and train in order to burn it out of his body.

She had liked it. She said she loved it. She loved anything that was exciting, that involved a change of scene, where there were new people and where things were pleasant. And he had felt the illusion of returning strength of will to work. Now if this was how it ended, and he knew it was, he must not turn like some snake biting itself because its back was broken. It wasn't this woman's fault. If it had not been she it would have been another. If he lived by a lie he should try to die by it. He heard a shot beyond the hill.

She shot very well this good, this rich bitch, this kindly caretaker and destroyer of his talent. Nonsense. He had destroyed his talent himself. Why should he blame this woman because she kept him well? He had destroyed his talent by not using it, by betrayals of himself and what he believed in, by drinking so much that he blunted the edge of his perceptions, by laziness, by sloth, and by snobbery, by pride and by prejudice, by hook and by crook. What was this? A catalogue of old books? What was his talent anyway? It was a talent all right but instead of using it, he had traded on it. It was never what he had done, but always what he could do. And he had chosen to make his living with something else instead of a pen or a pencil. It was strange, too, wasn't it, that when he fell in love with another woman, that woman should always have more money than the last one? But when he no longer was in love, when he was only lying, as to this woman, now, who had the most money of all, who had all the money there was, who had had a husband and children, who had taken lovers and been dissatisfied with them, and who loved him dearly as a writer, as a man, as a companion and as a proud possession; it was strange that when he did not love her at all and was lying, that he should be able to give her more for her money than when he had really loved.

We must all be cut out for what we do, he thought. However you make your living is where your talent lies. He had sold vitality, in one form or another, all his life and when your affections are not too involved you give much better value for the money. He had found that out but he would never write that, now, either. No, he would not write that, although it was well worth writing.

Now she came in sight, walking across the open toward the camp. She was wearing jodphurs and carrying her rifle. The two boys had a Tommie slung and they were coming along behind her. She was still a good-looking woman, he thought, and she had a pleasant body. She had a great talent and appreciation for the bed, she was not pretty, but he liked her face, she read enormously, liked to ride and shoot and, certainly, she drank too much. Her husband had died when she was still a comparatively young woman and for a while she had devoted herself to her two just-grown children, who did not need her and were embarrassed at having her about, to her stable of horses, to books, and to bottles. She liked to read in the evening before dinner and she drank Scotch and soda while she read. By dinner she was fairly drunk and after a bottle of wine at dinner she was usually drunk enough to sleep.

That was before the lovers. After she had the lovers she did not drink so much because she did not have to be drunk to sleep. But the lovers bored her. She had been married to a man who had never bored her and these people bored her very much.

Then one of her two children was killed in a plane crash and after that was over she did not want the lovers, and drink being no anæsthetic she had to make another life. Suddenly, she had been acutely frightened of being alone. But she wanted some one that she respected with her.

It had begun very simply. She liked what he wrote and she had always envied the life he led. She thought he did exactly what he wanted to. The steps by which she had acquired him and the way in which she had finally fallen in love with him were all part of a regular progression in which she had built herself a new life and he had traded away what remained of his old life.

He had traded it for security, for comfort too, there was no denying that, and for what else? He did not know. She would have bought him anything he wanted. He knew that. She was a damned nice woman too. He would as soon be in bed with her as any one; rather with her, because she was richer, because she was very pleasant and appreciative and because she never made scenes. And now this life that she had built again was coming to a term because he had not used iodine two weeks ago when a thorn had scratched his knee as they moved forward trying to photograph a herd of waterbuck standing, their heads up, peering while their nostrils searched the air, their ears spread wide to hear the first noise that would send them rushing into the bush. They had bolted, too, before he got the picture.

Here she came now.

He turned his head on the cot to look toward her. "Hello," he said.

"I shot a Tommy ram," she told him. "He'll make you good broth and I'll have them mash some potatoes with the Klim. How do you feel?"

"Much better."

"Isn't that lovely? You know I thought perhaps you would. You were sleeping when I left."

"I had a good sleep. Did you walk far?"

"No. Just around behind the hill. I made quite a good shot on the Tommy."

"You shoot marvellously, you know."

"I love it. I've loved Africa. Really. If *you're* all right it's the most fun that I've ever had. You don't know the fun it's been to shoot with you. I've loved the country."

"I love it too."

"Darling, you don't know how marvellous it is to see you feeling better. I couldn't stand it when you felt that way. You won't talk to me like that again, will you? Promise me?"

"No," he said. "I don't remember what I said."

"You don't have to destroy me. Do you? I'm only a middle-aged woman who loves you and wants to do what you want to do. I've been destroyed two or three times already. You wouldn't want to destroy me again, would you?"

"I'd like to destroy you a few times in bed," he said.

"Yes. That's the good destruction. That's the way we're made to be destroyed. The plane will be here tomorrow."

"How do you know?"

"I'm sure. It's bound to come. The boys have the wood all ready and the grass to make the smudge. I went down and looked at it again today. There's plenty of room to land and we have the smudges ready at both ends."

"What makes you think it will come tomorrow?"

"I'm sure it will. It's overdue now. Then, in town, they will fix up your leg and then we will have some good destruction. Not that dreadful talking kind."

"Should we have a drink? The sun is down."

"Do you think you should?"

"I'm having one."

"We'll have one together. Molo, *letti dui* whiskey-soda!" she called.

"You'd better put on your mosquito boots," he told her.

"I'll wait till I bathe . . ."

While it grew dark they drank and just before it was dark and there was no longer enough light to shoot, a hyena crossed the open on his way around the hill.

"That bastard crosses there every night," the man said. "Every night for two weeks."

"He's the one makes the noise at night. I don't mind it. They're a filthy animal though."

Drinking together, with no pain now except the discomfort of lying in the one position, the boys lighting a fire, its shadow jumping on the tents, he could feel the return of acquiescence in this life of pleasant surrender. She *was* very good to him. He had been cruel and unjust in the afternoon. She was a fine woman, marvellous really. And just then it occurred to him that he was going to die.

It came with a rush; not as a rush of water nor of wind; but of a sudden evil-smelling emptiness and the odd thing was that the hyena slipped lightly along the edge of it.

"What is it, Harry?" she asked him.

"Nothing," he said. "You had better move over to the other side. To windward."

"Did Molo change the dressing?"

"Yes. I'm just using the boric now."

"How do you feel?"

"A little wobbly."

"I'm going in to bathe," she said. "I'll be right out. I'll eat with you and then we'll put the cot in."

So, he said to himself, we did well to stop the quarrelling. He had never quarrelled much with this woman, while with the women that he loved he had quarrelled so much they had finally, always, with the corrosion of the quarrelling, killed what they had together. He had loved too much, demanded too much, and he wore it all out.

* * *

He thought about alone in Constantinople that time, having quar-
relled in Paris before he had gone out. He had whored the whole
time and then, when that was over, and he had failed to kill his
loneliness, but only made it worse, he had written her, the first one,
the one who left him, a letter telling her how he had never been
able to kill it. . . . How when he thought he saw her outside the
Regence one time it made him go all faint and sick inside, and that
he would follow a woman who looked like her in some way, along
the Boulevard, afraid to see it was not she, afraid to lose the feeling
it gave him. How every one he had slept with had only made him
miss her more. How what she had done could never matter since
he knew he could not cure himself of loving her. He wrote this let-
ter at the Club, cold sober, and mailed it to New York asking her
to write him at the office in Paris. That seemed safe. And that night
missing her so much it made him feel hollow sick inside, he wan-
dered up past Maxim's, picked a girl up and took her out to supper.
He had gone to a place to dance with her afterward, she danced
badly, and left her for a hot Armenian slut, that swung her belly
against him so it almost scalded. He took her away from a British
gunner subaltern after a row. The gunner asked him outside and
they fought in the street on the cobbles in the dark. He'd hit him
twice, hard, on the side of the jaw and when he didn't go down he
knew he was in for a fight. The gunner hit him in the body, then
beside his eye. He swung with his left again and landed and the
gunner fell on him and grabbed his coat and tore the sleeve off and
he clubbed him twice behind the ear and then smashed him with
his right as he pushed him away. When the gunner went down his
head hit first and he ran with the girl because they heard the M.P.'s
coming. They got into a taxi and drove out to Rimmily Hissa along
the Bosphorus, and around, and back in the cool night and went
to bed and she felt as over-ripe as she looked but smooth, rose-
petal, syrupy, smooth-bellied, big-breasted and needed no pillow
under her buttocks, and he left her before she was awake looking
blousy enough in the first daylight and turned up at the Pera Palace
with a black eye, carrying his coat because one sleeve was missing.

That same night he left for Anatolia and he remembered, later
on that trip, riding all day through fields of the poppies that they
raised for opium and how strange it made you feel, finally, and all

the distances seemed wrong, to where they had made the attack with the newly arrived Constantine officers, that did not know a god-damned thing, and the artillery had fired into the troops and the British observer had cried like a child.

That was the day he'd first seen dead men wearing white ballet skirts and upturned shoes with pompons on them. The Turks had come steadily and lumpily and he had seen the skirted men running and the officers shooting into them and running then themselves and he and the British observer had run too until his lungs ached and his mouth was full of the taste of pennies and they stopped behind some rocks and there were the Turks coming as lumpily as ever. Later he had seen the things that he could never think of and later still he had seen much worse. So when he got back to Paris that time he could not talk about it or stand to have it mentioned. And there in the café as he passed was that American poet with a pile of saucers in front of him and a stupid look on his potato face talking about the Dada movement with a Roumanian who said his name was Tristan Tzara, who always wore a monocle and had a headache, and, back at the apartment with his wife that now he loved again, the quarrel all over, the madness all over, glad to be home, the office sent his mail up to the flat. So then the letter in answer to the one he'd written came in on a platter one morning and when he saw the handwriting he went cold all over and tried to slip the letter underneath another. But his wife said, "Who is that letter from, dear?" and that was the end of the beginning of that.

He remembered the good times with them all, and the quarrels. They always picked the finest places to have the quarrels. And why had they always quarrelled when he was feeling best? He had never written any of that because, at first, he never wanted to hurt any one and then it seemed as though there was enough to write without it. But he had always thought that he would write it finally. There was so much to write. He had seen the world change; not just the events; although he had seen many of them and had watched the people, but he had seen the subtler change and he could remember how the people were at different times. He had been in it and he had watched it and it was his duty to write of it; but now he never would.

* * *

"How do you feel?" she said. She had come out from the tent now after her bath.

"All right."

"Could you eat now?" He saw Molo behind her with the folding table and the other boy with the dishes.

"I want to write," he said.

"You ought to take some broth to keep your strength up."

"I'm going to die tonight," he said. "I don't need my strength up."

"Don't be melodramatic, Harry, please," she said.

"Why don't you use your nose? I'm rotted half way up my thigh now. What the hell should I fool with broth for? Molo bring whiskey-soda."

"Please take the broth," she said gently.

"All right."

The broth was too hot. He had to hold it in the cup until it cooled enough to take it and then he just got it down without gagging.

"You're a fine woman," he said. "Don't pay any attention to me."

She looked at him with her well-known, well-loved face from *Spur* and *Town & Country*, only a little the worse for drink, only a little the worse for bed, but *Town & Country* never showed those good breasts and those useful thighs and those lightly small-of-back-caressing hands, and as he looked and saw her well-known pleasant smile, he felt death come again.

This time there was no rush. It was a puff, as of a wind that makes a candle flicker and the flame go tall.

"They can bring my net out later and hang it from the tree and build the fire up. I'm not going in the tent tonight. It's not worth moving. It's a clear night. There won't be any rain."

So this was how you died, in whispers that you did not hear. Well, there would be no more quarrelling. He could promise that. The one experience that he had never had he was not going to spoil now. He probably would. You spoiled everything. But perhaps he wouldn't.

"You can't take dictation, can you?"

"I never learned," she told him.

"That's all right."

There wasn't time, of course, although it seemed as though it telescoped so that you might put it all into one paragraph if you could get it right.

There was a log house, chinked white with mortar, on a hill above the lake. There was a bell on a pole by the door to call the people in to meals. Behind the house were fields and behind the fields was the timber. A line of lombardy poplars ran from the house to the dock. Other poplars ran along the point. A road went up to the hills along the edge of the timber and along that road he picked blackberries. Then that log house was burned down and all the guns that had been on deer foot racks above the open fire place were burned and afterwards their barrels, with the lead melted in the magazines, and the stocks burned away, lay out on the heap of ashes that were used to make lye for the big iron soap kettles, and you asked Grandfather if you could have them to play with, and he said, no. You see they were his guns still and he never bought any others. Nor did he hunt any more. The house was rebuilt in the same place out of lumber now and painted white and from its porch you saw the poplars and the lake beyond; but there were never any more guns. The barrels of the guns that had hung on the deer feet on the wall of the log house lay out there on the heap of ashes and no one ever touched them.

In the Black Forest, after the war, we rented a trout stream and there were two ways to walk to it. One was down the valley from Triberg and around the valley road in the shade of the trees that bordered the white road, and then up a side road that went up through the hills past many small farms, with the big Schwarzwald houses, until that road crossed the stream. That was where our fishing began.

The other way was to climb steeply up to the edge of the woods and then go across the top of the hills through the pine woods, and then out to the edge of a meadow and down across this meadow to the bridge. There were birches along the stream and it was not big, but narrow, clear and fast, with pools where it had cut under the roots of the birches. At the Hotel in Triberg the proprietor had a fine season. It was very pleasant and we were all great friends. The next year came the inflation and the money he had made the year before was not enough to buy supplies to open the hotel and he hanged himself.

You could dictate that, but you could not dictate the Place Contrescarpe where the flower sellers dyed their flowers in the street and the dye ran over the paving where the autobus started and the old men and the women, always drunk on wine and bad marc; and the children with their noses running in the cold; the smell of dirty sweat and poverty and drunkenness at the Café des Amateurs and the whores at the Bal Musette they lived above. The concierge who entertained the trooper of the Garde Republicaine in her loge, his horse-hair-plumed helmet on a chair. The locataire across the hall whose husband was a bicycle racer and her joy that morning at the crémerie when she had opened L'Auto and seen where he placed third in Paris-Tours, his first big race. She had blushed and laughed and then gone upstairs crying with the yellow sporting paper in her hand. The husband of the woman who ran the Bal Musette drove a taxi and when he, Harry, had to take an early plane the husband knocked upon the door to wake him and they each drank a glass of white wine at the zinc of the bar before they started. He knew his neighbors in that quarter then because they all were poor.

Around that Place there were two kinds; the drunkards and the sportifs. The drunkards killed their poverty that way; the sportifs took it out in exercise. They were the descendants of the Communards and it was no struggle for them to know their politics. They knew who had shot their fathers, their relatives, their brothers, and their friends when the Versailles troops came in and took the town after the Commune and executed any one they could catch with calloused hands, or who wore a cap, or carried any other sign he was a working man. And in that poverty, and in that quarter across the street from a Boucherie Chevaline and a wine cooperative he had written the start of all he was to do. There never was another part of Paris that he loved like that, the sprawling trees, the old white plastered houses painted brown below, the long green of the autobus in that round square, the purple flower dye upon the paving, the sudden drop down the hill of the rue Cardinal Lemoine to the River, and the other way the narrow crowded world of the rue

Mouffetard. The street that ran up toward the Pantheon and the other that he always took with the bicycle, the only asphalted street in all that quarter, smooth under the tires, with the high narrow houses and the cheap tall hotel where Paul Verlaine had died. There were only two rooms in the apartments where they lived and he had a room on the top floor of that hotel that cost him sixty francs a month where he did his writing, and from it he could see the roofs and chimney pots and all the hills of Paris.

From the apartment you could only see the wood and coal man's place. He sold wine too, bad wine. The golden horse's head outside the Boucherie Chevaline where the carcasses hung yellow gold and red in the open window, and the green painted co-operative where they bought their wine; good wine and cheap. The rest was plaster walls and the windows of the neighbors. The neighbors who, at night, when some one lay drunk in the street, moaning and groaning in that typical French ivresse that you were propaganded to believe did not exist, would open their windows and then the murmur of talk.

"Where is the policeman? When you don't want him the bugger is always there. He's sleeping with some concierge. Get the Agent." Till some one threw a bucket of water from a window and the moaning stopped. "What's that? Water. Ah, that's intelligent." And the windows shutting. Marie, his femme de ménage, protesting against the eight-hour day saying, "If a husband works until six he gets only a little drunk on the way home and does not waste too much. If he works only until five he is drunk every night and one has no money. It is the wife of the working man who suffers from this shortening of hours."

"Wouldn't you like some more broth?" the woman asked him now.

"No, thank you very much. It is awfully good."

"Try just a little."

"I would like a whiskey-soda."

"It's not good for you."

"No. It's bad for me. Cole Porter wrote the words and the music. This knowledge that you're going mad for me."

"You know I like you to drink."

"Oh yes. Only it's bad for me."

When she goes, he thought, I'll have all I want. Not all I want but all there is. Ayee he was tired. Too tired. He was going to sleep a little while. He lay still and death was not there. It must have gone around another street. It went in pairs, on bicycles, and moved absolutely silently on the pavements.

No, he had never written about Paris. Not the Paris that he cared about. But what about the rest that he had never written?

What about the ranch and the silvered gray of the sage brush, the quick, clear water in the irrigation ditches, and the heavy green of the alfalfa. The trail went up into the hills and the cattle in the summer were shy as deer. The bawling and the steady noise and slow moving mass raising a dust as you brought them down in the fall. And behind the mountains, the clear sharpness of the peak in the evening light and, riding down along the trail in the moonlight, bright across the valley. Now he remembered coming down through the timber in the dark holding the horse's tail when you could not see and all the stories that he meant to write.

About the half-wit chore boy who was left at the ranch that time and told not to let any one get any hay, and that old bastard from the Forks who had beaten the boy when he had worked for him stopping to get some feed. The boy refusing and the old man saying he would beat him again. The boy got the rifle from the kitchen and shot him when he tried to come into the barn and when they came back to the ranch he'd been dead a week, frozen in the corral, and the dogs had eaten part of him. But what was left you packed on a sled wrapped in a blanket and roped on and you got the boy to help you haul it, and the two of you took it out over the road on skis, and sixty miles down to town to turn the boy over. He having no idea that he would be arrested. Thinking he had done his duty and that you were his friend and he would be rewarded. He'd helped to haul the old man in so everybody could know how bad the old man had been and how he'd tried to steal some feed that didn't belong to him, and when the sheriff put the handcuffs on the boy he couldn't believe it. Then he'd started to cry. That was one story he had saved to write. He knew at least twenty good stories from out there and he had never written one. Why?

"You tell them why," he said.

"Why what, dear?"

"Why nothing."

She didn't drink so much, now, since she had him. But if he lived he would never write about her, he knew that now. Nor about any of them. The rich were dull and they drank too much, or they played too much backgammon. They were dull and they were repetitious. He remembered poor Julian and his romantic awe of them and how he had started a story once that began, "The very rich are different from you and me." And how some one had said to Julian, Yes, they have more money. But that was not humorous to Julian. He thought they were a special glamourous race and when he found they weren't it wrecked him just as much as any other thing that wrecked him.

He had been contemptuous of those who wrecked. You did not have to like it because you understood it. He could beat anything, he thought, because no thing could hurt him if he did not care.

All right. Now he would not care for death. One thing he had always dreaded was the pain. He could stand pain as well as any man, until it went on too long, and wore him out, but here he had something that had hurt frightfully and just when he had felt it breaking him, the pain had stopped.

He remembered long ago when Williamson, the bombing officer, had been hit by a stick bomb some one in a German patrol had thrown as he was coming in through the wire that night and, screaming, had begged every one to kill him. He was a fat man, very brave, and a good officer, although addicted to fantastic shows. But that night he was caught in the wire, with a flare lighting him up and his bowels spilled out into the wire, so when they brought him in, alive, they had to cut him loose. Shoot me, Harry. For Christ sake shoot me. They had had an argument one time about our Lord never sending you anything you could not bear

*and some one's theory had been that meant that at a certain time
the pain passed you out automatically. But he had always remembered Williamson, that night. Nothing passed out Williamson
until he gave him all his morphine tablets that he had always
saved to use himself and then they did not work right away.*

Still this now, that he had, was very easy; and if it was no worse
as it went on there was nothing to worry about. Except that he
would rather be in better company.

He thought a little about the company that he would like to
have.

No, he thought, when everything you do, you do too long, and
do too late, you can't expect to find the people still there. The people
all are gone. The party's over and you are with your hostess now.

I'm getting as bored with dying as with everything else, he
thought.

"It's a bore," he said out loud.

"What is, my dear?"

"Anything you do too bloody long."

He looked at her face between him and the fire. She was leaning back in the chair and the firelight shone on her pleasantly
lined face and he could see that she was sleepy. He heard the
hyena make a noise just outside the range of the fire.

"I've been writing," he said. "But I got tired."

"Do you think you will be able to sleep?"

"Pretty sure. Why don't you turn in?"

"I like to sit here with you."

"Do you feel anything strange?" he asked her.

"No. Just a little sleepy."

"I do," he said.

He had just felt death come by again.

"You know the only thing I've never lost is curiosity," he said
to her.

"You've never lost anything. You're the most complete man
I've ever known."

"Christ," he said. "How little a woman knows. What is that?
Your intuition?"

Because, just then, death had come and rested its head on the foot of the cot and he could smell its breath.

"Never believe any of that about a scythe and a skull," he told her. "It can be two bicycle policemen as easily, or be a bird. Or it can have a wide snout like a hyena."

It had moved up on him now, but it had no shape any more. It simply occupied space.

"Tell it to go away."

It did not go away but moved a little closer.

"You've got a hell of a breath," he told it. "You stinking bastard."

It moved up closer to him still and now he could not speak to it, and when it saw he could not speak it came a little closer, and now he tried to send it away without speaking, but it moved in on him so its weight was all upon his chest, and while it crouched there and he could not move, or speak, he heard the woman say, "Bwana is asleep now. Take the cot up very gently and carry it into the tent."

He could not speak to tell her to make it go away and it crouched now, heavier, so he could not breathe. And then, while they lifted the cot, suddenly it was all right and the weight went from his chest.

It was morning and had been morning for some time and he heard the plane. It showed very tiny and then made a wide circle and the boys ran out and lit the fires, using kerosene, and piled on grass so there were two big smudges at each end of the level place and the morning breeze blew them toward the camp and the plane circled twice more, low this time, and then glided down and levelled off and landed smoothly and, coming walking toward him, was old Compton in slacks, a tweed jacket and a brown felt hat.

"What's the matter, old cock?" Compton said.

"Bad leg," he told him. "Will you have some breakfast?"

"Thanks. I'll just have some tea. It's the Puss Moth you know. I won't be able to take the Memsahib. There's only room for one. Your lorry is on the way."

Helen had taken Compton aside and was speaking to him. Compton came back more cheery than ever.

"We'll get you right in," he said. "I'll be back for the Mem. Now I'm afraid I'll have to stop at Arusha to refuel. We'd better get going."

"What about the tea?"

"I don't really care about it, you know."

The boys had picked up the cot and carried it around the green tents and down along the rock and out onto the plain and along past the smudges that were burning brightly now, the grass all consumed, and the wind fanning the fire, to the little plane. It was difficult getting him in, but once in he lay back in the leather seat, and the leg was stuck straight out to one side of the seat where Compton sat. Compton started the motor and got in. He waved to Helen and to the boys and, as the clatter moved into the old familiar roar, they swung around with Compie watching for warthog holes and roared, bumping, along the stretch between the fires and with the last bump rose and he saw them all standing below, waving, and the camp beside the hill, flattening now, and the plain spreading, clumps of trees, and the bush flattening, while the game trails ran now smoothly to the dry waterholes, and there was a new water that he had never known of. The zebra, small rounded backs now, and the wildebeeste, big-headed dots seeming to climb as they moved in long fingers across the plain, now scattering as the shadow came toward them, they were tiny now, and the movement had no gallop, and the plain as far as you could see, gray-yellow now and ahead old Compie's tweed back and the brown felt hat. Then they were over the first hills and the wildebeeste were trailing up them, and then they were over mountains with sudden depths of green-rising forest and the solid bamboo slopes, and then the heavy forest again, sculptured into peaks and hollows until they crossed, and hills sloped down and then another plain, hot now, and purple brown, bumpy with heat and Compie looking back to see how he was riding. Then there were other mountains dark ahead.

And then instead of going on to Arusha they turned left, he evidently figured that they had the gas, and looking down he saw a pink sifting cloud, moving over the ground, and in the air, like the first snow in a blizzard, that comes from nowhere, and he knew the locusts were coming up from the South. Then they began to climb and they were going to the East it seemed, and then it darkened and they were in a storm, the rain so thick it seemed like flying through a waterfall, and then they were out and Compie turned his head and grinned and pointed and there, ahead, all he could see, as wide as all the world, great, high, and unbelievably white in the sun, was the square top of Kilimanjaro. And then he knew that there was where he was going.

Just then the hyena stopped whimpering in the night and started to make a strange, human, almost crying sound. The woman heard it and stirred uneasily. She did not wake. In her dream she was at the house on Long Island and it was the night before her daughter's début. Somehow her father was there and he had been very rude. Then the noise the hyena made was so loud she woke and for a moment she did not know where she was and she was very afraid. Then she took the flashlight and shone it on the other cot that they had carried in after Harry had gone to sleep. She could see his bulk under the mosquito bar but somehow he had gotten his leg out and it hung down alongside the cot. The dressings had all come down and she could not look at it.

"Molo," she called, "Molo! Molo!"

Then she said, "Harry, Harry!" Then her voice rising, "Harry! Please. Oh Harry!"

There was no answer and she could not hear him breathing.

Outside the tent the hyena made the same strange noise that had awakened her. But she did not hear him for the beating of her heart.

17a.

Item 702, Ernest Hemingway Collection, John F. Kennedy Library and Museum, Boston. Early typescript of "The Snows of Kilimanjaro," titled "The Happy Ending" in pencil, with pencil corrections.

The Happy Ending

"The marvellous thing is that it's quite painless," he said. "That's how you know when it starts."

"Is it really?"

"Absolutely. I'm awfully sorry about the odour though. That must bother you."

"Don't. Please don't."

"Look at them," he said. "Now is it sight or is it scent that brings them like that?"

The cot the man lay on was in the wide shade of a mimosa tree and as he looked out past the shade onto the glare of the plain there were three of the big birds squatted obscenely, while in the sky a dozen more sailed, making quick-moving shadows as they passed.

"They've been there since the day the truck broke down," he said. "Today's the first time any have lit on the ground. I watched the way they sailed very carefully at first in case I ever wanted to use them in a story. That's funny now."

"I wish you wouldn't," she said. ~~"It isn't as though I could do anything. Why should you want to make me feel worse?"~~

~~I don't," he said. "Really I don't."~~ "I'm only talking," he said ~~just the way I feel~~. "It's much easier if I talk. ~~Only~~ But I don't want to bother you."

"You know it doesn't bother me," she said. "It's that I've gotten so very nervous not being able to do anything. I think we might make it as easy as we can until the plane comes."

"Or until the plane doesn't come."

"Please tell me what I can do. There must be something I can do."

"You can take it off and that might stop it. Or you can shoot me. You're a good shot now. I taught you to shoot didn't I?"

"Please don't talk that way. Couldn't I read to you?"

"Read what?"

"Anything in the book bag that we haven't read."

"I can't listen to it," he said. "Talking is the easiest. We quarrel and that makes the time pass."

"I don't quarrel. I never want to quarrel. Let's not quarrel any more. No matter how nervous we get. Maybe they will be back with another truck today. Maybe the plane will come."

"I don't want to move," the man said. "There is no sense in moving now except to make it easier for you."

"That's cowardly."

"Why Can't you let a man die as comfortably as he can without calling him names. What's the use of slanging me?"

"You're not going to die."

"Don't be silly. I'm dying now. Ask those bastards." He looked over to where the huge, filthy birds sat, their naked heads sunk in the hunched feathers. A fourth planed down, to run quick-legged and then waddle slowly toward the others.

"They are around every camp. You never notice them. You can't die if you don't give up."

"Where did you read that? You're such a bloody fool."

"You might think about some-one else."

"For Christ sake," he said. "That's been my trade." He lay then and was quiet for a while and looked across the heat shimmer of the plain to the edge of the bush. There were a few Tommies that showed minute and white against the yellow and far off he saw a herd of Zebra white against the green of the bush. This was a pleasant camp under big trees against a hill, with shade, good water and, close by, a nearly dry water hole where sand grouse flighted in the mornings.

"Wouldn't you like me to read?" she said. She was sitting on a canvas chair beside his cot. "There's a breeze coming up."

"No thanks."

"Maybe the truck will come."

"I don't give a damn about the truck."

"I do."

"You give a damn about so many things that I don't."

"Not so many, Harry."

"What about a drink?"

"It's supposed to be bad for you. It said in Blacks to avoid all alcohol. You shouldn't drink."

"Molo!" he shouted.

"Yes Bwana."

"Bring whiskey-soda." ~~Bwana has gangrene.~~

"Yes Bwana."

"You shouldn't," she said. "That's what I mean by giving up. It says it's bad for you. I know it's bad for you."

"No," he said. "It's good for me."

So now it was all over, he thought. So now he would never have a chance to finish it. So this was the way it ended in a bickering over a drink. Since the gangrene started in his right leg he had no pain and with the pain the horror had gone and all he felt now was a great tiredness and anger that this was the end of it. For this that now was coming he had very little curiosity. For years it had obsessed him but now it meant nothing in its-self. It was strange how ~~very easy~~ being tired enough made it.

~~Now he would never write all the things that he was going to write.~~ Now he would ~~not~~ never write the things that he had saved to write until he knew enough to write them well. Well, he would not have to fail at trying to write them either. Maybe you could never write them, and that was why you put them off and delayed the start-ing. Well, he would never know now.

"I wish we'd never come," the woman said. She was looking at him holding the glass and biting her lip. "You never would have got-ten anything like this in Paris. You always said you loved Paris. We could have stayed in Paris or gone anywhere. I'd have gone any-where. ~~We had enough money and~~ I said I'd go anywhere you wanted. If you wanted to shoot we could have gone shooting in Hungary and been comfortable."

"Your bloody money," he said.

"That's not fair," she said. "It was always yours as much as mine. I left everything and I went where you wanted to go. I left everything ~~in my life~~ and I went wherever you wanted to go and I've done what you wanted to do. But I wish we'd never come here."

"You said you loved it."

"I did when you were all right. But now I hate it. I don't see why that had to happen to your leg. What have we done to have that happen to us?"

"I suppose what I did was to forget to put iodine on it when I first scratched it. Then I didn't pay any attention to it because I never infect. Then, later, when it got bad, it was probably using that weak carbolic solution when the other antiseptics ran out that paralyzed the minute blood vessels and started the gangrene. What else?"

"I don't mean that."

"If we would have hired a good mechanic instead of a half baked kikuyu driver he would have checked the oil and never burned out that bearing in the truck."

"I don't mean that."

"If you hadn't left your own people, your goddamned Long Island, Saratoga, Palm Beach people to take me on—"

"Why I loved you. That's not fair. I love you now. I'll always love you. Don't you love me?"

"No," said the man. "I don't think so. I never have."

"Harry what are you saying? You're out of your head."

"No. I haven't any head to go out of."

"Don't drink that," she said. "Darling please don't drink that. We have to do everything we can."

"You do it," he said. "I'm tired."

Now in his mind he saw a railway station at Karagatch and he was standing with his pack and that was the headlight of the Simplon-Orient coming in at night cutting the dark now and he was leaving Thrace then after the retreat. That was one of the things he had saved to write, with in the morning at breakfast, looking out the window and seeing snow on the mountains in Bulgaria and Nansen's Secretary asking the old man if it were snow and the old man looking at it and saying, No, that's not snow. It's too early for snow. And the Secretary repeating to the other girls, No, you see. It's not snow. And them all saying, It's not snow. We were mistaken. But it was the snow he sent them on into when he evolved exchange of populations. And it was snow they tramped along until they died that winter.

It was snow too that fell all Christmas week that year up in the Gauertal, that year they lived in the woodcutter's house with the big stove that filled half the room, and they slept on mattresses filled with beech leaves, the time the deserter came with his feet bloody in the snow. They gave him woolen socks and held the gendarmes talking until the tracks had drifted over. In Schruns on Christmas day the snow so bright it hurt your eyes when you looked out from the weinstube and everyone coming home from church and walking up the sleigh smoothed road along the river with the steep pine hills. And ski-running down the glacier toward the Madlener-haus, the snow as smooth to see as cake frosting and as light as powder and the noiseless rush the speed made as you dropped down like a bird. Snow bound a week in the Madlener-haus that time in the blizzard playing cards in the smoke by the lantern light, the stakes higher all the time as Herr Lent lost more. Until he lost it all. Everything. And you had won it. There was always gambling then. When there was no snow you gambled and when there was too much you gambled. All the time in his life he had spent gambling. Yet he had never written a line of that nor of that cold, bright Christmas day, with the mountains showing across the plain that Barker had flown across the lines to bomb and shoot up the Austrian leave train. Machine gunning them as they scattered and ran. Barker afterwards coming into the mess and starting to tell about it. And how quiet it got and then somebody saying, "You bloody shit." Those were the same Austrians that he skied with that year. Hans had been in the Kaiser-Jägers and when they went hunting hares together up the little valley above the saw-mill they had talked ~~about~~ of the fighting on Pasubio and of the attack on Pertica and Asalone and he had never written a word of that. How many winters in the Vorarlberg and Arlberg? The man who had the fox to sell when ~~we~~ they had walked into Bludenz, that time to buy presents, the taste of good kirsch, the fast-slipping rush of running powder snow on crust, singing "Hi Ho said Rolly" as you ran down the last stretch to the steep drop, taking it straight then running the orchard in three turns and out across the ditch and onto the icy road behind the inn. Knocking your bindings loose, kicking the skis free and leaning them up against the wooden wall of the inn, the lamp-light coming from the window and inside they were playing the accordeon.

"Where did we stay in Paris?" he asked.

"At the Crillon. You know that."

"Why do I know that?"

"That's where we always stayed."

"No. Not always."

"There and at the Pavillion Henri-Quatre in St. Germain. You said you loved it there."

"Love is a ~~pile of shit~~ (dung hill)," said Harry. "And I'm the cock that gets on it to crow."

"If you have to go away," she said, ~~She never could use the word die~~ "is it absolutely necessary to kill off everything you leave behind? I mean do you have to take away everything? Do you have to kill your horse, and your wife and burn your saddle and your armour."

"Yes," he said. "Your damned money was my armour. My Swift and my Armour." ~~Fleishman's yeast and Fleishman's vest. Vest is vest."~~

~~"I think your getting better. Now you sound more like yourself."~~

~~"More like Willie Howard."~~

"Don't."

"All right. I'll stop that. I don't want to hurt you."

"It's a little bit late now."

"All right then. I'll go on hurting you. It's more amusing. The only thing I ever really liked to do with you I can't do now."

"No, that's not true. You liked to do a lot of things and everything you wanted to do I did."

"Oh for Christ sake stop bragging will you?"

He looked at her and saw her crying.

"Listen," he said. "Do you think that it is fun to do this? I don't know why I'm doing it. It is trying to kill to keep yourself alive I ~~guess~~ imagine. I was all right when we started talking and now I'm crazy as a coot and being as cruel to you as I can be. Don't pay any attention darling to what I say. I love you, really. You know I love you. I've never loved anyone else the way I love you," he slipped into the familiar lie he made his bread and butter by.

"You're sweet to me."

"You bitch," he said. "You rich bitch. That's poetry. I'm full of poetry now. Rot and poetry. ~~Oh one rich bitch will have the itch.~~ Rotten poetry."

"Stop it. Harry why do you have to turn into a devil now?"

"I don't like to leave anything," the man said. "I don't like to leave things behind."

It was evening now and he had been asleep. The sun was gone behind the hill and there was shadow all across the plain and the small animals were feeding close to camp; quick dropping heads and switching tails, he watched them keeping well out away from the bush now. The birds no longer waited on the ground. They ~~all~~ were all perched heavily in a tree. There were many more of them. His personal boy was sitting by the bed.

"Memsahib's gone to shoot," the boy said. "Does Bwana want?"
"Nothing."

She had gone to kill a piece of meat and knowing how he liked to watch the game she had gone well away so she would not disturb this little pocket of the plain that he could see. She was always thoughtful, he thought. On anything she knew about, or had read, or that she had ever heard. It was not her fault that when he went to her he was already over. How could a woman know that you meant nothing that you said; that you spoke only from habit and to be comfortable. After he no longer meant what he said his lies were more successful with women than when he had told them the truth.

It was not that he lied as that there was no truth to tell. He had had his life and it was over and then he went on living it again with different people and more money with the best of the same places and some new ones. You kept from thinking and it was all ~~fine~~ marvellous. You were equipped with good insides so that you did not go to pieces that way, the way most of them had, and you made an attitude that you cared nothing for the work you used to do, not that you could no longer do it. But in yourself you said that you would write about these people; about the very rich; that you were really not of them but a spy in their country; that you would leave it and write of it and for once it would be written by some-one who knew what ~~they were~~ he was writing of. But ~~you~~ he would never do it because each day of not writing, of comfort, of being that which ~~you~~ he despised dulled ~~his perceptions~~ his ability and softened his will to work so that, finally, he did not work at all. The people he knew now were all much more comfortable when he did not work.

Africa was where he had been happiest in the good time of his life so he had come out here to start again. They had made this safari with the minimum of comfort. There was no hardship; but there was no luxury and he had thought that he could get back into training that way. That in some way he could work the fat off his soul the way a fighter went into the mountains to work ~~and sweat it from~~ in order to burn it out of his body.

She had liked it. She said she loved it. ~~He knew the country and he always could go to any place he had been to once. It was much more exciting being out without a white hunter to take all responsibility and they had led a pleasant, healthy life and he had felt the illusion of returning strength of will to work.~~ She loved anything that was exciting, that involved a change of scene, where there were new people and where things were pleasant. And he had felt the illusion of returning strength of will to work. Now if this was how it ended, and he knew it was, he must not turn like some snake biting its-self because its back was broken. It wasn't this woman's fault. If it had not been her it would have been another. If he lived by a lie he should try to die by it. He heard a shot beyond the hill.

She shot very well this good rich bitch, this kindly caretaker and destroyer of his talent. Nonsense. He had destroyed his talent himself. Why should he blame this woman because she kept him well? He had destroyed his talent by not using it, by betrayals of himself and what he believed in, by drinking so much that he blunted the edge of his perceptions, by laziness, by sloth and by snobbery, by pride and by prejudice, by hook and by crook. What was this? A catalogue of ancient books? What was this talent anyway? Yes, it was a talent but instead of using it he had traded on it. It was never what he had done, but always what he could do. And he had chosen to make his living with something else instead of a pen or a pencil. It was strange too, wasn't it, that when he fell in love with another woman, that woman should always had more money than the last one? But when he no longer was in love, when he was only lying, as to this woman now who had the most money of ~~any~~ all, who had all the money ~~in the world~~ there was, who had had a husband and children, who had taken lovers and been dis-satisfied with them, and who loved him dearly as a writer, as a man, as a companion and as a proud possession, it was strange that when he did not love her at all and was lying, that he should be able to give her more for her money than when he had really loved. We must all be cut out for what we do, he thought. However you make your living is where your talent lies. ~~And~~ He had sold vitality, in one form or another, all his life and when your affections are not too involved you give much better value for the money. He had found that out but he would never write that, now, either.

Now she came in sight walking across the open toward the camp. She was wearing jodhpurs and carrying her rifle. The two boys had a Tommie slung. She was still a good looking woman, he thought, and she had a pleasant body. She had a great talent and appreciation for the bed, she was not pretty but he liked her face, she read ~~a great deal~~ enormously, liked to ride and shoot and, certainly, she drank too much. Her husband had died when she was still a comparatively young woman ~~but too old she had thought~~ and for a while she had devoted herself to her two just-grown children, who did not need her and were embarrassed at having her about, to her stable of horses, to books, and to bottles. She liked to read in the evening before dinner and ~~drink~~ she drank scotch and soda while she read. By dinner time she was fairly drunk and after a bottle of wine at dinner she was usually drunk enough to sleep.

That was before the lovers. After she had the lovers she did not drink so much because she did not have to be drunk to sleep. But the lovers bored her. She had been married to a man who had never bored her and these people bored her very much.

Then one of her two children was killed in a plane crash and after that was over she did not want the lovers and ~~there were not enough book, they did not come out fast enough, and~~ drink, being no anesthetic, she had to make another life. Suddenly she had been acutely frightened of being alone. But she wanted someone she respected with her. He, Henry Walden, had become that life. It had begun very simply. She liked what he wrote and she had always envied the life he led. She thought he did exactly what he wanted to. The steps by which she had acquired him and the way in which she had finally fallen in love with him were all part of a regular progression in which she had built herself a new life and he had traded away what remained of his old life. He had traded it for security, for comfort too, there was no denying that, and for what else? He did not know. She would have bought him anything he wanted. He knew that. She was a damned nice woman too. He would as soon be in bed with her as anyone, rather with her, because she was richer, because she was very pleasant and appreciative and because she never made scenes. And now this life that she had built again was coming to a term because he had not used iodine two weeks ago when a thorn had scratched his knee as they moved forward trying to photograph a herd of water-buck standing, their heads up, peering while their nostrils searched the air, and their ears spread wide to hear the first noise that would send them rushing into the bush. They had bolted, too, before he got the picture.

Here she came now.

"Hello," he said.

"I shot a Tommy ram," she ~~said~~ told him. "He'll make you good broth and I'll have them mash some potatoes with the Klim. How do you feel?"

"Much better."

"Isn't that ~~fine~~ lovely. You know I thought perhaps you would. You were sleeping when I left."

"I had a good sleep. Did you walk far?"

"No. Just around behind the hill. I made quite a good shot on the Tommy."

"You shoot marvellously you know."

"I love it. I've really loved Africa. Really. If you're all right it's the most fun that I've ever had. You don't know the fun it's been to shoot with you. ~~Imagine being at Palm Beach now.~~ I've loved the country."

"~~We don't play much backgammon do we?~~ I love it too."

"Darling you don't know how marvellous it is to see you feeling better. I couldn't stand it when you felt that way. You won't talk to me like that again will you? Promise me?"

"No," he said. "I don't remember what I said."

"You don't have to destroy me. Do you? I'm only a middle-aged woman who loves you and wants to do what you want to do. I've been destroyed two or three times all ready. You wouldn't want to destroy me again would you?"

"I'd like to destroy you a few times in bed," he said.

"Yes. That's the good destruction. That's the way we're made to be destroyed. The plane will be here tomorrow."

"How do you know?"

"I'm sure. It's bound to come. The boys have the wood all ready and the grass to make the smudge. I went down and looked at it again today. There's plenty of room to land and we have the smudges ready at both ends."

"What makes you think it will come tomorrow?"

"I'm sure it will. It's overdue now. Then in town they will fix up your leg and then we will have some good destruction. Not that dreadful talking kind."

"Should we have a drink? The sun is down."

"Do you think you should?"

"I'm having one."

"We'll have one together. <u>Molo letti dui whisky-soda</u>!" she called.

"You'd better put on your mosquito boots," he told her.

"I'll wait till I bathe."

While it grew dark they drank and just before it was dark but when ~~it was too dark~~ there was no longer enough light to shoot, a hyena crossed the open on his way around the hill.

"That bastard crosses there every night," the man said. "Every night for two weeks."

"He's the one makes the noise at night. I don't mind it. They're a filthy animal though."

Drinking together, with no pain now except the discomfort of lying in the one position, the boys lighting a fire, its shadow jumping on the tents, he could feel the return of acquiescence in this life of ~~doing nothing~~ pleasant surrender. ~~It was a pleasant life and~~ She <u>was</u> very good to him. He had been cruel and unjust in the afternoon. She was a fine woman, marvellous really. And just then it occurred to him that he was going to die.

It came with a rush; not as a rush of water nor of wind; but of a sudden ~~hollow darkness~~ evil smelling emptiness and the odd thing was that the hyena slipped lightly along the edge of it.

"What is it, Harry?" she asked him.

"Nothing," he said. "You had better move over to the other side. To windward."

"Did Molo change the dressing?"

"Yes. I'm just using the boric now."

"How do you feel?"

"A little wobbly."

"I'm going in to bathe," she said. "I'll be right out. I'll eat with you and then we'll put the cot in."

So, he said to himself, we did well to stop the quarreling. ~~There isn't much time now.~~ He had never quarreled much with this woman, while with the women that he loved he had quarreled so much they had finally, always, killed it off. ~~He did not think of this now except as part of what he should have written.~~ He had loved too much, demanded too much, and he wore it all out.

[There is a note in the margin in pencil to "redo" the entire following paragraph.] Along in Constantinople that time, having quarrelled in Paris before he had gone out, he had whored the whole time and then, when that was over, and he had failed to kill his loneliness, but only made it worse, he had written ~~Frances~~ her ~~a letter,~~ the first one he'd loved, the one who left him, a letter telling her how he had never been able to kill it. How when he thought he saw her outside the <u>Regence</u> one time it made him go ~~all~~ faint and sick inside and that he would follow a woman who looked like her in some way a mile along the Boulevard, afraid to see it was not her, afraid to lose the feeling that it gave him. How every one he had ever slept with since had only made him miss her more. How what she had done could never matter since he knew he could not cure himself of loving her. He wrote this letter at the Club, cold sober, and mailed it to New York asking her to write him at the office in Paris. That seemed safe. And that night missing her so much it made him feel sick, he wandered up past Taxim's picked a girl up and took her out to supper. Went to dance with her afterward, she danced badly, and left her for an Armenian wench he took away from a British gunner subaltern after a row. The gunner asked him outside and they fought in the street on the cobbles in the dark. He ~~nailed~~ hit him twice and when he didn't go down he knew it was a fight. The gunner hit him in the body, then beside his eye. He ~~nailed him the gunner~~ swung with his left again and ~~as he fell forward the gunner~~ landed and the gunner fell on him and grabbed his coat and tore the sleeve off and he ~~slammed~~ clubbed him twice behind the ear and then got him cleanly with his right as he pushed him away. When ~~he~~ the gunner went down his head hit first and he ran with the girl because they heard the M.P.s coming. They got into a taxi and drove out to Rimmily Hissa along the Bosphorus and around and back in the cool night and went to bed and she felt just as over-ripe as she looked but smooth as hell, rose petal syrupy smooth bellied big breasted and he left her before she was awake looking blousy enough in the first day-light and turned up at the Pera Palace with a black eye carrying his coat because one sleeve was missing. That same night he left for Anatolia and he remembered, later on that trip, riding all day ~~that other time~~ through ~~the~~ fields of poppies that they raised for opium and how it made you groggy, and it seemed to affect the horse too, to where they had made the attack with the newly arrived Constantine officers that did not know a god-damned thing and the artillery had fired into the troops and the British observer had cried like a child. That was the day he'd first seen dead men wearing white ballet skirts and upturned shoes with pom poms on them. The turks had come steadily and lumpily and he had seen the skirted men running and the officers shooting into them and running, then, themselves and he and the British observer had run too until his lungs ached and his mouth was full of the taste of pennies and they stopped behind some rocks and there were the turks coming as lumpily as ever. Later he had seen the things that he could never think of and later still he had seen much worse. So when he got back to Paris that time he could not talk about it or stand to have it mentioned. And there in the café as he passed was Malcolm Cowley with a pile of saucers in front of him and a stupid look on his face talking about the dada movement with a Roumanian who said his name was Tristan Tzara who always wore a monocle and had a head-ache and back at the apartment with his wife that now he loved again, the quarrell all over, the office sent his mail up to the flat. So then the letter ~~from Frances~~ in answer to the one he'd written came in on a platter one morning and when he saw the hand writing he went cold all over and tried to slip the letter underneath another. But his wife said, "Who is that letter from, dear?" and that was the end or the beginning of that. He remembered the good times with them all and the quarrells and why had they always quarrelled when he was feeling best? They always picked the finest places to have the quarrells. ~~And~~ He had never written any of that because at first he never wanted to hurt anyone and then it seemed as though there was enough to write without it. But he had always thought that he would write it finally. There was so much to write. He had seen the world change; not just the events; although he had seen many of them and had watched the people, but he had seen the subtler change and he could remember how the people were at different times. He had been in it and he had watched it and it was his duty to write of it; but now he never would.

"How do you feel?" she said.

"All right."

"Could you eat now?" He saw Molo behind her with the folding table and the other boy with the dishes.

"I want to write," he said.

"You ought to take some broth to keep your strength up."

"I'm going to die tonight," he said. "I don't need my strength up."

"Don't be melodramatic, Harry, please," she said.

"Why don't you use your nose? I'm rotted half way up my thigh now. What the hell should I fool with broth for? Molo bring whiskey-soda."

"Please take the broth," she said gently.

"All right."

The broth was too hot. He had to hold it in the cup until it cooled enough to take it and then he just got it down without gagging.

"You're a fine woman," he said. "Don't pay any bloody attention to me."

She looked at him with her well known, well loved face from Spur and Town and Country only a little the worse for drink, only a little the worse for bed but Town and Country never showed these good breasts and those useful thighs and as he looked and saw her well known pleasant smile he felt death come again. This time there was no rush. It was a puff as of a wind that makes a candle flicker and the flame go tall.

"They can bring my net out later and hang it from the tree and build the fire up. I'm not going in the tent tonight. It's not worth moving. It's a clear night. There won't be any rain."

So this was how you died, in whispers that you did not hear. Well, there would be no more quarreling. He could promise that. The one experience that he had never had he was not going to spoil it now. He probably would. You spoiled everything. But perhaps he wouldn't.

"You can't take dictation can you?"

"I never learned," she said.

"That's all right."

There wasn't time, of course, although it seemed as though it telescoped so that you might put it all into one paragraph if he could get it right.

There was a log house chinked white with mortar on a hill above the lake. Behind the house were rolling fields and behind the fields was the timber. A line of Lombardy poplars ran from ~~it~~ the house down to the dock. Other poplars ran along the point. A road ~~ran~~ went up the hills along the edge of the timber and along that road he picked blackberries. Then that log house was burned down and all the guns were burned and afterwards their barrels with the lead melted in the magazines and the stocks burned away lay out on the heap of ashes that were used to make lye for the big iron soap kettles and you asked Grandfather if you could have them to play with and he said, No. The house was rebuilt in the same place out of lumber now and painted white and from its porch you saw the poplars and the lake beyond but there were never any more guns. The barrels of the guns that had hung on the deer feet on the wall of the log house lay out there on the heap of ashes and no one ever touched them.

Then in the Black Forest after the war we rented a trout stream and there were two ways to walk to it. One was down the valley and around the valley road in the shade of the trees that lined the white road and then up a side road that went up through the hills past many small farms, with the big Schwartzwald houses, until that road crossed the stream, and that was where our fishing began. The other way was to climb steeply up to the edge of the woods and then go across the top of the hills through the pine woods and then out to the edge of a meadow and down across this meadow to the bridge. There were white birches along the stream and it was not big but narrow, clear and fast, with pools where it had cut under the roots of the birches. At the Hotel in Triberg the proprietor had a fine season. It was very pleasant and we were all great friends. The next year came the inflation and the money he had made the year before was not enough to buy supplies to open the hotel and he hanged himself.

You could dictate that but you could not dictate the Place Contres carpe where the flower sellers dyed their flowers in the street and the dye ran over the paving where the autobus started and the old men and the women always drunk on wine and bad marc and the children with their noses running in the cold; the smell of dirty sweat and poverty and drunkenness at the Cafe des Amateurs and the whores at the Bal Musette they lived above. The concierge who entertained the trooper of the Garde Republicaine. The locataire across the hall whose husband was a bicycle racer and her joy that morning at the Cremerie when she had opened L'Auto and seen where he placed third in Paris-Tours. His first big race. She had blushed and laughed and then gone upstairs crying with the yellow sporting paper in her hand. The husband of the woman who ran the Bal Musette ~~who~~ drove a taxi and when he had to take an early plane the husband knocked upon the door to wake him and they each drank a glass of white wine at the Zinc of the bar before they started. He knew his neighbors in that quarter then because they all were poor. Around that <u>Place</u> there were two kinds; the drunkards and the sportifs. The drunkards killed their poverty that way; the sportifs took it out in exercise. They were the descendants of the Communards and it was no struggle for them to know their politics. They knew who had shot their fathers, their relatives, their brothers, and their friends. And in that poverty and in that quarter across the street from a boucherie chevaline and a wine co-operative he had written the start of all he was to do. There never was another part of Paris that he loved like that, the sprawling trees, the old white plastered houses painted brown below, the long green of the auto-bus in that round square, the sudden drop down the hill of the rue Cardinal Lemoine and the other way the narrow crowded world of the rue Mouffetard. There was the street that ran up toward the Pantheon and the other that he always took with the bicycle, the only asphalted street in all that quarter, smooth under the tires, with high narrow houses and the cheap tall hotel where Paul Verlaine had died. There were only two rooms in the apartment where they lived and he had a room on the top floor of that hotel that cost him sixty francs a month where he did his writing and from it he could see the roofs and chimney pots and all the hills of Paris.

From the apartment you could only see the wood and coal man's place. He ~~also~~ sold wine too, bad wine. The golden horse head outside the Boucherie Chevaline where the carcasses hung yellow gold and red in the open window, and the green painted co-operative where they bought their wine; good wine and cheap. The rest was plaster walls and the window of the neighbors. The neighbors who, at night, when some one lay drunk in the street, ~~would~~ moaning and groaning in that typical French ivresse that you were propaganded to believe did not exist, would open and then the murmur of talk. "Where is the policeman? When you don't want him the buggar is always there. He's sleeping with some concierge. Get the <u>Agent</u>." Till someone threw a bucket of water from a window and the moaning stopped. "What's that? Water. Ah, that's intelligent." And the windows shutting. Marie protesting against the eight hour day saying, "If a husband works until six he gets only a little drunk on the way home and does not waste too much. If he works only until five he is drunk every night and one has no money. It is the wife of the working man who suffers from this shortening of hours."

"Wouldn't you like some more broth?"

"No thank you very much. It is awfully good."

"Try just a little."

"I would like a whiskey-soda."

"It's not good for you."

"No. It's bad for me. Cole Porter wrote the words and the music. This knowledge that you're going mad for me."

"You know I like you to drink."

"Oh yes. Only it's bad for me."

When she goes, he thought. I'll have all I want. Not all I want but all there is. Ayee he was tired. Too very tired. He was going to sleep a little while. He lay still and death was not there. It must have gone around another street. It went in pairs and moved absolutely silently on the pavements.

No he had never written about Paris. Not the Paris that he cared about. ~~Of two other countries he had written well and of the place where he had been a boy he had written well enough. As well as he could then. But what about the rest?~~

~~What~~ Nor had he ever written about the ranch and the silver gray of the sage brush, the quick clear water in the irrigation ditches, and the heavy green of the alfalfa. The trail went up into the hills and the cattle in the summer were shy as deer. The bawling and the steady noise and slow moving mass raising a dust as you brought them down in the fall. And behind the mountains and the clear sharpness of the peak in the evening light and riding down along the trail in the moonlight bright across the valley. And coming down through the timber in the dark holding the horses tail when you could not see and all the stories that you meant to write. The half wit chore boy left at the ranch that time told not to let anyone get any hay and that old bastard from the Forks who had beaten ~~him when~~ the boy when he had worked for him stopping to get some feed. The boy refusing and the old man saying he would beat him again. The boy got the rifle from the kitchen and shot him when he tried to come into the barn and when you came back he'd been dead a week frozen in the corrall and the dogs had eaten a big part of the body. But the rest you packed on a sled wrapped in a blanket and you got the boy to help you haul it and the two of you took it over the road on skis and sixty miles down to town to turn the boy over. He having no idea that he would be arrested. Thinking he had done his duty and that you were his friend and he would be rewarded. He'd helped to haul the old man in so everybody could know how bad ~~he'd~~ the old man had been and how he'd tried to steal some feed that didn't belong to him and when the sheriff put the handcuffs on him he couldn't believe it. Then he'd started to cry. That was one story he had saved to write. He knew ~~fifty~~ at least twenty good stories from out there and he had never written one. Why?

"You tell them why," he said.

"Why what, dear?"

"Why nothing."

She didn't drink so much, now, since she had him. But if he lived he would never write about her he knew now. Nor about any of them. The rich were dull and they drank too much, or they played too much backgammon. They were dull and they were repetitious. He remembered poor Scott Fitzgerald and his romantic awe of them and how he had started a story once that began, The very rich are very different from you and me. And how he had said to Scott, Yes, they have more money. But that was not humorous to Scott. He thought they were a special glamorous race and when he found they weren't it wrecked him just as much as any other thing that wrecked him.

He had been contemptuous of those who wrecked. You did not have to like it because you understood. He could beat anything, he thought, because no thing could hurt him if he did not care.

All right. Now he would not care for death. One thing he had always dreaded was the pain. He could stand pain as well as any man until it went on too long but here he had something that had hurt frightfully and just when he had felt it breaking him the pain had stopped.

He remembered long ago when Williamson, the bombing officer,

had been caught coming in through the wire that night and screaming had begged everyone to kill him. He was a fat man, very brave,
and a good officer although addicted to fantastic shows. ~~But after
seeing a fat man~~ But that night he was caught in wire, with a flare
lighting him up and his bowels spilled out into the wire, so when they
brought him in, alive, they had to cut him loose. Shoot me, Harry.
For Christ sake shoot me. They had had an argument one time about
the Lord never sending you anything you could not bear and some
one's theory had been that meant that at a certain time the pain
passed you out automatically. But he had always remembered Williamson. Still this now that he had was very easy and if it was no
worse as it went on there was nothing to think about. Except that he
would rather be in better company.

He thought a little about the company that he would like to
have.

~~No, he had written some things pretty well. And he had had good
friends. He had slept with every woman that he really wanted since
he was nineteen and if he had bitched his life it had not been for lack
of opportunity.~~

No, he thought, when everything you do you do too long and do
too late you can't expect to find the people still there. The people all
are gone. The party's over and you are with your hostess now. I'm
getting as bored with dying as with everything else, he thought.

"It's a bore," he said out loud.

"What is, my dear?"

"Anything you do too bloody long."

He looked at her face between him and the fire. She was leaning
back in the chair and the fire-light shone on her face and he could see
that she was sleepy. He heard the hyena make a noise just outside the
range of the fire.

"I've been writing," he said. "But I got tired."

"Do you think you will be able to sleep?"

"Pretty sure. Why don't you turn in?"

"I like to sit here with you."

"Do you feel anything strange?" he asked her.

"No. Just a little sleepy."

"I do," he said. He had just felt death come by again.

"You know the only thing I've never lost is curiosity," he said to her.

"You've never lost anything. You're the most complete man I've every known."

"Christ," he said. "How little a woman knows. What is that? Your intuition?"

Because, just then, death had come and rested its head on the foot of the cot and he could smell its breath.

"Never believe any of that about a scythe and a skull," he told her. "It can be two bicycle policemen as easily, or be a bird. Or it can have a wide snout like a hyena."

It had moved up on him now but it had no shape anymore. It simply occupied space.

"Tell it to go away."

It did not go away but moved a little closer.

"You've got a hell of a breath," he told it. "You stinking bastard."

Just then it was morning and had been morning for some time and ~~they~~ he heard the plane. It showed very tiny and then made a wide circle and the boys ran out and lit the fires, using kerosene, and piled on grass so there were two big smudges at each end of the level place and the morning breeze blew them toward the camp and the plane circled twice more, low this time, and then glided down and levelled off and landed smoothly and coming walking toward him was old Compton in slacks, a tweed jacket and a brown felt hat.

"What's the matter old cock?" he Compton said.

"Bad leg," he ~~said~~ told him. "Will you have some breakfast?"

"Thanks. I'll just have some tea. It's the puss moth you know. I won't be able to take the Memsahib. There's only room for one. Your truck is on the way."

Helen had taken ~~him~~ Compton aside and was speaking to him. Compton came back more cheery than ever.

"We'll get you right in," he said. "I'll be back for the Mem. Now I'm afraid I'll have to stop at Arusha to refuel. We'd better get going."

"What about the tea?"

"I don't really care about it you know."

The boys had picked up the cot and carried it around the green tents and down along the rock and out onto the plain and along past the smudges that were burning brightly now, the grass all consumed and the wind fanning the fire to the little plane. It was difficult getting him in but once in he lay back in the leather seat and the leg was stuck straight out to one side of the seat where Compton sat. Compton started the motor and got in. He waved to Helen and to the boys and as the clatter moved into the old familiar roar they swung around with Compie watching for wart hog holes and roared, bumping, along the stretch between the fires and with the last bump rose and he saw them all standing below, waving, and the camp beside the hill flattening now and the plain spreading, clumps of trees, and the bush flattening while the game trails ran now smoothly to the dry waterholes and there was a new water that he had never known of, the zebra, small rounded backs now and the wildebeeste, big headed dots seeming to climb as they moved in long fingers across the plane, now scattering as the shadow came toward them, they were tiny now, and the movement had no gallop, and the plain as far as you could see, gray yellow now and ahead old Compie's tweed back and the brown soft hat. Then they were over the first hills and the wildebeeste were trailing up them and then they were over mountains with sudden depth of green rising forest and the solid bamboo slopes and then the heavy forest again sculptured into peaks and hollows until they crossed and hills sloped down and then another plain, hot now, and purple brown, bumpy with heat and Compie looking back to see how he was riding. Then the other mountains dark ahead. And then instead of going on to Arusha they turned left, he evidently figured that they had the gas, and lookin[g] down he saw a pink sifting cloud moving over the ground, and in the air, like the first snow in a blizzard, that comes from nowhere, and he knew the locusts were coming up from the South. Then they began to climb and then it darkened and they were in a storm, the rain so thick it seemed like flying through a water fall, and then they were out and Compie turned his head and grinned and pointed and there all he could see, as wide as all the world, great, high and unbelievably white in the sun, was the square top of Kilimanjaro. And then he knew that there was where he was going.

The hyena stopped whimpering in the night and started to make a strange, human, almost crying sound. The woman heard it and stirred uneasily. She did not wake. In her dream she was at the house on Long Island and it was the night before her daughter's debut.

Somehow her father was there and he had been very rude. Then the noise the hyena made was so loud she woke and for a moment she did not know where she was and she was very afraid. Then she took the flashlight and shone it on the other cot that they had carried in after Harry had gone to sleep.

Somehow he had gotten his leg out and it hung down alongside the cot. The dressing had come down and she could not look at it.

"Molo," she called. "Molo! Molo!"

Then she said, "Harry. Harry." Then her voice rising, "Harry. Please. Oh Harry!"

Outside the tent the hyena made the same strange noise that had awakened her. But she did not hear him for the beating of her heart.

17b.

Item 706, Ernest Hemingway Collection, John F. Kennedy Library and Museum, Boston. Untitled pencil manuscript beginning "At that time of year there were no foreigners in Schruns . . ." Penned by Ernest Hemingway on the first page "Use in The Happy Ending." Hemingway had intended this flashback description of Austria for "Snows of Kilimanjaro" but decided against including it.

At that time of year there were no foreigners in Schruns. There was snow on the tops of the mountains and in the valley there was frost on the ground and the roads were frozen hard. The sun shone on the frost over the valley in the morning and in the village the frost was melted by the sun. Even when the sun was shining you could see your breath walking in the town and at two o'clock in the afternoon the sun went behind a mountain of gray rock and it was suddenly cold. Later, just before it got dark, the sun came out from behind the mountain and shone high up on the valley and lighted the pine trees and the meadows where the grass was dead and the brown mountain houses and the green and white church against the pine trees. Coming down into the valley down the side of the mountain it was very steep ~~and~~, there were low stone walls beside the ~~trail~~ path and the sun was shining on the brown fields and through the birch trees with their leaves fallen. There were bush leaves and beach [*sic*] and oak leaves on the path and on the frozen ground and below was the valley with ~~smoke~~ the village and directly below along the valley the line of the river with a stony bed and different channels and a covered wooden bridge to Tchaggam across the valley were the mountains. ~~their shapes and then changing their positions along with~~ Coming down the path the mountains across the valley changed in the evening. At first there were the high mountains, far behind, white with the snow fields. Then going down the path those could no longer be seen and there were only the nearer mountains that ~~went up~~ made the other side of the valley. ~~There were woods and straight brown lines through the~~ They ~~were rose~~ were steep and there were pastures and huts for the herdsmen and the cattle and above the fields there were woods and above the woods other fields with cabins like little black squares on a map.

17c.

Item 704, Ernest Hemingway Collection, John F. Kennedy Library and Museum, Boston. Titled pencil manuscript drafts of the epigraph for the "The Snows of Kilimanjaro."

The Snows of Kilimanjaro

Kilimanjaro is a snow covered mountain 19,710 feet high and is said to be the highest mountain in Africa. ~~The Western Summit of Kilimanjaro~~ Its Western Summit is called by the Masai the House of God. Close to the Western Summit ~~at three thousand feet above the permanent snow line on the Southwest slope, above the highest abode of animal life,~~ there is the dried and frozen carcass of a leopard which has been there for many years. No one ~~who climbs the mountain disturbs it nor does anyone~~ knows what the leopard was seeking at that altitude.

"The difficulties, he said, were not in the actual climbing. It was a long grind, and success depended not on skill but on one's ability to withstand the high altitude. His parting words were that I must make the attempt soon, before there was any risk of the rains setting in."

[The following is on a separate page.]

Kilimanjaro is a snow covered mountain 19,710 feet high and is said to be the highest mountain in Africa. ~~It is not~~ Its western summit is called by the Masai the House of God. At three thousand feet ~~a haz-~~ ~~ardous mountain to~~ above the snow line on the S.W. slope there is the dried and frozen carcass of a leopard which has been there for many years. No one knows what the leopard was seeking at that altitude.

"The difficulties," he said, "were not in the actual climbing. It was a long grind, and success depended not on skill but on one's ability to withstand the high altitude. His parting words were that I must make the attempt soon, before there was any risk of the rains setting in."

Acknowledgments

To Patrick Hemingway, I extend my deepest appreciation for his guidance, thoughtful discussions of the short stories, and his eloquent foreword. I am grateful to Michael Katakis for his vision and support. Sincere thanks to Susan Moldow and my editors at Simon & Schuster, Nan Graham, Liese Mayer, Daniel Loedel, and Katie Rizzo, as well as their colleagues Jeff Wilson, Brian Belfiglio, and Yessenia Santos. I am especially grateful to Tom Putnam, former director of the John F. Kennedy Library and Museum in Boston, and to Susan Wrynn, former curator of the Ernest Hemingway Collection at the Kennedy Library, Hilary Kovar Justice, curator of the Ernest Hemingway Collection, as well as their colleagues Laurie Austin and Maryrose Grossman of the Audiovisual Archives and particularly Stacey Chandler of the Textual Archives for their unfailing professionalism and steadfast support without whom this work could not have been accomplished. For permission to publish from my grandfather's letter in the United States I am grateful to the Ernest Hemingway Foundation and to Professor Kirk Curnutt for his kind assistance. I am grateful to Robyn Fleming of the Thomas J. Watson Library at the Metropolitan Museum of Art for assisting me with interlibrary loan requests during my research for this book. I would also like to acknowledge the following individuals: Joseph and Patricia Czapski, Angela Hemingway Charles, Carol Hemingway, Valerie Hemingway, Liisa Kissel, John Michael Maas, Sandra Spanier, H. R. Stoneback and his students, and my daughter Anouk Anji Hemingway. I am particularly grateful to my wife,

Colette C. Hemingway, who assisted me in the editing of the selections for this volume and read and edited a draft of my introduction. Beyond these professional tasks, Colette has been a constant support for this important work and my inspiration.

The paperback edition is an abridgement of the hardcover edition, published in 2017. I am grateful to Patrick Hemingway, Susan Moldow, Nan Graham, Daniel Loedel, Hilary Justice, Sandra Spanier, and H. R. Stoneback and his students for their thoughtful suggestions, which helped me form the selection presented here.

Notes

Introduction

1. For scholarly discussion of "Judgment of Manitou," see Charles Fenton, *The Apprenticeship of Ernest Hemingway: The Early Years* (New York: Farrar, Straus & Young, 1954), 15–16; Peter Griffin, *Along with Youth: Hemingway, the Early Years* (New York: Oxford University Press, 1985), 26–27; Michael Reynolds, *The Young Hemingway* (New York: W. W. Norton & Company, 1986), 73. No manuscript of the story is preserved.

2. Declan Kiely, curator of literature at the Morgan Library in New York, suggested in his 2015 exhibition "Ernest Hemingway: Between Two Wars" that this was the first Nick Adams story, even though the protagonist's last name is Grainger. Philip Young and Joseph Flora have suggested that "Summer People" is the first story to feature the character Nick Adams. See Philip Young's preface in Ernest Hemingway, *The Nick Adams Stories* (New York: Charles Scribner's Sons, 1972), 7; Joseph M. Flora, *Hemingway's Nick Adams* (Baton Rouge: Louisiana State University Press, 1982), 8 and 181–87. Michael Reynolds, however, dates the writing of "Summer People" to 1926, much later than other Nick Adams stories such as "Indian Camp," even though "Summer People" is based on events of 1920. See Reynolds, *The Young Hemingway*, 123–24.

3. See Paul Smith, "Hemingway's Apprentice Fiction: 1919–1921," *American Literature* 58, no. 4 (1986): 574–88. See also David L. Anderson, "Hemingway's Early Education in the Short Story: A Bibliographic Essay on Brander Matthews and Twenty Volumes of Stories at Windemere," *The Hemingway Review* 33, no. 2 (2014): 48–65.

4. "Ernest Hemingway, The Art of Fiction 21," *The Paris Review*, no. 18 (Spring 1958): 70. See also Steve Paul, *Hemingway at Eighteen: The Pivotal Year That Launched an American Legend* (Chicago: Chicago Review Press, 2018).

5. *The Kansas City Star Style Book*; quoted from Ernest Hemingway's personal copy in the Ernest Hemingway Collection at the John F. Kennedy Presidential Library and Museum.

6. The most comprehensive analysis of the manuscripts of Ernest Hemingway's short stories appears in Paul Smith, *Reader's Guide to the Short Stories of Ernest Hemingway* (Boston: G. K. Hall & Company, 1989), in which

the manuscripts are discussed story by story. Smith's book remains an invaluable resource for future studies.

7. Ernest Hemingway, *A Moveable Feast: The Restored Edition* (New York: Scribner, 2009), 17.

8. Paul Smith, "Three Versions of 'Up in Michigan': 1921–1930," *Resources for American Literary Study* 15, no. 2 (Autumn 1985): 163–77.

9. Ernest Hemingway to Sherwood Anderson, March 9, 1922, in Sandra Spanier and Robert W. Trogdon, eds., *The Letters of Ernest Hemingway*, vol. 1, *1907–1922* (Cambridge, UK: Cambridge University Press, 2011), 330.

10. See Michael Reynolds, *Hemingway: The Paris Years* (New York: W. W. Norton & Company, 1989), 109–11.

11. Edmund Wilson, *Dial*, October 1924.

12. For the 1930 Scribner's edition of *In Our Time*, Hemingway added "On the Quai at Smyrna" as a kind of introduction.

13. Agnes von Kurowsky's diary, which recounts the affair from her perspective, is preserved in the Ernest Hemingway Collection at the John F. Kennedy Presidential Library and Museum, where it was gifted after her death. See also Matt Hlinak, "Hemingway's Very Short Experiment: From 'A Very Short Story' to *A Farewell to Arms*," *The Journal of the Midwest Modern Language Association* 43, no. 1 (Spring 2010): 17–26.

14. For a discussion of the manuscripts, see Smith, *Reader's Guide to the Short Stories of Ernest Hemingway*, 34–35.

15. Robert Paul Lamb, *The Hemingway Short Story: A Study in Craft for Writers and Readers* (Baton Rouge: Louisiana State University Press, 2013), 3–85.

16. Jeffrey Meyers, "Hemingway's Primitivism and 'Indian Camp,'" *Twentieth Century Literature* 34, no. 2 (Summer 1988): 211–22.

17. Hemingway, *A Moveable Feast*, 17.

18. The only other manuscript of "The Three-Day Blow" is a typescript with a few emendations in the author's hand, preserved as item EHPP-MS18-015 in the Ernest Hemingway Collection at the John F. Kennedy Presidential Library and Museum.

19. Ernest Hemingway, *Death in the Afternoon* (New York: Charles Scribner's Sons, 1932), 192. On Hemingway's iceberg principle, see also "Ernest Hemingway, The Art of Fiction 21," 84.

20. For a detailed analysis of the composition of "Big Two-Hearted River," see Hilary K. Justice, "Tragic Stasis: Love, War, and the Composition of Hemingway's 'Big Two-Hearted River,'" *Resources for American Literary Study* 29 (2003–4), 199–215.

21. Ernest Hemingway to Dr. C. E. Hemingway, March 20, 1925. Quoted from Carlos Baker, ed., *Ernest Hemingway: Selected Letters 1917–1961* (New York: Scribner, 1981), 153.

22. Ernest Hemingway to Maxwell Perkins, April 15, 1925. Quoted from Baker, ed., *Ernest Hemingway: Selected Letters 1917–1961*, 156. See also Matthew J. Bruc-

coli, ed., *The Only Thing That Counts: The Ernest Hemingway–Maxwell Perkins Correspondence* (Columbia: University of South Carolina Press, 1999), 33–34.

23. On the making of *The Sun Also Rises*, see Seán Hemingway's introduction in Ernest Hemingway, *The Sun Also Rises: The Hemingway Library Edition* (New York: Scribner, 2014), xi–xx, and Lesley M. M. Blume, *Everybody Behaves Badly: The True Story Behind Hemingway's Masterpiece* The Sun Also Rises (Boston: Eamon Dolan/Houghton Mifflin Harcourt, 2016).

24. For an excellent general introduction to *Men Without Women*, see Joseph M. Flora, *Reading Hemingway's* Men Without Women: *Glossary and Commentary* (Kent, OH: The Kent State University Press, 2008).

25. For a thoughtful discussion of Hemingway's use of dialogue in "The Killers," see Robert Paul Lamb, *Art Matters: Hemingway, Craft, and the Creation of the Modern Short Story* (Baton Rouge: Louisiana State University Press, 2010), 90–93. See also Ron Berman, "Vaudeville Philosophers: 'The Killers,'" *Twentieth Century Literature* 45, no. 1 (Spring 1999): 79–93.

26. Smith, *Reader's Guide to the Short Stories of Ernest Hemingway*, 140–41.

27. For an expansive selection of the best war stories of all time, see Ernest Hemingway, ed., *Men at War* (New York: Crown, 1942).

28. On the importance of war as a subject in Hemingway's writing, see Seán Hemingway's introduction in *Hemingway on War* (New York: Scribner, 2003), xix–xxxvi.

29. For an insightful discussion of Hemingway and Cézanne, see Colette C. Hemingway, *in his time: Ernest Hemingway's Collection of Paintings and the Artists He Knew* (Boston: Kilimanjaro Books, Inc., 2009), especially 1–10. For a thoughtful study of the manuscripts of "Hills Like White Elephants," see Hilary K. Justice, "'Well, Well, Well': Cross-Gendered Autobiography and the Manuscript of 'Hills Like White Elephants,'" *The Hemingway Review* 18, no. 1 (Fall 1998): 17–32.

30. Carol Hemingway, "907 Whitehead Street," *The Hemingway Review* 23, no. 1 (Fall 2003): 8–23.

31. Michael Reynolds, *Hemingway: The 1930s* (New York: W. W. Norton & Company, 1997), 135.

32. William Shakespeare, *The Tempest* (ebook, Playshakespeare.com, 2014), act 1, scene 2, lines 396–401.

33. For a more detailed discussion of the manuscripts of "A Way You'll Never Be," see Smith, *Reader's Guide to the Short Stories of Ernest Hemingway*, 268–71. Smith notes interesting similarities between the first draft and both *A Farewell to Arms* and, especially, "A Natural History of the Dead."

34. Carlos Baker, *Ernest Hemingway: A Life Story* (New York: Charles Scribner's Sons, 1969), 228; and Smith, *Reader's Guide to the Short Stories of Ernest Hemingway*, 268.

35. See Smith, *Reader's Guide to the Short Stories of Ernest Hemingway*, 277–88, for a careful summary of the debate. See also Paul Smith, "A Note on a

New Manuscript of 'A Clean, Well-Lighted Place,'" *Hemingway Review* 8, no. 2 (Spring 1989): 36–39.

36. George Monteiro, "Hemingway on Dialogue in 'A Clean, Well-Lighted Place,'" *Fitzgerald-Hemingway Annual* (1974): 243.

37. For another example of this, see Hemingway, *A Moveable Feast*, 9–10 and 221–25.

38. For a discussion of the large body of scholarship on "The Short Happy Life of Francis Macomber," see Smith, *Reader's Guide to the Short Stories of Ernest Hemingway*, 327–48. See also Charles M. Oliver, *Critical Companion to Ernest Hemingway: A Literary Reference to His Life and Work* (New York: Facts on File, 2007), 329–34.

39. For a more detailed discussion of the manuscripts of "The Short Happy Life of Francis Macomber," see Bernard Oldsey, "Hemingway's Beginnings and Endings," *College Literature* 7, no. 3 (Fall 1980): 213–38, especially 224–34.

40. For a transcript of the safari notes, see Ernest Hemingway, *Green Hills of Africa: The Hemingway Library Edition* (New York: Scribner, 2015), 243–45.

41. George Eastman, *Chronicles of an African Trip* (privately printed for the author, 1927), 9. Eastman was a client of Philip Percival's before Ernest Hemingway. For Percival's own account of their two safaris together, see Philip H. Percival, *Hunting, Settling and Remembering* (Agoura Hills, CA: Trophy Room Books, 1997), 123–25.

42. Hemingway, *Green Hills of Africa*, 203–36, especially 220–21.

43. Hemingway made the leopard's quest more mysterious by stating that it was unexplained. Scholars have shown that the epigraph is based on an actual leopard that was hunting a mountain goat. See John M. Howell, *Hemingway's African Stories: The Stories, Their Sources, Their Critics* (New York: Charles Scribner's Sons, 1969), especially 99–100. See also Smith, *Reader's Guide to the Short Stories of Ernest Hemingway*, 354–55.

44. See Robert W. Lewis Jr. and Max Westbrook, "The Texas Manuscript of 'The Snows of Kilimanjaro,'" *Texas Quarterly* 9 (Winter 1966): 66–101. A complete transcription of the manuscript at the University of Texas at Austin has been published; see Robert W. Lewis Jr. and Max Westbrook, "'The Snows of Kilimanjaro' Collated and Annotated," *Texas Quarterly* 13 (1970): 64–143. In addition to the first draft transcribed in this edition, an intermediary typescript is preserved at the University of Delaware. For a discussion of the manuscripts, see Smith, *Reader's Guide to the Short Stories of Ernest Hemingway*, 349–51.

45. Mary Welsh Hemingway, *How It Was* (New York: Alfred A. Knopf, 1976), 469. For the Lillian Ross interview, see Lillian Ross, *Portrait of Hemingway*, Modern Library edition (New York: Random House, 1999), first published in the *New Yorker* in 1950. Ernest Hemingway's "The Art of the Short Story" was first published in the *Paris Review* in 1981.

46. Some of the stories discussed in "The Art of the Short Story" are not included in this edition. They can be found in *The Complete Short Stories of Ernest*

Hemingway, the Finca Vigía Edition (New York: Simon & Schuster, 1987). The date provided after the titles of the stories featured in this edition is the year the story was first published, except for the "Untitled Milan Story," which is published in its entirety for the first time in this book. In that case, the date is the year that Ernest Hemingway wrote the story.